DON'T SAY A WORD

BOOKS BY AMBER LYNN NATUSCH

Dare You to Lie

Don't Say a Word

DON'T SAY A WORD

AMBER LYNN NATUSCH

TOR TEEN

A TOM DOHERTY ASSOCIATES BOOK
NEW YORK

This is a work of fiction. All of the characters, organizations, and events portrayed in this novel are either products of the author's imagination or are used fictitiously.

DON'T SAY A WORD

A Tor Teen Book
Published by Tom Doherty Associates
120 Broadway
New York, NY 10271

www.tor-forge.com

Tor® is a registered trademark of Macmillan Publishing Group, LLC.

The Library of Congress Cataloging-in-Publication Data is available upon request.

ISBN 978-0-7653-9771-3 (hardcover)
ISBN 978-0-7653-9772-0 (ebook)

Our books may be purchased in bulk for promotional, educational, or business use. Please contact your local bookseller or the Macmillan Corporate and Premium Sales Department at 1-800-221-7945, extension 5442, or by email at MacmillanSpecialMarkets@macmillan.com.

First Edition: September 2019

Printed in the United States of America

0 9 8 7 6 5 4 3 2 1

To two people, without whom I'm not sure I would have survived high school,

Richard Berry, thank you for creating a safe space for your students to escape from everything else in their lives.

Shannon Hall, thank you for creating a drama-free space where I could just dance and forget.

DON'T SAY A WORD

PROLOGUE

When I was eight, I learned what evil was.

Not the generic kind of evil that people use to describe bad things, but real and true evil of the most biblical sense. The kind that defies explanation. The kind that you can never scrub from your mind once you encounter it.

Dad and Gramps had taken me to Matthew's Ice Cream Shop after a baseball game that day. I'd finally won after a six-game losing streak. Dad thought that win was worthy of celebrating, so the three of us crammed into the two-person booth in the back of the shop with an ice cream sundae, equipped with spoons longer than my forearm. I was three bites in when Dad's phone rang. I watched his proud expression fall to one of horror before he masked it with his official FBI face. The one that gave nothing away. But it was too late. I'd already seen the truth behind the lie.

"Where is she?" he'd asked, staring off past where Gramps and I sat. "I understand. I'll be right in." He hung up the phone, then slid out of the booth. "I'm so sorry, Kylene. You and Gramps will have to celebrate without me. It's work . . . I have to go."

He turned to walk away, but Gramps stopped him in his tracks.

"They found that Woodley girl, didn't they, Bruce?"

My father looked over his shoulder to Gramps, his lips pressed into a thin, grim line. He nodded once, and I could feel Gramps go tense beside me. That nod had meant far more to him than it had to me. I mean, finding the girl who had been missing from one town over was a good thing, right? She'd been gone for a long time; shouldn't they have looked happier? Wasn't that something worth celebrating?

I would find out later that it wasn't something to celebrate at all.

Gramps and I watched as my father's pace hastened on his way to the car. I turned to Gramps and started my interrogation. I'd always been my father's daughter.

"Is Daddy going to bring her home? Is that why he had to leave?"

Gramps' expression softened, and he wrapped his arm around me, pulling me close to him.

"No, Junebug. That's not why he had to go."

"Then why?"

"Well, I reckon your daddy's gonna go find the person that took that girl away. He's gonna keep him from ever doin' that to anyone else ever again."

"Because Daddy stops the bad guys, right?"

"He sure does, Junebug. He sure does."

"Okay. . . ."

"Now, eat your ice cream before it makes a big ole mess of this table."

He scooped some onto his spoon and took a bite, smiling as he swallowed it. But that smile never reached his eyes, and even at that young age, I knew something was wrong. I sat up on my knees and grabbed his face in my hands. It was then that I saw the unshed tears still welled in the corners of his eyes.

"Gramps, what's wrong?" He forced a laugh and kissed me

on my forehead to dismiss my concerns. But even at eight, I was not so easily derailed. "Tell me why you're sad, Gramps."

When he realized I had no intention of dropping it, he sighed.

"Because every time your father gets one of those calls, it reminds me that there are people in this world—truly evil people that don't belong."

"You see those people, right? In the prison?"

He nodded. "I sure do. And your daddy helps put 'em there."

"Gramps, how do you know someone is a bad guy?"

He looked at me thoughtfully for a moment, tucking a stray piece of hair behind my ear.

"You don't, Junebug. Ain't no way to know for sure 'til it's too late."

I remember letting those words soak into my mind—trying to give them context when I had none for them. They sank to the bottom of my consciousness until later that night when I sat at the top of the stairs and eavesdropped on my parents' conversation. I heard my father recount the vivid details of what had happened to Sarah Woodley. How she'd been taken after school never to be seen alive again. How her body showed that she'd been tortured and beaten before she died. He used words I didn't recognize at the time. Words I didn't understand fully until I was older.

When I learned them, I remembered what my father said that night and my stomach roiled with realization.

At the tender age of eight, I learned that a monster could be lurking behind every passing smile, every friendly neighbor, every pillar of the community. It cast the world in a much darker light. Made me question everything.

It was those suspicious traits that had made my father an amazing investigator, but even he'd fallen victim to a faceless evil. And that truth was a wake-up call. It wasn't enough for me to be as smart as my father—I needed to be smarter. If I wasn't, he would rot in prison—or die long before his murder sentence was served.

And I could end up as dead as Sarah Woodley.

ONE

I shot awake in an uncomfortable hospital chair, my neck throbbing. With a jolt, my hand went to my throat, visions of being stabbed with a needle rampant in my mind. My heart pounded against my fractured ribs—the soundtrack from the night I'd been attacked. The same as the day my father's verdict had been handed down. Apparently, some memories don't fade with time.

The pain brought me back to the present, and I realized it was just a nightmare—the same one I'd been having ever since Donovan Shipman and Luke Clark tried to kill me. Two attempted homicides in one night; a stretch by even Jasperville standards.

My best friend, Garrett, lay in the hospital bed with wires and machines attached to him. I could finally hear the beeping and chirping over the blood pounding in my ears. It had been only a few days since his surgery, but he had already been downgraded from the ICU, which meant I could visit him. Finally.

Those few days had felt like a lifetime.

Quietly, I stood up and walked over to him, slipping my hand in his. I gave it a squeeze to see if he'd reflexively do the same, but I felt nothing. He hadn't woken up once. At least not while I was conscious.

My other hand drifted to his face to brush his dark hair aside. I lightly grazed the few pale parts around the edge of it that weren't an awful shade of bruised. Even though it had been over a week since the attack, it was still shocking to see him like that. He'd been beaten so badly that I knew it would take a while for the rest of the swelling to go down. I'd gotten off easy in comparison. My arm was no longer in a sling but it was stiff and sore, and my ribs still hurt when I breathed too deeply. Both injuries seemed like hangnails compared to Garrett's. The doctors told his father that he was lucky he'd pulled through. His internal bleeding had been substantial.

Though they expected him to make a full recovery, I couldn't help but worry. The only reason Garrett had been with me that night was because he didn't want me to go alone. He wanted to have my back, as always. His need to keep me safe had nearly cost him his life—that was a bitter pill to swallow.

As I stared at his injured face, his eyes flickered a few times before slowly opening. He looked up at me with utter confusion and I stifled a squeal. His brown eyes darted around the room, undoubtedly trying to figure out where he was.

"It's okay, Garrett. You're in the hospital. You've been unconscious for a while . . ."

"Hospital . . . ?" he asked, his voice hoarse and garbled, like he had cotton balls in his mouth.

"You need some water." I ignored his question and grabbed the cup next to his bed. I angled the straw so he could take a sip without moving more than necessary. Once he'd drained the entire thing, he looked at me, awaiting an answer. I hesitated, unsure of how much to say. "Yeah, you're in the hospital. . . . Do you remember what happened after homecoming?"

His brow scrunched with concentration. It took a moment, but when his eyes went wide, I knew he did. They were filled with fear.

"Are you all right?" he asked. It was like a blow to the chest. After all he'd suffered, he was still worried about me. Tears ran down my face. "Are you crying? Why are you crying?"

"Could you back off for a minute and just let me enjoy the fact that you're awake?" I answered, choking on a laugh. "And of course I'm crying, you jerk! I thought you were going to die!"

It must have hurt him to do it, but he smiled. "Drama queen."

"Screw you, Higgins! If you'd found my near-lifeless body like I found yours, you'd be a hot mess over it."

"True." His smile faded. "I'm glad I didn't." His fingers brushed against mine, and I took his hand again, gripping it tight. I didn't want to let go. "When Donovan attacked me, all I kept thinking about was if he'd somehow gotten to you already. I tried so hard to get away, but that son of a bitch hit me from behind. I never really stood a chance. Then I saw his attention snap back toward the road and I knew you were okay—that he hadn't found you yet. It was little consolation, but it was something to cling to."

Tears rolled down my cheeks again. "I'm so sorry, Garrett. I'm the reason you're in here."

He shook his head, the movement slow and careful, but clear.

"I chose to go with you. I knew it was risky."

"Right—risky because we could have gotten caught breaking and entering Mark Sinclair's house. Not because Donovan was going to try to kill us."

Before he could reply, one of the machines next to me blared, damn near giving me a heart attack. A moment later, a nurse came in.

"You're awake," she noted with a smile. "I'll let the doctors know."

"Do I have to go?" I asked, sounding a little more desperate than I'd meant to. I wasn't ready to leave just yet.

Sympathetic eyes took me in, then fell to where our hands were clasped.

"No, honey. You can stay," she said, clearly misreading the situation. But I didn't care. She could assume we were dating if it got me what I wanted. "Just go easy on him, and if anything changes before the doctor arrives, you come running, okay?"

I nodded, and she left.

"So, what happened?" Garrett asked. "With Donovan?"

"The short version is that Donovan was arrested for assault with a deadly weapon and attempted murder, amongst other things. He was shot, not fatally unfortunately, and I found you and brought you to the hospital. The end."

He looked at the faint bruises on my face and his eyes narrowed. "What's the long version?"

"That's something I'll tell you when you're lounging on Gramps' couch assuming your role as remote control hog, okay?"

He rolled his eyes. It was about the only movement he could make without hurting himself.

"Are you at least gonna tell me who shot the bastard?"

I hesitated for a second. "Some FBI agent. I guess Striker had him keeping an eye on me. Thank God he showed up when he did."

He looked content with my reply but I wasn't sure how he'd take the news I still had to share. I took a deep breath, unsure how to brace him for the truth. But Garrett was a lot like me. Sometimes sugarcoating it only made things worse.

"There's something else you should know—about AJ." Garrett somehow managed to look menacing in a hospital johnny. "He never took those topless pictures of me. Donovan told me—he was the one that did it. He used AJ's camera to cover his ass." Garrett said nothing for longer than I was comfortable with, and I squeezed his hand to make sure he hadn't lapsed into an eyes-open coma. "Garrett . . . say something."

"Oh my God. . . ."

"I know. It's a lot to take in."

"Yeah." Garrett's expression went blank, and I worried I'd have to run and get the nurse in a minute if he didn't perk up. Beneath the shades of green and blue engulfing his expression, Garrett went pale.

"You know what? We can talk about this later. It's hard to drop bombs on you like this when you're hooked up to all these machines. You look so pitiful."

Garrett laughed, which quickly turned into a painful cough, and I grabbed my water bottle to help ease it.

"Do you want me to call your dad? Let him know you're awake?" I asked. He shook his head. "Garrett, he's your father—"

"And he's partly the reason I'm in here."

"So am I."

"That's different."

"Not really."

I hesitated for a second and Garrett saw right through me. No traumatic brain injury could stop him from that.

"What's going on?" Garrett asked, trying—and failing—to shift his torso over on the bed. I reached over to help him, but he waved me off with a weak flick of his wrist.

"It's about your dad, Garrett. He knows that I know about him—about the bribe he took." I hesitated for a moment to let those facts sink in before continuing. "But there's more. Your dad is somehow involved with my dad's case. He knows my dad is innocent, Garrett. He told me so."

Before Garrett had a chance to respond, a female doctor in a white coat swept into the room and started checking his monitors.

"I need to speak with the patient and run a few tests," she said to me over her shoulder. "Do you mind waiting in the reception area?"

"No, that's fine. I was just leaving." I looked down at Garrett, then bent over and gently kissed his forehead. "I'll be back soon, okay? Get better. I need you back at that godforsaken school. I can't survive it without you."

"Don't worry. I'll be back on my feet in no time."

"And that's exactly what I'm trying to assess, so if you two are finished," the doctor said, giving me a stern look.

"Sorry. I'll see you later, Garrett."

"Later it is. Love you, Ky."

I swallowed hard against the surge of emotions that shot through me.

"Love you, too."

I wiped my damp eyes the second I stepped out into the hallway. As I did, Sheriff Higgins approached, wearing his uniform, firearm and all. The strongest flash of déjà vu went through my mind, dragging up unwelcome memories. Memories of a hospital room, a syringe, and a deranged killer—the one the sheriff helped save me from.

Things between the two of us had been strained before that night, mainly because of his behavior during the photo scandal two years earlier. But following homecoming, they'd been tense at best. We had a secret to keep, one that kept him from being tied to Luke Clark's death. One that would keep him in the clear with the faceless evil, the Advocatus Diaboli, who was responsible for framing my father and Luke's attempt on my life—but it came at a cost. We had to keep up appearances, which proved easier than I'd have thought.

He was good at being a dick.

"Kylene," he said by way of greeting as he stopped in front of me.

"Sheriff."

"I got a call. They said he's awake."

"He is," I replied with a genuine smile. "And he's perfect. Same old Garrett."

The sheriff let out a breath. "Thanks for being here. I'm glad he wasn't alone when he woke up."

He gave me a tight nod and headed for his son's room.

I hurried out of the hospital, needing to escape the reminder of what had happened to me the night of the attack. Now that Garrett was awake and going to be okay, I realized going back there would be damn near impossible. I wished I could erase it from existence and take my memories along with it.

TWO

The sun was low in the sky when I pulled up to Gramps' tiny ranch house. I hopped out of the car, the crisp fall wind blowing my hair into my face, but it couldn't obscure the sight of Gramps sitting on the front porch in his rocking chair, staring back at me. I tried to convince myself he hadn't been posted there, awaiting my return.

"Hey," I said, walking up the path to the house. Gramps smiled in response, but there was a wariness to that smile that made my heart plummet. I hadn't left him a note or a message on his phone telling him I'd gone to see Garrett. To Gramps' credit, he was trying not to smother me after the attack—checking up on me all the time—so he hadn't called. That fact only made me feel worse.

With tears pushing against the backs of my eyes, I ran to Gramps and bent over to wrap my arms around his neck.

"I'm okay, Gramps. I promise."

"Maybe so, but that poor Higgins boy ain't, is he?" I pulled away to look at him. Sharp lines cut through his expression—harsh like the anger he felt. "I saw guys in Nam walk away from war in better shape. . . ."

"That's where I went. I'm so sorry I forgot to leave you a note." He nodded once, accepting my apology. "He's awake now," I continued. "I was there when he came to."

"He gonna be all right?"

"Yes—I mean, he's still pretty banged up, but he was talking and making sense. His memory of that night is pretty clear, which is good because the doctors were worried about that."

"The boy's body was beaten to a pulp. He's damn lucky he's alive. Forgettin' things could have been the least of his worries." He hesitated for a beat. "Yours too . . ."

Those two words hung there between us, an almost physical barrier. We'd never had anything get in the way of our relationship, and the thought of the choice I'd made to go after Donovan dividing us hurt more than I could express. Sorry was never going to be enough for what I'd done. And it wasn't going to be enough for things I was likely going to do.

"I love you, Gramps."

"Aw, Kylene, you know I love you more than life itself, but the parts of you you got from your daddy are gonna put me in an early grave. You gotta be smart about the battles you fight and the ones you walk away from. You can't right all the wrongs in this world. Ain't no man alive that can."

I choked on a laugh, my throat tight with emotions.

"Guess it's a good thing I'm not a man then, huh?"

He smiled and shook his head as I dragged my sleeve across my face to catch the tears that had finally escaped. As much as I hated to admit it, Gramps was right. I did need to be smarter about who I took on and who I let be. I needed to rein in that fiery temper of mine before I really got into trouble. The kind you don't walk away from. Ever.

"Girl, you are a piece of work, I swear. . . ."

"But I'm all yours."

"That you are."

I forced a smile before heading toward the front door. I had it halfway open when Gramps' words halted me.

"You been over to see your daddy yet?" he asked, the clear

ring of knowing in his tone. He was aware I hadn't been and was testing me. He rarely if ever did that, and the fact that he'd chosen that moment and that subject to bust out his subtle interrogation style gave me the chills.

"No. Not yet, but I talked to him a few days ago. I told him everything that happened."

"Everything?"

"I mean, I'm sure I unintentionally left out some details, but yes . . . as much as I could think to at the time."

"You need to see him, Kylene." Not a request, but a demand from Gramps.

Hell was getting frosty.

"I will soon, I promise."

"Good. Now, go do whatever homework you need to before bed."

"I'm on it."

"Atta girl. I'll be in soon."

He turned his gaze to the sunset and rested his head back in the chair. Again, my heart fell to my stomach. He looked so much older—so stressed. Knowing that I was a big part of that filled me with guilt. The fact that I knew I was likely to cause him more before I solved my father's case made me feel worse.

With that albatross around my neck, I pushed the door open and stepped into our modest home. A cling-wrapped plate sat on the kitchen counter waiting for me, so I grabbed it along with a fork and made my way down the hall to my small den-turned-bedroom. I flopped down on the bed and crossed my legs, propping the plate in my lap. I ate in silence, contemplating what the next day would bring.

For various reasons, I hadn't been back to school the week after the attack. Between Donovan's arraignment, my injuries, police interrogations, and a general desire to avoid the backlash of an all but ruined football season, Gramps and I thought it best I lay low for a bit. Unfortunately for me, there were standardized tests coming up that I couldn't miss.

I wasn't looking forward to going back to Jasperville High. Though my return should have been easier, I knew it wouldn't be. The stares and whispers would remain, even if the reasons for both were different. With Donovan's arrest, the football team lost an integral player. Our season would rest solely on the strengths of our offensive line—and AJ, our quarterback. Since I had inadvertently led to Donovan's incarceration, I was clearly to blame. The fact that he'd nearly killed Garrett and me seemed to get lost in the articles about him. It was crazy how quickly the narrative turned from drug abuse and attempted murder to lost games and crushed hopes of a state championship run.

With the potential fallout swirling in my mind, I focused on the one positive I'd find within the walls of JHS—Tabby. My female partner in crime. The lanky redhead from Canada. Tabby had a way of making everything seem better—and that was something I desperately needed.

THREE

Gramps called down the hall to tell me he was headed to the store for groceries and that he'd be back in a bit. The second I heard the door close, I put my homework away and pulled out the witness list from my father's case, cross-referencing it with the court transcripts and depositions I'd spread out across the bed. Something about one of them didn't quite add up. A vagrant in the area had allegedly heard the entire event unravel. But reading through his testimony and the questions asked by my father's attorney, a niggling sensation crawled along the back of my mind. His replies sounded a little too perfect. Too practiced.

And entirely fishy.

With highlighter in hand, I started to mark up the records in front of me along with the photos that were submitted into evidence of the crime scene. When I was done, I took a step back to survey them. Then a knock at the front door interrupted my work.

I stormed down the hallway to the door. I didn't bother to look through the peephole before opening it, instead choosing to just throw it open and scowl at whoever was waiting on the other side. That scowl deepened when I found rookie FBI agent Cedric Dawson standing there, looking smug as ever. "I've never been more disappointed to not find a Jehovah's Witness on my porch," I said. My expression did little to hide my irritation at his presence.

He'd been calling and texting since Donovan's arraignment. I'd been avoiding him like the plague, hoping this moment would never come.

"Nice to see you, too, Danners. You alone?" I made a big show of looking back into the house and then at the only car parked in my driveway. He seemed to take the hint. "Good. We need to talk. We have to hammer out the details of our cover story."

"You mean *your* cover story. I don't need one, remember? You made that very clear when you dropped this bomb of insanity on me."

"It's not insane. It's genius, and it's going to make it easier to catch whoever is behind this underage sex ring and put him behind bars sooner than later. I thought you'd want that. Isn't that your thing: justice for those who can't get it for themselves?"

His smug delivery had me taking a cleansing breath and reminding myself that assaulting a federal officer was a serious offense. But so was having to put up with Dawson's sense of superiority. Maybe if I only punched him once, they'd call it even.

Then again, maybe not.

Instead of replying, I took a step back and swept my arm out in a grand gesture for him to enter. He laughed as he stepped through the door, shaking his head.

"You're going to have to drop the hostile act if we're going to pull this off, Danners."

"It's hardly an act, and you're going to have to stop calling me by my last name if you want anyone to believe we used to date, *Dawson*."

He smiled at me, but there was little joy in it—kinda like the man himself.

"Used to?" he asked. "You mean 'are currently dating,' right, *Kylene*? That's my cover."

"Were you dropped on your head as a child? We're exes, remember? That's the story I gave Garrett when you met—Tabby too—and that story is going to stay."

"Why would I be transferring to your school if we're exes?"

"That's your story to write, not mine," I said, walking away. "Besides, doesn't most of the sheriff's department know who you are after you interrogated Dr. Carle? How are you going to keep a lid on that?"

"I'm not. The head of the bureau for Ohio, Special Agent in Charge Bob Wilson, will." I stopped in my tracks to turn and face him. "He's already been to visit Sheriff Higgins and his crew. He threatened them with prison time if my identity was leaked. Apparently he made quite an impression."

"I bet," I said, remembering just how intimidating that man could be. He was tough but fair, and had done everything he could for my father until even he couldn't refute the evidence against him. I had no doubt that the sheriff and his minions weren't going brush off Agent Wilson's warning. "So what else do I need to know, if all that's covered? I have things to do and Gramps will be home soon. This can't take forever." He slipped his leather jacket off and threw it onto Grams' well-worn recliner, then kicked off his shoes. "By all means, make yourself at home."

"Thanks," he said, heading for the sofa in the living room. With a lazy, graceful move, he plopped himself down on it, draping his arms along the back edge in man-sprawl fashion. It was impossible not to notice his roguish good looks—from his focused hazel eyes to his long, toned frame and perfectly styled brown hair—but eye-candy status aside, he still irritated the hell out of me.

Even if he had saved my life.

I walked behind him, rounding the arm of the couch to sit as far away from him as possible.

Looking at him, it was hard to see the young FBI agent that had come to my aid the night Donovan tried to kill me. He'd risked his life to cross a flooded bridge just to get to me, even though I seemed to be little more than a thorn in his side. That was the thing about Dawson that I just couldn't figure out. One minute, he looked at me like he loathed my existence. The next, he was putting his life in danger to save me. Maybe his sense of justice was just as strong and reckless as mine. Maybe we weren't so different after all.

Except I wasn't a smug bastard who thought my father was guilty and he most certainly was. There was still that.

"So here's the deal: We started dating after you moved away to Columbus. We were off and on at first because your temper and my aloof nature were like fire and gasoline, but we got close after everything with your father started. It really solidified our relationship."

"Ha!" I barked out my response so loud that I startled myself.

"Anyway," he continued, looking annoyed. "I come from a rich family—"

"Of course you do—"

"My parents are both in big business and are gone a lot. I'm eighteen and on my own most of the time. When I heard about the attack, I told them I was transferring schools for the rest of the year. They grudgingly agreed. The only reason we broke up was because you knew you were going to have to move and couldn't handle the pressure of long distance along with everything going on with your dad. I think that story will be believable. I don't think anyone in this town will question it."

"Wow, are you actually *trying* to be an asshole right now, or does it just come this naturally?"

"The latter," he replied without pause. "So, this will explain why you didn't mention me to your friends here or your grandfather—it hurt too much."

"That still doesn't explain why you're moving here to go to school."

"I'm worried about you," he said. "And we're trying to get back together. That shouldn't be so hard to sell."

"Clearly you don't know my friends. They can smell bullshit from ten miles away."

"Then I guess you'd better be on your A-game."

I pinned my deadliest stare on him. He didn't even flinch.

"So you're saying your cover story is that you're worried about my safety so you moved down here to keep an eye on me?" He nodded. "Yeah . . . that's not creepy at all."

"I'd been in boarding schools in the past. My parents don't care if I'm around or not. It makes total sense."

"I guess. . . ."

"Do you have a better idea?"

"Yeah. You could just be the new kid."

"I could, but I know your feelings about me are too strong to act like you don't know me. You can't hide that level of intensity, Danners. And since Garrett and Tabby know me as your ex, you're kinda stuck with being part of my cover."

He was right, and I hated him for it.

"Why do you even have to go undercover? What are you trying to find at JHS?"

He stared at me for a moment, clearly assessing if he should tell me or not—if it was a small price to pay for my role in closing his case.

"There's a girl—the *recruiter.* She's the one bringing the girls in. We're pretty sure she works directly with whoever's in charge. I need to find her."

I had no flippant response to that one. Knowing that one of

my fellow students was involved in the exploitation of others made my skin crawl. I wanted to find her just as badly as he did.

"Fine. I'll be a part of this ridiculous charade, but only if I get to help with the case."

"Absolutely not!"

"Then no deal, Dawson. Find your own way."

"Even if I wanted to let you in, I don't have the authority to do that."

"Whatever. Those are my terms, Dawson. I either get to help or you're on your own. It's that simple."

His expression was murderous.

"Are you really that childish? You'd risk these girls' safety for your own gain?"

"Not childish. *Practical.* Don't forget, I brought down a prescription drug ring on my own and found out that there's some sociopathic Wizard of Oz out there pulling criminals' strings. Hell, I handed you the lead that broke open the case that you're now undercover on. I'm good at this, whether you want to admit it or not. So, I'll help you if you help me."

"I don't have the authority to do that," he repeated, no shortage of anger heating his face.

The smile that crept across mine was full of challenge.

"Afraid to break the rules a bit for the greater good, Dawson?"

"Your father broke the rules, Danners. That didn't work out so well for him."

"My father," I shouted, launching myself up from the couch, "was framed somehow—forced to shoot Reider—and I'm going to prove it." I stormed to my room to retrieve the trial evidence that was sprawled out in an organized mess. "Look!" I said as I walked back to the living room and jammed my finger at the transcript of the vagrant's deposition. "Read this. Doesn't this seem a bit convenient to you? That a man with no history of military or police training was able to keep his wits about him when he heard a gunshot right near where he slept? That he actually stayed and remembered the events so clearly that he could account for this much detail?"

I stared at Dawson's profile as he read the text in question. Wrinkles formed at the corners of his eyes as they narrowed, focusing on the paper.

"Even if what you're saying is true, that he lied about what he saw or was fed this information, it hardly negates the mountain of evidence showing that your father was sabotaging federal cases."

"If what I'm saying is true, then that's grounds for a mistrial—possibly charges of witness tampering and coercion."

He turned to face me, a mess of emotions warring in his eyes.

"You're fighting a losing battle with this, Danners. You know that, right? Maybe it's time you surrender the childish fantasy that your father is some noble enforcer of the law and entertain the idea that he actually did what he was convicted of because he was about to be indicted for various other crimes."

"No." My voice was cold and angry, my answer final.

He shook his head, putting the paper back down. "You're going to make yourself crazy doing this, you know that, right?"

"Maybe, but no crazier than I'll be if I do nothing." His expression softened just a touch. "Tell me you wouldn't do the same if your mentor was in my father's shoes. That you wouldn't be trying to prove his innocence." His lack of immediate reply spoke volumes.

"Okay, Danners. Here's the deal I'll make you: You keep my cover story and I'll keep you apprised of how the case is going. No major details. No investigating. Maybe I'll let you get me coffee on occasion—"

"And you'll listen to any evidence I find to exonerate my father." Not a question—a demand.

His eyes narrowed. "Fine. But this is a one-time offer, Danners. Take it or leave it."

I could tell by the tone of his voice and the set of his jaw that he hated offering me anything at all. Inside, I did a little victory dance.

"I'll take it."

"Good. Now, let's iron out a few more details before I show up at school tomorrow."

"Tomorrow?"

"Yes. Tomorrow."

I exhaled heavily and flopped back onto the couch.

For the next few minutes, we went over our extensive backstory, ranging from first kiss to favorite foods to craziest stories. By the time we finished, I was exhausted. If I'd gone along with his original dating cover story, I'd have already wanted to break up.

"You need to watch out for Tabby," I said as he slipped his coat back on, preparing to leave. "She's goofy but she's smart. Surprisingly astute. Your life will be easier if you get on her good side."

"Noted."

"And Garrett will be super protective of me—once he's back." I couldn't hide the sadness I felt when I said his name.

"He should be. That's what friends are for," he said with conviction. I nodded as he stepped toward the door. "Anyone else I need to watch out for?"

I hesitated, not wanting to bring up AJ.

"Yeah. AJ Miller—my *other* ex-boyfriend. I think it's fair to say he still has feelings for me. I'm not sure how he's going to react, having my most recent ex trying to win me back. We broke up because I thought he was the one that took those topless pictures of me. Then I found out it was Donovan. That asshole taunted me with the truth right before you showed up."

"That kid at homecoming. The one you were running away from—"

"Yep. That was AJ," I replied. His lips pressed to a thin line. "And you will do your best to be nice to him, because I would have told you that I found out he was innocent."

"Yeah. I guess you would have." He got quiet for a moment, looking at me with his intense hazel eyes. Something was brewing in that mind of his—I could feel it. But when he finally opened his mouth, I hadn't planned for what came out. "What you did homecoming night—" He cut himself off before finishing, those words dying off into the silence that followed them. Just when I thought I'd have to say something to ease the tension growing in the room, he spoke. "That was reckless, Kylene. You and Garrett could have been killed."

"Yes, well, had we known that going in, we might have acted differently."

"Or not." His words were backed with such confidence that I squirmed a little. Maybe Dawson knew me better than I thought. His profiling skills were on point.

"What about you?" I asked, turning the heat in his direction for a moment. "You're the one who scaled a flooded bridge railing to cross it on foot—in a *suit*."

"I had no other choice. You, however, had options."

"You had other choices."

"Like what?" he asked, his harsh tone forcing me back a step.

"I don't know . . . helicopter?"

"You reached out to me for a reason. I wasn't going to leave you to fend for yourself, Danners." He said those words matter-of-factly, but I couldn't help but feel there was something else behind them. Something warmer and softer and unfamiliar to me coming from him. I had to look away for a moment to clear my head.

"Gramps will be back any minute. You should probably go."

"All right," he said, turning to leave. "I'll see you tomorrow."

"Can't wait," I replied, following him to the door.

I watched him disappear down the driveway and into his car. I wondered how in the hell I was going to pull off this stunt. Tolerating Dawson was one thing, but liking him was another thing altogether. It would take a herculean effort to convince my friends and Gramps that I was once in love with the rookie agent.

Possibly even a miracle.

FOUR

Monday morning, my anxiety was through the roof, the whole Dawson fiasco starting to finally sink in. I wasn't sure I could pull it off. He suggested (read: threatened) to pick me up that morning, but I declined, reminding him that we were exes and I didn't want to ignite rumors on my first day back. Obviously, he saw right through my argument, but let it go.

Gramps was up making breakfast for me by the time I got out of the shower, so I quickly got dressed and threw my long blond hair into a ponytail so I could join him. I loved mealtimes with Gramps. They made me feel like a kid again.

"Mornin' Kylene."

"Hey Gramps," I replied, going over to kiss him on the cheek while he pulled bacon from the pan. Gramps made the best bacon. Not too crispy. Not too limp. I'd become convinced after attempting to cook it a couple of times that it was an art form and a grossly underappreciated one at that.

"You sure you're up to this today?" he asked with a frown. "It's been just over a week since—" He cut himself off and I pretended not to notice.

"I think so. I'm still a bit sore, but capable of taking a swing at someone if necessary."

He shot me a look over his shoulder and I winked back.

"Girl, your apple didn't fall far from your daddy's tree."

"Did it even fall at all?"

"That right there is a good question." He put a plate in front of me, then sat down and took a bite of his eggs. "That ex-boyfriend of yours you mentioned, is he starting school soon?" he asked. I nodded, looking none too happy about it before I practically kicked myself under the table. With bashful blue eyes, I looked up at him, trying to force my pale cheeks to rosy.

"Today."

"I'll be at work tonight, and I don't want him over here alone. I don't really want you over there, either, since he's livin' by himself."

"Gramps, it's not like that at all, but that's fine. I'll only have him over if Tabby is here, okay?"

It was his turn to nod. "Or the Higgins boy once he's outta the hospital and well enough to visit."

"When Garrett is out, I want him all to myself for a bit."

"I wonder how everyone else will feel about that. . . ." Gramps let his unspoken words hang in the air around us. I struggled for the proper response.

"Everyone else?" I asked, taking a bite of bacon.

"I think you have a couple of exes that seem mighty interested in getting back with you."

I wanted to argue that point but couldn't. I took another bite of my food and chewed it dramatically to buy me time.

Gramps just laughed.

"Oh, to be young again. . . ."

I glanced up at the clock and realized I was going to be late.

"As much as I want to have this conversation with you, Gramps, I gotta run. Thanks for breakfast!" I snatched a piece of toast and gave Gramps a hug before hurrying to grab my bag and keys. I broke through the front door at a jog, slamming it behind me. Moments later, I was in the car, begging her to start. "Come on, Heidi . . . don't let me down today."

Thankfully, she sputtered to life without argument and we were on our way.

I pulled up to the school to find Tabby heading in. She saw me and waited at the edge of the parking lot. I was a mess, hurrying while trying to put my backpack on. I dropped my keys and fumbled them again when I tried to pick them up a second time. Yeah, I was on edge about the Dawson thing, and it was affecting my basic abilities to function, which I needed to survive JHS. I knew right then that this undercover investigation wasn't going to end well for me.

I actually cringed when I saw Tabby come running toward me, watching what could be best described as a baby giraffe trying to sprint. She managed to make it to me injury free—somehow.

"Kylene!" she screamed in true teenage girl fashion—all high-pitched and screechy.

"Don't squish me!" I replied, backing away from the open arms headed my way. "My ribs still hurt!!"

She stopped short, smiling like a creepy clown. "Oh my God, I'm so happy you're here!"

"Good to see you too, Tabs."

"I'm so sorry I couldn't come visit you—Dad wouldn't let me."

"No worries. I wasn't very good company. Showering while injured was a pain in the ass, so . . . let's just say I've smelled better."

"You smell great now," she said, realizing how awkward that sounded right after it slipped out. Classic Tabby.

"Yes, well, that took far longer to accomplish than you should probably know."

She laughed, then gently wrapped her skinny arms around me and gave me a light hug.

"I'm so glad you're okay." The sun reflected off her glistening blue eyes, and I had to look away.

"Me too."

"And Garrett's awake! Things are going to be back to normal soon."

"He's awake, but he won't be in school for a while. I'm hoping to find out when in the next couple days."

She nodded thoughtfully. "We should probably go inside. The first bell is about to ring."

As if on cue, it did just that. We followed the herd of kids entering the building, engulfed by the cacophony. Tabby and I parted ways on the second floor, and I made my way up to room 333, Mr. Callahan's den of doom—or physics, as some called it.

He wasn't waiting by the door like he usually did, which gave me a moment's relief, but the second I rounded the corner to enter, that disappeared. I saw Garrett's empty seat and my chest tightened.

"Ms. Danners," Callahan called from his desk. "I have your missed assignments here." For once, he looked less smug about doling out homework. Maybe he actually felt sorry for Garrett and me. "I'm assuming a week will be sufficient to get all caught up."

Nope. Not sorry at all.

"Yeah. Sure."

I took the stack of papers from him and made my way to my seat. Thankfully physics wasn't one of the classes we had testing in that day, but I hated being there all the same. I hated the sound of Callahan's voice and the groans of the students around me. But most of all, I hated the fact that Garrett wasn't there to suffer with me. Instead, he was suffering in an entirely different and unacceptable way on his own.

Because of me.

For the rest of the class, I zoned out, letting my eyes glaze over while I stared at the front of the room. I wondered if maybe I wasn't ready to come back to school yet.

Tabby and I got separated during our study period and I had to sit out in gym class because I wasn't cleared for activity until the next day, so it wasn't until lunch that I had a chance to really talk to her. We quickly grabbed some food and made our way outside, headed for our usual table. I couldn't help but think of how lonely Tabby had been when Garrett and I were gone.

I realized on our way that there were some additions to the lunch area. Some of The Six—the boys originally accused of taking those topless pictures of me—had abandoned their parking lot luncheons in favor of joining the masses. Mark Sinclair and Jaime Chavez sat with some of the other popular kids while Eric Stanton and Scooter Brown surrounded themselves with football players only.

I walked past the football table only to be greeted with a bunch of smartass comments, none of which were favorable. I turned to face their ridicule, my muscles rigid with adrenaline, ready for a fight. But before I could start in, Mark intervened.

"Why don't you guys shut the fuck up. If you don't, I'll gladly sit back and watch her kick your asses. She may be small but she's fierce. Consider this your warning—you should probably thank me for it."

Silence fell over everyone.

I looked over at Mark, who gave me a sharp nod, then sat down next to Jaime.

Dumbfounded, Tabby and I continued to our table.

"So," she said, twisting open her bottle of water. "As you can see, not much has changed."

"Or has it? Seems like there's a rift in Jockland."

"Maybe. Mark and Jaime were really nice to me while you were gone. They've been worried about you and Garrett."

"So weird. Don't get me wrong, I like this turn of events, but it feels strange. I'd kinda just hoped everything would be normal when I got back."

"That's impossible now that 'roid-raging Donovan Shipman is gone."

"Thank God for small blessings."

"Small?" she asked. "I'd say that's huge."

"And it came at a huge price, too," I replied, my voice quieter.

Her smile fell. "He's going to go away for a long time, right?"

I nodded. "Seems like his get-out-of-jail-free cards have all been used. No big bad guy is coming to save him this time. He's on his own. Last I heard, there was a plea deal on the table, which would be fine with me. I just want him behind bars for a long time. Frankly, he'd be smart to take anything they gave him."

"Well, I hope he has a really burly cell mate named Bubba who likes to snuggle."

I nearly shot soda out of my nose as I choked on it.

"One can only hope," I said before clearing my throat. "Hey, do you think you can help me get caught up a bit on my assignments, providing we don't keep getting separated in study hall?"

"Of course. No worries."

"Great. I feel like I'd just dug myself out of that hole and now I'm right back in it."

"You might have to hang up your cape for a while—at least until you're back up to speed."

"Agreed."

The two of us ate and laughed and gossiped our way through lunch. It felt good. It felt normal. At least until I paid attention to the empty spot on the bench next to me. Then it felt like shit.

But that bench didn't stay empty the whole lunch period. Nope. That would have been way too simple. And my life didn't do simple.

Instead, I looked up at the door to the cafeteria to see AJ Miller making his way outside. The second he caught sight of me, I knew there'd be no avoiding what was headed my way. Ready or not, here came trouble.

"Hey Tabby," he said, propping a foot up on Garrett's usual seat. Tabby's eyes darted to me, waiting for a cue. AJ, sharp little cookie that he is, took one look at Tabby staring at me and started pleading his case. "Ladies, I couldn't help but notice that you both were looking a bit like someone had run over your dog, and I think I know why." He indicated the bench beneath his foot. "So I have a proposition for you. I know I'm a poor substitute for the infamous Garrett Higgins. I'm not quite as tall, dark, or handsome, but my gift for sarcasm, unparalleled charm, and ability to discuss the latest fashion trends should suffice in his absence." Once again, Tabby's eyes darted over to me, then back to AJ. "And," he said, an impish grin taking over his expression, "if all else fails, my face serves as a pretty good punching bag."

He gave her a playful wink for good measure.

"About that," Tabby started, squirming in her seat. "I should apologize."

"No need, Tabby. You thought I'd hurt Ky. You were being a good friend. A great one, actually. I'd have hit me, too, if I were you." His piercing green eyes fell on me. "I'd punch anyone that hurt her."

Tabby's freckled face flushed. The poor girl was swooning so hard I feared she would faint. She'd always liked AJ—thought he was noble for standing up to Donovan on my behalf. And, yeah, that changed in a blink when she found out what we'd thought he'd done, but the second she learned the truth, she was all about him and me getting back together. Honestly, I thought she would have rolled out the red carpet for him when he came to join us. The fact that she hadn't spoke to how much she cared about me—how loyal she was.

My cheeks might have warmed a bit at the thought.

AJ was still hovering when I pulled away from my musings long enough to notice. He was waiting for approval to stay.

"Are you really in this much of a hurry to commit social suicide?" I asked.

He looked around the outdoor eating area full of staring students and shrugged. "They can like it or not. I don't really care. Most of them are sheep anyway. If I like you, they'll accept you."

"Wow," I said with a laugh. "If your ego inflates any more, you'll float away. Is the view different from way up there?"

His playful expression sobered for a moment. "It's pretty damn good." I held his gaze for as long as I could until I finally broke and grabbed the pizza from my tray.

"Wait," I said, mouth full of the bite I'd just taken. "This isn't even your lunch period! Don't you TA for Callahan now? Shouldn't you be up doing his evil bidding or something?"

"I'm supposed to be organizing some after-school thing for him."

"Sounds awful."

"It is."

"So, to avoid it, you're skulking around the school looking for me?"

He shrugged. "Guilty as charged."

I sighed in my most put-upon way. "Well . . . it is Callahan, so I can appreciate the desire to bail."

"Totally," Tabby added, nodding a little too enthusiastically.

"So now that I'm officially Garrett's second-rate understudy, what do you need me to do, ladies? Brood? Act misunderstood? Be a feast of manly eye candy for you?"

Tabby giggled like a schoolgirl, covering her face with her hands. She was clearly going to be no help where AJ was concerned.

"Manly eye candy?" I asked, my tone incredulous.

He feigned offense. "Kylene, I spend at least five minutes a day in the gym actually working out, thank you very much."

"Five, huh? I would have thought someone with your DNA could have achieved those washboard abs in less time than that. Unless, of course, you don't have them anymore. . . ."

Without batting an eyelash, he whipped up his shirt. Washboard abs, check. But along with them were pecs I didn't remember, and lats that seemed to fan out wider than they had before. Yep, AJ Miller had grown up and filled out while I was away.

Maybe he wasn't so far off about the eye-candy thing.

"Well," he said, pulling his shirt back down. "Now that we have that settled."

"We sure do," Tabby said, her voice distant and awestruck.

"The bell is going to be ringing soon, and just in the nick of time," I said, gathering up my things. "Because I for one was starting to think that Garrett number two over here was about to lose more than just his shirt." Tabby's eyes widened at the thought. "Down, girl. Gonna need you to find a poker face, Tabs. And wipe that drool off your chin."

"It looks like my job here is done," AJ announced, smiling like he couldn't have been more pleased with his lunchroom interruption. And, as much as I wanted to put a damper on his parade, I couldn't. Was he Garrett? No. But in those five minutes spent joking with him, I'd seen the AJ Miller I'd fallen in love with once. The boy that used to make me laugh and blush and so much more. The boy that had stolen my heart. And even though I'd blamed him for breaking it, I knew I had to let those memories go, or at least try to. It wasn't fair to hold a false past against him. Once my dad was free and his name cleared, I wouldn't want people to hold his incarceration against him, either. AJ had pointed out the similarities between him and my father to me once, and he'd been right.

But knowing the truth didn't turn back time—didn't grant us those two and a half years we'd both lost. I had no idea if AJ thought we could pick up where we'd left off, but I didn't think even he was that delusional. At some point, we'd both have to acknowledge that we were different now. Changed by the events of that night and the fallout. The question that begged to be asked was: Were we changed for the better, or worse? AJ seemed to be the kid I remembered, wrapped up in a fancy, upgraded package. I, on the other hand, had pieces of the old me tucked away in an armored shell. I was tougher. Harsher. And far more prickly. It seemed like AJ's endgame was to be with me, but would the me he got be the one he actually wanted? I pondered that while I walked down the hall to my next class, uncertainty clinging to me like a wet shirt.

My only saving grace was that even if I'd wanted to rekindle something with AJ, I couldn't—not easily, anyway. Agent Dawson, code name Alex Cedrics, wouldn't make that easy. My new-to-town ex-boyfriend was there because of me, and, like it or not, that said something publicly, even if we weren't dating. There wasn't much room for AJ in that equation.

Even if I wanted there to be.

FIVE

I made it to final period before I even saw Dawson.

When I did, I had to look twice. He was in full hipster mode, and it totally worked. I'd only ever seen him when he was working or crashing my homecoming dance, so I had no clue what he normally dressed like. I'd always joked about him looking like he'd stolen his dad's clothes in the morning for work. In that moment, I wasn't laughing. Everything about his style suited him, from the fitted jeans to the threadbare vintage tee he'd paired with it. His hair was edgier looking than it was when he was working—more high-end and less buttoned-up. Agent Dawson was hot, there was just no denying it.

And it seemed the girls of JHS had quickly come to the same conclusion.

He moved through the hall like a shark cutting through a school of guppies. Those girls were babies compared to him—they lacked both the maturity and the intellect to hang. And even though I knew he had zero interest in their attention, it irritated me to see them flirting with him. Maybe it was because he wasn't doing a great job not flirting back. I wondered exactly what kind of reputation he was hoping to earn at my school.

Then he saw me, and his eyes lit up. He stopped talking to the harem following him through the halls and made a beeline for me. I'd barely gotten the word "hi" past my lips when he leaned in and nuzzled my cheek with his nose. Heat shot through me for a moment as if the reality of the situation had evaporated—as if we were two teenagers in love. Then I looked up at his haughty, mocking expression, and reality slammed back down.

"Hi yourself," he replied, his face still hovering close to mine. I looked away from him to see a gaggle of glaring lower classmen focused on me. Without thinking, I wrapped my arm around Dawson's waist and leaned into him, turning my gaze up to face him. Even though I knew who I was standing with and that a small part of me loved to hate him, I relished the feeling of shutting those girls up. They already hated me, that much was for sure, but letting them hate me for this particular reason was so much more rewarding.

Even if it was a lie.

"Do I need to explain to you how exes behave?" I said to him, quietly enough that only he could hear me in the chaos of class change. "Because you seem a bit confused."

His eyes drifted over in the direction the girls had been. A wry smile spread across his face.

"Friends of yours?"

"Hardly. And they're the only reason your balls are still intact."

He looked back down at me, a more serious expression taking over his face.

"Where are you headed now?"

"Spanish. You?"

The smile returned. "Same."

"Super. Can't wait."

"Maybe I can get a seat beside you. We can pass notes all class."

I dropped my arm from his waist.

"Seriously, how old *are* you? Nobody does that anymore. We *text* with *cellular phones*," I explained, overemphasizing the words.

"Good to know. Wouldn't want that to blow my cover. Now, which way are we going?"

"Follow me." I started off in the direction of the stairs and he trailed behind.

Once we got to our class, I took my seat next to Jaime Chavez while Dawson handed his schedule to Mrs. Stewart. She smiled at him, then announced him to the class. Not surprisingly, nobody but the girls cared. It was funny watching them perk right up at the sight of the new guy.

He was given a desk two rows over from me. I suddenly became overly self-aware. I needed a distraction.

"Who's the new kid?" Jaime asked, leaning toward me.

"That's Alex. My ex-boyfriend."

I could practically hear Jaime's surprise. I turned to find his eyebrows high on his forehead.

"Why's he here?"

"He transferred here because he was worried about me."

"Are you getting back together?"

His curiosity in the matter was unnerving.

"Why? Did you want a crack at dating me, Jaime?"

He frowned. "No." I tried not to laugh. "Does AJ know about him?"

"I don't know."

Jaime leaned back in his seat. "I don't want to be the one to break that news," he mumbled to himself.

That made two of us.

* * *

Thankfully, no notes were passed by Dawson that class. When the bell rang, I got up to leave and felt him hovering at my side, behind me just enough to let me out.

"Where to now?" he asked.

"Home, genius. School's over."

"And I was having so much fun. . . ."

His deadpan answer almost worked, but when I turned to face him, I could see the loathing hiding just below the surface. He hated being there almost as much as I did. Maybe more. It was hard to blame him, though. He'd survived high school once. Having to do it again seemed inhumane.

I had no idea what to say, which was rare, so I let it go and made my way out of the room.

"Did you learn anything interesting today?" I asked, hoping my casual question wouldn't arouse suspicion in anyone passing by. I looked back to find Dawson scowling at me as we descended the stairs.

"No. Just getting the lay of the land. Taking notes. The real work will start tomorrow."

"Ah . . ." His double entendre wasn't lost on me.

"Am I coming over later?" he asked as we made our way through the main doors and into the mass of people waiting for their buses.

A few of them shot me curious looks, then started whispering with those around them.

"Dude!" I said, pulling him closer. "You can't say things like that here. Everyone will always assume the worst about every comment. They'll read into everything. You might as well have just asked if we're having ex-sex tonight!"

A pause.

A smile.

"*Are* we?"

I looked to the sky. "I feel like there should be a special spot in heaven for me after this. . . ."

"All right, *Kylene*. You've made your point."

"Good."

"Let me try again. Can we meet up to do some *homework* tonight?"

I shot him a wary glance. "Better. Not perfect, but better. And I don't know. I have to get some things done at home. I'll call you."

"Getting your hooks in the fresh meat before he learns your reputation, Danners?" a male called out, followed by the laughter of those around him. I turned to find Scooter Brown high-fiving some kid I didn't recognize. I sighed heavily in preparation for the battle I was about to wage—but, for the second time that day, it never came. Instead, I heard Dawson's voice ring out over the laughter, shutting it down.

"I've known her for two years. I have no concerns about her reputation. This town's, however . . ." He grimaced, sucking air through his teeth. "If I were you, I'd be a bit more worried about that."

As if dismissing them entirely without a care in the world, Dawson turned his back and walked away, leaving them, and me, speechless for a moment.

"I'd watch your mouth, man!" Scooter shouted after him. Dawson just waved his hand in the air in a yeah-okay-I-got-it kind of way, never breaking his stride. The shock and awe of those that saw it was palpable. You didn't tell off football players in Jasperville. Not unless you wanted to live in fear for the rest of your school years. But Dawson had done just that and in a way that silently flipped the bird at them in the process. It was clear that Scooter and his crew had no idea what to do in response. Every attempt at a comeback came off weak. Every threat died on their tongues.

On Dawson's first day of school, he'd managed to shut down a legacy of bullying that predated the Internet like it was nothing. I frowned as I walked toward the parking lot, trying to deny the jealousy I felt. I'd barely survived my return to JHS from the moment I set foot in the place.

And Dawson, in one day, all but owned it.

SIX

I was exhausted when I got home. My body was almost healed from the attack, but my mind, if I was honest, wasn't faring nearly as well. Sleep had been elusive at best since that night, and my general level of anxiety was a five out of ten at any given moment. I felt like I was hovering on the edge of a cliff, constantly warring with myself as to whether or not I should jump or run from it screaming. The in-between was maddening.

The only thing I'd found to help was keeping busy, which meant not allowing myself to slow down. Sleep was slowing down on crack, so that just didn't work. Insomnia, however, wasn't proving a great long-term solution, either. I needed a distraction of a healthier variety.

Luckily for me, one called me around dinnertime.

I picked up Gramps' landline—the one he insisted he still needed. I didn't recognize the number on the caller ID.

"Hello?"

"Is this Kylene Danners?" a muffled voice replied.

"Who wants to know?"

"You can call me Jane."

"What can I do for you, *Jane*?" I replied, my dubious tone calling out her fake name.

"I want your help."

Silence.

"Help with what?"

"I need you to get me out of somethin'—before it gets me killed."

That got my attention. "What 'something' are we talking about here?"

More silence.

"I—I needed cash, and at the time this seemed the best way to get it . . ."

"How did you get it?" I asked, my heart in my throat.

"I . . . I had sex for money—*have* sex for money."

My hair bristled. *She's one of the girls* . . . "Are you working for someone else?" I asked, hoping she'd have the answers Dawson needed.

"Yeah, but I don't know who."

"Listen, I'd love to help you out, but you need to go to the police."

Her laugh was full of bitterness and contempt. "You can't be serious. You aren't that dumb, Kylene. You have no idea who the johns are. How powerful. How untouchable."

"Then how can I do anything?"

"You brought down Donovan Shipman without the help of the cops and exposed that shady doctor in the process. I'm willing to bet you can get me what I need to get outta this."

"Maybe," I said, leaning back into the couch. "But I'm hardly a PI or muscle for hire. I nearly died."

"Listen, I'm desperate," she said. "I can't bring down whoever is behind this and I don't trust the cops to, either. I've had my share of run-ins with Higgins and his crew." The tone of her voice told me she knew that the sheriff's department wasn't on the up-and-up—she just didn't know why like I did—the photo scandal had exposed the sheriff's shadiness almost as much as it had my boobs.

"I wouldn't trust the locals, either, but I know for a fact that the feds are looking into it."

"Really?"

"Yes."

"Well, that's great and all, but I'm not sure what they're gonna find. They might be able to track the johns—maybe identify some of the girls—but everything is done through disposable phones and direct deposits. I have no idea who's behind this. Neither do they."

I bit my lip, wondering if I should play the Dawson card, then decided not to. There had to be another way to get a lead.

"*Someone* has to know who he is," I said, letting my words hang between us.

The longer she took to reply, the more my anxiety spiked. My heart raced and my hands sweated, and I wondered if I'd just made a terrible mistake—pushed her too hard.

"Someone did . . . ," she said, her voice shaky with nerves. "She tried to get out. She's dead now."

Adrenaline shot through me.

"Jane, you need to go to the feds—"

"No!" she shouted before lowering her voice. "*No*. No cops. I can't risk it."

"Okay," I said in a calm tone. "But let's say I agree to help, what is it you want me to do? You need to tell me something about this mess you're in that I can use, or my hands are tied."

She was silent for a minute, undoubtedly weighing out her options. It was clear that she was smart—distorting her voice. Not giving me her real name.

Or maybe she was just scared.

"I need you to understand somethin', Kylene. I don't trust *anyone*—not anymore. I can't afford to." She paused for the briefest of moments. "But I need you to bring down whoever is doing this to me," she said, anger building in her tone. "You're my ticket outta this hell."

Hell was something I understood.

I thought about how bad things had to be for her—how desperate she must have been to have willingly gone into prostitution. My topless pics seemed like someone took my ball away from me on the playground in comparison. I'd gotten all the justice I ever would for myself. I wanted to do the same for her.

"Here's the good news, Jane. I don't need you to trust me," I said, sitting up straighter. "I need you to give me a damn clue so I can start bringing this asshole down."

"Danielle Green," she said so quietly that I barely heard her over the din in the background.

"*Danielle Green?*" I repeated.

She scoffed. "You don't know who she is, do you?" I shook my head as if she could see me. "That figures. People like you never see girls like us. It's like we don't even exist."

"Who is she?" I asked, trying not to flinch at her jab.

"She's the one that got me into this. The one in contact with the guy running the show."

My heart raced. "The recruiter."

She didn't reply. She didn't have to.

"I knew others, too—the ones before Danielle. They've gone missing over the years, but I never put together why until Danielle was killed. I thought they'd just run away to escape it all. Turns out that ain't the case."

"Who else—"

"Do yourself a favor and Google search for runaways in this area over the past few years. You'll find quite a few—too many, in my mind. Not a single one was ever heard from again."

"Give me the names, Jane," I said, trying to keep the panic from my voice.

"*Shit*," she breathed into the phone. "I have to go. Do what I told you to do. I'll call you soon."

I blurted out my cell number and she grunted in acknowledgment before the line went dead.

I sat in silence for a solid minute, my mind reeling from what had just gone down. This was the clue Dawson needed—the one he'd come to Jasperville for—and she was dead. Now he was left with an informant that wouldn't work with the feds—only me. He was stuck letting me in on the case whether he liked it or not.

With a heavy exhale, I grabbed my bag and keys and headed for Dawson's place. I was about to bring him the lead he needed.

A dead one.

SEVEN

I drove to the address Dawson had given me in one of his many texts I never responded to in the week following the attack. I knew exactly where his rental house was—a tiny neighborhood of small, slab-style ranch homes. It wasn't the fanciest place to live, but rental homes were few and far between. There were far worse in town, and even worse still the farther from town you got.

The redbrick house was the last on a dead-end street, which made for easy parking. I rolled up in front of 68 Willow Lane to find the lights on inside. Dawson stood in front of the picture window, scowling out into the darkness. I hadn't told him I was coming over. But did a fake ex-girlfriend really need to?

By the time I headed up the short concrete walkway, the front door was open. He leaned against the doorjamb, looking every bit his normal cocky self. His first day at school had done little to bruise his ego. In fact, it was bolstered by the drooling girls who did nothing to hide their desire for fresh meat. The fact that the fresh meat was there for me sure didn't help the lack of Ky Danners love in that place.

If looks could have killed, I'd have been six feet under.

"Miss me already?" he asked, plastering on a smile that looked more menacing than playful.

"I am a glutton for punishment," I replied, pushing past him into the house—without invitation.

"Come on in, *babe*—"

I stopped dead in my tracks. "Call me babe again and I'll bury your balls somewhere deep inside your abdomen. Got it?"

He laughed. "Isn't that what all high school kids say to the loves of their lives?"

"*Ex*-love of your life," I corrected. "And I wouldn't know. Go do some research, undercover wonder. See what you come up with."

"Did I hit a nerve? Memories of a bad relationship past?"

"No. Memories of bad eighties movies my parents made me watch. You sound like a douche when you say it. The fact that you obviously don't mean it only makes it worse. I literally want to peel my skin off when I hear it leave your mouth."

"Wow. Really?" He looked not at all unnerved by that statement. Unfortunately, it seemed to fuel his desire to repeatedly use that Neanderthal term of endearment. Or ownership, however you wanted to view it.

"Yes. Really."

"What about Loverboy?" he asked. "Does he get to call you *babe*?"

"Have you been spying on me?" I asked, my tone incredulous.

"Hardly. You were eating lunch. I was getting a water. No spying necessary."

"Listen, AJ is my issue to deal with, not yours."

"A fact I'm well aware of, but I can't stand watching him stare at you with those puppy dog eyes. Just put him out of his misery. It's the humane thing to do."

"More blood on the Danners family's hands? You'd like that, wouldn't you?"

His eyes narrowed to slits as he glared at me. "I'm not really a big fan of murder."

"Yeah, I got that message when we met."

His jaw tightened, the muscles of it straining while he clenched his teeth, undoubtedly an attempt to hold back whatever retort he was dying to throw my way.

"You may be a lot of things, Danners, but you're no murderer."

I leaned into him, our bodies close. "That's where you're wrong, Dawson. I am capable of murder and probably worse. You think I wouldn't have shot Donovan dead if I'd had a gun? That I wouldn't have beaten him to death with his bat for what he did to Garrett? I'd do it now if I had the chance. Premeditated and all. There are few things I won't do for the people I love, Dawson, because it's a short list of names. I don't have friends—I have family. With me, you're either in or out. And if someone comes after my family, don't think for one second that I won't do whatever I have to to stop them."

Whether it was from the set of my face or the strength of my words, for a fraction of a moment, Dawson looked shocked. Like for the first time since he'd met me, he realized that I wasn't all talk. This bitch had bark *and* bite.

Then the moment passed, and his expression returned to its steely resolve.

"Admitting that to an officer of the law isn't the wisest move, Danners."

"Oh, but you're not, remember, *babe*?" I looped my arms around his waist, pressing my body to his while I pushed up onto my tiptoes to whisper in his ear. "And I'm far too smart to ever let you catch me."

I pushed him away, and, just as expected, his expression was murderous. Irony at its finest.

Silence stretched out between us until he shook his head and walked into the living room.

"I know you're here for a reason, so why don't you just fill me in." He sat down and casually draped his arms over the back of the couch. But there was nothing casual about his stare.

"I got a call tonight. It was a girl—one of *the* girls." I waited for realization to settle in, then continued. "She said she wants me to help her. She won't go to the cops. She's too paranoid, not that I blame her."

"She wants *your* help? Why you?"

The desire to slap him was hard to curtail. "Maybe because I brought down a prescription drug ring all on my own?"

He seemed unimpressed by my argument. "Maybe." I opened my mouth to argue but he stopped me with a raised palm. "Tell me what she said. Don't leave anything out."

So I did. I relayed every tidbit she'd given me. Even those she didn't. I profiled her as best I could from our conversation—that she was white, likely poor due to her need for money, and around my age—so he could get a sense of who we were dealing with. Then I told him the bad news about his recruiter.

He let out a slow exhale.

"Listen, I know that's a blow to your case, but at least you have a name now—someone to investigate."

He nodded slowly. "I'll have someone discreetly search her residence—see if Sheriff Higgins can get into her locker after hours so rumors don't start flying. We need to keep this under wraps for as long as possible. We don't want the killer to know that we know. And this girl—Jane—you have to gain her trust. Keep her working with you. We need all the information you can get from her since you're convinced she won't come forward."

"I can do that," I replied with certainty.

He gave me a wry smile. "Pretty sure of yourself there,

Danners. That high opinion is almost warranted. Almost. Pull this off and I might be willing to let that character flaw slide in the future."

"Oh, I highly doubt that, Dawson. That would mean you'd have to eat shit with a smile, and I don't imagine you'd like the taste much."

"I've eaten it once before. I'll manage."

It took a second for his words to fully register. Dawson admitted to being wrong about someone or something in the past. Very wrong. The way he said it was so acerbic that I could practically feel how much he hated it. Dawson was a lot like me in that regard. Being wrong wasn't something we did well.

It wasn't something we did often, either.

"I shall have a spoon ready for you, then," I said.

Again with the malicious smile. "I prefer a fork."

"Of course you do." I sat down on the far end of the couch and stared at him. "So, where do you want to start?"

Without a word, he got up and disappeared down the hallway leading to the bedrooms. The floor plan of the home was similar to Gramps', albeit a decade or two newer. Ranch homes never deviated much from that layout.

He returned with a laptop and sat down beside me, pulling the coffee table over so he could place the computer down. We were so close that our legs kept brushing; I made a point to cross mine away from his. I tried not to notice the upturn at the corner of his mouth when I did.

I watched as he typed in a general search for missing girls in our region of southern Ohio over the past five years. A list of names appeared, far longer than I expected. It made my stomach turn. He looked at me, his tight features telling me he felt the same, then asked if any of the names looked familiar.

A preliminary scan revealed three that I could identify. Two were older than I was. One was much younger. Danielle's was nowhere to be seen.

For an hour and a half, Dawson dug into whatever information was available online, from the most general demographics to whatever mentions there were—if any—regarding their disappearances. Most of those were found on social media sites and were posted by friends. And there were painfully few of those.

That got me thinking.

"Dawson," I began, still staring at the screen. I could feel his body shift to face me. I kept my eyes fixed straight ahead. "How does someone go missing—or run away—and next to nobody cares? Not the family? Or the media?"

His silence disturbed me enough for me to turn and look at him. When I did, I could see the anger in his eyes.

"Because you don't matter."

I could feel the blood drain from my face. "That's it, isn't it? That's the connection between all these girls? That's the profile." He nodded once, a slow deliberate movement that made my heart stop. "Jane's right. The ones she knew—they really didn't run away. . . ." This time, a shake of his head, his nose slashing a horizontal line in the air.

Some of those girls—their names little more than a reminder of their existence—were gone, and I could think of only two fates they'd met. The first being that they had just run away. The second being the more obvious given Jane's insistence on the use of past tense when describing them. Death had found them because either they were no longer of use to whoever was exploiting them, or—like Danielle—they'd tried to leave and got caught. How they'd gotten caught was what left me the most unsettled. Jane had said she couldn't go to the cops because nobody would believe her, but maybe it was deeper than that. Maybe she couldn't go because she, like me, knew that the corruption in this town ran far too deep and was far too insidious to navigate. One wrong word to the wrong person and you were dead. Jane hadn't called me because she thought nobody else would believe her.

She feared the wrong people would.

EIGHT

Mr. Callahan wasn't a complete dick when I rolled into class late Tuesday morning. My surprise must have been evident in my expression because he actually made a point of telling me to sit down before he had second thoughts and decided to send me down to the main office. I could get my poker face on to avoid a trip down to Mrs. Baber's lair of doom. No problems there.

At least, not until gym class.

The second I set foot in the gymnasium, I knew I was in trouble. Instead of the track-pants-clad teacher I expected to greet me, I found a balding, misogynist football coach standing in the middle of the gym talking to a couple of his players. He glanced over at me and scowled. Coach Blackthorn was hardly a Kylene Danners fan, since I'd screwed his perfect season.

Nothing good could come of his substituting for Ms. Davies.

"Looks like the trash won't stay out," he said to the kids around him, loud enough for me to hear. Which, of course, was his intention.

"Sure doesn't," I replied, eyeing him up.

"Tell me something, Danners. Did Shipman really hit you or did you give yourself those bruises so you could get yourself some sympathy 'round here? You don't look that banged up. He would have done more damage than that. . . ."

My cheeks flushed with anger just as the rest of the class started filing in from the locker rooms. Exactly what I needed—an audience.

"What would you know about it? You've probably never taken a real hit before in your life—not without a full set of pads on."

His eyes flashed with anger. My insult had hit the appropriate nerve.

"You ain't so tough."

"Neither is your boy Donovan. At least not without his steroids," I said.

It was so quiet in the gym you could have heard a pin drop.

His face turned red with anger, and I wondered if he'd explode or have a heart attack if he didn't calm down. I didn't want his blood on my hands—or the rest of me, for that matter—so instead of prodding him further, I turned and headed for the locker room to get my backpack.

"Get out of my class!" he shouted after me.

"Gladly."

I went straight to Principal Thompson's office, Coach's implied destination when he tossed me from class. Mrs. Baber looked at me suspiciously when I walked in. I raised my hands as I stepped up to her massive wooden fortress of a desk.

"I didn't start it," I said. "Coach sent me to see Principal Thompson."

She eyed me tightly for a second before picking up her phone and buzzing his office—the office that was only ten feet away.

"I have Kylene Danners here. Okay . . . I'll send her in."

With a jerk of her hair-helmeted head, she granted me safe passage to the principal's office.

I opened the door to find the forty-something salt-and-pepper-haired man awaiting me. He was leaning back casually in his chair—an attempt to look less official, no doubt. When I walked in, he stood up and indicated that I take a seat in one of the two mismatched chairs.

Then he came around to sit on the edge of his desk in front of me.

"To what do I owe the pleasure, Kylene?" His tone was full of optimism I knew he couldn't have felt. Me showing up at his office was an ominous sign at best. At worst, he already knew what I'd said in gym class, thanks to the efficiency of the JHS rumor mill. I hesitated at first, wondering what my best angle was.

Eventually, I decided on blunt-force truth.

"Coach Blackthorn and I got into it in gym class."

His brow furrowed at my revelation. "What happened?"

I told him what Coach had said to set me off. His anger at the scenario was thinly veiled.

"Before you say anything," I said, warding off his reply, "I should tell you that I may or may not have, in fairly colorful language, told him off."

Principal Thompson looked at me for a moment before his gray-blue eyes sparkled with amusement.

"Exactly how colorful *was* your language?" he asked, maintaining a straight face. It was no big secret that Thompson wasn't a fan of Coach Blackthorn. To his credit, he did his best to remain professional, though I was pretty certain he was cursing the fact that he wasn't there to see our little showdown.

"I mean. . . . on a scale of pale pastel to electric rainbow, I'd say it was a vibrant watercolor."

He had to turn away and cover his laughter with a cough. Then he sat down in his chair and leaned his elbows on the desk.

"You know I can't sanction that kind of behavior, Kylene." When I opened my mouth to apologize, he stopped with a raised index finger. "But, I know how Coach can be, and he was clearly in the wrong here, so I'll make you a deal. You keep that colorful mouth of yours closed during gym, and I'll make sure he does the same. Okay?"

Okay? It sounded too good to be true.

"You drive a hard bargain, sir, but I'm in."

"Good. Now, is there anything else I can do for you?"

"Nope. I'm just going to go wait for lunch to be served."

He stood. "Then I won't keep you. I believe it's burger day."

"Wouldn't want to miss that. . . ."

"Definitely not." He walked me to the door and opened it for me. "Please come see me anytime, Kylene. My door is always open."

"Providing you can get past the front desk," I said quietly enough that Mrs. Baber wouldn't hear me.

At that, he laughed.

"I'll let her know you get a free pass."

He gave me a little wave before heading back to his desk to do whatever it is that principals do when they're not disciplining unruly students like myself. I headed down to lunch, hoping I had enough time to at least get a few calories in me before the second half of the day. If not, I would fall asleep in class for sure.

I was certain Principal Thompson didn't want to see me again that soon.

NINE

I tore out of the cafeteria as fast as I could, needing to stop by my locker on the way to class—a detour I rarely, if ever, took. As I slammed the metal door shut, I found Dawson looming.

"Jesus!" I shouted.

"Any phone calls?" he asked, his voice hushed, his hazel eyes keen. I glared at him for a moment, trying to calm my breathing.

"No. Did you hear anything yet?"

He shook his head no, letting his façade fall for a split second, revealing his frustration.

"Hopefully I'll hear from my contact later today."

That made two of us. Something good needed to come from the search of Danielle's home and locker.

While possibilities ran through my mind, Dawson's arms wound their way around my neck. I glared up at him like he'd lost his mind and he smiled. We looked like a couple at an eighth-grade dance. People were rushing past us, staring baldly as they did, and it was all I could do not to knee him in the balls just to get away from their scrutiny, but I didn't want to cause an even bigger scene. Had we been alone, his nuts would've required an ice pack.

Possibly two.

Remembering to play the role of someone who had once

loved him—possibly still did—I beamed up at him, a sure warning of what was to come from anyone who really knew me. Then I remembered that Dawson may have known things *about* me—facts he'd read and profiling he'd done—but he didn't really *know* me. Not the way Garrett or Gramps or my dad did—AJ, too. But he was about to learn.

I mimicked his gesture, looping my arms around his neck while making sure they were inside of his. I reached up on my tiptoes so I could cup my hands around the back of his head right where it met the neck, then I started applying pressure, pulling his head down toward me. He resisted, as I knew he would. Leaning in closer, I continued my controlled attempt to pull him into a clinch.

"I think now is a good time to set some rules, *Alex*," I said, my words like shards of ice. "I don't do the word 'babe' and I also don't do public displays of affection—ever. Got it?"

"You did yesterday," he countered, his voice strained.

"You caught me off guard yesterday, and I capitalized on the moment to piss some people off."

"So what don't you do under normal, nonpetty circumstances?"

"No hugging. No kissing. No holding hands. No ass grabbing, or arms over my shoulder. Nothing that resembles you attempting to claim territory in any way. I'm not a tree to piss on. Try again and you'll see."

I adjusted my hands and pulled down harder, his head jerking for a split second before he resisted with ample force to maintain an upright position.

"You done?" he asked, his voice straining slightly.

"That depends. Are you?"

I took his lack of response as a yes and let go. Dawson's face was flushed, which could have been played off as my charming effect on him, but I knew otherwise. He'd had to work a lot harder than he'd expected to against my hold. He hadn't planned on my Muay Thai training, that much was certain.

I glanced over my shoulder to make sure we hadn't unintentionally made the wrong kind of scene—that we looked like exes flirting between classes. From what I saw, students were just stealing glances at the new kid and his train wreck ex-girlfriend. I was thankful for that, because I feared if we'd made a spectacle of ourselves, I would have been forced to do something drastic to dig our way out of it. I shuddered to think about how deeply that would have offended my PDA rules.

"So basically, I'm not allowed to act like I like you?" he clarified, his lips at my ear.

"Yes. That."

He pulled away, shaking his head in frustration. Then the warning bell rang and the halls began to clear.

"You know your plan will never work, right? Teenagers are like dogs in heat. They're all over each other—especially when they're trying to get back together."

I cocked my head at him. "Are you implying I'm a bitch?"

His incredulous glare made him look so terribly put-upon. "At the moment, no. But my point, that you so obviously missed, is that your rules aren't even remotely believable."

"You have met me, correct? Do I scream warm and cuddly, 'get your free hugs here' to you?" I stared at him in awe for a second, wondering how he ever became a detective if he was truly that clueless. "Saying that me not partaking in PDA isn't believable is like saying it's not believable that a junkyard dog tore your arm off when you stuck it through the fence to pet it."

Silence. "Now who's making the bitch reference—"

"Focus, Dawson," I said, pointing two fingers at my eyes.

"*Alex*—" he corrected with a smile.

"Whatever the hell your name is, just listen up. Touch me like that again and we're going to have a problem. Got it?"

He looked like he wanted to say something smart then thought better of it, reining in the response before it could escape. Instead, he nodded in agreement, shocking the hell out of me. Apparently, I did a crap job of hiding that fact, which seemed to leave him satisfied.

His smug smile returned.

"I can't wait until we have a public fight and I get to slap that look off your face," I muttered under my breath.

"What? I can't even smile at you?"

"That wasn't a smile. It's too glib to be a smile. But, yes, you can smile at me. Sparingly. And no googly eyes."

"Do I look like I make googly eyes at anyone?"

It was a fair point. "No, but I do have a certain charm. . . ."

"Not enough, Danners," he said, choking on a laugh. "Definitely not enough."

His smile widened before he turned and strode off. He never looked back to see what state he'd left me in, but I had a feeling that Dawson rarely looked back. He was an "eye on the prize" kind of guy, singularly focused on the task at hand. He'd do whatever he had to in order to shut down the sex ring in town.

Even if that meant having to tolerate me and my rules.

TEN

After school, I did what I'd promised Gramps I'd do: I went to see my father. He sat down at the seat across the glass panel from me at Logan Hill Prison, looking as if he'd aged a year since I'd last seen him. His hair was grayer than I remembered, and his normal rosy pink undertone had gone sallow. I knew I was the cause of at least some of that stress. I didn't want to think about what the others were.

"Hi, Dad."

He looked at me for a moment before speaking. "I was wondering when you'd finally get around to coming down here." His eyes narrowed further. "Judging by that hint of yellow on your cheek, you waited long enough for the bruises to fade."

Dammit. Busted.

"I didn't want you to get more worked up about it—"

"Worked up?" he shouted, before his gaze snapped to the guard on the far side of the room. He took a deep breath to calm himself, fully aware of the consequences if he didn't. "I told you to lay low—to come to me before you did anything!"

"I didn't have time—"

"You could have died, Kylene!"

"I know that, Dad. We've already gone over all this on the phone. There's no point in rehashing it now."

"There is a point—to make the reality of what nearly happened to you finally sink in!"

"Dad," I said, taking a deep breath of my own. I'd never heard of a visitor being dragged from the prison before, but I didn't want to find out that it was possible. "I'm buried in that reality. Every single time I look in the mirror or move the wrong way or visit Garrett in that hospital, it's burned into my consciousness."

"Then imagine what learning about this event has done to the people that love you, Ky. I'm stuck in here, unable to protect you. Do you have any idea how hard that is for me?" I didn't bother to answer his rhetorical question. I had a pretty damn good idea what it had been like, because I knew how I would have handled it. In truth, I was amazed my dad hadn't scaled the walls to try and escape.

"If I'd thought for one second that what happened that night was going to happen, I never would have gone."

"You should have called the sheriff," he said, though it looked like it pained him to even suggest it.

"Yeah . . . ," I said, exhaling hard. "I guess it's time I fill you in on a few other things since you're already mad."

So I did. I told him that Sheriff Higgins had been paid off and that there was an underage prostitution ring in Jasperville and that somehow those two things were tied back to an unknown bad guy—someone that went by the name Advocatus Diaboli. And then I told him that the sheriff knew he'd been set up/framed/whatevered. Shock flashed in his eyes until his cop face fell into place as he mulled over my story, swirling it around to see if it felt right or not. He leaned forward, propping his elbows up on the table, wanting to get a better look at me. To read me like I was a suspect in interrogation. Even behind the thick glass panel, my father was intimidating.

"How do you know all this?"

I hesitated for a moment. "I may or may not have illegally

listened in on an FBI interrogation." His eyebrows shot up. "Long story short, turns out Luke Clark knew Higgins was indebted to the AD as well. Seems this asshole has his hooks in a lot of powerful people around Jasperville."

My father's expression darkened. "And beyond, apparently. . . ." He leaned back in his chair for a moment, stretching his arms behind his head. "Kylene, I want you to listen to me. I know you want to get me out of here, and nothing would make me happier than to be with you, but you cannot continue down this road. I forbid it. Proving who took those pictures of you was one thing, but this? This is something else entirely. If this Advocatus Diaboli has high-powered people willing to off teenage girls, then you don't need to put yourself in his sights again, got it?"

I had no idea how to respond. I wanted to say, "Yes, Dad. I'll stay away," but my knee-jerk reaction when threatened was to do the opposite of what I should. Smart? No, not at all. But that didn't make it any less true. The new school district psychologist had expressed concerns about how I was dealing—or not dealing, as the case seemed to be—with the attack homecoming night; I'd been nearly killed twice in the span of an hour. She said my frankness about the event was a coping mechanism, and that I hadn't really begun to peel that away so I could deal with the emotional fallout. In fact, she thought it might be making me more reckless—a fair assessment. Maybe if I'd told her about the night terrors and insomnia I'd had since that night, she'd have gone a little easier on me.

I looked at my father sitting on the other side of the glass awaiting my response. There was only one thing I could say to him.

"I'll agree to your terms, but only if you let Meg and I help you get your appeal. That doesn't involve angering sketchy criminals. We just have to find a technicality to get you off on."

His jaw flexed. "I'll consider it."

An uncomfortable silence grew between us until I decided to change the subject. I filled Dad in on how Garrett was doing, my return to school, and, eventually, the AJ conundrum. By the time I was done venting, he looked positively overloaded. I wondered if he wanted to go back to discussing criminals instead.

"Well I'll be damned," he muttered to himself.

"Dad. You're in prison. You are damned."

He laughed. "I guess I just never expected to discuss AJ in this manner again."

I shrugged. "Neither did I."

"How's he taking it all?"

A sad smile overtook my expression. "Like AJ takes everything—in perfect stride. He doesn't want to make a big thing out of it. But, Dad, I think about the things I said to him—how I treated him—"

"Ky, you can't be responsible for the things you don't know. That applies to AJ, too."

"I guess. . . ."

"Listen, if he's willing to forgive and forget, then let him. There's no sense in making yourself crazy over it." An awkward parental pause stretched out between us. "So . . . does this mean you're getting back together?"

"Dad—"

"I just want to know."

"No, Dad. We're not getting back together."

"Why not?"

"It's complicated."

He quirked an expectant brow at me. I hadn't planned to bring Dawson, aka Alex, up; guess I screwed the pooch on that one.

"My ex from Columbus moved to town. He wants to get back together, hence the complication. . . ."

"Am I allowed to ask questions about this ex-boyfriend I've never met before?"

"I'd rather you didn't."

"But that's what fathers do."

"Dad, trust me when I say that you don't want to this time, okay?" I hesitated for a second before continuing, knowing that what I was about to say would hurt him. "We got close when all the trial stuff was going on. You weren't around much then."

The way he exhaled back into his chair meant my sleight had hit home. No way would he be digging deeper into that story. He looked like I'd punched him in the gut.

"Would I approve of him?"

No.

"Yeah. I think you'd like him. He's smart and driven. A real go-getter."

"And he's good to you?"

Not especially, unless you count the time he saved my life. . . .

"The best."

He looked thoughtful for a moment. "How old is he?"

Twenty-three.

"Eighteen."

"Then he'd better keep his damn hands to himself."

"I'll be sure to tell him you said that."

The officer in the room gave us a warning that our visit was nearly up, breaking our moment of normalcy.

"So," I said, squirming in my seat. "About your case—"

"I said I'll think about it."

"I could give Meg the transcripts I have. It can't hurt to have her look them over. And I'm not technically involved then, which is a total bonus for you."

He bit the inside of his cheek as he mulled over my suggestion.

"Maybe."

"Time's up, Danners," the officer called, coming over to retrieve my father.

"Will I see you soon?" my father asked as he got to his feet.

"Of course. Love you, Dad. And be careful."

He shot me a look that was full of determination and a hint of mischief.

"Always."

I watched as he was led away through the security doors and ultimately back to his cage, the one I had to free him from. Though he hadn't exactly given me permission to share the transcripts with Meg, he hadn't forbidden it, either. A "maybe" was as good as a "yes" in my books. In truth, a "no" would have been, too.

One way or another, I was going to get my father out of that place—even if it damn near killed me.

ELEVEN

I pulled into the driveway at Gramps' house just in time for my phone to start buzzing. Knowing who the caller likely was, I yanked my cell out of my bag and answered in a flash.

"Hello?"

"Did you learn anything?" Jane asked. She wasn't messing around. I had to admit I liked her style.

"I think so."

"And?" She did nothing to hide her impatience.

"All the girls that I found were declared runaways because they didn't seem to have anyone that cared enough about them to try and find them. They were loners—outcasts. For the most part, lower income families with sordid histories—abuse, drugs . . ." *Fathers in prison* . . . "There was no media coverage of most of their disappearances, except for a couple, and I doubt there'd be much at the sheriff's office regarding them, either—not that I have access."

"I'm sure that cute friend of yours could get you what you needed," she said. My hair stood on end and my heart stopped. How could she possibly know about Dawson?

"My friend?" I replied, my voice low and thin.

"Yeah. Garrett. The sheriff's kid." I let out an exhale as I collapsed against my car. "I'm sure he can help you get whatever you need."

"Not from a hospital bed."

"I meant when he gets out, obviously."

"Maybe you haven't spent much time at the sheriff's department, but I can assure you, just because your dad runs the show there doesn't mean you can walk in and start looking through whatever you want, assuming there's anything there to look through in the first place."

"Reports had to have been filed on at least a couple girls, otherwise the media wouldn't have known."

"And I'm willing to bet that report is all there is in those files."

Silence. "Fine. Maybe you're right, but he's gotta be your best bet for getting at those records. We don't have time to waste—I think I might be the next recruiter. . . ."

"Why?" I asked, my anxiety spiking.

"I knew Danielle the best. She trusted me. The person in charge had to know that."

"But she tried to get out," I argued.

"Right, which could be even worse for me if he thinks she told me who he is."

Yeah. Total catch-22.

"All right," I said, sighing hard as I wondered how I was going to use Garrett as my cover for whatever Dawson was able to dig up. But keeping all these lies and cover stories straight was sure to get me caught in the end. It was a tall order, especially with my current state of mind. "I'll talk to Garrett and see what he can do."

"But he can't know why," she blurted out, almost interrupting me.

"That's going to prove challenging, don't you think?"

"He was with you when you went after Donovan, right?"

"Yeah, but he also knew why I was doing it."

"Well, I'm sure you can figure it out."

"I'll make it work," I grumbled, pretending to be irritated.

"You can't tell him anything, Kylene. Nobody can know what we talk about, got it? Not even that new kid you're hanging around with."

"Tabby?" I asked, surprise in my voice.

"Well, yeah, her too, but the guy. The one that looks like he's too good for the rest of us."

"That's my ex-boyfriend. . . ."

Silence. "You sure about that?" she asked. "He doesn't look so 'ex' to me."

"Then maybe you should look closer."

At that, she laughed. "Maybe in a different life, we could have been friends."

"Or maybe we could now."

She went silent again. "A girl like you wouldn't be friends with me." Her voice was soft and low, but that didn't mask its acerbic tone. If Jane thought she ranked lower on the social hierarchy than I did, then her circumstances were more unimaginable than I could fathom.

The line went dead.

I let out an exhale that had my lips flapping wildly, raspberry style. Then I let my head loll back so I could stare up at the sunroof. How in the world was I going to use Garrett as a cover when he was still in the hospital? I couldn't wait until he was out. As far as I was aware, he had no concrete release date, and I knew damn well Dawson wouldn't wait until he did.

Then I wondered how I was going to work with an informant who trusted no one. A ghost of a girl who'd fallen through the cracks into the hands of a criminal, ready to exploit her. Anger rushed through me at the thought. Though Jane was no typical victim, she was a victim nonetheless. If I had to play the game by her rules for the time being, I would. But Dawson didn't have to, and I doubted he would. He had resources I could only dream of and a handler back in Columbus who could look into all kinds of leads on his behalf. All I could do was hope that somehow, in our quest to save Jane and the rest of them, we didn't lose her.

Or worse.

I had planned to just call Dawson about my chat with Jane but decided it would be easier to go over and tell him in person. I seemed to be more convincing live than on the phone. Lucky me.

The front door opened after I parked Heidi and killed her engine. Her exhaust system was struggling as of late, so you could hear her coming from a solid block away, which would explain why Dawson stood in his doorway looking amused. In the car department, he had me beat.

"Something important to tell me or have you come to take me back?" he asked as I walked up to meet him.

I rolled my eyes. "The former, clearly."

"And?" He moved back enough to let me in the house.

"Jane just checked in."

"You came all the way over here to tell me that?"

"No. I came over here to tell you that she's pushing for me to use Garrett to get into the sheriff's office and snag the files on her dead friends. I guess the good news is that she thinks I'm capable of such a feat. The bad news is that I have no clue how I'm going to maintain the façade of not working with the cops but getting this kind of information."

"So you're asking me for help?"

His rhetorical question was duly noted.

"I can't do this on my own," I said, narrowing my eyes. "But neither can you."

He closed the door and walked into the living room, plopping himself down with an exhale.

"I need her, Danners. The search of Danielle's house was a total bust. The FBI couldn't find anything tying back to the prostitution ring at all. Everything else we've compiled so far has led nowhere. All the suspected johns lead to dead ends. They've traced the bank accounts they pay to an offshore account at the kind of bank that doesn't answer to FBI requests. The only girls we've ever tracked down all refuse to talk because they're afraid they'll be the ones arrested. This is the first big case I've gotten to work on since I joined the bureau—I can't afford for it to end badly." For a moment, I felt the immense pressure he was under. For the victims; for himself. "I've already got the information Jane wants you to look up, but it's paltry at best. Good ole Sheriff Higgins didn't dig too far into those girls' disappearances. There's nothing there. It's like he didn't even consider for one second that they didn't run away."

"Interesting. . . ."

I let my voice trail off, which garnered his attention.

"Say what you're thinking."

"I'm thinking that offshore accounts smack of someone a little higher brow than anyone in this town. That maybe our good friend, the AD, might be behind the scenes, pulling the strings. That maybe it's time we corner Higgins and get the unofficial findings on their cases. See if he intentionally covered something up."

"You think the AD made him overlook their cases?"

"At this point, I'm not putting anything past him or anyone in this town, for that matter. Jasperville is built on a shady foundation. We can't afford to trust that the cops did their jobs."

"No," he sighed. "We can't. Which is unfortunate, given that he's the one that searched Danielle's locker."

As if on cue, Dawson's phone rang.

"Yeah," he said in a gruff voice. "You found a cell phone? Is it a burner? Did you look through the messages—you know what? Leave it. I'll look myself—"

Silence fell heavy in the room. I could hear the mumble of the sheriff's voice on the other end but couldn't make out the words. Judging by Dawson's increasing pallor, they weren't good.

"I see. . . . Yeah, okay. I'll be there in fifteen."

He hung up without saying goodbye.

"What'd he say?" The young fed's eyes fell on me, still a bit wild, then he shook his head and headed for the door. "Hey!" I said, grabbing his arm as he brushed past me. "What's going on?"

"It's official business. I can't tell you." His dismissal was obvious, but I was having none of it. I jumped in front of him, blocking the door.

"Can't or won't?"

"Both, now move."

"Something he said has you spooked. It's written all over your face. Should I be worried, too?"

"Yes" was his only response.

I tried to let it wash over me and failed. The cold hand of fear trailed its way across my neck, making me shiver.

"What did Higgins find, Dawson?" I asked, my voice barely a whisper.

He hesitated for a moment. "He searched her text history. Lots of times and dates on there—things he expected to find." Another pause. I leaned in closer. "But the final text—the last one she received before she died—had a name in it. *Your* name."

The fear took hold, choking off my air as I struggled to breathe.

"My name?"

He nodded. "With a question mark after it. It was from the same phone number all the other texts were from—most likely the pimp. You're on his radar, Kylene."

Not good. So not good.

"What do we do?"

"*We* don't do anything. *I'm* going to go meet with the sheriff and go over the evidence. I'll have a plan put together after that."

"Okay. . . . Be careful."

"Me? I'm not the one whose name's on that phone."

"Right, but if we're worried about the sheriff's potential cover-up of the girls' disappearances, then your meeting could be an ambush—especially if the AD is involved. He cleans up his messes, Dawson. I know that all too well."

"I'll be careful," he said, giving me a wan smile. "Thanks for your concern."

"Well," I said, taking a deep breath to try and shake the dread growing inside, "you *are* my ex-boyfriend and all. I don't want to have to fake cry at your real funeral if you get yourself killed."

"Mmm . . . that would be awful. I'll try not to put you out like that." He continued to stare at me as I hovered awkwardly near the entryway. There was always such a weight to his gaze—like he was far older than his twenty-three years. Like he'd weathered so much pain in his short lifetime. I wondered if maybe he had. Then I wondered if he saw the same in me. "I'm going to follow you home before I meet up with Higgins—make sure you get there all right. I know how you love a dramatic car chase."

I forced a laugh.

"So, does this mean you'll be dropping your cover story now? If Danielle was your purpose for being there, then . . ."

"I don't know yet. I don't get to make that call. There could still be a connection at the school and until I hear otherwise, I'm going to push to stay put—especially with that text on Danielle's phone."

He pinned me in place with his stare.

"And here I was hoping to be rid of you," I joked, though my tone lacked any hint of humor.

"Afraid not, Danners." He lingered for a beat, then reached past me for the door. "I should probably go."

"Yeah . . . I have homework to do tonight, anyway. I'll see you tomorrow." I slipped through the door he'd just opened and headed for my car.

"What's this?" he asked, following me out onto the front step. "No goodbye kiss?"

His smug smile was back, but I could see it didn't quite reach his eyes. The notes of green in them always seemed to flare whenever he was trying to get under my skin. But I did appreciate his attempt to lighten the mood.

"I don't kiss my exes, Dawson."

He laughed. "Might want to tell AJ that."

I shook my head. "See ya later."

"Good night, Danners."

I drove home trying to convince myself that my name in that phone wasn't really a big deal. Danielle was gone, and though she was a victim, that fact was somewhat overshadowed by the role she'd played in exploiting other young girls. She was a predator—a trafficker in her own right. I was certain she had solid reasons for her involvement, but they died with her.

I'd never learn her story.

With her gone, she couldn't leverage me into the sex trade, but the fact that the person in charge knew me well enough to know that my circumstances were not good was unnerving.

That person had knowledge of my personal life that they shouldn't have, and I couldn't help but scroll through a mental index of who that could be.

I spent the whole night pondering just that.

TWELVE

The next morning, Tabby nearly attacked me in the hallway on our way to gym to ask why Alex wasn't in first period with her. I hesitated before giving her some lame excuse about him texting me saying he didn't feel well—that he wasn't up to coming. She seemed satisfied with my response, but I wasn't. I was jealous that he could blow off classes to go do whatever he was doing. Given the night's events, I knew he hadn't just randomly slept in.

Coach was subbing for Ms. Davies again, but, not surprisingly, he took a very different tone with me, ignoring me entirely. I could live with that. I felt like I should stop by and deliver Principal Thompson a fruit basket or something.

When lunch rolled around, we took our seats at our usual table—the one farthest away from everyone else. While I poked at what appeared to be some kind of loose meat sandwich, Tabby rattled off everything that I'd missed in her first period class. Apparently, some girl had attacked another one over (yep, you guessed it) a boy, and poor Mr. Andrews—the tiny history teacher—had to pry them apart while dodging blows. Tabby seemed floored by this behavior, but I knew it was nothing new. JHS was like a zoo full of wild animals. It was only a matter of time before a fight broke out amid the different species.

"Anything exciting happen to you today?" she asked, daring to take a bite of the lunch special du jour.

"I found a quarter by my locker. . . ."

She shot me an unimpressed look. "Are you going to text Alex and see how he's doing?"

"Why would I?" I asked, sounding confused. "He's my ex, Tabs, not my boyfriend."

"You're not worried?"

I could feel the weight of her stare as I took a bite of my food.

"No. He's not dying, Tabby. He's just under the weather."

I dared a glance her way. I was met with a sour expression, those sharp eyes of hers narrowed, assessing me in a way I knew I would soon regret.

"You don't seem like you care very much about him, Ky."

"I care!" I argued, feigning offense. "But we're not together anymore."

She hesitated. "He clearly still likes you. Why else would he have come here?"

"Poorly made decisions?" I offered.

"Do you want to get back with him?"

"I want to eat my lunch."

"You totally bailed on him at homecoming—"

"To go find evidence at Mark's house, Tabby! Not to avoid him."

"You never talk about him—"

"Because I don't want to be *that* girl!"

"Or light up when he's around—"

"I'm not a neon sign, Tabby. And I don't really get excited about anyone, in case you haven't noticed. In fact, this is me excited, see?" I pointed to a forced grin, and she laughed.

"Well . . . you have a point there. It's just that—"

"Tabby," I interrupted. "Alex and I are complicated. Always have been. Probably always will be. We left on . . . *interesting* terms. Our history isn't all rainbows and unicorns."

"Okay. . . ."

"Really. I used to light up when I was around him," I said, leaving out the "especially when he left" portion of that truth for obvious reasons. "A part of me is glad he came to school here. It's just hard to adjust. My life in Columbus was different. Inserting him in Jasperville isn't so simple."

Her eyes drifted off toward the school, then back to me. A tiny smile tugged at her lips.

"Is it your difficulty inserting him into your life that's making it hard for you, or is it the return of someone else that's complicating things?"

Before I had a chance to puzzle out what she was implying, a tall dark shadow engulfed me. I turned around to find her meaning standing behind me.

AJ, the lunch crasher, was back.

"You're not actually going to eat that, are you?" he asked, straddling the bench to sit beside me. He stared down at my tray for effect, his features twisted with disgust. I stifled a laugh—his face had always been highly animated.

"Nope, I bought it on the off chance you'd be joining us."

His brow furrowed. "I can't tell if that was an act of kindness or aggression."

I shrugged. "Guess you'll never know."

I popped a fry into my mouth and grinned.

"I'm glad you came to join us again," Tabby said, drawing our collective attention. The twinkle in her eye as she stared at us told me I was going to want to kill her before the lunch bell rang. "We were just talking about you."

"Were you?" he asked, snatching a fry off my tray before I

could bat his hand away. Stealing a fry from me was tantamount to asking to be flayed alive. AJ knew that, which meant only one thing. He, too, was testing me.

"Not really," I replied, sliding my tray out of reach. "Tabby was talking about boys she wanted to see naked. I mainly nodded and smiled to placate her." I dared a glance over at my pale friend whose face had turned a scarlet red. "Care to weigh in?" I asked him. "Although you've probably seen most of what JHS has to offer in the locker room already, so this might be a boring conversation for you."

"Well, Chris Tomlinson does have an impressive eight-pack," he said, reaching past me to grab another fry off my tray. Again. I would have snapped him into a headlock if I'd been thinking clearly, but the feeling of his body brushing against my chest seemed to temporarily short my circuits. By the time the thought of defending my food occurred to me, he was sitting upright in his seat, munching away on his pilfered fry.

"Awesome. I'll see if I can get him to flash me in Spanish."

"You won't be disappointed," he said with a wink. A clear challenge.

"And if I am?" I replied, shifting closer to him in my seat. Challenge accepted.

"I'll find something better to show you."

"Promises, promises." I dismissed him with a wave of my hand.

"You know me well enough to know I always deliver on my promises."

"Oh really?" I replied, my tone thick with incredulity. "Like you did that night at Garrett's when you said you'd run through the woods naked if I beat you at arm wrestling?"

"You totally cheated!" he said, feigning affront.

"And the night you said you'd moon the grandstand at the Pumpkin Festival when we were riding the freshman float?"

"That was a wardrobe malfunction. I was wearing button-fly jeans and I couldn't get them down in time!"

"Mm-hmm," I said, staring at him as I took a long sip of my fountain pop. I let the straw linger in my mouth for a second too long, and I could feel the weight of AJ's gaze fall on my lips before returning to my eyes. "What about the night at Matthew's Ice Cream Shop when you promised to streak around the building if I out-ate you?"

He swallowed hard. "I'll take a rematch on that one anytime. . . ."

"All I hear is a lot of talk, AJ."

"You calling my bluff, Ky?"

I took a bite of a French fry, never breaking my stare. "I'm just stating the facts."

He leaned in closer. "Name the place. Name the dare."

I felt a rush of blood fill my face as my body remembered how easy it was to be with him. How easy it was to want to be near him. To want him to touch me.

"The cafeteria's a pretty public spot," I said, my voice low and husky. "Lots of people to see you in all your glory."

"Is that the challenge then? Drop trou and run through the tables?"

I quirked a brow. "Think you got it in you, Miller?"

He leaned in closer still. So close that I could feel his breath on my face when he spoke.

"Depends on the prize."

Seconds seemed like years in that moment. I didn't want to be the one to flinch first, but reality had crashed into me and I knew I had to. I wasn't just flirting with AJ. I was courting disaster at best. At worst, total scandal.

"No prize," I said, pulling away from him. "Just you making good on your past bets."

I doubt he felt it, but for a split second, his expression fell with the sudden turn of our conversation. It was clear that he'd wanted a different outcome—expected it, even.

"Another time. Maybe in a couple weeks—for your *eighteenth birthday*," he replied, forcing a smile.

"Your birthday is coming up?" Tabby asked, unable to curb her excitement.

"Yeah. Two and a half weeks from today, I can officially adult."

She cringed. "That makes it sound less appealing."

AJ laughed as he stood up. "Ladies, I'm going to leave so you can eat your dubious lunches without the distraction of me streaking—*today*."

He looked at me for a moment before stepping over the bench and walking away.

"Bye, AJ!" Tabby yelled after him. I, however, remained silent, scared to open my mouth for fear of what might tumble out. I needed super glue, and lots of it. Then the redhead's eyes fell on me and I knew I was in trouble.

"So that ex-boyfriend of yours," she started, unable to conceal her delight at what had just taken place.

"Which one?"

"Exactly . . . ," she replied with a fiendish smile.

"Tabby—"

"I'd say you and Alex just found yourself another relationship complication."

"No, I'd say I wandered a little too far down memory lane with AJ. That's all."

She shook her head.

"That's not what it looked like to me."

"Then maybe you need glasses."

"Sorry, Ky. My eyesight is 20/20, and it's telling me that you're in one hell of an ex-boyfriend mess."

I exhaled heavily, letting my lips flap with the force.

Although I would have loved to argue her observation, hindsight was 20/20, too, and I knew damn well I'd lose—especially after what she'd just witnessed. It had always been so easy with AJ. Easy to joke. Easy to laugh. Easy to love. Until it wasn't. But that hurdle was no longer on the track, and the farther I ran, the clearer I could see him standing at the finish line. Distance and distraction would be the only cure for my AJ situation, and that was going to prove difficult—maybe even impossible. With he and I having made amends, he would be unavoidable for sure.

The only solution I could see was to pick a side—and, given the case, I knew which side that would have to be. Simple in theory, but not so in application. My lunch hour left me vulnerable to AJ's stealth attacks, and since Tabby was clearly flying the #TeamAJ banner, she'd be no help at all. I had to somehow convince my redheaded wingman that Dawson was the guy for me.

Her and me both.

THIRTEEN

With still no word from Dawson, I decided to swing by the law office of Stenson, Marcus, and Clark to see Meg. I found the secretary, Marcy, at her control center, fielding a call when I walked through the door. She looked up at me and her face went pale in an instant. I waved at her, hoping it would make us both feel less awkward. It didn't, but it was worth a shot anyway.

I stood there until she hung up.

"Is Meg in?"

She nodded, forcing a smile, then picked up the receiver to buzz her boss. Seconds later, swift and determined footfalls echoed from the hall of offices. Meg stepped into the front area with a look of guilt and relief on her face.

"Come on back," she said, waving me over. I joined her and the two of us made our way back to her office in silence. No playful remarks. No witty repartee. For once, the gravity of a situation pressed down on us far too heavily for that.

She closed the door behind me, shutting us into her office for privacy. Meg had worked on my behalf to clear me of any potential charges regarding her dead colleague, Luke. The one I'd killed in self-defense. She'd managed to keep my name out of the papers because I was a minor, and she may have threatened every single person at the sheriff's department with legal action if my name was ever leaked. But it was Jasperville—some version of the truth would eventually come out. One the town could spin to its liking.

Everyone would think I was a murderer, just like my father.

"So," I said, unable to bear the silence between us or the parental look of fear and guilt on Meg's face, "do I still have a job here, or what?"

She broke out into a laugh that nearly camouflaged her sob.

"Jesus, kid . . . do you really want one after everything that happened?" she asked.

I nodded. "I do, but I could use a brief hiatus, if that's okay with you. I've gotta get caught up on the schoolwork I missed last week—even if my bank account disagrees."

"Of course," she said, her sympathetic smile making me look away. "And, just so you know, the Sinclairs confirmed today that they wouldn't be pressing any trespassing charges against you for being on their property the night of homecoming. I spoke to Sheriff Higgins about it yesterday."

"What about Luke . . . ?"

She paused. "I told you before, Ky. The sheriff was never going to go after you for that."

"So I'm in the clear—in the eyes of the law, at least."

Her expression fell to one of sad understanding. "Yes. But I'm guessing the court of public opinion has been far less than forgiving about Donovan Shipman."

"That's a painfully accurate assumption."

"Have a seat," she said, indicating the club chair reserved for clients. I fell back into the tasteful gray upholstery and exhaled. She sat down on the other side of the desk from me and tented her fingers against her mouth. "How are you doing with all of this, Ky? And don't give me your canned response. I want the truth."

"Surprisingly well, I think. I'm having trouble sleeping, but that seems normal given what happened."

"Are you seeing a therapist?"

"The school psychologist—just once."

"Did it help?"

"Maybe?"

"How's Gramps taking everything?"

"I mean . . . as well as can be expected."

"And your father?"

"Let's just say I'm surprised he didn't go postal and land himself in solitary."

"That is shocking." Her laughter trailed off until she stared thoughtfully at me for a moment. "I'm glad you did what you had to do, Ky."

I hesitated for a moment, pushing from my mind the memory of Luke holding a needle to my neck.

"I didn't have a lot of options at the time."

"No. you didn't." Her eyes narrowed, assessing me from across her desk.

"What? Why are you making that face at me?"

"Because," she mused, leaning forward in her chair. "I can't help but feel like even though I'm your acting counsel, I don't know everything that happened that night."

I shifted in my seat. "Because you don't. . . ."

"Attorney-client privilege still applies."

I thought about what my dad had said—how he didn't want me to investigate his case. Then I thought about how alike Meg and I were. How she hated cover-ups and conspiracies as much as I did. Telling her the truth about that night would rope her into a case far bigger than the lot of us, but she at least had an avenue that could best lead to my father's release.

So I took a deep breath and told her everything.

By the time I finished filling her in about the sheriff, the prostitution ring, and the AD, she looked genuinely shocked. Possibly a little scared, too. I wasn't sure how to handle the Agent Dawson bit, but I opted to tell her about his involvement in the girls' case, but not his undercover mission. Not that Meg would have, or could have, told anyone, but I thought it best to keep that to myself. It would have only led to more questions I couldn't answer, especially about my involvement.

"So you think this Advocatus Diaboli is somehow tied to your father's case?"

"Yes. Sheriff Higgins all but said he was."

"This is very circumstantial evidence."

"I know. I need more before I can try to get Dad's ruling overturned, or case reopened, or whatever it is that would happen if new damning evidence came to light."

Meg shot me an incredulous look. "You need an attorney to look into his case again? Because I spent the first ten years of practice working at the DA's office, Kylene. I know a lot about prosecutorial law. If I think we can get this case reopened, I'll do it. In a heartbeat."

"I was hoping you'd say that," I said reaching into my backpack. I pulled out a copy of the transcripts Striker had given me and dropped them on the desk. "You'll need these. I've highlighted some suspicious testimony and made notes in the margins about some of the witnesses."

She smiled at me, amused. "You sure you don't want to be a lawyer, kid?"

"And sully my pristine reputation?" I asked indignantly. "Not a chance."

Our laughter rang through the room, the soundtrack to our newly founded partnership. Meg was the ally I'd needed to help my father, and now I had her. Together, we would free my dad—maybe even get him reinstated to the FBI. But Meg was definitely right about one thing. The court of public opinion was far crueler than Lady Justice herself.

Maybe my dad would never be able to shed the skin of his murder conviction.

FOURTEEN

Sleep finally came, but it wasn't kind. I shot up in bed three times, my recurring nightmare of Luke plunging the needle into my neck playing on a loop in my brain. I might as well not have slept at all. And, judging by the late-night text I'd gotten from Dawson, I figured he wasn't much better off.

I doubted he'd be in school the next day.

Since I woke up at five, I got to school early for once in my life. I stopped by my locker to unload whatever books I didn't need that morning. When I threw open the door, my cell started ringing. I quickly glanced around the hall before answering.

The second I heard Jane's voice, I froze.

"I don't have a lot of time, so I need you to shut up and listen," she said by way of greeting. "I told you the other night that Danielle was dead. What I didn't tell you is I know that because I saw her die with my own eyes. I watched a man cut her throat, bend down and grab her by the ankles, then throw her into the river like she was nothing. She hasn't been reported missing yet—and she died about two weeks ago. I know this because I followed her that night. She'd told me she was going to meet her contact and tell him that she wanted out. She was sober now and this way of life wasn't for her anymore."

I fell back a step into the locker behind me.

"Don't ask me why I followed her," she continued. "I think you of all people know what it's like to just get one of those feelings that you can't ignore. So I did it. I don't know what I hoped to get from going—if I just wanted to make sure she was safe or see who was in charge so I could maybe use it against him somehow, but none of that matters now. What I learned—or confirmed—is that there is no way to leave this hell. That if I want to get out alive, I need leverage or I need him shut down."

"That's why you need me," I whispered.

"I was going to tell you the names of the other girls I knew that were in this—old recruiters. Write these down," she said and I yanked a pen out of my bag. "Kit Casey, Rachel Fray, Angela Mercy, and Samantha Dunkley." I scribbled them down on my hand as quickly as I could. "After seeing what happened to Danielle, I know they were killed, too. This guy doesn't leave loose ends."

Every hair on my body shot up at her words. Luke would have still been alive at the time Danielle was killed—maybe he was responsible for her death. Maybe Dawson's whole case was over before his undercover mission really got started.

The warning bell rang, jarring me from my thoughts. I could hear it echo through from Jane's line as well.

"I have to go—"

"Wait!" I shouted. "I need the date and time that you last saw Danielle." She rattled off both and I wrote those down on my hand too.

Then she hung up.

With no time to waste, I took a picture of the information on my hand, then ran to the bathroom to wash it off. If Dawson's recruiter was killed by the very person she worked for—the one he was hoping to find so he could get closer to the man running the show—then processing Danielle's crime scene, investigating her life, would be his best bet at finding the killer. Once we had him, we had the asshole responsible for exploiting and discarding girls like the ones Jane had mentioned. The ones who nobody seemed to care about.

The Throwaway Girls.

As I rushed down the hall, I sent Dawson a text: GET YOUR ASS HERE NOW! WE NEED TO TALK. Then I ran into Callahan's class just as he was closing the door.

I hadn't heard back from Dawson by lunchtime, so I decided it was time for drastic measures. Instead of heading to the cafeteria, I bolted for my car and drove off, hoping I wouldn't get caught in the process. Dawson's house wasn't far away, so I knew I could make it back before lunch was over, but the margin for error was minimal at best.

When I pulled up to his house, not a light in the place was on. I ran up to the door and started pounding on it. If anyone had seen me, I'd have just looked like a crazy ex-girlfriend—not out of the ordinary for Jasperville. It took a solid thirty seconds before the deadbolt turned and the door flew open to reveal a half-naked, totally disheveled-looking Dawson.

"What the hell, Danners—"

"Do you ever check your phone?" I asked, pushing past him through the doorway.

"I was sleeping."

"Yeah, well, it's time to wake up."

I rambled off every detail from my phone call, his intense stare never faltering. Then I shoved the picture on my cell phone of the girls' names in his face. He grabbed a pair of glasses off a wooden end table and looked them over. I watched as realization dawned in his expression. He recognized every one of them from our search the other night.

"What's the date and time for?" he asked, though I suspected he already knew and just wanted confirmation.

"Danielle's murder."

He let out a breath. "I need to know where that crime scene is," he said, running his hand through his hair as he made his way down the hall. Without invitation, I followed. "I need to process it for forensic evidence."

"But it's been two weeks," I countered. "And we've had some crazy thunderstorms in that time."

"You watch too many cop shows," he said, storming down the hall to his bedroom. He grabbed a T-shirt off the bed. As he pulled it over his head, his half-naked status finally registered. It seemed wrong to stare at his abs while discussing a murder, but for the briefest moment, I did.

And they did not disappoint.

"We just need to use a different chemical to find any traces of blood. And we can process it for DNA. Whoever killed her is most likely the same person prostituting the girls. If we get a hit, it could be case closed for two different crimes. But I can't do that without the location of the crime scene. The number on Danielle's phone is no longer in service, therefore untraceable. Another dead end."

I followed Dawson out of his room into what he'd set up as an office across the hall. And by office, I mean a desk under the window and an enormous whiteboard lining the far wall. It was covered with names and photos and profiles of the girls we'd found after Jane's initial call—the Throwaways—each with a picture at the top and a trail of information underneath. Some of those trails were painfully short. How it was possible to find so little information on a person was unthinkable. It was like they'd never existed.

"I've been combing what little evidence was obtained from Danielle's home and locker to see if she can be tied to any of the other runaways. Now that Jane has come forward with these other potential homicide victims, I can work to tie them all together and build a list of suspects solely based on who they all had in common."

"If you can manage that." I pointed at the meager details he had so far.

"That's just a preliminary workup on them. Now that I know we're likely looking for someone who they all had in common, I can dig deeper. Jane said the other girls were recruiters, too. That's how the sex trade often works. The people in charge use someone—usually a former victim—to reach out to girls they've predetermined to be easy prey. They would have to have known these girls well enough to know that they could be leveraged into doing what he made them do."

His response, though harsh, made a lot of sense.

"Okay. What do you need from me?"

"I need you to do exactly what you're doing. Keep feeding me information and work on gaining Jane's trust." His business expression fell for a moment, revealing a softer edge. "She's smart and a survivor. You two have that in common."

An uncomfortable silence closed in around us for a moment until I couldn't breathe. I had to break it.

"What are you going to do?"

"I'm going to sit here and dig up everything I can on the girls. Until Jane contacts you and tells you something about the crime scene, I'm stuck with that."

"You planning on making an appearance at school anytime this week?"

"Yes, I'll be back. Agent Wilson wants me to get whatever I can on teachers the girls had in common so I can share it with the bureau's profiler. Hopefully narrow down the suspect list."

"Good. I'm not prepared to keep covering for you to keep the rumors at bay."

His brow quirked. "Rumors?"

"I'm sure there are some good ones already."

"Can't wait to hear them."

"You're no help at all."

Any hint of amusement fell from his face. "I have a case to solve, Danners. I can't be worrying about high school bullshit."

"I wish I didn't have to," I muttered under my breath. "Anyway, I need to get back before our lunchtime meeting quickly becomes the afternoon topic of conversation." He shot me a curious look. "Like we had a quickie . . . make-up sex, maybe?"

"Alex Cedrics doesn't do quickies."

I fluffed past that statement as fast as I could. "That's great, but I should probably still go."

"Or you could cut class and help me out."

My eyes went wide at his words—the stickler for the rules baiting me into breaking them.

"Are you trying to get me into trouble?"

He scoffed. "Like you need help with that."

"You really want me to stay?"

"I have homework assignments that need to be done. You could do those so I can investigate."

While I stared at him, struck by the audacity of his idea, he walked down the hall to the coffee table and grabbed his laptop. He plopped down on the couch and went straight to work as though he didn't have to do anything else to convince me to stay—or maybe he didn't care either way.

With my blood pressure rising, I pulled my phone out and called Mrs. Baber to tell her I didn't feel well and went home for the day. I rode out her riot act about policy and procedure and following the rules, then hung up.

Dawson glanced up at me, a mischievous look in his eyes.

My eyes narrowed in return.

"You wanted me, you got me. Now . . . where do I start?"

* * *

Hours later, I needed a break. My resentment for doing homework while Dawson investigated was making me angry—or maybe I just needed food.

"You got any snacks in this place?" I asked as I passed him at the kitchen table.

"Chips are in the pantry."

I opened the long cupboard door to see the chips in question. I was not impressed with what I found.

"Aww . . . what's up with this hippie crap? No nacho chips? Cheese doodles?"

"That stuff is nothing but chemicals."

"Yeah. And?"

He let out a put-upon sigh. "Try those. You'll like them."

"I highly doubt it," I mumbled, pulling out the bag of hipster puffs. "If this is made with some kind of vegan cheese crap, I'm going to throw them up all over your rug."

With snacks in hand, I returned to my spot on the couch and picked up my books.

"You puke, you clean."

"Can you not talk while I'm doing *our* homework, which, by the way, is so unfair that I don't even really know where to begin my rant. You do realize that Tabby basically does my physics for me, right? You're going to fail that class. I hope that goes down on your permanent record. . . ."

"It won't."

Dick. "Shhhh . . . studying."

A low laugh escaped him, but I didn't bother to look up. I was on the brink of understanding electrical current and resistance. The power of the ohm was strong with me in that moment. No need to disrupt that (pun totally intended).

Dawson sighed and got up from the kitchen table to join me

on the couch. He reached for the snacks, then grabbed the remote. He turned on the TV to a prison documentary in progress, highlighting all the horrible things that happen there. I quickly snatched the remote and shut it off. For a moment, we sat in silence, the crunch of my hippie-not-really-cheese-puffs the only sound in the room.

"You know those are always an overdramatization of prison life," he finally said.

I found little comfort in his words. "Yeah . . ."

"Your dad will be removed from most of what goes on anyway because he's not in the general population."

My anger spiked. "You sure about that, hotshot? Because up until the last time I saw him, he was. Some bullshit about paperwork not being filed properly or a holdup or missing something—basically, someone was screwing with him."

When Dawson didn't respond right away, I turned to face him. His gaze was fixed on me, dark questions brewing behind his warm hazel eyes.

"What do you mean?"

"I mean he was in gen pop. He had the war wounds to show for it. Hell, he threw himself down a flight of stairs to be put in the infirmary just to be isolated for a few days. That's desperation at its finest, even if he did his best to play it off as a strategic move and nothing more."

His eyes narrowed further. "Even if there was some sort of clerical error, it shouldn't have taken long to fix," he said, puzzling something out in his mind. "When did he get pulled from gen pop?"

"I don't know. The last time I saw him, he didn't say and I forgot to ask. I was a little preoccupied, fielding his parental anger regarding my near-death experiences."

"I'm sure you were."

"In fairness, I think he took it about as well as any father who's in prison and can't keep his daughter safe would."

"You have to understand why."

I exhaled hard. "I do."

"The way you operate under the motto 'do first, think later,' Danners—it's not working out so well." I had no snappy comeback for that one. It hit too close to home. "Tell me more about the hospital room with Luke," he said gently.

"I'm sure you read the report," I replied, looking away from his assessing gaze.

"I know he attacked you and you got away after stabbing him with a needle full of potassium chlorate—a needle he'd planned to murder you with to tie up loose ends, I assume. What I can't understand is how a girl much smaller than Luke, wounded badly enough to be hospitalized, was able to fight him off and incapacitate him long enough to stab him with his own weapon."

Silence.

"I waited until he made a mistake," I explained, pinning heated blue eyes on him. "Men get cocky when they only see you as prey."

"True, but that's not it. Something else happened in that room."

"No—"

"I think you're covering for someone."

"No—"

"And I want to know who."

"I should go," I said, stuffing my books into my bag. Dawson's gentle hold on my arm stopped me.

"You have to trust me, Kylene." I looked over at him to find earnest eyes staring back. "It's the only way this arrangement will work."

I took a deep breath. "Sheriff Higgins found us. He's the reason I'm alive, but he didn't kill Luke. That was me. I sent him out of the room and told him to come back only once I started screaming for help. I need whoever has him under his thumb to think that he's not involved."

"You did it to cover for him?" he asked. I couldn't be sure, but I thought I heard a hint of awe in his voice.

"He knows my father is innocent, Dawson. I need him, like it or not."

He released my arm. "Thank you," he said. I nodded as I looked away, unable to meet his gaze. "Now, I think you should stay here and finish our homework. Maybe once you're done, you can help me follow up on the leads I found."

My eyes darted to him. "I'm willing to fail if you are."

He smiled at me. It was full of mischief.

"Then let's get back to work."

FIFTEEN

After I left Dawson's, I went home only to find it dark and empty. Instead of sticking around, I grabbed my duffel bag of sparring gear and drove into town. The silence in my car allowed my thoughts to take center stage—something I tried not to let happen since the night of the attack. The school psychologist said that I needed to find a healthy outlet for my emotions to help alleviate any anxiety I was having. My current strategy, intentional or otherwise, was to hurl myself into whatever distraction I could, a convenient plan given my life was riddled with investigations to occupy my mind. But it was the quiet moments I couldn't escape, no matter how hard I tried.

They threatened to break me.

To drown it out, I sang to myself, wishing I had the money to put a stereo in my ailing Honda. Heidi was really letting me down when it counted most.

I pulled up to Kru Tyson's Muay Thai gym, hoping that my workout could drown my raging thoughts. In truth, I was willing to bet that kicking things would prove to be better therapy than my counseling session. Maybe sitting around talking about things worked for some, but for me—not so much. I was a physical girl. I needed a physical outlet.

Mark Sinclair and some other guys were all jumping rope

to warm up, so I quickly changed in the bathroom and joined in. My ribs tweaked a bit with my deep breathing but not enough to pose a problem. The pros of being there outweighed the cons, big-time.

"How you feelin', Danners?" Tyson asked as he stepped out of the ring, headed for me.

"Not one hundred percent, but better."

"Anybody givin' you shit at school?"

"A couple kids, but nothing major. Coach Blackthorn, on the other hand . . ."

"What did that hillbilly do?"

"Ran his mouth about me being trash . . . said I was lying about my injuries to get sympathy."

Tyson's expression turned murderous. "Did you shove your foot up his ass?"

"Tempting, but no. I just told him off until he kicked me out of class."

A small smile tugged at the corner of his mouth. "You didn't back down."

"I didn't back down."

"Because fuck him, right?"

I nodded. "Because fuck him."

"You be sure to let me know if I need to go pay the coach a little visit. Maybe set him straight."

"I will totally do that."

A few of the guys laughed at our exchange, then Tyson told us to hang up the ropes and started assigning people to various activities. Once he was done, he motioned for me to follow him over to the far side of the gym.

"You wanna tell me how you're really doin'?" he asked, his voice gentler than I'd ever heard it.

"I mean . . . it's a lot, I won't lie about that. I don't know how you handled two tours overseas."

"I was highly trained, Danners. Combat was second nature to me. You're not military." He eyed me closely and I tried not to squirm. "You talkin' to someone about this?"

"I had to see a counselor last week. They wouldn't let me come back to school until I did."

"The fallout from something like this—you can't mess around with it. I mean it. That shit will send you into a spiral if you let it. I got buddies who never got over what they went through in the Middle East. Don't let that be you." I nodded, unsure what to say. If Tyson was worried about me—and he didn't worry about anything—then maybe I should have been far more worried about myself. "Training will help settle your mind. I started boxing in the military for that reason. Muay Thai basically saved my life. So, injured or not, you need to be in here, got it?"

"Train through the pain, right?" I asked, forcing a smile.

"Life doesn't wait for you to feel better before it comes at you again. It'll knock you down and stomp on you, but you can't give up. You keep fighting until the fight's over, you feel me?"

I nodded again, the macabre thought of me fighting Donovan flashing through my mind. That had almost been the end, and though I didn't want to tell Tyson the gory details, he would have loved to know that it was his voice in my ear that kept me alive that night—that drove me forward when I wanted to quit. I planned to use that voice to help get me through the fallout of that night, too.

"Will it always be like this?" I asked him. "Will I always view life through this filter?"

"I wish I knew the answer to that," he said. "I've still got mine."

Before I could press the issue, he told Mark to come hold pads for me. I watched as Mark sauntered over, his lean but muscled frame stopping in front of me. He looked at me with sympathetic eyes as Tyson told him what would happen to him if he pushed me too hard. None of it sounded pleasant.

Mark looked honest-to-God nervous.

"It'll be fine," I said, taking my stance. "He won't *actually* bury his hand in your face."

"Yeah . . . I'm not so sure about that." He held the pads at waist height and I landed a body kick. My ribs tweaked with the rotation, but I breathed through it, allowing the muscles to calm down rather than spasm. "You okay?" he asked.

What a loaded question that was.

"I will be."

I hoped that was true.

The next thirty minutes was spent trading blows and kicking the heavy bag. Not once did the dread creep in. Not once did I think of Donovan or Luke or everything that happened that night. It was then that I really started to believe that things could one day be normal again. That maybe, just maybe, Tyson was right.

Muay Thai could save me, too.

About ten minutes before training was done for the night, the squealing of car tires cut through the loud music in the gym. The screech of breaks just outside the building got our collective attention—as did the slamming door and car peeling out down the street.

Tyson and I were the first out the door. I looked down the road to see taillights disappear around a corner. Then I turned to find what had been dumped out.

A young dark-haired girl was scrambling to collect her belongings and stuff them back into her purse. Some of the guys were already headed her way. I watched her recoil from their approach.

"Hey!" I shouted. "Give her some space." I ran over to ward off their good intentions that were undoubtedly scaring her more. That's when I saw the freshly split lip on her face and swollen red mark on her cheek. It would be a deep shade of purple when she woke up.

"What happened?" Tyson asked her. She said nothing in response.

"Let me handle this," I told him. "You guys head in. I'll be right there." He eyed me like he wanted to argue, but I flashed him a look that said I meant it. He nodded, then barked orders at the others to do as I said. I turned to face the girl, who'd headed off around the building. "Wait!"

"I can't talk to you," she said, never looking back.

"Can I take you somewhere? Home? The sheriff's department?"

She wheeled on me, her features twisted into a nasty snarl. "Back off!"

I took a step in retreat, hands up. "Just trying to help."

At that, she scoffed. "You can't help me. No one can. . . ."

She took off in a run, the shadows of the alley swallowing her up.

If I'd been a betting girl, I'd have put a lot of money on her being caught up in Jane's world. Hell, maybe she *was* Jane. Either way, it gave a face to the situation. A boost of reality that I needed. These girls' lives were in danger.

Dawson and I had to help them.

SIXTEEN

Friday afternoon proved torturous. We got out of final period early so we could file into the gym and show our school spirit at yet another pep rally. Because I had no spirit to speak of, I thought it was a great time to make a break for it. I headed toward the door nearest the parking lot. Unfortunately for me, Mr. Callahan had positioned himself there in case students like myself got any wild notions of skipping out early.

"Miss Danners . . ."

"I was just going to go put my bag in my car so I didn't have to haul it into the gym," I said without skipping a beat. If he'd thought he was going to sweat the truth out of me, he was sorely mistaken. I'd faced death square in the face before. Mr. Callahan didn't stand a chance.

"Let's go," he said, putting his arm out to block my way and usher me back the way I'd come.

"It'll take two seconds. I promise."

"To the gym, Ms. Danners." He put a little heat in his tone that time. It wasn't too shabby an effort. I had to give him credit for that.

"Fine," I said, turning back around to head down the hall. Along the way, I tried stopping off at the girls' bathroom, but Mr. Callahan saw right through me.

"I don't think so," he said, closing the door before I could enter. "There's a bathroom right by the gym."

"But I have to go now!"

"If you'd had to go that badly, you wouldn't have made it to your car and back without peeing your pants. Keep walking."

I huffed and turned toward the gym again, walking as slowly as possible.

"You know, I thought you would have learned something after what happened to you and Garrett—that when you go looking for trouble, you'll eventually find it. I'm sorry to see that you didn't. Hopefully I can say more for Garrett when he returns."

I bristled at his words, wishing I could whip around and bury my shin into the side of his face, but that wouldn't have panned out well for me for multiple reasons.

"And here I thought we were turning a new leaf," I said, scowling at him.

"Girls like you never change, Ms. Danners. I know that all too well. You won't stop until you end up in jail or dead."

Wow. He wasn't pulling any punches.

"Girls like me, huh?" I asked, wheeling around on him.

"*Kids* like you. Troubled homes. No stable parental figures. Nobody to keep track of your comings and goings."

"You don't know anything about me or my home life."

He quirked a brow at me. "I think I know way more than you'd like. I've known many girls like you over the years. Their stories don't end happily."

"Well, sir, that's what too many years in the public school system will get you. Maybe you should retire . . . no time like the present!"

While we stood in the middle of the dimly lit hallway (JHS's nod to going green), staring one another down, I heard footsteps approaching from behind me. They were getting louder by the moment.

"I wondered where you went," Dawson said, closing in to find Mr. Callahan and I embroiled in a silent battle.

"I just wanted to drop my bag off at my car before getting my pep on," I explained, pulling my gaze away from Mr. Callahan long enough to force a smile at Dawson.

"I'll take it," he said, reaching out his arm. I let him lift the bag from my shoulder and tried not to notice him assessing Callahan and me in the process. He had such a calm, cool expression while he did it. I had to admire his skill.

It was clearly one I lacked.

"I'll make sure she gets to the rally, sir," he said, smiling at Mr. Callahan. "I know she's trouble sometimes, but she's totally worth it."

He put his hand on the small of my back and directed me down the hall toward the gym. Callahan, not trusting either of us, followed behind until we reached the bleachers and started to climb the steps in search of a place to sit. Tabby stood and waved frantically at us from up near the top, so we headed that way. It wasn't until we were committed to sliding past other students to join her that I saw who she was with. AJ Miller sat on the far side of her.

Not good. So not good.

"I was hoping I'd find you!" she shouted over the cries of the crowd.

"Yeah. Me too. This is way better than my planned escape."

She looked at me curiously before realizing my meaning. "You tried to bail, didn't you?"

"Yep. And got busted by Callahan."

We sat down in between the two boys, AJ to her left and Dawson to my right. I prayed that if I just sat there still enough, maybe neither one would say anything. It seemed foolproof in my mind. Sadly, that was the only place it was.

"Callahan is all over you," AJ said, leaning forward to look past Tabby. "I heard him talking about you to someone the other day. Neither one seemed to be a fan."

"You don't say."

"You should probably lay low where he's concerned."

"Who was the other teacher?" Dawson asked, sitting on the edge of the bleacher to see past me to AJ.

AJ looked to me and then back again to Dawson. His expression was a mix of emotions I could barely decipher. Uncertainty, anger, and jealousy were just a few that I managed to catch.

"AJ, I don't know if you've officially met Alex yet—my ex-boyfriend . . ."

"She means soon-to-be-boyfriend-again."

AJ hesitated for a second, eyeing Dawson up. Dawson eventually reached his hand out toward AJ to shake his, showing he could be the better man. AJ looked irritated that Dawson had beaten him to it but took what he offered with a smile.

But I knew that smile—and it didn't reach his eyes.

"It was Coach Blackthorn," AJ said, pulling his hand away.

"Well, that's not surprising," I muttered under my breath. "I got him in trouble with Principal Thompson and basically ruined his championship run." Coach and a long list of faithful JHS football boosters hated me. Them and about 90% of the entire town.

"What did they say?" Dawson asked, leaning closer to hear over the din in the gymnasium.

AJ looked at him suspiciously for a moment. "I don't know how she came up in conversation—I'd been listening to a message on my phone—but when I finally heard them talking,

Callahan was going off about Ky's attitude, and how she's a lost cause now that her dad's in . . ."

The awkwardness that fell upon us was thick and heavy and suffocating.

"It's fine, AJ. You can say it. We all know."

He looked unsure.

"Now that your dad's in prison and you're living with Gramps, who he doesn't think is fit to take care of you. Coach seems to think it would be best if you just disappeared from Jasperville—that the town would be better off."

"Such gratitude for taking a psycho 'roid-rager off the streets. I'm really feeling the love."

"How can they say things like that?" Tabby asked, her disbelief and disgust plain in her tone. "She's a child!"

"I'm technically emancipated now, but they don't know that, not that it matters."

"If anything," she continued, not at all derailed by my words, "they should have sympathy for her situation—not be assholes about it!"

I snapped my head to my left and stared at the ginger. She was pissed. Really pissed. Swearing, for God's sake.

"Bring it down a notch, Tabs. I know they're offending your naïve sense of right and wrong, but that's how it is around here. You want sympathy for the victim, you're in the wrong place—not if the victim doesn't have the right last name or the right connections."

"That's such crap," she said, her voice lower.

"How do grown men say things like that about a student?" Dawson asked. At first, I thought it was his way of fitting into the conversation. But at second glance, I could see he was assessing how callous they'd been. How kill or be killed it could be at JHS.

"Coach is a misogynist, so nothing he says surprises me.

Callahan . . . I have to say, I'd had high hopes when I first returned to physics class. He seemed to have sympathy in his eyes—maybe respect. But I guess not."

"Yeah, no," AJ quickly added with a shake of his head. "Definitely not."

"What I don't understand is why those two were talking at all. It's no secret that they're not friendly," I said.

"Why not?" Dawson asked.

"Mainly because Callahan won't let the football players in his class off easy—the few that dare take it. He doesn't subscribe to the turn-the-other-cheek grading policy that is standard in some classrooms."

"I thought that was only a thing in college sports," Tabby asked.

"Nope."

"So you've managed to bring two people who dislike one another together because they both dislike you more?" she asked. "That's impressive, Ky. Even for you!" She added a smile to her comment, but it didn't soften the blow. Joking or not, she was right.

"Did they say anything else?" Dawson asked, working his profiling no doubt.

AJ looked thoughtful before speaking. "Coach asked if she was basically on her own. Callahan said it seemed that way from what he could tell. Then Mrs. Petri came in and told Coach one of his players was down in the principal's office, and he hauled ass out of the room."

I could feel Dawson's stare boring into the back of my head as I looked at AJ. I knew he wanted to share some sort of unspoken message, but I just wanted to let it go. We needed a subject change—or the pep rally to end early.

"So Tabby, want to go get an ice cream sundae at Matthew's tonight?"

Her face lit up like a Christmas tree for a whole second before the lights went out.

"I don't think I can." Her shoulders rounded in embarrassment. "My dad still isn't keen on us hanging out after everything that happened—he was willing to let you come over to our house, but I'm not sure I can swing an outing together. Not yet. He needs to get to know you better first—get to know the you that I know." I tried to give her a reassuring smile, but she saw right through it. "He's just nervous, Ky. It's not personal."

"I can't blame the man for not wanting you to get beaten with a baseball bat because you hang out with me."

"He'll come around eventually," she said, looping her arm around my shoulders.

"Not if he ever figures out how bad an influence I am on you." I managed a laugh with that comment and it earned me one in return.

"True. . . ."

"I don't see how he can't already know that if he's met you," AJ added with a wink, trying to further lighten the mood.

"I don't think you're giving Ky enough credit," Dawson replied, putting his hand on my knee—a clear infraction of the aforementioned no PDA rule. "I think Ky is great at hiding things from others when it suits her purpose—at making them see what she wants them to see."

"Are you calling her a liar?" AJ sat up a little straighter, his body rigid.

"I'm saying she has layers. That she's complex and not easily read. It's obvious to see if you pay enough attention."

Sweet Baby Jesus, help me. . . .

"I've known Ky since we were kids," AJ said, his voice low and threatening. "I know all there is to know about her."

"Funny," Dawson replied, sounding smooth as silk. "Doesn't seem that way."

"Hey look," I shouted, pointing at the basketball court. "The badger mascot—" I threw my arms up in the air and cheered as loudly as I could. It garnered some curious looks from everyone around me, but it did what I'd hoped it would. It shut down the brewing man-fight between my ex and the fed. Regardless of my warning to Dawson that he'd have to try to get along with AJ, he clearly had another plan in mind. "Is it just me or does the badger look more like a prairie dog?"

"Maybe," Tabby said, actually contemplating what I'd said. The boys, however, were not.

The four of us sat in silence as the cheerleaders performed their competition routine they'd be taking to regionals. We barely spoke at all as Coach Blackthorn blathered on about school pride and salvaging the season and weathering the blow he took in losing Donovan. *Losing him*—as if he'd gone missing like the Throwaway Girls Dawson was investigating. I could feel my rage boiling up within me as he continued to talk, his grating drawl making me want to claw my way out of my skin.

Blackthorn represented everything that was wrong with Jasperville.

"I gotta get out of here," I mumbled, pulling my bag out from between my legs.

Just as I started to stand, Dawson clamped his hand down on my thigh and held me in place.

"Don't let him get to you," he said quietly enough for only me to hear. "Don't let any of them *ever* see that they're wearing you down."

He let me go without another word, and I sat there for the final few agonizing minutes of the rally, wondering exactly why he'd said what he did. Was it to keep me from drawing attention to myself? To keep me from plummeting deeper down the rabbit hole of social exile? Or was it something else entirely—something Dawson understood from personal experience?

"Hey!" Tabby cried, bouncing in her seat, her smile beaming. "What if we all go out tonight? I can tell Dad that I'm meeting up with AJ. And if you two just happen to show up, I can hardly be held accountable for that, right? I mean, this town is really small. . . ."

"Um, Tabs, I don't—"

"Sounds good to me," AJ said, staring across us to Dawson.

"I was just about to say the same," he replied.

"Don't you have a football to throw tonight?" I asked AJ.

"I can go after."

"Perfect!" Tabby said, her elation at her plan plain in her smile. "Meet there once the game is over?"

The boys quickly agreed while I sat there slack-jawed and begging to be abducted by aliens. What had sounded like a fun night for Tabby and me had suddenly become a nightmare. Dawson and AJ passive-aggressively sparring all night was sure to send me into a blind rage. Doling out headlocks was imminent.

While I sat in my silent stupor, the final bell rang. Students quickly dispersed, but I stayed where I was, hoping that if I didn't move, I wouldn't have to go on the date I hadn't meant to sign up for. Dawson stood up beside me, reaching a hand toward me. With my mind still reeling, I took it. He pulled me to my feet, my body close to his.

"Why don't you come by my place before we go out tonight?" He looked down at me with a smile, but his eyes were sharp. I got the subtext loud and clear.

"Yeah, sure. I just have to go home first. I'll be over later." I turned to say goodbye to Tabby and AJ, and found the latter staring past me at Dawson. "See you guys tonight." I waved before walking away. Somehow the vast gymnasium started to feel a bit claustrophobic.

By the time I was outside, I was practically gasping for air. Dawson, who'd caught up, looked over at me with concern.

"You gonna be okay, Danners?"

"Yep. Just need a sec to recover from what just happened."

"Your ex doesn't seem to like me very much."

I glanced over to find him wearing his trademark smug grin. "You think? Can't imagine why. . . ."

"Probably because he's jealous."

"Noooooooo," I replied, pouring every ounce of sarcasm I possessed into that single word. "And you didn't do anything to egg that on, did you?"

He simply shrugged. "Just trying to keep things believable."

"Well, could you find a way to make it believable without being excruciating for me?"

Another shrug. "I'll see what I can do."

We parted ways in the parking lot. I climbed into Heidi and just sat there for a moment, emotions swirling around in my tightened chest. How in the world I was going to survive the two of them that night was beyond me. Morbid though it was, the thought of spending an evening in the pressure cooker that AJ and Dawson created made me wish we could investigate Danielle's crime scene instead.

At least something good would come of that.

SEVENTEEN

Tabby tried to double down and strong-arm me into going to the football game one town over, citing that it was the last away game for the season. I hit back (below the belt), playing the "it's too traumatic" card. She dropped the subject immediately but made sure I wasn't bailing on ice cream. I promised I'd be there with Dawson in tow.

With hours to kill before what promised to be the world's most awkward un–double date ever, I went home and waited for Dawson to call. He'd texted me to tell me that he had to meet up with the profiler and he'd let me know when he was done. That left me alone with way too much time on my hands and too few distractions.

Not a winning combination.

At first, I tried to watch a movie. When that didn't work, I ransacked the boxes in my room, deciding that I should finally finish unpacking. That successfully killed an hour and a half, but even once I'd finished and reorganized my closet by color, I still hadn't heard from Dawson. If he didn't hurry, it would be time for our date, and I'd be stuck flying solo, undoubtedly having to explain why Alex wasn't there—much to AJ's delight, no doubt.

After eating some dubious leftovers from the fridge, I flopped down on the couch. I was running on empty, and I knew I couldn't do that forever. Trying to outrun the fallout of that night was a crappy plan. My denial was waning with every night's sleep lost, and I feared my demons would escape their cage any day.

The longer I laid there, the more sleep tugged at me, begging me to follow. I closed my eyes, hoping my memories wouldn't haunt my dreams as they had since homecoming night. Then something unexpected—something else entirely—drifted into my mind, a scene I hadn't revisited since my father's arrest.

The night of Agent Jim Reider's death.

My father looked at me as he left, hovering at the door longer than usual.

"I love you, kiddo. You know that, right?"

I blew him off like he was being overly sentimental for some bizarre reason—not seeing the sincerity in his eyes.

"Yeah, Dad. Now go or you'll be late." He opened the door. "Where are you going, anyway? Isn't it kind of late for a meeting?"

"I have to go to the north side of downtown. I shouldn't be long." That was all he said before rushing out the door.

Mom was working late, so I watched a movie—some paranormal thing that scared the pants off me. An hour and a half later, right at the climax of the film, my father burst through the back door. He locked it behind him and said a quick hello as he rushed past me to his office, then into the basement.

"You nearly gave me a heart attack," I yelled after him, sitting up on the couch.

He didn't respond as his footfalls echoed down the steps, then disappeared.

A knock on the front door came about the time the credits started to roll. I'd had the TV up so loud that I doubted my father even heard it from his subterranean hideaway. I answered the door to find his boss and two other agents standing on the front porch.

"Hello, Kylene," Special Agent in Charge Wilson, his boss, said. He sounded far too formal for my liking. "Is your father home?"

"Yeah, he just got back a little while ago. Why?"

The three of them shared a knowing look before returning their attention to me. I never heard my father come up from the basement, but in a flash, he was at my side, staring at his colleagues.

"Kylene, I want you to call your mother and tell her to come home right now."

"Dad? What's going on?"

"Just do as I say, Kylene. Everything's going to be fine."

I didn't believe him.

"Bruce, we need you to come down to the bureau with us."

My mind finally caught up with what I was hearing.

"Wait! Are you taking him in?" I asked, the disbelief of a child clear in my tone.

None of them answered—not even my father. Instead, he stepped outside to join them. Two of them took him by the elbows and led him out to one of the three vehicles parked outside.

Now in a full state of panic, I raced to the living room and grabbed my phone. I didn't do what my dad had asked. Instead, I called his partner, Striker. If anyone would know what to do, it was him.

"Kylene?" he said, his smooth, deep voice sounding confused.

"They just took my dad! They're bringing him down to the bureau. Nobody will tell me what the hell is going on. Is this about the meeting Dad had just now? The one downtown?"

Striker grew alarmingly silent.

"I don't know anything about a meeting." My heart plummeted to the floor. "What did you tell them when they came for your dad?" Striker's tone was all business, which wasn't a good thing. He was calm but commanding, and I frantically tried to remember how everything had gone down.

"They asked if he was home . . . I said he'd just come in. SHIT!

I should have lied, Striker. I should have said he was home all night!"

"I'm going to go down to the bureau now and see what I can find out, okay? In the meantime, you are going to stay put and wait to hear from me, got it?"

I nodded, then realized he couldn't see me.

"I understand."

"I'll call you soon."

Then the line went dead—just like Reider's and my father's future.

I exhaled loudly, sitting up on the couch. I rubbed my face with my hands, my mind running over and over the events of that night. What I could have done differently. How I could have helped cover for my father. Then I thought about him running to the basement and my hackles stood on end.

Over the course of my father's arrest and subsequent trial, warrants had been issued for our home. They'd come through and emptied his office. They'd ransacked the better part of our home, including my bedroom. They'd searched the basement, too, but not like I'd expected. Then again, I never mentioned that Dad had gone down there when I was interrogated, and my father might not have, either. At the time, it didn't really register, but in my mania-induced insomnia, my brain put it together. Dad had spent a long time down there before his colleagues had shown up to take him away. I'd always assumed he was cleaning himself up in the downstairs bathroom, but now I wondered. . . .

I ran outside and opened up the garage door. It was full of stuff Mom didn't take out west with her, so there it sat, taking up the better part of Gramps' one-car garage. I plowed through the boxes in search of anything marked BASEMENT. They were buried in the back, of course, but I eventually maneuvered my way to them.

Forty-five minutes later, I found what I was looking for: an old file box full of tax reports and other important financial papers. If my dad had done what I thought he had, I'd soon find out. I'd have a clue I could use for his case.

With shaking hands, I shuffled through the papers, hoping as I neared the back that I hadn't struck out. That my mind wasn't failing due to lack of sleep. But the second my index finger landed on the blank tab of a manila folder, I felt a surge of adrenaline shoot through me. I pulled it out, looking over my shoulder to see if the feds had sneaked up on me like a good little paranoid girl.

Once I was comfortable that I was alone, I opened it up. In it were sheets of papers with columns of numbers on them. Hand-scribbled notes were tucked everywhere. Sticky notes galore. And, in the back, some surveillance photos of men I didn't recognize, the date and time stamp printed in the top corner.

"What is all this, Dad?" I asked the silence. I didn't have a clue what to make of it all, but I knew that it was what I'd been looking for.

I carefully put everything except the file away, making it look as undisturbed as possible, and then I closed the garage. With an excitement I could barely contain, I ran to my room and locked the door. I stashed the file by taping it to the bottom of my dresser drawer, then grabbed my phone to text Dawson. I wanted to tell someone about my find, but then I remembered he wasn't a great candidate. He wouldn't be nearly as thrilled about it as I was.

So I texted someone else instead.

Striker, my dad's old partner and ally, replied immediately. He agreed to meet up in Columbus the next day for lunch. I didn't need to tell him why I wanted to see him. He knew me well enough to suspect I was up to something.

As I walked back to the living room, a text from Dawson finally came in. He was almost in town and would be over shortly. Given how late it was, we weren't going to have a lot of time to get caught up on what he'd been up to before our date. I exhaled in frustration, then perched myself on the kitchen counter and waited for him to arrive. With any luck, he had found a break in the case—something about one of the girls Jane had named. If so, I wasn't sure I'd make it through our date without dragging him into a closet and making him spill it.

I was too on edge to pull that off.

EIGHTEEN

A knock on my door jarred me from my thoughts, and I hopped down from the kitchen counter just as Dawson let himself in.

"Are we already on that level?" I asked, doing nothing to hide my mock disbelief. "Shouldn't you need a warrant or something to just march into a home?"

"Cute, Danners," he replied. He was not amused, and I could only imagine why. Either he'd found something ominous during his investigation that night, or he'd struck out. Or maybe he was about as excited about our date as I was. All were likely options. "We should go. The game should be done by now, right?"

"Yeah," I replied, grabbing my coat and purse. "And we wouldn't want to be late for this." He choked on a laugh. Yep, definitely not excited about our plans. "So, how was your meeting with the profiling guy?"

"She's not a guy, and it was fine until the head of the bureau dropped in."

"Agent Wilson?"

He nodded. "He wanted to be brought up to speed on the case."

"And?"

He shrugged. "I told him about Danielle and the inside informant, who knew some of the other girls—girls she suspects are now dead, too. I told him I'm working her to get the location where Danielle was killed. Obviously, I left your connection to Jane out of it, for both our sakes. By the time I was done briefing him, I couldn't tell if he was pleased or disappointed."

"You know you can't afford for him to be the latter, right? Screwing up your first major case is a career killer."

"I'm well aware, but I appreciate the concern."

I locked up the house as he walked to his car. Once we were on our way, he turned the focus of conversation to me.

"What did you do while I was gone?" he asked.

I thought about the file I'd found, and my adrenaline spiked. Telling him about that was a surefire way to start a fight, and I wasn't up for that. Especially not before our date with AJ, which would have me refereeing the second we sat down. Dawson was a little too good at playing his role of possessive ex-boyfriend when AJ was around. I couldn't tell if he did it to torture AJ or me—possibly both.

"I cleaned up my room, did some homework . . . nothing crazy."

He eyed me sideways as he pulled onto the main road through town. He didn't bother responding.

"So, what exactly have I signed on for tonight?" he asked, his tone uncertain.

"I have no idea. My guess is a total shit show."

And, boy, did that prove to be true.

When we pulled up to Matthew's Ice Cream Shop, the lot was packed. I secretly hoped that there wouldn't be a seat in the place and we'd have to bail, but no such good luck. Instead, we walked in to find Tabby and AJ sitting in a booth together. She jumped up and waved when she saw us, and I knew we were sunk.

"After you," Dawson said, stepping aside so I could lead the way. The entire place seemed to be staring, and, unless my ears were playing tricks on me, I'd say a hush fell over the room. Whispers soon followed—some I could discern, others not so much. It didn't matter though; I knew what they were about.

By the time we reached Tabby and AJ, the whisperers had grown bold.

"It was one hell of a game tonight," some underclassman I didn't recognize called out.

"Yeah. No thanks to her," another replied. I stopped dead in my tracks, doing all I could to curb my rising temper, but I was failing miserably. As others joined in, putting me on blast, I felt my hands ball up into fists.

"Hey!" AJ shouted, jumping up on his seat. "I have news for all of you. Our season didn't rise or fall based on one player. It takes a whole team to win. And that player tried to kill her and put Garrett—his former teammate—in the ICU because he beat him with a baseball bat!"

Silence dropped on the room like a concrete slab.

I tried to ease the tension in my shoulders, but Dawson's lips were soon at my ear—they did nothing to help.

"The kid that throws the football is the town hero and the girl that catches a would-be killer is public enemy number one?" he asked. I nodded. "This is one ass-backward town, Danners."

Couldn't argue with logic like that.

Once AJ was satisfied everyone was done, he sat back down. Tabby looked at me with her big moony eyes and I sighed. If she hadn't been before, she was full-on #TeamAJ after that performance. Dawson was in for a long night.

"I take it you won?" I asked, sliding into the booth.

"Barely," AJ replied with a smile. "But yeah. We did."

"Congrats," Dawson said.

AJ hesitated before replying. "Thanks."

Just as the awkwardness started to settle in, Tabby shot up

and offered to go to the counter and order for us all. I suggested I should go with her, but she shut me down. The redhead was officially on my shit list.

The three of us made painful small talk until Tabby returned with a mountain of type 2 diabetes on a tray.

"Good Lord, Tabs! My extreme-ice-cream-eating days are over. Just ask AJ. The last time I tried that, it didn't end so well for me."

"Boys eat a lot," she argued, placing the food down on the table.

Thankfully, with food in our faces, conversation was sparse. I tried to drag the eating process out as long as I could, hoping that the night wouldn't end up a total debacle if I succeeded. But then the topic of my childhood came up, and both Tabby and Dawson were too eager to listen. AJ, having always loved an audience, was more than happy to feed them stories of me growing up while I sunk lower and lower in the booth, hoping maybe I could just slide under the table and slither away unnoticed.

"So Ky was a fighter?" Dawson asked. I shot up at attention hearing his incredulous tone.

"Yeah," AJ answered before I could launch into my rant. "She's been training in Muay Thai since she was little. . . . You didn't know that?" The note of amusement in AJ's tone was impossible to ignore.

Dawson turned at me and smiled. "No. She never told me."

"I didn't really train when I was in Columbus," I said, trying to fluff over the subject. "That's why."

"She was really good," AJ continued. "I think her record is still 12 and 0."

"You went to her fights?" Tabby asked. "Was that when you were dating or before?"

Yep. The ginger was going down.

"Both, actually. I loved watching them, but it was so hard seeing her get hit, especially in the face."

"Funny," Dawson said before taking a long sip of water. "I'd have been far more worried about a head injury than how she looked."

Oh boy . . .

"I cared about both," AJ replied, his expression darkening.

"Cared or *care?*" Dawson pressed. "I just want to be clear on where you stand."

The desire to run from the building screaming was hard to control. The dick-swinging contest had hit epic proportions, and I saw no sign of it stopping. The two of them calmly went back and forth until I reached under the table and squeezed Dawson's leg so hard my hand started to cramp.

"I've got to pee. Are you guys going to be good if I leave?" I asked, staring them both down.

"We're fine, Ky," AJ said.

"Just ironing some things out," Dawson added.

I looked over at Tabby, who seemed a bit overwhelmed by the turn of events but had nothing helpful to offer.

"Tabby, if they get out of hand, whack them with this," I said, handing her a long ice cream spoon. "Right over the knuckles. It hurts—a lot."

She clutched the spoon, smiling devilishly as she looked at the boys. I hoped for their sakes they behaved.

I hurried to the back of the building that housed the restroom and tried to devise an escape plan to implement when I returned. Once I did what I had to, I headed back down the hallway of photos. Taking my time, I scanned the pictures until I came upon one in particular, surrounded by countless others. Somehow, in all my years of going there with my family and friends, I'd never paid enough attention to realize who was in it. Two young men, late teens or early twenties, wearing army green pants and tees with dog tags around their necks looked back at me. The one had his arm slung over the other's shoulders while they posed for the camera, a medical tent in the background. One was a much younger Gramps. The other, upon deeper inspection, was a youthful, unscarred Mr. Matthew.

"This must be from Vietnam," I said to myself, realizing that's where the picture had likely been taken. I leaned in close to see the bloody bandage poking out from the hem of Gramps' sleeve—and the blood all over Mr. Matthew's hands. Gramps must have just been patched up.

I wondered if Mr. Matthew had saved him.

I'd heard bits and pieces about Gramps' time in the army, but he wouldn't talk about it much. Gram, either. She would always tell me those were dark times for my Gramps—Mr. Matthew, too, given the napalm burn he'd sustained on the side of his face and neck. Some things are better left alone, she'd say, so I never asked, and they never told.

Pushing that thought aside, I made my way back out to the main dining area, stopping at the front counter to order something to take home for my Vietnam vet. A little treat to say thanks for how hard he was working. I was surprised to see the other person from that photo restocking the cups and cones.

"Mr. Matthew! I didn't expect to see you here. Shouldn't you have teenage minions doing these kinds of tasks for you?"

He looked up and took me in for a moment, not realizing who I was right away. When recognition set in, he laughed, the puckered scars along the right side of his jaw tightening as he did.

"Well, I'll be damned. Kylene Danners, how are ya, girl?"

"Full, thanks to your banana split."

Another hearty laugh echoed through the building. "Then what is it that I can do for you if you're stuffed to the gills?"

"I wanted to get something I can take home for Gramps."

"How is that old dog, anyway?" he asked. "I haven't seen him 'round here in ages."

"He's been working more. A lot, actually."

His expression sobered, reading between the lines.

"I'm sorry to hear that. He should be taking it easy these days. Lord knows he's earned it."

"Well, our situation doesn't really lend itself to that right now."

"No," he replied. "I don't imagine it does with your daddy where he is."

"Yeah. . . ."

"How's your mama doin'?"

"I'm not sure. She's out west right now."

He hesitated for a second. "Got it." I could see his mind working on something while he stared at me. "You know, if you find yourself with too much alone time on your hands and in need of a job, you let me know. I'm sure I can find somethin' for you to do."

"Like be your cones-and-cups-refilling minion?"

He smiled wide. "Maybe more than that, if you can be trusted." He threw in a wink at the end for good measure, making me laugh.

"I think I could make a mean sundae. . . ."

"I'll just bet you could. Now, what can I get you to take home for your gramps? Anything you want—it's on the house."

"Oh, you don't have to—"

"You wanna argue with a Vietnam vet, or you wanna tell me what flavor you want to take home for that old coot?"

"Chocolate chip, sir!" I said, snapping to attention.

His smile grew to a grin. "Atta girl."

He turned to grab a cup from the stack he'd just restocked, then bent down to scoop Gramps' ice cream from the display freezer. I shot a wary glance over to where AJ, Tabby, and

Dawson were sitting, wondering if leaving those three alone together for so long was a good idea. But then I saw Tabby throwing her head back in laughter and AJ actually smiling at whatever Dawson had said and let out a sigh of relief.

Maybe that spoon had come in handy.

"Here you go, Kylene," Mr. Matthew said, pushing the ice cream across the counter to me.

"Are you sure I can't pay you for this?"

"Downright positive, young lady. And you remember what I said. If you need some extra cash, you let me know. Always somethin' around here that needs doin'."

"I will. Thanks again for the ice cream."

"Tell your gramps I said hi."

"Yes, sir!"

I saluted him with my free hand and made my way back to the table where my friends and Dawson sat. Tabby's laughter had died, and AJ's smile had faded. My anxiety spiked for a moment until Dawson looked over his shoulder at me with ice cream in hand and waved.

"You ready to go, Kylene?"

Kylene, not babe. The boy could be taught.

I waved the ice cream in the air.

"Yep. I need to get home before this turns into chocolate chip soup, so let's get a move on."

Tabby got up to give me a hug goodbye while AJ just looked on, a strange expression on his face. I told them to behave, then rushed Dawson toward the exit before the moment could sour.

"I see why you like Tabby so much," Dawson said, opening the door.

"She's a good egg."

"She is. And downright nasty with that spoon. . . ."

I laughed at that. "You two deserved it. Not sure what in the hell all that was, but I'm glad it's over."

"Just playing my role, Danners," he said, leading the way to his car. "How many teenage boys would be overly gracious with the competition?"

Fair point.

"I know, it's just so awkward and uncomfortable."

He turned to smile at me, pure wickedness in his eyes. "Not for me."

I groaned as we climbed into his car. "Could you maybe bring it down a few notches from now on? For my sake? Please?"

He let my question linger for a solid minute before answering. He fired up his car and backed out in silence. I nearly crawled out of my skin in the interim.

"I'll dial it down a bit—*for you*."

"Thanks," I said with an exhale.

"But I don't think that's going to solve your problem."

"I know," I muttered under my breath.

"For what it's worth, I'm sorry that you're in this spot. I don't envy you."

I turned and looked to see if his expression matched his sentiment. Much to my surprise, it did. His profile was tight, like the situation I was in bothered him more than it should have. Maybe Dawson was more capable of sympathy than I'd thought. Or maybe he was a hopeless romantic wrapped in a barbed-wire shell. I could relate to that.

He drove me home, then pulled into Gramps' driveway and put the car in park.

"I'm going to be busy working on the case this weekend," he said, his gaze fixed on my garage door.

"Okay. . . ." I stared at his profile, but it gave nothing away. "Was that an invitation?"

A muscle in his jaw feathered. "I'm not sure."

"I'll be out of town in the morning," I said. "I'm not sure when I'll be back."

He took a deep breath. "Come over when you are." My jaw dropped. "Now close your mouth and get out of my car before I come to my senses and change my mind."

I was halfway out the door in a second.

"See you then," I said before slamming his door and running to the house. I didn't look back, not wanting him to see the grin I wore. He'd have reneged his offer if he'd seen it.

With my luck, he would anyway.

Like a good date, Dawson made sure I got into the house safe before taking off. I dropped my stuff on the kitchen table and put Gramps' ice cream in the freezer, then walked over to the couch and flopped down. My sugar high was too great to even attempt going to bed. Instead, I tried for the second time that night to distract myself with a movie.

I hoped that time it would work.

NINETEEN

I woke up the next morning to find Gramps in the kitchen. It felt like ages since I'd seen him.

"Did ya have a nice night out?" he asked, flipping the eggs in the pan.

"Yeah. For the most part."

He looked over his shoulder, trying to read the subtext in my expression.

"You wanna talk about it?"

"It's nothing. I went for ice cream with Tabby, AJ, and Alex."

"I saw my present in the freezer. Thanks for that," he said with a devilish smile.

"Mr. Matthew told me to tell you hi."

"I should try to get by there and see Grant soon. It's just been hard to find the time."

I gulped down my guilt. "I saw the picture of you two in the hallway there last night—from the war." He stilled in front of the stove, spatula in midflip. "You looked like you were close."

He nodded. "We were before we left. Even closer when we got back." He didn't say anything else for a minute or two. Once he plated our breakfasts, he came to join me at the table. "So, enough about me and Mr. Matthew. Why don't you tell me why your night wasn't all it shoulda been. Is it because Garrett wasn't there?"

"No—I mean, yeah, that always puts a damper on things, but that's not the only reason." He looked at me expectantly, and I took a deep breath. "AJ and Alex . . . they don't really get along."

"Oh," Gramps said, leaning back in his chair. "Well now that's not that surprisin', is it?"

"Not really."

"Did ya have to pry 'em apart?"

"Nothing like that. It was just tense, that's all."

"It was, or you were?" he asked, quirking a brow at me.

"Both?"

He looked as though he wanted to say more but took a bite of his eggs instead.

"That ain't an easy situation to navigate—but you'll find your way."

"Thanks, Gramps," I said.

We finished our breakfast and I cleared the table.

"I have to run up to Columbus today to see Striker. He wants to make sure I'm doing all right after everything."

"And are ya?" Gramps asked, the tension in his tone palpable.

"I'm getting there," I replied. I walked over and kissed him on the cheek, then grabbed my purse and headed for the door.

"You gonna be home late?"

"No, but I promised Alex I'd help with his homework. Poor boy can't speak Spanish for beans."

"At his place?" he asked, squaring his shoulders as though preparing for a fight..

"We're not together, Gramps. It's homework. Nothing more."

He frowned. "I want you home no later than ten, okay?" Gramps said, his business voice in full force. "Emancipated or not, I don't want you over there late. No sense courtin' a whole new kind of problem, if you get my drift."

"Gramps!" I shouted, totally mortified. "I am not sleeping with Alex. And, even if I was, I'm pretty sure we could have sex before 10:00 P.M." He turned to shoot daggers at me over his shoulder. "But, we're not, so it's a moot point."

"Best you keep it that way, young lady."

I shook my head. "I'll text you and let you know what the plan is, okay?"

"All right. You tell Striker I said hello."

"I will! Love you, Gramps."

"Love you too, girl."

I closed the door behind me and tried to shake off the icky feeling I had from talking about sex with Gramps. Some topics should be fully off-limits for grandparents. Sex was definitely at the top of the list.

The drive to Columbus was uneventful, and an hour and a half later, I found myself parked outside of the mom-and-pop restaurant Striker and I'd met at before. The same one I'd met Dawson in front of a couple weeks earlier. It seemed so long ago.

I found Striker sitting in his favorite booth near the back, his massive frame taking up the bulk of one side. He waved me over with a bright smile that contrasted his deep umber skin, and I hurried to meet him. I gave him a half hug so he didn't have to get out, then sat down across from him.

"How ya doin', kiddo? Everything all right down there in Hicksville?" he asked before waving the waitress over. We placed our orders (they really made the best grilled cheese ever there), and then got down to business.

"I'm good. Trying to get back into the swing of things."

"That can be hard to do," he said. "You've been through hell."

"Hell seems to be my status quo," I replied. I let out a little laugh, but it was mirthless. The truth was my hell started the second my naked pictures ended up online freshman year and just kept on going through my father's trial right into the Donovan disaster. I wasn't sure how much Striker knew about Dawson's case or if he knew that he was undercover, so I didn't bring it up. When he didn't ask, I assumed he didn't.

"Well, I sure hope that changes for you."

"I'm wondering if this will help," I said, pulling out the file I'd found and slapping it down on the table. Striker eyed it for a second before picking it up to flip through it.

"What is it?" he asked, his dark brow furrowed.

"Dunno. Check out the pictures in the back," I said, waiting for him to find them. I knew the second he did because his eyebrows shot up in disbelief.

"That's Reider. . . ."

"Yeah. I wondered if he was one of them. But who's the other guy and why did my dad have this photo?"

Striker took a sip of coffee while he continued to stare at the picture.

"Let me run it through our facial recognition software and see what I can find. If I can figure out who he was meeting with, I might be able to figure out where this was taken and what it means. Where did you find this file?" he asked.

I leaned forward, wanting to keep my voice low.

"It was in a file box from the basement. I think my dad stashed it there the night Reider died. He was hiding it. I just don't know why."

Striker's expression fell. "Because he knew they were coming for him."

"But why hide evidence that could help you? And why not give it to his attorney?"

"Maybe it wouldn't help him. Maybe it damns him somehow. . . ."

I pulled away from Striker in disbelief. "What the hell does that mean?"

He shook his head. "What I'm trying to say is that maybe this is stuff Reider was using against him and he somehow got his hands on it. There's no way to know until I figure out what it all means."

I relaxed a bit, leaning back in my chair. The waitress returned with our food and I took a huge bite of my sandwich, the hot cheese burning the roof of my mouth.

"How long will it take to find out?"

"Not long if this guy's in the system. If he's not, longer."

"Are we talking hours or days?"

"Hopefully the former. I'll let you know as soon as I have something concrete."

"What about the rest of it? The papers with all the numbers?"

"That," he said with an exhale, "is going to take more work. Maybe if I can ID the guy, the numbers will make much more sense."

"You can't show this to anyone else, Striker. This stays between you and me."

His eyebrow quirked. "Does your father know you found this?"

"Hell no! And you're not telling him. He's been super cagey about his case after everything that happened homecoming night. He wants me to give up on it, but you know I can't do that. You know why, too."

He nodded. "Okay. I'll keep this to myself—for now."

"Thank you," I said, losing the edge my tone had held.

"So what else is going on with you? School any easier? Got yourself a boyfriend?" I choked on my drink, nearly spitting it out all over our food. "Did I hit a nerve?" he asked, smiling as he leaned forward on his elbows, watching me squirm.

"Kind of."

"Kind of?"

"It's complicated."

"With kids these days, it always is."

We ate the rest of our lunch while we got caught up. He asked me about counseling, and I told him I'd meet with the school psychologist again soon. He seemed satisfied with my response and changed the subject. While he talked about his daughter and her scholarship to Dartmouth and not being sure about having her so far away, my mind drifted off into the forbidden zone. If Luke had succeeded, I wouldn't have had to worry about college applications and moving away from home. That reality had been so close it was as if it tainted me somehow. Marked me with ink I couldn't rub off.

I broke from my stupor when Striker uttered Dawson's name.

"Sorry?" I said.

"I asked if you've seen Dawson. He's still working that case down there. I know it's a small town, so I wondered if you'd run into him."

"Um, yeah. A couple times," I said, trying to play off my anxiety.

"You haven't told anyone how you know him, have you? It's best if he keeps a low profile."

"No. I didn't have to. I wasn't with anyone when I saw him."

"Good," Striker said, satisfied with my answer. "I know you helped him get that break in the case. With any luck, he can find the person running the operation soon and help those girls."

Those girls . . . If only Striker knew.

"I hope he does," I said, my voice a little thin and empty.

"Well, I hate to run, kiddo, but I have somewhere I need to be shortly." He got up and threw some money down on the table. "We should do this again soon, though, okay? I'd be lying if I said I wasn't worried about you."

"I'm hanging in there, Striker. You know me, I'm a fighter."

"Damn right you are, and don't you forget it. But just because you're tough doesn't mean you have to take on everything alone. It's okay to need help, Kylene. After all you've been through, I don't doubt that you do."

"Message received," I said with a nod.

"Good, now text me when you get home so I know you arrived safely. People drive like idiots these days. Make sure you're not on your phone while driving, got it?"

"Yes, Dad."

He shook his head and laughed. "Just what I need, another teenage daughter trying to put me in an early grave."

I gave Striker a hug and thanked him for lunch, then made my way to my car. I texted Dawson to see if he still wanted me to come right over, but he didn't reply. His house was sort of on my way home, so I figured it wouldn't hurt to swing by and check in like he'd suggested.

Had I known what I was about to walk into, I might have rethought my plan.

TWENTY

Dawson didn't answer when I knocked, so I walked in and called his name. He shouted something unintelligible from the back of the house, and I made my way there. In his office, I found him with marker in mouth, staring at the whiteboard that looked quite different than it had the last time I saw it.

The columns of information on the girls had been erased, replaced with Danielle's name encircled at the center of the board. Another concentric ring containing the names of the four girls Jane gave me was just outside of the bull's-eye. Beyond that was a much larger ring with the names of all the girls we hadn't yet been able to tie to the sex ring—the rest of the girls.

All along the wall were pages of notes, photos of suspects, and string pulled tight between them and the circles of names on the whiteboard. Dawson had gone full-on *A Beautiful Mind* up in that room. I wasn't sure if I should be impressed or worried.

"Well you've been busy," I said. He didn't even balk at my sarcastic tone. Instead he turned slowly to look at me, and every second that passed as he silently stared was torture. Then he turned back to the board.

I headed for the door.

"I've dissected the lives of Kit Casey, Rachel Fray, and Danielle Green," he said, halting me. "I still have more to do with Angela Mercy and Samantha Dunkley. I need you to go through the school records for all five girls. Outline their class schedules. Make note of all teachers they had, any disciplinary measures, extracurriculars, etc. We've got to cross-reference all of this with the three I've already gone through. I'm digging into police records now, with the help of your favorite small-town sheriff."

"I'm on it!" I said, plopping down on the floor. I heaped their files into my lap, thinking Dawson would be less inclined to snatch them away if they were there, and started thumbing through them.

"Start with Kit and Rachel. They were the same age and at the same school. The other three weren't."

"Sounds good, but shouldn't we do this kind of search on *all* the girls that allegedly ran away?"

Dawson shook his head. "We could, but we'll start here with the girls Jane mentioned. Anything farther back than five years makes it hard to get school records for. Until we need to broaden our search, we'll stick with those."

It felt wrong not to include the others—like somehow they didn't matter—but if Dawson thought this was our best bet, then I'd trust his judgment and do what I could with the victims we had. If they weren't enough, I'd see what I could dig up on the others.

I hunkered down with the pile of personal files in front of me and started paging through them. I started with the girls Dawson suggested, who were the same age and had attended Ash Haven School together. Kit disappeared in the winter of their junior year and Rachel, the summer following the completion of senior year.

AHS no longer existed as it did when they attended. Their class was the last to graduate from the K–12 school. After that, grades 9–12 were shipped over to Jasperville. The town of Ash

Haven was even smaller than ours and unable to sustain a high school on its own, but over recent years, its population had increased enough for the existing school to be overrun. The state threatened to shut it down for overcrowding, so the two towns and the powers that be hashed out a way for those eighty or so students to attend JHS. Ash Haven would pay taxes to help cover the expense of having them there, and JHS got a nice new addition, partially funded by the state. It turned out to be a win/win for everyone.

While I was compiling a list of the faculty the girls all shared, I realized pretty quickly that if you were on staff at AHS, the students had you as a teacher at some point. There was just so much overlap. Basically, every teacher and administrator there was on the short list.

Frustrated, I moved on to Angela and Samantha (aka Sam). They had disappeared after Kit and Rachel, and both had attended JHS. I was starting high school around the time that Angela went missing. She'd just graduated that spring. Sam, I remembered. She had been a junior my freshman year. She was pretty unremarkable. I had no real interaction with her. She'd disappeared after I'd moved to Columbus, so I never heard anything about her having run away. But, then again, I didn't think I would have even if I'd still been at JHS. None of the girls had made more than the slightest ripple in the world when they went missing.

I swallowed back the bile rising in my throat and got back to work.

After about an hour, I'd mapped out and cross-referenced the lists of school staff that the girls all had in common. Some were thinly connected, but I left them in place regardless. Thanks to the JHS victims, the AHS list was whittled down significantly. That said, there were still quite a few names on the list.

Mr. Callahan, who'd transferred in the spring of Ash Haven's final year of K–12 operation. He'd left to cover for Ms. Langley, who had to go out early for maternity leave. When she decided not to return the following year, Callahan obtained her full-time position. He'd had both Angela and Sam in his class, though both dropped out at some point. Whether that was because physics or Callahan wasn't for them remained to be seen.

Coach Blackthorn had also come over from AHS, though he came the year before the school transferred its high school students. His ability to coach football was rivaled only by his ability to be a complete and utter chauvinistic asshole, so it was no wonder that Jasperville had wanted him the second they'd realized the young coach showed real promise. The state championship would be in sight with someone of his coaching prowess.

Maybe early graves for ostracized girls would be, too.

Ms. Davies and Principal Thompson had both come over from AHS as well, but from what I could tell, all of them had started the fall after Angela Mercy had graduated. They would have been at JHS during only Sam's and Danielle's time there. They had no connection to Angela at all.

I breathed a sigh of relief.

"How you doing over there, Danners?" Dawson asked as he pinned another paper up to the wall. A news clipping I hadn't seen before.

"Well, I went through their class schedules and connected at least two teachers to all of the girls. It gets a little hairy with the transfer of students and some teachers from a nearby school the year after Rachel went missing, but I think I got that all sorted out."

He shot me a confused look, so I did my best to explain how Jasperville essentially absorbed the high school student body from Ash Haven's school. Once he'd grilled me on the particulars, he seemed satisfied with what I'd collected.

"How did you know about Blackthorn and Callahan going over early? Was there something in the files about it?" he asked, a hint of uncertainty in his voice.

I shot him an incredulous look. "Dawson, let me make something very clear to you. The arrival of Coach Blackthorn at JHS was a town-celebrated event. We held a parade for him. The football team qualified for the state quarterfinals in his first season. I'm surprised there wasn't a statue erected outside the front steps of the school in his honor."

"Point taken," he said, smirking at me. "What about Callahan?"

"Ah, now that one was a bit more insidious, given that I wasn't yet in high school, but rumor of his assholedom and anal-retentiveness spread quickly amongst students. It eventually trickled down to the middle school—a warning for what we'd one day be in for. And let me tell you, he lived up to the hype."

"Kinda like you?" he asked with a laugh. I merely scowled at him in response. "You did good, Danners. Now, make sure you go through the rest of their files to be sure none of them had ties to any other teachers you might have ruled out. Could be extracurricular stuff—maybe tutoring or detentions. Something like that. We don't want to overlook any small detail."

I spent the next couple of hours scouring their records for suspensions or other disciplinary actions, of which there were many for all five girls—their attendance records were abysmal. None of them were involved in sports or clubs of any sorts. Notes on their family situations were abundant and grim, and I cringed when I read them. Their circumstances made perfect sense of why they'd agree to something as unthinkable as selling your body for money.

Right before I was set to give up, I found something in Angela's file—a transcript for summer school attendance. I looked it over, wondering if I'd find anything of value, but it was a total bust. Nothing there either exonerated our suspects or implicated anyone new. I stuffed it back in and stood up to stretch.

"I need to figure out if I can find something with official start dates for Davies and Thompson. They transferred to JHS when Ash Haven closed grades nine through twelve. I just want to make sure it's safe to cross them off the school staff suspect list."

Dawson looked thoughtful for a moment. "I'll have Sheriff Higgins make a call. He can come up with a story to cover why he's asking for it. It's not private information, so it shouldn't be a big deal. It would be nice to narrow the field a bit," he said with an exhale. "The list is still pretty long."

He pointed to a vertical list along the far edge of the whiteboard. It went all the way from top to bottom. I stood so I could get a closer look at it, and the second I did, my eyes went wide. The names read like a who's who of Jasperville (and a couple surrounding towns). Some of them were pillars of the community.

"Tell me these are not all viable suspects," I said, my eyes still taking in the names.

"They are until I can narrow down the field."

"Mr. Matthew, the ice cream man? And Tim Bailey, the movie theater owner? Dawson, the man is wheelchair bound! I'm pro-ableism all the way, but there is literally no way he could have slit Danielle's throat the way Jane described!"

"That means he's not the murderer, that's all. He stays."

He took his marker and started jotting down the names I'd mentioned from my school records search while I scanned the list.

"Kru Tyson? Seriously? Dawson, I've known him since I was four years old. I grew up in his gym!" I looked over at him while he stared back, unfazed by my outburst. "It's just so hard to wrap my head around. . . ."

"Just because he has ties to some of the girls doesn't make him guilty. But it doesn't make him innocent because you think he's a good guy, either."

"I know that. I do—it's just messing with me seeing his name up there. My rational mind understands that it could be anyone, but my gut is really struggling with some of these names. . . ."

"Knowing evil can exist in anyone isn't a black-and-white concept. It gets muddied by our feelings—our emotions—especially when that evil resides in someone close to us. What we want to believe and what's actually true are rarely if ever the same thing, Danners. . . ."

I took a deep breath and moved on, unwilling to admit how right he was.

"How am I supposed to train with him knowing he's a suspect in this case?" I asked.

"You're not," he replied, as if that point should have been perfectly clear.

"But it's—" I cut myself short, not wanting to tell Dawson that I needed the gym to survive. That my mental health might hang in the balance.

"It's what?" he asked, stepping closer.

"Nothing. It's fine. I won't go for now. Not until he's cleared."

Dawson's eyes narrowed, his dissatisfaction with my response clear in his taut features.

"Good."

I turned back to the board to avoid his scrutiny.

"The problem I'm having," I said, pointing to the list, "is that all of this is circumstantial at best. I mean, yeah, we've made connections, but some suspects will have more than others by nature of their jobs. Some will be harder to dig up, possibly because someone doesn't want them to be found—just look at Callahan and Coach, for example. Both had access to the girls and their files, which, let me tell you, are some colorful reading when you start thumbing through the nonacademic stuff, but that's hardly a smoking gun. And if we can't actively tie them to Jane, it doesn't even matter."

"True, but it's hard to ignore the fact that JHS girls seemed to go missing once those teachers transferred," he countered. "That's a pattern. This is how we start to establish a hierarchy to the suspect list."

"What about the other girls?" I looked up at the widest circle on the whiteboard and all the names it held.

"We can't assume all these missing girls were killed by this guy," he said. "That said, a lot of them were from AHS, and they were all before the first JHS girl disappeared."

"Except for Sarah Woodley," I argued, remembering the circus surrounding her disappearance and retrieval of her body. Even at the tender age of eight, that memory was burned into my consciousness.

"I don't believe she fits the profile or the MO of the killer," he said. "I talked it over with Erin and she agrees, so I've excluded Sarah from the victim pool."

"Erin?"

"The profiler at the bureau."

"Ah . . . got it."

I could feel my brow furrow as I focused on everything I'd heard my dad say the night they'd found Sarah's body. All the things not released to the papers.

"What's up, Danners? What are you thinking?" Dawson stepped in front of me, quietly demanding my attention.

"I'm not sure . . . I just—I remember that night so clearly.

The night they found her. I can't explain it, but I just feel like her death is related somehow."

He looked thoughtful for a moment, not dismissing me right off. A small victory in and of itself.

"Well, let's say she was one of his victims, then we need to go back and try to tie her to the suspect list, which will be more challenging given how long ago she was killed."

"Get me what you can on her case and I'll go through it with a fine-tooth comb to see what I can find," I said, straightening my spine. "I just can't shake the feeling that she's involved."

He bit the inside of his cheek, then nodded.

"Deal. Now, break's over."

He handed me employment records for Matthew's Ice Cream Shop dating back as far as Sarah Woodley's disappearance, and I sat back down on the floor, ready to riffle through them. If this was real police work, I was all for it. There was a certain excitement that built with every turn of the page—every potential newfound piece of information. It may not have been a sexy process, but it was necessary, and doing it only made me sharper and more skilled for solving my dad's case.

Even if he didn't want me to.

TWENTY-ONE

It was late by the time I got home from Dawson's; I was totally exhausted. Gramps had fallen asleep on the couch, so I tossed a blanket on him and headed for bed. The second I closed my eyes, I felt my mind begin to race, then slow. Then the bad thoughts started again.

I couldn't beat them back if I tried.

My eyes shot open, my only real defense against them, and I looked over to find the time on my phone taunting me. It was midnight and I was wide awake, a million and one ideas running through my mind, none of them coherently tied to another. It was as though my brain had taken to switching the channels in fast-forward—a pesky side effect of its inability to handle what had happened. Part of me was happy that at least it had adapted in some way, but the other part realized that I needed to get control of it before it was too late. The school psychologist had told me my symptoms would evolve as time went on, and that if I wanted the best outcome possible, I needed to do my best not to ignore the signs.

Clearly, she didn't know me. I had two coping mechanisms—three, if you counted sarcasm. Extreme denial or all-out fixation/obsession were the main ones, neither of which she would approve. Maybe that's why I hadn't followed up with her.

In the spirit of trying, I closed my eyes and did the deep

breathing exercise she'd suggested. In through the nose, deep into the belly, with a long exhale through the mouth. I did this several times, trying to will my mind to calm. Eventually it did, but with it came clarity, and that was far less welcome. When my brain quieted, it chose to focus on Donovan raising his bat above me to smash my head in. I did all I could to breathe through that memory—to break the instant fight-or-flight cycle it, and others like it, reflexively brought about, but I failed. Instead, I jumped out of bed and began pacing my room, scrubbing my face with my hands.

Distraction—I needed one ASAP. Calling Tabby wasn't an option for multiple reasons. Neither was Garrett. Gramps was asleep and waking him would have only raised red flags and stressed him out more than he already was, something he definitely didn't need. That left only two options, and both came with serious drawbacks. Pissing Dawson off because I'd woken him up after he hadn't slept for two days didn't seem worth the fallout. But calling AJ would send the wrong message—especially at that hour. After a few minutes of rationalization, I decided it would be okay if I texted to apologize for blindsiding him with the whole Alex thing. He'd taken it well at the time, sporting a brave face, but I knew it had hurt him. He'd told me homecoming night that he still loved me.

He deserved an explanation at minimum, even if it was all a lie.

I grabbed my phone and sent a harmless text asking if he was still awake. My phone vibrated seconds later with his reply: Yeah. What's up?

I took a deep breath before answering: I owe you an apology.

He quickly responded: For what?

I literally laughed out loud at that. I mean really, I wasn't certain I could ever apologize enough for everything I'd said and done to him, even though I'd tried.

I stared at the screen, trying to figure out how best to apologize for the Alex situation, then I wondered if that was even possible. Maybe I should have left well enough alone.

Just as I went to text him back, the phone started to vibrate with an incoming call.

AJ.

"Hey," I said, putting him on speaker.

"What's this midnight apology about?" His voice sounded sleepy, and I felt like a total ass for waking him up.

"You were sleeping!" I said. "Go back to bed. We can talk about it another time."

"I'm awake now, Ky. Might as well just tell me. It must be one hell of an 'I'm sorry' if you couldn't wait until Monday."

I took a deep breath and flopped back onto the bed.

"I just—I wanted to apologize for not telling you about Alex before." He stayed silent, and that quiet made me antsy and my mind started to race. Then my mouth let all those thoughts out in one run-on sentence that would have had Ms. McManus cringing. "I mean, I know we weren't exactly on good terms until recently, but I should have found time to let you know, but the case and Donovan and Garrett in the hospital and this therapy I'm supposed to be doing that I'm avoiding because I'm not sure it'll help because I can't seem to turn my brain off long enough to get some sleep, because if I do all I can see is Garrett all beaten up and then—"

"Ky!" AJ said, his voice forceful enough to cut me off but still filled with concern. "Slow down. Please." I took a few deep breaths to calm my breathing. "First, tell me you're okay right now."

"I'm good," I said, still sounding winded. "But I had no idea that talking so fast was a cardiovascular activity."

"Well, now you won't have to work out tomorrow."

"Bonus."

"Seriously though, are you okay?"

"As well as can be expected under the circumstances, yes."

His silence told me he wasn't sold on my response. "You know if you ever need me, I'll be there, right?"

I smiled. "I know."

"Great. Now, about that apology you owe me . . ."

"I really am sorry that I didn't warn you about Alex. It was shitty to just dump him on you like that. I didn't want it to go down that way—it just sorta happened."

"Ky," he said, his voice full of sympathy. "I'm a big boy. I can handle the fact that you dated what's his name, who thinks you're getting back together."

I think his lack of frustration and anger with the situation somehow made it worse.

"Okay, well . . . that's all I wanted to say. Sorry for waking you up."

"Wait!" he said. "We're up. Why not fill me in on the last two and a half years of your life?"

I choked on a laugh. "Well, one of those years was in the news constantly, so I think you already know that part of the story. The rest of it was pretty boring. Just school."

"And Alex?"

Crap.

"Yep, him too." Another awkward silence fell between us before I broke it. "What about you? Fill me in on all the JHS shenanigans I missed."

Surprisingly, he did. He filled me in on his family drama, the fallout from my photo scandal, and school life in general. By the time he was done, it was one in the morning.

"That's about it," he said with a yawn.

"Go to sleep. You're going to be exhausted tomorrow."

"What about you?"

"Me? I'm getting used to my zombie insomniac state. I'll be fine."

"If you say so," he replied with a laugh. "Try to remember to brush your hair when you get up. Not sure what happened yesterday, but it was interesting to say the least."

"Dick!" I said, trying not to shout the name at him. "You'd better not show up at lunch on Monday because you'll be wearing mine if you do."

"I'll take my chances."

"Good night, AJ."

TWENTY-TWO

Early Sunday afternoon, I went to visit Garrett. He'd been transferred to a specialized therapy facility to get him back on his feet. Once I found the room, I knocked lightly on his door before poking my head in. I was met with a wave of his hand, urging me to come in.

"Are you alone?" he asked, sounding all suspicious. I literally looked behind me for a second, suddenly wondering if maybe I wasn't.

"Um, yeah? I think so."

"Good."

No further explanation given.

"What's with the paranoia, big guy? They giving you too many painkillers and now you're getting all twitchy?"

He scowled at me. "Hardly. I just wondered if, you know, AJ or Tabby was with you."

"Nope. Sorry to disappoint. It's just me." He eased back in his bed, carefully rearranging himself to make a little room for me. Then he patted the barely vacant spot next to him. "Garrett, you're freaking me out right now. Is something wrong? I feel like we're in a Lifetime movie and you're about to tell me that the good news is that you're healing, but the bad news is they found a brain tumor on your latest CT scan."

"Just sit, would you?" I shut my mouth and did as he asked. Garrett was rarely that serious. "I need to ask you something."

"No, I will not make out with you!"

"Ky—"

"I'm sorry! You know I joke when I'm nervous! I'll get it together, I promise. Now, what do you want to know?"

"You said my dad knows your dad is innocent. . . ."

"Yeah. And?"

He hesitated for a second, biting his lip as his dark eyes drifted off to the door and back to me.

"I overheard him on the phone the other day. He thought I was asleep, but even still he was talking low and carefully choosing his words." Another pause. "He sounded scared, Ky. You know my dad—nothing scares him."

"He was scared about losing you—"

"No. Not like that. He was like that with my mom, too. But this was different. He was doing a lot of explaining—about Donovan, and other things. And he said your name twice. . . ."

Not good. So not good.

"Who do you think he was talking to, Garrett?" His sharp gaze was answer enough. "The blackmailer?" He nodded once. "What else did he say?" I asked, sweat running down my spine.

"Nothing much. It was vague and evasive."

"There's no way anyone else could know what I did," I thought aloud, wishing I hadn't immediately after the words left me.

"*Did?*" he asked. I remained silent. "What did you do, Ky?"

I sighed heavily and got up to close the door to his room, locking it behind me. Then I sat down beside him, leaning in close enough to whisper in his ear.

"Promise me you won't freak out."

"Ky—"

"Keep your voice down," I said, hoping his paranoia would kick back in. We couldn't be sure no one was listening in—not until we knew more about who we were dealing with. "Promise me or I'm not saying anything. I don't need you having a damn heart attack."

"Fine. Just tell me."

I took a deep breath and grabbed his hand.

"You were in surgery at the time. I'd been checked into the hospital to be treated for minor injuries. I had to go to the bathroom, so I made my way there, when someone ushered me into a room and locked us in."

His face went pale beneath his fading bruises. "What happened . . . ?"

"Luke Clark, the attorney I worked with at Meg's office, tried to kill me. He was the one behind Donovan and the prescription drugs. He was trying to tie up loose ends."

"Jesus . . ."

"I was hurt and weak, and he was too strong for me. He had a syringe full of something to stop my heart. Your dad found us. Luke threatened to expose your father. They fought and then Luke tried to take me out. Your father knocked him off me . . . and then I grabbed the needle and stabbed Luke with it." Garrett said nothing, just stared at me in utter disbelief. "I knew if your dad was found with me that he'd be in a shit spot because the person blackmailing him is the same one backing Luke. He goes by 'the Advocatus Diaboli,' and he seems to be leveraging all kinds of people into doing shady things around here."

"Like kill my best friend," Garrett said, squeezing my hand.

"But he didn't," I replied with a smile, squeezing him right back.

"So you killed Luke?" His question was gentle, as was the look in his brown eyes.

"I did—but that's not exactly a secret. I wasn't named in the papers because I'm a minor, but people here—at the hospital—they knew. Word's going to spread soon enough if it hasn't already."

"So what's the secret?"

I took a deep breath. "That I ordered your dad to leave after I did it and told him not to come until the hospital staff came to my aid when I started screaming."

"You took a bullet for him. . . ."

I nodded. "He told me he later collected all the CCTV tapes just in case and edited them, just to cover his tracks. All they showed was me being dragged into the room and then coming out screaming. Garrett, I'd be dead if it weren't for your dad. And he'd be dead if it weren't for me. Like it or not, he and I are allies now. He doesn't want to be mixed up with this guy any more than I do."

"Well this changes things a bit."

"Yes, but I need you to act normally or he'll know that you know."

"I can do that."

"Good, now, let's talk about something else. I'm getting all wigged out just thinking about that night."

"Then tell me all about what I'm missing at school," he said, wrapping his arm around my shoulder.

"I'm really starting to think you *do* want to make out with me."

"Sorry, Ky. My stance on blondes remains, even after my acute brain trauma."

"I swear my life would be way less complicated if we did date. We'd be the most hilarious couple ever."

He smiled at me, then kissed my forehead.

"True, but it would be hard for you to date me since I'd be the better looking one in the relationship."

My mouth shot open, jaw hanging in disbelief.

"Garrett Higgins!" I slapped his hand and he flinched, laughing and wincing at the same time.

"I'm just screwing with you, Ky. Now tell me all the gossip."

I sat there, enjoying the feeling of being near him. All joking aside, I felt closer to Garrett than anyone my age. I trusted him with everything—including my life. It hurt to know that over the next few weeks, or however long it took for Dawson and me to solve the case, I'd have to lie to him. I hoped he wouldn't be mad when he found out I was covering for Dawson. I hoped he would forgive me. More than anything, I prayed it wouldn't change things between us. I needed Garrett's grounding presence in my life.

I couldn't afford to lose him.

"They said I can go home on Tuesday," Garrett said. He'd only been fixated on his official discharge from the second he regained consciousness. Well, that and his hot physical therapist. "Dad's getting everything ready for me."

"Not everything." The mischievous twinkle in my eye told him exactly what I'd meant.

"No, Kylene. No party. Absolutely not—"

"But it'll be fun—"

"No—"

"And small—"

"No—"

"And totally lame—"

"Not happening—"

"Just me, Tabby, AJ—if you guys have sorted things out—and a movie. And food, of course, because I've seen the stuff you've been eating lately and I hardly think it counts."

"Ky. . . ."

"Really. It'll be no big deal. I promise."

His dubious glare said he wasn't buying my story. "I'm going to live to regret this, aren't I?"

"I mean . . . that's totally possible, but . . ."

"Fine. But only you three. That's it."

"Great. It's settled. I'll call Tabby and let her know the plan."

"Why do I think giving her advance notice about this is a bad idea?"

"Because you've met her." I winked at him as I dialed her number. All I had to do was say the word "party" and she was a squealing incoherent mess. At best, I understood every third word she said before she hung up, leaving Garrett and me both staring at each other.

"This is going to be a shit show," he muttered under his breath.

"Agreed."

He opened his mouth to complain when his long-legged physical therapist walked in. Her pale brown eyes sparkled when she looked over at him. Like magic, his irritation disappeared.

As she approached, I noticed her hair.

"I thought you didn't go for blondes," I mumbled under my breath, leaning toward him in conspiratorial fashion.

He flashed me an impish grin.

"Rules were made to be broken."

On my way home from the hospital, I got a text from Dawson telling me that ten of the suspects on his list had been cleared. Unfortunately, none of those suspects were ones I was hoping to see eliminated. And that got me wondering . . .

We knew who had opportunity, but what about motive? And, even better than that, leverage to be puppeted into the whole deal? If the AD was pulling the strings behind the scenes, which it seemed he was, then what could he possibly have on those suspects to make them do his bidding?

Those questions haunted me well into the night.

TWENTY-THREE

Motive.

That one word churned over and over in my mind while I watched Mr. Callahan, looking pompous as ever, at the front of physics and Coach shouting at some kid who tripped while doing sprints in gym. By the time lunch rolled around, I couldn't stand it any longer. I had to do something.

On my way to the cafeteria, I blurted out something to Tabby about needing to talk to Principal Thompson and bolted before she could ask why. I ran down the hallway, her questions slowly dying in my wake. I didn't stop running until I found myself standing outside room 333. Callahan had been connected to every victim we knew of so far. All we needed was hard evidence to tie him to them or a viable motive. I had no idea what I thought I might find in his office, but I knew I had to look. And since his TA had a thing for me, I thought I might be able to use that connection to get me in there.

Shitty? Yes. Practical? Also yes.

The door was open, so I poked my head in to find AJ sitting at Mr. Callahan's desk, headphones on. I tried calling his name twice to no avail, then walked up beside him and tapped his shoulder. He jumped in his chair and turned to look at me with wild eyes. I stifled my giggle. AJ always had scared easily.

"Now who's stalking whom?" he asked, slipping his headphones off.

"I thought I'd turn the tables on you. Keep you on your toes."

His broad smile told me how much he approved. "You feel sorry for me because I'm stuck up here."

"Maybe."

I heard voices in the hall. Not wanting to be disturbed, I ran over to shut the door. Once I did, AJ's interest most certainly piqued.

"Do we need privacy?" he asked. The sultry tone in his voice sent shivers up my spine.

"Maybe."

"Is that the only answer I'm getting out of you today?" he asked, sliding off his stool. He walked toward me slowly as if I were a cornered animal—like he was afraid he'd spook me.

". . . maybe." I added a wry smile for good measure, and he took the bait. "Okay, no, it's not the only answer. And I'm here because I kinda need a favor."

"What kind of favor?"

There was far too much heat in his stare when he asked that question—a dangerous amount.

I took a deep breath to steel my nerves. "The kind that lets me into Callahan's back office."

He stopped dead in his tracks. "Ky—"

"I know what I'm asking of you, AJ. I need you to trust that it's for a good reason. A *noble* one."

I'd played the white knight card, knowing he'd have a hard time saying no to that.

"Are you in trouble?" he asked in a hushed tone.

"No. It's not about me, I promise. Can you help me, AJ?"

He glanced to the back of the classroom where the door to

Callahan's private office stood closed, then back to me. I could see the conflict in his eyes. Duty versus cause.

"What are you going to do in there?" he asked.

"I'm not sure, to be honest."

His lips pressed to a grim line. "He'll be back here in about fifteen minutes. You need to be long gone before that," he said, heading to the office door. He pulled out a key and unlocked it for me. I slipped past him to enter and he stopped me short with a hand on my shoulder.

"Fifteen minutes, Ky." I nodded in response. "Please don't make me regret this."

"I'll owe you one," I said with a smile. In a flash, that heated gaze was all over me.

"Deal."

He closed the door, leaving me in a room full of old lab equipment, a row of file cabinets, and Callahan's desk. For such a small space, it was an overwhelming amount of stuff, and I felt hemmed in by it. I set the timer on my phone for thirteen minutes, then set about ransacking the place as quickly and quietly as possible. I rummaged through all his desk drawers for anything incriminating, and any open file cabinet I could find. The one labeled "TESTS" was locked, not surprisingly. I didn't have time to try to jimmy it open, so I went back to his desk, focusing on the piles of crap he had on top.

Folder upon folder of uselessness was stacked there, and I searched through them for anything obvious like "PROSTITUTION 101" or "WHERE I BURIED THE BODIES" but found nothing. Then my eyes fell upon his day planner and an idea struck. If I couldn't find motive, maybe opportunity would suffice.

I riffled through it, looking for the day of Danielle's murder. I searched the pages for anything damning, my eyes wild and darting all around until they landed on two little letters. Letters that seemed so innocuous on their own, but once combined with the knowledge of Danielle's death had unmeasurable gravity.

There, on the day she was murdered, were the initials "DG."

With my heart in my throat, I started thumbing back through the planner, looking at the days before she died. On multiple occasions the initials "DG" appeared with no further explanation.

I whipped out my phone and started snapping pics of all the pages I could find with her initials on it. I was about halfway through when my alarm went off.

"Nooooo!" I groaned, shutting it off. Seconds later, I could hear footsteps outside, undoubtedly AJ coming to drag me from my search, but a voice cut both his approach and my breathing short.

"Did you get those assignments ready for me?" a muffled Mr. Callahan asked AJ.

"Yes, sir. I was just going to go drop them on your desk," AJ replied, sounding calm and cool.

"I'll take them," Mr. Callahan said, his heavy footfalls nearly paralyzing me. Then I snapped out of it.

In a quiet scramble, I straightened up his desk and bolted for the door that led directly to the hallway from his office. But as I rounded his desk, I knocked a stack of files over. I froze instantly, blind panic rocketing through my veins.

"What was that?" Mr. Callahan asked, hurrying toward his office door.

The one I hadn't locked.

I dropped to the floor and reached for the handle, turning the lock as quietly as possible before crawling toward the exit. The key in the lock was the soundtrack to my escape, and I flung myself out into the hallway just as I heard it turn. I pressed the door closed behind me, then bolted down the hall to the girls' room. I could hear Callahan shouting at AJ about something strange going on as he opened the door I'd narrowly escaped through to look for a potential intruder.

I listened to AJ explain that he'd been in there earlier to get something and that he must have bumped the stack, setting it off-balance. He apologized profusely, using his patented AJ charm. Mr. Callahan calmed down, and I breathed a sigh of relief. The last thing I wanted to do was get AJ in trouble.

I really did owe him big-time.

I wondered how long it would be before he came looking to collect.

TWENTY-FOUR

I texted Dawson the pictures as soon as I could and buried my phone in my bag just before Ms. McManus caught me using it. God forbid she opened my texts and asked me to explain the messages I'd sent. It would be another date with Principal Thompson for me.

Dawson was waiting for me outside our Spanish class, and it didn't take long for me to find myself embroiled in a mini-interrogation right there in the hall. His face was only inches from mine so he could keep his voice low, but his proximity was distracting. I kept trying to look around him to see if people were staring—I know I would have been.

"How did you get those pictures?" he asked, his voice low and harsh.

"That's not important—"

"I think a court of law may disagree."

"I didn't steal anything. I just took pictures. Pictures that make Callahan look a lot guiltier."

He had no clever response for that one.

"I'm going to have someone at the bureau start digging into his personal life and financials. I need to see what kind of secrets he's hiding."

"Like a shit ton of money and dead bodies?"

The warning bell rang.

"Something like that."

Without another word, he rushed toward the stairs.

"Where are you going?" I called after him.

He turned back and winked.

"My unexcused absences have earned me a date with Principal Thompson."

He disappeared down the stairs, leaving me behind. I hated being left behind. Always Watson to his Sherlock.

After school, I wanted to meet up with Dawson to see how it went with Principal Thompson, but I'd promised to run errands in town for Gramps first. By the time I finished, it was nearly dinner. I walked into the house, bags in hand and starving, to find that Gramps was nowhere to be seen. The only trace of him was a note on the table—his trademark move—that said he'd been called in early and hadn't had time to make dinner. Next to the note was a ten-dollar bill.

"Takeout it is," I muttered to myself, feeling bad that Gramps thought he'd had to do that. I thought for a minute about what I could get for that amount that would have leftovers for him the next day. My conclusion was a grim one. Marco's Pizza was a dubious mom-and-pop establishment famous for pizza coated in enough grease to give you a heart attack by the third slice. That said, it was amazing.

The owner, Marco, however, slightly less so.

He was a Sicilian-born Brooklyn boy who moved to Jasperville when I was in grade school. People tended to give him a wide berth when he walked down the street. Covered in tats—neck and all—and built like a Mack Truck, he was intimidating as hell. Rumor was he'd escaped the mob and been planted in Jasperville. And by planted, I mean by the feds—witness protection for snitching. But for all his scary attributes, he'd never been anything but nice to me, so I had no issue going to his joint to get a thin-crust special. Even if my arteries protested the whole time.

Marco's was only a few minutes from my house, so it wasn't long before I found myself walking in. The door still jingled when it opened, drawing the attention of the few people dining there. Most who went there always got takeout—because of Marco. He looked through the open kitchen at me and smiled, his gold tooth near the back gleaming in the fluorescent lights. He barked some orders at the poor kid working alongside him, then stepped to the counter.

"I recognize you . . ."

"Kylene," I replied with a smile to match his. A warm one tainted with trouble.

"You're Bruce Danners' kid, right?"

"Yep. A dubious honor to hold in this town, but I hold it proudly nonetheless."

He jerked his head in a nod. "Family is the most important thing." He sounded like the Godfather when he said that, and I had to stifle a laugh—because I wanted to live.

"Agreed."

"So, what can I get for you, Danners' kid?"

I scanned the menu, taking in the prices more than anything else. The ten dollars in my pocket was feeling light as I did.

"Just a small cheese, please. Extra thin."

"Like it should be," he said before turning to the kitchen and hollering out my order. "That'll be nine ninety-nine." I handed him the ten and took my penny change. "Have a seat. Should be out in a few minutes."

I nodded my thanks and crossed the room to a tiny two-person booth in the corner. Sitting there, I toyed with the crushed red pepper flakes jar, twirling it around and around in my hands. I was staring at it so intently that I didn't notice the man standing next to my table.

I looked up to find an average-looking guy with dad-bod, fidgeting with his keys.

"Are you waiting for someone?" he asked.

"Not unless that someone is a small cheese pizza, no."

He apologized for bothering me, then rushed out of the building.

"Weirdo," I muttered under my breath as I continued to twirl the pepper shaker, hoping it would distract me from the growing volume of the conversation across the tiny pizzeria. One that didn't surprise me. One I wasn't in the mood for.

"It's a shame what happened to that Shipman boy. Ain't nothin' wrong with takin' a few drugs to up yer game. And that nonsense about him tryin' to kill those kids . . . bullshit. That's all that is."

Twirl . . . twirl . . .

"It's that damn Danners girl," someone else said, his voice loud and pointed and, from what I could tell without looking, directed right at me. "Stuck her nose where it don't belong and got bit. But girls these days can say anythin' and police'll believe 'em. Damn feminists. Women are best for two things, and thinkin' ain't one of 'em."

"Gonna be a sad end to a great football season this year," the other man said, his voice now traveling directly over to me.

Twirl . . . twirl . . . twirl . . .

"Sure is, Earl."

Footsteps headed toward me.

Twirl . . . twirl . . . CRASH.

One of the guys knocked the shaker from the table to the

seat across from me. It didn't break, but it made one hell of a noise when it smashed into the plastic bench seat.

"You hear me, girl?"

I lifted my head enough to give him a sidelong glance.

"I hear you," I answered with venom in my tone. "I can't understand a damn thing you're saying because I don't speak hillbilly, but, yes, I hear you just fine."

The man sneered at me. "You think yer pretty damn smart, don'tcha, girlie?"

"I feel like that's a loaded question. . . ."

"If yer that smart, then maybe you should get your ass outta this town."

"Is that a threat?" I asked him, straightening my back against the weight of his warning. "Because, I gotta tell you, threatening me in a public place isn't really a great idea. You see these other people in here? They're called *witnesses*."

The two men exchanged a glance and laughed.

"Ain't nobody in this place seen nothin'. Not if Edson and me tell them they don't. You catch my meanin'?"

I did. And it wasn't good.

Not liking my position, I stood up, pushing my way out of the booth.

"All this over a lousy football team? You know we never would have held up against those big private schools from the city in the finals. Even you two aren't that dumb."

"Guess we ain't gonna find out now since you ruined everythin'."

"She didn't ruin shit," a gruff female voice said from across the room. "And you two rednecks know that."

They turned to face the tall brown-haired girl, who stood up well against their scrutiny. She had balls—I had to give her that.

"Why don't you and your friend drag yer skinny asses back to yer single-wides and yer junkie mamas, trailer trash bitches," Earl said, stepping closer to where she and her black-haired friend sat silent in the booth.

"Or maybe you should go make some money to pay for yer mama's habit," Edson added.

"Fuck you," she snapped, making a move for him. I cut her off on the way, giving her my best "not now" face. She seemed to read it loud and clear and stepped down.

"Now boys," I said, turning my attention back to them, "I can assure you that Donovan deserves to be in jail. He put the sheriff's son in the ICU—that's *the intensive care unit* for those not so stellar with acronyms. He tried to kill me, he beat his girlfriend, and he—" I cut myself off before blurting out that he'd taken naked photos of me, too. Somehow I doubted those two Neanderthals would see anything wrong with that. "But maybe you're more worried about football and the good ole boy system to care."

I was mad. Seething mad. And shouting, apparently, because I could see Marco coming out from behind the counter.

"We got a problem out here?" he asked, looking at the grown men and then the other girls and me.

"We was just expressin' our disappointment with the football season and she started shoutin'."

"Liar."

Edson smiled at me. "Takes one to know one."

"Your pie is ready," Marco said, his eyes now pinned on Edson. How that inbred piece of crap didn't run from the building screaming was beyond me. Maybe he was too stupid to know better. That seemed highly likely.

Eventually the two men turned and left. Marco hovered long enough to see them drive away. Brooklyn wasn't playing around. He was street smart, and I appreciated that fact. He also, apparently, had my back.

"Thanks," I said. That single word was full of so much meaning in that moment. I followed him to the counter and took the box that he handed me. I went to pull it away, but he held it firm for a second, pinning dark brown eyes on mine.

"What that kid did to you and your friend . . . it wasn't right. There's a code—a line you don't cross. He crossed it." He looked out the door after the two that had left. "And so did they."

There was so much subtext to his comment that I needed more time than I had to sift through it all. But what was loud and clear was that even Marco, who had clearly done bad things in his life, was on my side. At least for now.

"Thanks," I said again, taking the box from him and turning to leave. On the way out, I walked past the girl who had come to my aid and her friend. They both sat in the booth, glaring at me. Seeing their expressions, I opted not to say goodbye.

They were tough girls with what sounded like even tougher lives, and though I didn't recognize either of them, they were clearly local enough that guys like Earl and Edson knew exactly who they were. I remembered what they'd said to the one who'd spoken up—what her circumstances were—and I realized that she and her friend were just like the girls Dawson and I were investigating. *Throwaway Girls.* Then I thought about how many girls at our school were in similar predicaments: junkie parents, foster care gone wrong, no money or means of any sort.

The enormity of the situation slammed down on my shoulders.

If girls like those were indeed the target of the prostitution ringleader, then Jasperville County was ripe for the picking.

One of the poorest counties in the state that boasted a record-breaking opioid problem and rampant unemployment. So many in town were struggling. I wondered just how many girls were missing from Dawson's whiteboard.

I doubted we'd ever really know.

TWENTY-FIVE

At lunch the next day, Tabby and I had an unexpected visitor. I looked up from my soggy noodles to see Dawson storming toward our table like I'd just set his car on fire. I excused myself and got up to cut him off at the pass, not wanting Tabby to overhear us.

We found a quiet corner to tuck ourselves in before Dawson said a word.

"Callahan has some skeletons in his closet."

"Ha! No surprise there."

"Looks like he had a messy divorce when he was younger. His wife alleged that he was having sexual relationships with students."

"Holy shit!" I all but shouted, then slapped my hand over my mouth.

"That's not the best part."

"Well don't keep me in suspense!"

"It seems that everything regarding those allegations just went away overnight. The whole thing was dropped, just like that. Callahan moved down here to start over and the rest is history."

"The AD is good at making troublesome things go away," I said, realizing what had likely happened.

"Exactly. I've got to go to the bureau today and sit down

with my team so we can sift through his financials, his ex-wife's—see if the reported allegations named names, and, if so, follow up with them. We need to see how much of a cleanup job this was, if it was one at all."

"This is too much of a coincidence to actually be a coincidence, right?"

He looked at me for a moment, his sharp eyes boring through mine.

"I intend to find out. Until then, I want you to steer as clear of him as you can."

"With pleasure."

"You're on the pimp's radar—don't forget that. If it is Callahan, I don't even want you to be the last one in the room with him after class, got it?"

"Yeah. I got it."

He nodded, then flashed me a smile as he leaned into my ear. "I mean it, Danners. No more off-book stuff."

Then he left without another word.

I returned to find Tabby staring. Assessing. "What was that about?"

"Alex wants to talk to me about getting back together," I said, not knowing how else to satisfy her curiosity.

"Looks to me like you two already are. That's the rumor going around school. . . ."

"I'm sure it is."

"Do you want to? Get back together with him?" she asked, her tone so, so careful.

I hesitated before responding. I'd done everything I could to get out of playing Dawson's girlfriend, but with my late nights at his house and our intimate hallway convos, I wondered if it wouldn't be better if I just surrendered to the rumors. It'd be the fastest way to make them go away.

And salvage some shred of my reputation.

"Ky?" she said, concern etching her face. "You okay?"

"Yeah, sorry. I spaced out there for a sec. But, yes, I do want to get back together with Alex."

She forced a smile to hide her #TeamAJ disappointment. I forced one in return, wondering what Dawson's reaction would be when I filled him in on the change of plans. If history was any indication, I'd probably want to hit him.

Or break up.

After school on Tuesday, Tabby and I raced over to Garrett's house. I didn't ask about the monster-sized plastic bag of shiny things she'd pulled from her locker and stuffed in my trunk. I wanted to cling to plausible deniability when his interrogation set in. "No, Garrett, I had no idea that she was going to throw glitter confetti at you when you walked in. . . ."

We walked up to the house and knocked. Seconds later, Sheriff Higgins opened the door.

"Girls," he said with a nod. "Garrett said you all might be comin' by."

"I have decorations!" Tabby exclaimed, holding up her bag of shenanigans.

"Do you mind if we set up while you go to get him?" I asked, doing my best to act like this was a totally normal encounter. It wasn't, of course. Me taking the rap for Sheriff Higgins left his cover intact with whoever had his claws in him. It also left a tension between us so thick that I prayed Tabby's preoccupation with streamers would keep her from noticing.

"That'd be just fine," he replied, stepping aside to let us in. "I'm headin' out now. I'm afraid that doesn't leave you with too much time."

"Don't worry, sir. We won't need it." Before he could reply,

Tabby had dumped the entire contents of her bag on the floor, sorting through it to find what she wanted to start with.

"I'll see y'all in a little bit then. Kylene, could I have a quick word outside?"

"Sure thing," I replied. "You gonna be okay without me, Tabs?" She looked up from under a mountain of sparkly crap and smiled.

I took that as a yes and followed the sheriff out the door.

"You need something?" I asked, walking over to meet him by his cruiser.

"I want to check in with you—make sure you aren't gettin' yourself into any more trouble with that FBI kid."

"*Agent Dawson*?" I said, emphasizing his title. "Wouldn't dream of it."

"I know he's lookin' into some old runaway cases. I hope he isn't kickin' a hornet's nest with that."

"What do you know about them? Is this one of those times you looked the other way?" Even though I'd figured out that he couldn't have been involved in all their cases, given the timeline and when Sheriff Higgins had been roped in by the AD, I threw the jab out there anyway.

He scowled in response. "I know you don't think much of me after all that happened, Kylene, but you need to understand that I want the answers to what's goin' on around here, same as you."

"I'd like to believe that. I really would."

"But you don't."

I shook my head. "I'm just not sure I can trust you. Trust anyone, for that matter."

"What happened to you at the hospital—it's got you spooked." An observation, not a question. "You look tired, Kylene. Those black circles under your eyes say as much. You look skinny, too. You eatin'? Sleepin'?"

"I'm getting by," I said, folding my arms over my chest.

His eyes narrowed. "Has that fed got you helpin' him with this case?" he asked, leaning closer to me. He was angry, but not at me. It was that kind of anger parents shared when they were watching out for one another's kids. When I didn't answer, he bent down to level his gaze on mine. "I want you to listen to me, girl. If what he's gettin' into leads back to the AD, you don't want to be anywhere near that, you understand?"

"Who is this guy?" I asked, voice thin and soft.

"I don't know," he replied, resting his hands on my shoulders. "But I pray to God you never find out."

With that, he gave me a nod and climbed into his car. Seconds later, he was gone, leaving me in his driveway alone with my thoughts. Then the door opened and Tabby popped her head out.

"Hey! Are you going to help me, or what?"

"Yeah. I'm coming."

I walked back to the house, forcing a smile, but Tabby saw right through it.

"Is Garrett's dad mad at you about something?" she asked, draping her arm around my shoulders as she ushered me in.

"He's just worried about Garrett for the same reasons your dad is worried about you. Being around me seems to court a certain amount of disaster, you know? And, if I'm being honest, I don't do much to counter that."

She frowned, then tucked a stray piece of hair behind my ear.

"You stand up for what's right, Ky. That's not something you should apologize for."

"I should when it almost gets my best friend killed."

That truth gave her pause. "But all that's over now," she said, thinking she was pointing out the obvious.

Oh, how wrong she was.

"Yeah. I guess the sheriff will come around eventually."

"He will once he sees how awesome these decorations are!" she exclaimed, holding up a massive WELCOME HOME GARRETT sign. "Nothing says friendship like a well-decked-out party."

I had no choice but to laugh at that.

"Then I guess we'd better streamer the bejeezus out of this place to get me out of the doghouse."

We went to work on Tabby's creation until not a surface in the Higginses' living room was bare. Tabby took a step back into the kitchen to admire her vision come to life and gave a nod.

"I think it's ready."

I heard the crunch of tires on gravel in the driveway outside.

"And not a moment too soon."

I ran to the door and threw it open wide to find AJ making his way to the house. He smiled when he saw me and picked up his pace.

"Is he here yet?" he asked.

"No. I thought you were him, actually."

"Ah! That would explain the open-door treatment."

"It would," I replied, jokingly closing the door on his face. He caught it before it shut.

"That was harsh," he said, feigning affront. I merely shrugged in response.

"Hey, AJ!" Tabby called. "Glad you could come."

"I wouldn't have missed it."

It was then that AJ realized just how ridiculous the Higginses' living room looked. He turned his dubious expression to me, and I shook my head no. If I didn't get to rain on Tabby's parade, he didn't, either.

"Here they come!" Tabby shouted, jumping down from the couch.

"Are we supposed to hide or something?" AJ asked, looking at me confused.

"I'm pretty sure our cars in the driveway are a bit of a spoiler," I said. "She's just excited. Let it go."

Tabby threw the door open, bouncing on her toes as she waited for Garrett to slowly walk up to the porch.

"Easy girl," I cautioned. "You can't pounce on him. He's still not in great shape."

My warning went in one ear and right out the other. In two steps, she snatched him up in her skinny arms and hugged him like she'd been waiting to do it her whole life. Thankfully, she wasn't strong enough to do any damage, but Garrett still winced a little until I pried her off him and shooed her into the house.

"I tried to stop her," I said, smiling up at him. Then I gave him a hug, too.

"Well, I think we both know how in vain that effort was from the get-go."

He draped his arms around my shoulders and did his best to squeeze. I did my best not to be bothered by how weak it was.

"Hey, man," AJ said, coming up behind me. I slid out of the way so they could do their bro-hugging and backslapping, which was really more of a light tap on both their parts. I guess the two of them had hashed things out. It felt amazing to see them together and friends again. It felt right.

"Just wait till you see what Tabby did," I said. Noting my overly enthusiastic tone, Garrett shot me a sideward glance and I nodded. He knew how much she'd loved the decorations at homecoming. He'd already put two and two together.

"I love it, Tabs," he said as he walked in, eyes wide. "You girls have been busy."

"Do you really like it?" Tabby asked. The poor girl held her breath, like our approval meant the world to her.

"I do. I think it's awesome."

"Why don't we all let Garrett get settled on the couch," Sheriff Higgins said from behind his son. "He's home, but he still needs rest, and if you tire him out now, there won't be much of a party to speak of."

AJ helped Garrett over to the couch and the rest of us found places to sit. Tabby and I crammed onto the love seat while AJ perched on the arm of the sofa Garrett was stretched out on. Sheriff Higgins asked if we all wanted anything to drink, then came back with soda and cups.

Then he disappeared to give us some space.

"Hey, did you invite Alex?" Garrett asked. It was such a harmless question—one he didn't realize he shouldn't ask because he'd been isolated from the AJ/Alex drama. But given how tense everyone went at the mention of his name, Garrett sorted it out pretty quickly.

"He said he'd stop by if he could," I lied. "I think he's got some stuff to do out of town today."

Garrett gave a sympathetic look and nodded.

"I brought cake!" Tabby shouted, launching herself off the love seat. "Anybody want some?"

"I could use a sugar buzz," AJ replied, getting up to help her. Once the two left the room, Garrett struggled to sit up on the couch. He clearly was preparing to launch an interrogation—one that would have made my pretend boyfriend proud—but my phone began buzzing. I fished it out of my pocket to find a local number I didn't recognize on the screen.

"I've got to take this," I said, heading for the front door. The second it closed behind me, I answered. "Hello?"

"Did you get anywhere with the information I gave you?" Jane said, skipping the pleasantries.

"I did," I replied. "I've constructed a pretty elaborate timeline and cross-referenced the girls' lives to come up with a list of people they have in common. I need to run them past you to tighten up the suspects list."

"Fine," she replied. I rambled off every name I could remember from the list Dawson had amassed. Some she didn't recognize at all. Others she knew all too well. By the time we finished going through it, only a few remained. All the JHS staff that had been implicated were still in the running, though some more than others, along with Mr. Matthew, Kru Tyson, and Sheriff Higgins. I sighed, wishing a few of those names hadn't made the cut. "Kylene," she said, pulling me from my disappointment.

"Yeah?"

"I feel like you're missing a couple names from that list."

"How so?"

"Well, there was another teacher that came over the same year as Principal Thompson, Coach, and Callahan. You forgot Ms. Davies."

"I know, but I eliminated her because you said a man killed Danielle. That you *saw* him."

"I did, but that doesn't mean he's in charge, does it? That he couldn't be working with someone else?"

My heart sank to the gravel at my feet. As much as I prided myself on seeing men and women as equals, I'd completely overlooked the possibility that a female could be the kingpin behind the operation. And though the thought made me physically ill, that didn't make it any less plausible.

"You're right," I said. "You know what I really need right about now? Physical evidence—like from a crime scene."

"I can't give you that."

I hesitated for a second. "You could if you tell me where the murder took place." I looked over my shoulder to make sure I was still alone, then moved farther away from the house just to be sure. The last thing I needed was Sheriff Higgins overhearing me.

Silence.

"I can't. . . ."

"Do you want to end up the next recruiter? No? Then help me get something concrete."

"I don't want to end up like Danielle, which is what I'm afraid will happen if you go poking around that bridge, dusting for prints or whatever it is you think you're gonna do." I opened my mouth to argue, but she kept right on going. "And if you think I'm sittin' around here thinking 'hey, maybe I should drag this out a little longer . . . what's a few more nights on my back with some of Jasperville's finest grunting and sweating all over me,' you're not the girl I'd hoped you were."

I recoiled from her words. They were a slap I'd not only deserved but needed. The distance between Jane and me made it easy to forget that she was a kid, a girl being exploited. My cheeks flushed with the shame I felt in that moment. I knew all too well what it was like to be victimized by those with more power than I had.

"I'm sorry," I said softly.

"I don't want your damn apology or your pity. What I want you to do is find whoever is behind this so I can get out."

I took a deep breath. "Then you need to tell me, Jane. I can handle it—I promise. I need this. You do, too."

She hesitated, clearly weighing out the pros and cons. Her paranoia was blocking her way out of her hell. The longer she was silent, the more I knew she saw that. A minute later, I got what I wanted.

"Marchand Bridge," she whispered.

"Marchand Bridge," I repeated.

"In the middle by the north railing." I made a note of the

location in my phone. "What exactly do you hope to find there? You're not a CSI and you don't exactly have a DNA lab in your basement," she said, her tone harsh.

"I have friends at the FBI—friends who won't ask questions if I ask them to run a couple tests for me."

"How do you know you can trust them?"

I felt like that was the million-dollar question lately. How did I know I could trust anyone? Everyone on that list of suspects was either someone I'd known my whole life or one in a position to shape kids' futures—not steal their innocence, then murder them.

"Because he's my dad's old partner. He stood by my dad through everything. He's helping me find evidence to reopen my father's case. Is that good enough for you?"

She inhaled deeply, then let it out slowly. "It's going to have to be."

Then the line went dead.

I quickly copied the number Jane had called from and texted it to Dawson. It was a long shot, but if he could track her down based on it, it certainly wouldn't hurt our situation.

Tucking my phone away, I turned to head back inside only to find Garrett sitting on the porch bench, staring at me. The look on his face said it all. He'd heard at least part of my conversation with Jane, if not most.

I needed a shovel to dig myself out of the shit I was in.

TWENTY-SIX

"Which do you want to tell me first: Why you need Striker to run tests for you without questions or who that was on the phone? I'll let you decide."

The sting of his words combined with how tightly his arms were folded against his chest put me on the defensive. My jumbled mind, too addled by lack of sleep to process everything happening quickly enough, only made things worse. I looked on as Garrett pushed himself off the bench and carefully climbed down the steps. I walked over to meet him, hoping to save him some energy. He was going to use up a lot of it being pissed at me.

"I can't tell you who was on the phone, Garrett, but I want to."

"Then do it."

I shook my head. "I promised her I wouldn't tell anyone. Especially *you*."

He looked as though I'd slapped him. "Why not me?"

"Because of your dad."

"Oh. That."

"I'm sorry."

"Please tell me what you've gotten yourself into this time. Is it about your father's case? Did you find someone who has information on what went down?"

I tried to think back over the conversation I'd had with Jane and what Garrett could have overheard. Since he hadn't asked who Danielle was or mentioned anything about murder, it was entirely possible that I could play this whole encounter off as a call from an informant—someone willing to speak off the record about my dad's case.

"I did, but she's easily spooked, and she knows your dad has been bought off. She seems to have done her research on me before reaching out. I can't jeopardize this, Garrett. Not even to spare your feelings."

His lips pressed to a thin line. "You can't do this on your own, Ky. It's not safe. I mean, for God's sake, look at me. I just got out of the hospital and you're already heading down a path to land yourself in one."

I knew he hadn't said it to hit below the belt, but it knocked the wind out of me all the same. Mainly because he was right. Seeing him there, struggling to stand before me, gave me a moment's clarity that I desperately needed. It cut through my defenses and slapped me with reality.

Tears started to slowly roll down my cheeks.

"Aw, dammit, don't cry. I didn't say that to hurt you. You're just so thickheaded sometimes."

"I know," I sniffled, wrapping my arms around his waist.

"Can you at least tell Alex? You need someone to have your back."

"I have her back," a voice said from the doorway. I looked past Garrett to find AJ headed our way with Tabby not far behind.

"Why do you need someone to have your back?" Tabby asked, concern in her eyes.

"It's about the Donovan stuff," Garrett said, playing down how severe he thought things were.

"But that's all over," AJ replied. His brow furrowed with confusion.

"Didn't he take the plea agreement?" Tabby asked. "He's going to jail, Ky. He can't hurt you now."

Ah, the joys of balancing who in my life knew what. If I didn't royally mess that up at some point, I'd know for sure that God existed.

"Garrett's just worried," I said, pulling away from him. "He has more reason to be than anyone." Neither AJ nor Tabby dared argue that point.

"I'm getting kind of tired," Garrett said, turning to head in. "Can we just watch a movie or something?"

"Of course, man," AJ said, helping Garrett inside. Tabby and I followed without a word. Once in the living room, we turned on a comedy and watched in relative silence. While the others appeared to be enjoying it, I couldn't help but be on edge. I felt like the lies were starting to close in around me, and I had no way of escaping.

My dad and I both were imprisoned by them.

I sneaked into the bathroom to text Dawson about the crime scene. He called me back two seconds later.

"How do you know this?"

"How do you think, hotshot?"

I swear I heard him growl under his breath.

"How secluded is this place?" he asked.

"During the day? Not at all. There's way too much traffic along that stretch. We'll have to wait until dusk. The mine will be closed by then and the bridge will be basically untraveled."

"We?" His tone was incredulous. "*We* aren't going anywhere. *I* am going to go case the scene and see if I need to call in a team to process it. I don't want to risk exposure, but if there's enough evidence there, I don't have a choice."

"You wouldn't even know about this without me!" I argued,

knowing it wasn't likely to get me anywhere. By-the-book Dawson wouldn't bend the rules on this one.

"Maybe not, but that doesn't entitle you to tag along. Reading through some old files and processing a crime scene are two very different things." When I didn't say anything in response, I could practically hear his suspicion grow. "Danners, you are not to go anywhere near that bridge, do you understand me?"

I silently nodded.

"Danners?" he called, anger creeping into his voice.

"It's not like I'm going to race over there now with my Junior Detective kit so I can show you up."

"Good. Leave this to—"

"The professionals? Yeah. I got it. I'll go paint my nails and watch a chick flick—you know, kids' stuff."

I hung up without saying goodbye, then walked out into the narrow hallway to find AJ staring at me.

"Everything okay? I heard you yelling."

I sighed hard, knowing he must have overheard my conversation with Dawson and the frustration in my tone.

"Yeah, AJ. Everything's great."

"Was that Alex?"

"Uh-huh."

"You two have a fight or something?"

"No. Alex is just a bit moody, that's all. Sometimes when I talk to him I don't know if I'm getting Jekyll or Hyde."

His expression darkened. "That's not cool, Ky. You shouldn't have to put up with that."

No. I really shouldn't, and yet . . .

"I think the stress of being here and us not being a couple is just getting to him lately. If he doesn't snap out of it, I'll kick him in the junk. Does that make you feel better?"

His eyebrow quirked ever so slightly. "Maybe." We stood there awkwardly for a moment until he broke first. "Hey, my mom is working late shift this week. I thought maybe you'd want to come over one night. Maybe watch a movie?"

"Me? Like, just me?"

"No, like you and Tabby and Garrett. That sound better?"

"What about Alex?" I asked, my tone cautious.

"Not if he's a moody dick. . . ."

I started to squirm under the weight of his gaze. I'd basically just given him the ammo he'd turned on me, and there wasn't an easy way out of the line of fire.

"Maybe. I'll see if I can swing it."

"Cool."

He smiled at me, then pushed past me into the bathroom.

I let out the breath I'd been holding.

Of all the things I had to be worried about, a movie night at AJ's shouldn't have been high on the list. And yet, there it was, topping it in that moment. Navigating our relationship was like tiptoeing through a minefield. One wrong move and everything went BOOM! Even with the knowledge that Dawson would soon be headed to a crime scene to process evidence in Danielle's murder, I still couldn't push AJ's offer out of my mind. Maybe it was because the murder was too hard to wrap my head around. Maybe it was just too surreal to fully grasp. Or maybe I was desperate to occupy my mind with something else because the alternative scared the crap out of me.

I knew that, despite Dawson's clear directive, I was going to go to the place where a girl had her throat sliced before being tossed into the river below. Nobody should want to go there willingly, but I had to see it for myself—had to put myself in Jane's shoes. The desire to do it flew in the face of human survival instincts, but I was going, come hell or high water.

TWENTY-SEVEN

I arrived at Marchand Bridge a bit after dusk to make sure Dawson arrived first. I parked my car well off the road and quietly ran toward the bridge, hugging the tree line for cover. Every step closer put me in jeopardy of getting caught, but I needed to see—needed to know that he found something worth calling in the cavalry for.

From a distance, I watched as he sprayed the concrete and the railings, swabbing various parts and dropping the swabs into evidence packages before sealing them up. I dared another step closer, edging toward a patch of brush perfect for hiding behind. The snap of a twig underfoot made my heart rate rocket. He looked in my direction, squinting to see what was there, but I was hidden.

He dialed his phone quickly, then put it to his ear. I hoped he was calling headquarters. I hoped I was close enough to hear the plan.

Instead, I heard the wild buzzing of my phone in my pocket.

"Shit!" I ground out through my teeth.

By the time I turned it off, Dawson was halfway over to me. The look on his face could have melted glass.

"What about *not* coming here did you fail to grasp, Danners?"

I stared baldly at the bag of evidence in his hand.

"Is that blood residue?" I asked, my voice thin and weak.

His scowl deepened. "Yes."

I opened my mouth to say something—anything—in my defense, but the words died on my tongue. The feeling of dread rising in my stomach became too hard to ignore, and it took every ounce of energy I had to tamp it down. Was it wrong to have hoped that Jane had been lying about Danielle's murder? That it was a prank of epic proportions? I managed to keep those possibilities alive until I was standing there, Dawson lecturing me about protocol and contaminating the scene, holding a cotton swab drenched with fluorescein and Danielle's blood. The prayer that maybe I'd wake up from all of this and realize it was a bad dream was killed in an instant.

I looked out over the river. Because of recent storms, it was flowing hard, churning up all kinds of debris. Maybe even Danielle.

"How far do you think this carried the body?" I asked, interrupting him mid ass-reaming. The hollowness of my voice seemed to get his attention. His anger bled to concern as he stared at me.

"There's no way to tell. Her remains will likely show up at some point, way downstream."

I thought about what Jane had told me, mulling her words over and over. I couldn't help but think that the killer had been so careful over the years. That he'd taken such great lengths in picking his victims and disposing of them so that he didn't get caught. So why then would he haphazardly just toss a body into the river, knowing that it would eventually surface? Yeah, maybe it wouldn't have tied back to him, but still—it seemed careless, and nothing about this guy (or woman) seemed careless. In fact, quite the opposite.

I tried to focus on what Jane had said about how Danielle was tossed over the bridge.

"Dawson," I said softly, still puzzling things together as I spoke. "Jane said the killer bent down and picked her up by the ankles, then threw her over. . . ." I looked up at him. "But why not just push her over? Why caber toss her in?"

He stepped closer to me, the slow movement only adding to the tension I felt.

"What are you trying to say?" he asked.

"What if she didn't go downstream at all? What if the killer tied something around her ankles to weigh her down and her body is below the bridge right now?"

His gaze cut to the river, its strong current running down the middle. Then he took off toward his supplies on the bridge. I raced after him, visions of a dead girl floating through my mind.

He riffled through his duffel bag, looking for something. When I spotted the flashlight poking out from beneath the bag, I grabbed it, terror driving my actions. He looked up to me as I took a step backward.

"Give me the flashlight."

I held it tight to my chest. "What are you going to do, Dawson?"

"Just give me the flashlight, Danners," he replied as he stripped his jacket off, followed by his shirt.

"You can't go in there, you cocky son of a bitch. You'll get swept away!"

"Not if I dive deep enough. I'll be fine. Just give me the flashlight. I need to see if you're right."

"And if I'm wrong, you might die trying to prove it!"

"I need to know what kind of reinforcements to call in, Danners." He stood with his hand outstretched, reaching for the flashlight. "You have to trust me," he said. "I know what I'm doing."

I clutched that stupid flashlight like it was a lifeline. Handing it over willingly made me feel like I was accepting his harebrained plan, which I most definitely was not. I didn't want to stand by and watch Dawson die because I overthought something and shared it with him. I couldn't let someone else get hurt because of my bad judgment.

Dawson, seeing my distress, lowered his hand slowly and closed the distance between us.

"*Kylene*," he said gently, resting his hands on my shoulders. "I can hold my breath underwater for at least two minutes. I swear to you that nothing bad is going to happen to me. And, if for some reason it did, it wouldn't be your fault, okay? But I need that flashlight or I won't be able to see if she's there. Can you give it to me, please?"

I forced myself to look at him, fighting to wipe the fear I felt from my expression. With a deep breath, I relinquished the light and took a step back. Then I watched as he ran down the bridge to where it met the embankment and started his precarious descent. I wished we had a rope or something—anything to tether him to me. Once he went under, I had no way of knowing if he was all right or not.

When he reached the water's edge, he looked up at me, the dying light highlighting his tight expression. I held my breath as he waded in waist deep, fighting the pull of the current already. Moments later, he was gone.

I started the timer on my phone. The second it hit two minutes, I was calling the sheriff if Dawson didn't resurface. While I looked on, my fingertips bit into my smartphone and the bridge's railing. My eyes darted everywhere, desperate for something to focus on, but found nothing. With thirty seconds left, I felt my eyes well with tears. I ran to the opposite railing to see if he'd popped up downstream, but still, I found nothing. No trace of Dawson. No smug grin staring up at me, telling me just how pleased he was that he'd nearly scared me to death.

Then the sound of repetitive beeping shot adrenaline through my veins.

His time was up.

"Dawson!" I screamed over the surging water, dashing back and forth between the rails, hoping to catch sight of him. But it was hard with blurry vision, my eyes filled with tears that I could no longer hold back. "Dawson! Answer me!"

I looked down at my phone. Thirty seconds had passed since the two-minute mark. With shaky fingers, I started to dial the sheriff.

"Danners!" he called, from somewhere downstream. I dropped my phone and darted toward the embankment. By the time I reached it, Dawson had climbed halfway up, hacking and coughing along the way.

"Jesus Christ!" I shouted at him, sliding down the few feet to meet him. Once I regained my footing, I flung my arms around his neck and crushed my body to his, holding on to him for dear life as my clothes sucked up the bitterly cold water. I felt my breath hitch as I held back a sob. Then I felt Dawson's arms wrap around me, one hand rubbing up and down my spine.

"I'm okay," he said softly. "I'm all right." When I didn't let him go, he pulled away from me, leaning down to look me in the eyes. "You were right. She's down there."

I sniffled and wiped my eyes with my sleeves.

"Glad your pants didn't get soaked for no reason," I said, hoping to lighten the moment, but my tone was too acerbic for that. "So, what now?"

"I need to call the bureau, then the sheriff. I have to hash out a plan for how we can deal with this. The body could still have forensic evidence on it and I'm sure as hell not leaving that to the locals to recover. But we can't afford for this discovery to be leaked, either. I don't need a circus down here or my cover will be blown." He stood there thinking for a moment, his body shivering with the cold.

"How about you solve that mystery with your clothes on." I turned and stormed up the hill, my anger creeping in as my adrenaline slipped away. Without an argument, he followed until we were back on the bridge. I grabbed my phone and answered a text from Tabby while he put his dry shirt and jacket back on. At least half of him would be warm.

I tried not to overhear his conversation with the sheriff, but it was impossible not to. When he started to describe the degree of decay, I had to leave. I soon found myself dry heaving against a tree.

When I was sure my stomach was done, I went and sat on the hood of his car, hands crammed between my knees to keep them from shaking.

"Danners," Dawson called as he headed my way. "Sheriff is coming out now to secure the scene until the feds can come process it. I can't leave, but you shouldn't stay here. You don't need to see this."

"I'm fine. My nerves are just shot, that's all. I really thought you'd—"

I cut myself off, unable to say the word "drowned" without my emotions betraying me. My gaze fell to my bouncing knees—the ones that still held my hands captive. Dawson's eyes must have followed, because those hands were soon freed, taken by his for inspection. The second he saw how violently they shook, he ushered me toward the driver's side of his car.

Then he started to pace.

"Shit!" he said under his breath. "I can't leave the crime scene, but you can't be here when the sheriff shows up and shouldn't be driving right now. You're too shaken up—"

"Dawson, I'm fine—"

"Really?" he asked, his tone incredulous. "I don't think so."

"You also think you're always right, so you can see my conundrum at the moment." I forced a smile and he stopped wearing a path in the dirt.

He pinned narrow eyes on me.

"What do you think of my car?" he asked.

I looked at him like he had three heads. "I think it's great for someone who enjoys an early-bird special and mall walking."

"What did you want to do to me the first day we met?"

I cocked my head at him. "I feel like that answer is fairly obvious."

He hesitated for a second before asking one final question.

"How badly do you want this case to be over so I'm out of your hair?"

My smile fell slightly. "I see what you're doing, Dawson—trying to distract me—but it's unnecessary. I'm okay. Just let me go. . . ."

His features hardened, all sharp angles and shadows.

"I'm not sure I can do that."

A strong gust of wind shot between us, blowing my hair wildly across my face. He pushed aside a stray lock of hair, tucking it safely behind my ear.

"I should go," I said, just as headlights cut through the trees around us.

He hesitated for a moment before escorting me to my car. Once in, I fired her up and pulled away. As I drove off, I saw him in the rearview mirror, watching me. His expression was as unreadable as ever.

TWENTY-EIGHT

I didn't sleep at all that night, visions of a faceless girl floating in the river depths plaguing my mind. Every time I began to drift off, I could see myself diving into the river to find Danielle but when I reached her, the dark hair that danced wildly around her would pull back to show me something else, something far more terrifying—my face where hers should have been. After the third time I shot up in bed, breathing hard and scrubbing at my face to try and erase that image, I gave up.

I made my way to physics, lamenting my lack of sleep. Then I saw Garrett waiting for me outside Callahan's room and everything was right with the world, if only for a moment.

"Hey!" I shouted, running to meet him. "What are you doing here? I thought you were staying at casa de Higgins for the next week doing the homeschool thing until you were fully healed up."

"My dad is making me nuts. I can't sit there and watch him watching me anymore. I won't stay all day—I get tired pretty easily—but I thought I could make it until lunch and then head back. Get a break from the sheriff."

"You need to rest," I scolded as we walked into the classroom. Callahan looked up from his desk, true shock on his face at the sight of Garrett. In fairness, his face was still bruised, and he had tape covering his stitches. Reconstructing part of his right cheek had taken two surgeries and a specialist. They said he'd be totally fine once it fully healed—but I couldn't help but cringe at the thought of his face being permanently scarred because of what Donovan had done to him.

Because he'd gone with me that night.

"Garrett!" Mr. Callahan said, sounding every bit as shocked as he looked. "It's great to see you. How are you feeling?"

"Tired—sore."

"I have your homework for you, but I don't want you to worry about that. Take all the time you need. Kylene can probably help you get caught up."

I shot him a look of sheer, unadulterated outrage, but Callahan didn't even bother to glance my way.

"Thanks, sir. I'll do my best to get it done soon."

Garrett took the pile from Callahan, then made his way to his seat, welcomed back by everyone he passed. While I was elated for him—he deserved a hero's welcome—I couldn't help but be bitter. Nobody rolled out the sympathy wagon for me when I'd returned. In fact, it was quite the opposite. Garrett, having put two and two together, shot me a look of understanding. I guess my anger was written all over my face.

Class started, but I drowned out Callahan's monotone lecture on the physics of electricity with thoughts about Jane and the case. I hoped Dawson was busy ignoring his classwork as well in favor of plotting things in his mind. With a suspect list ripe with opportunity, we needed either physical evidence or motive—preferably both. And since walking up to Coach or Callahan and asking them straight up if they killed Danielle and where the murder weapon was or what the AD had on them wasn't a viable option (though a tempting one, just to see the looks on their faces), we had to take the insidious route.

I think I preferred mine more.

* * *

Garrett was looking rough by lunchtime, but he toughed it out just to have that time with Tabby and me. She glowed like a mythical creature when he came and sat down, her excitement at his return plain. Few people had the ability to make you feel truly cared about. Tabby was one of them.

"I'm just so excited!" she squealed, frantically clapping her hands. "Things can go back to normal now."

"That might be too much to ask," I mumbled under my breath.

"I take it Callahan wasn't as gracious upon your return, judging by how you fumed all through class," Garrett said dryly, poking at his food like he wasn't sure eating it was the best idea.

"That's a fair assessment."

"He's a grump," Tabby said, dismissing Callahan's assholeness. "Just ignore him."

I sighed. "If only it were that simple."

"So Ky," Garrett said, braving a bite of his food. His expression soured and he dropped his fork, clearly regretting his choice. "How's your dad's case coming along?" He pinned me with a knowing glance and I looked away.

"Have you been working on that?" Tabby asked, perking up yet again. "Do you need me to help?"

"What's this?" Garrett asked, feigning affront. "You let the Canadian help but not me?"

"I was busy letting you help me with the Donovan thing."

"Glad to see you're keeping it even," he replied, staring me down. After our interaction outside his house the day before, he knew I was poking around where I shouldn't be—and likely doing so alone. His displeasure with that was clear in the set of his jaw and furrow of his brow.

"I am," I said to him before turning to Tabby, "and no, I haven't really been. I kinda hit a wall with his transcripts, and when I last went to visit him, he didn't seem too keen on me digging around anymore. Not after everything that happened with Donovan."

"I can't say I blame him, Ky. Having you out there, possibly putting yourself in harm's way, would be a nightmare for a parent," Tabby said.

"Yeah." I tried to hold her gaze, but it was too full of worry. "I'm going to give it a rest for now. I'll check in with his old partner soon and see if maybe he has some insight."

And he should have had just that. It had been days since I gave him the file I'd found. Facial recognition didn't take long to run and given that both men in the picture were white males, it made it more accurate. All I could hope was that he'd gotten multiple matches and was weeding out false positives. Whoever Reider was talking to in that photo had been important enough for my father to tail him and snap off pictures. We just needed to know why.

Just as Tabby started to fill Garrett in on everything he'd missed, my phone started buzzing. I excused myself when I saw an unfamiliar number and walked to an open area for privacy.

"Hello?" I said quietly.

"Did you find anything?" Jane asked, cutting to the chase.

Man, that was a loaded question.

"Yeah. A lot, actually." I filled her in on all the samples gathered that had already been shipped off for testing. Then I let her in on the rest. "I also found Danielle. . . ."

I heard a loud crash on the other line. Jane had dropped the phone.

"You what?" she replied, sounding winded.

"I found her. She was weighed down under the bridge."

"Dammit," she muttered under her breath repeatedly. "You can't keep that quiet, Kylene!"

"I know. I would have called you and told you, but—"

"Does the sheriff know?"

"He does. I called it in anonymously."

"Dammit!" she shouted before lowering her voice. "Once this goes public I'm screwed, you know that, right? We all are!"

"The FBI was already investigating the prostitution, Jane. The sheriff isn't the one handling this. I know you don't trust any of them, but I trust my contact at the FBI, and he's all over this, okay? This is a good thing. If they find DNA on her body, then they can find the killer and send him away for life."

"Or he'll know one of us saw him murder Danielle and get rid of us all for causing trouble."

I wanted to refute her point but couldn't.

"I'm doing everything I can, Jane. Having the feds involved with this is going to help. They're not wrapped up in our small-town politics."

"You hope. . . ."

I left that one alone, too.

"Did Danielle have connections to any of the other suspects we discussed before? I know about all the faculty at school, but what about outside of there?"

"Maybe. She had a friend who'd sneak her into the movies all the time. She got busted a lot but never got in trouble with the owner. Before she got caught up in all this mess, she said she was cleaning the ice cream shop for Mr. Matthew, but I figured she was using that as a cover for hooking. I mean, it made sense: late nights, working alone."

"I never saw her on his employment records. . . ."

"Exactly my point."

"What about the others?"

She was quiet for a moment before responding. "No. If she was connected to them, I didn't know about it."

"All right," I said, glancing back at my friends, who were now staring at me. "I should go."

"Yeah. Me, too." Another silence. "Thanks, Kylene."

She hung up, and I returned to the lunch table.

"Who was that?" Garrett asked.

"Just Gramps. He wanted to check in. He's still a bit uneasy."

Garrett nodded. "I get it."

I tried to eat my lunch without entertaining the awful thoughts invading my mind. What if the killer did suspect the girls? What if he did clean up his mess before he was caught? Dawson couldn't protect someone he didn't know. I wondered if finding Danielle was the clue we'd needed to track down a murderer or a death sentence for the girls he was abusing.

Suddenly, I wasn't very hungry.

TWENTY-NINE

I was ill-prepared for the shit storm I walked into at school the next day.

News that a body was recovered from the river had finally been leaked, and in true Jasperville fashion, the halls were filled with whispers and rumors. I knew that the details hadn't been intentionally released, but that didn't matter. All it took was a few nosy people and a loose-lipped secretary at the sheriff's department to take care of that. Though Danielle's identity was never mentioned, it wouldn't be long before that came out, too. The sheriff couldn't keep that secret forever.

By lunchtime, the conspiracy theories had hit epic levels. Aliens, Bigfoot, and a few other urban legends were all in the running. I sat down at our table, prepared to weather Tabby's thoughts on the matter as well as her interrogation of Garrett. She'd undoubtedly assume that he knew something about the body his dad had fished out of the river.

"I just can't believe it," she said, pushing her red hair back. "A real dead body . . ."

"Some drunk probably fell in," Garrett said before taking a bite of his sandwich.

"Yeah," I replied. "Makes sense."

"But wouldn't someone have reported that person missing?"

Tabby asked. The naïveté of her question stung, and I tried not to flinch.

"Maybe it was a vagrant," I said.

"Do we even have those here?"

I shrugged. "We get random wanderers. People from the backwoods that only come to town when they need something."

She stared at me like I had three heads. "What I'm trying to say is that it's not out of the question."

Tabby opened her mouth to argue, but AJ's arrival cut her off.

"Did you hear about the body in the river?" he asked, sitting down next to Tabby. "Crazy, right? I wonder who it is."

"Can we talk about something else?" I asked, dropping my sandwich. "This isn't great lunchtime conversation."

AJ looked to Garrett and then back to me with concern in his eyes.

"It's a mystery, Ky. . . . You live for those."

"Well, maybe I don't live for the kind involving waterlogged, bloated corpses."

Tabby's face turned a little green. Her sandwich hit the table, too.

"All right," AJ said, putting his hands up in surrender. "New topic. How's this: Ky and I discussed a possible movie night at my place this weekend. Tabby? Garrett? You in or what?"

"Sounds fun!" Tabby's enthusiasm was impossible to miss.

"Yeah, man. I can swing that."

"Perfect. I'll text you guys later. For now, I gotta run. Callahan has me on a tight leash lately. I don't feel like listening to another lecture."

"Good call. They're the worst," I said.

"They really are," Garrett grumbled.

"What would you know about it? He's so far up your ass right now it's not even funny!"

"True. At least getting the shit beaten out of me wasn't totally without an upside."

Nervous laughter broke out among the group, then AJ gave a nod and ran back to the main building. I tried not to watch him go but there'd always been something captivating about the way he moved. A confidence that only someone who gave zero fucks could have.

"Enjoying the view?" Garrett said, yanking my attention from AJ. I didn't bother answering him. Instead, I stole a chip from his plate and chewed it dramatically. I wasn't about to get into AJ drama in front of Tabby. With my luck, she'd have pulled out little AJ flags and started waving them or ripped her shirt open to a #TeamAJ tank underneath. Yeah, no. I'd take a hard pass on that any day.

While Garrett and Tabby hashed out the logistics of who'd be driving whom to AJ's, I kept my head down and tried not to think about Danielle's dead body, instead focusing on its potential for the killer's DNA. Dawson hadn't answered any of my texts. I prayed that no news was good news.

THIRTY

It was the end of the day before I heard from Dawson. He texted me then came tearing into the building before the bell for final period rang. The two of us eyed each other across the hall for a moment. His lack of expression forced my heart into my throat. Then he stormed toward me, intercepting me by the classroom door. He hauled me into the corner, then whispered in my ear.

"We found DNA."

Holy. Shit.

"Are you sure?" I said under my breath, his face too close to mine.

"Positive. There were still some skin cells found deep under her fingernails. It's been processed and is currently being run to see if it matches anyone in the system."

Deep under her fingernails . . . Danielle had put up a fight.

Excitement surged through me at the realization that she'd have left marks on the murderer—physical evidence that could narrow our list. Then my hopes crashed seconds later when I remembered what Jane had said. That she'd died two weeks earlier. Any markings left on the perpetrator would have long since healed.

Another dead end.

"Do you think you'll get a hit?" I asked, my voice soft and

empty. Images of the dead girl clawing to get away from the man that ultimately killed her played over and over in my mind.

Dawson looked around at the student-filled hallway, then grabbed my hand and led me to the stairs. The two of us rushed out the door to the parking lot. Once there, he filled me in.

"Maybe, but I can't bank on it. At minimum, we have something to run against any suspects when they're brought in."

I looked at him curiously. "Can you get DNA from suspects if they're not charged with a crime?"

The smile I loved to hate spread across his face. "It's not standard protocol, but there are ways."

"Like taking the soda can or cup they used?" I asked, thinking of my favorite crime shows. He nodded. "So that's really a thing. . . ."

"It is. Now, whether or not it's admissible is a gray area, but we'll deal with that when the time comes."

"Okay."

"I've got to get home and do some paperwork. Will you be over later?"

"Yeah, maybe. I've got a paper due tomorrow that I can't blow off any longer. But if I get it done early enough, I'll be over. Gramps is home tonight though. . . ."

"Maybe I should come over to your place, then," he said with a wicked grin.

"Nope. I like that he knows *about* you but doesn't *actually* know you. I'm going to keep it that way as long as I can."

His smile faltered for just a second.

"I'll let you know if I hear anything," he said before he walked away, headed for his car. I watched as he sped off, then let out a breath. I hated feeling left behind—out of the action. That was the only thing keeping me going.

As I headed back toward the school, the bell letting me know I needed to stop by the main office for a tardy note, I passed my car. A paper tucked under my wipers caught my attention, and I walked over to get it, thinking Jane might have put it there. But when I saw what it said, I knew it wasn't from her.

You'll end up just like her . . .

The note fell from my hands to the ground, my body coiled to either fight or run. Flashbacks of bricks through my window and files of my topless pictures raced through my mind. My chest tightened like a snake was squeezing the life out of me. I leaned against Heidi, struggling for air as my vision went spotty, frozen with panic.

I was losing the fight.

Breathe, a voice in my head said softly. In through the nose, out through the mouth. I repeated this over and over again, breathing deep down into my diaphragm—the way I'd learned to when I trained. The way my counselor had shown me. I could feel my chest ease slightly the longer I did it.

Once I regained control of my body, I snatched up the note and jumped into my car. I grabbed my phone to call Dawson, then stopped. I needed a minute to think. After my near meltdown the night before and the text on Danielle's phone, there was no way Dawson would let me anywhere near the case if he saw the note. But if it had physical evidence on it, I couldn't possibly withhold it—it could match the DNA found on Danielle. I needed an angle to play that would keep me on the team but get us evidence if there was any to be found.

The second an idea hit me, I peeled out of the parking lot.

"I feel like you're making a real habit of showing up here unannounced," Dawson said, stepping back to let me in.

"About that," I said, readying myself for the first bomb drop of my visit. "For the sake of my reputation and sanity, I've made the executive decision that we're dating now. Half the school thinks we already are, anyway. Might as well just succumb to the rumors and be done with it. It's not like it really changes anything. It just makes my late-night drop-ins far less scandalous."

The corner of his mouth twitched. "I thought you loved a good scandal."

"I do, but not when I'm at the heart of it. Could you please not be a dick about this right now? We have other shit to deal with." I held the folded note out to him using my sleeve to protect it, and he took it doing the same. "You need to process this for DNA. See if any matches what they found on Danielle."

His eyes went wide when he read it, and they quickly turned to me.

"How did you get this?"

I took a deep breath. "Jane left it on my car for me with an explanation. Someone sent it to her." How easily that lie flew off my tongue. "I don't know anything beyond that, so don't ask. Just process it, okay?"

Those shrewd eyes of his searched my face for something—maybe the truth I was withholding. But he never found it.

"I'll take it up there now."

"Great. I hope there's something on it—that it matches Danielle's killer."

"And that he's already in the system."

"Either way, it could be helpful."

"Yeah," he said, his voice drifting off. "I'll let you know. See you later, *girlfriend*."

His attempt to sarcastically confirm our relationship fell flat. His whole body was rigid, his eyes full of unasked questions, and I could feel them on me as I got into my car and drove off—like he was afraid to look away. Like if he did, I would disappear just like Danielle.

My phone rang during dinner, and I dared a glance at the screen under Gramps' watchful eye.

"I've got to take this," I told him, jumping out of my seat and heading down the hall before he could read me the riot act about no phones at the table. I closed the bedroom door behind me and answered Striker's call. "Hey Striker! What—"

"I don't know how your dad got this photo or how he knew to get it in the first place, but you've come across a real land mine here, Kylene." I couldn't come up with a reply fast enough, my mind racing with possibilities. "The guy in that picture with Reider? He's with the Mafia in Jersey. One of the bigger families. What I've been able to gather in this short amount of time is that Reider had a little too much fun in Atlantic City. . . . He was in debt, Ky. Lots of it—and with the wrong people. The kind that make you pay in broken body parts and threats against your family. Possibly favors, if you're in the right profession."

Like an FBI agent in cybercrime.

"Holy shit—"

"And, from what I can tell, this was going on for some time."

"That's it, Striker! Dad knew Reider was the dirty one. That he was indebted to this Mafia family and was manufacturing evidence against my dad because he was getting too close!"

I was shouting, my adrenaline and excitement too much to contain. Seconds later, Gramps was knocking on my door.

"What's all this shoutin' about?" he asked, poking his weary face in.

"Striker found a break in Dad's case!" I replied.

"'Bout damn time somebody did. Tell him good job—and keep it up."

I couldn't ignore the sense of urgency in Gramps' tone when he delivered those final words. They made me cringe.

"Kylene," Striker said, drawing my attention back. "I have a few more things to look into, but this file you found—it's *huge*."

He hung up without another word.

I looked over to where Gramps stood. "Why did you sound so desperate when you said that? About Striker keeping it up?"

"It's nothin', Junebug. Just rumors spreadin' through the prison. Can't take them too serious. Those inmates ain't got nothin' but time on their hands to come up with wild stories to tell. And your daddy ain't in with most of them anyway."

My eyes narrowed at Gramps' careful choice of words. He wouldn't lie to his *Junebug*—at least not outright. But he'd sure as hell paint a prettier picture than the one that existed to keep my worries at bay.

"You think they could get to him if they wanted to?"

Out of the frying pan. Into the fire.

I'd cornered Gramps, and, judging by the look on his face, he knew it. He scrubbed at his chin stubble for a moment, trying to find a way out, then exhaled hard when he realized he didn't have one.

"There's always a way if you want one bad enough," he finally said. My blood ran cold. "Only way to avoid that is to get him out. Sooner than later."

He walked down the hall, leaving me with that bombshell. I needed Striker to come up with a way to tie Reider's gambling issues to my dad's case, and fast. Apparently, the clock was already ticking.

THIRTY-ONE

Dawson texted me early the next day to say that the paper was clean. No DNA or fingerprints to be found. Though I wasn't surprised, I was still disappointed. For all our sakes, I'd hoped to catch a break with that note.

I ran out of the bathroom just after the bell rang and nearly collided with Principal Thompson.

"Just who I wanted to see," he said in a friendly tone. "Please join me in my office, Kylene."

I followed him there and hovered by a chair while he closed the door.

"Have a seat," he said, indicating one in front of his desk. I did as he asked, trying to keep my curiosity from my expression. Neutrality was best when facing authority. Indifference was hardest to interpret and the least damning. "I wanted to talk to you about some of your recent behaviors."

"Okay . . ."

"I've heard that not all your homework assignments have been turned in yet. You've also been cutting classes and showing a general disregard for your schoolwork—"

"I let Mrs. Baber know I wasn't feeling good!"

He gave me a look of disappointment.

"That may be the case, but signing yourself out is not a power you should abuse to suit your . . . personal interests. . . ."

He let his words trail off while he tried to figure out how best to call me out on what I'd done.

"Personal interests?" I asked, irritation seeping into my tone. So much for neutrality. "Which ones might those be? The nap-and-chicken-noodle-soup kind?"

"No, the going-over-to-your-boyfriend's-house kind."

Adrenaline shot through me and I tried to school my features to keep my face from giving me away.

"Not sure why you think that's where I went—"

"Please don't insult my intelligence. Alex Cedrics is your boyfriend, correct?"

"What does he have to do—"

"You of all people should know this is a small town that likes to talk. How long did you think it would take before your whereabouts when you skipped school got back to me?" I stared at him, trying to think of something to say, but Mr. Thompson just kept on going. "That boy has been absent more than present since he started here. His teachers have noted his aloof nature in class. His poor participation. How easily distracted he seems to be."

"Your point?"

His expression soured.

"My point is I think he's a poor influence on you, Kylene, especially at this . . . *delicate* time in your life."

A cool numbness crept its way through my body.

"What are you suggesting?"

"That maybe you consider your current situation and decide if he's helping or hurting it."

I leaned forward in my chair as a thought popped into my head.

"Why do you care so much?"

He looked honest-to-God shocked at that question.

"It's my job to care, Kylene."

I scoffed, thinking about how little he'd likely "cared" for Danielle Green. How he hadn't followed protocol for her chronic truancy. How either he'd let her fall through the cracks because of who she was, or maybe—just maybe—he'd wanted her disappearance to go unnoticed because he was the one who'd caused it.

"While I appreciate your concern," I said, my tone sounding anything but thankful, "Alex is basically all I have at this point. If I break up with him, I have nobody."

"What about your grandfather?"

"He's always working. We need the money. . . ."

"What about Garrett? You two were close before—"

Time to let the lies fly. . . .

"He nearly died because of me. That's kind of a relationship killer."

"And Tabby? I always see you two together in the halls."

"She's taking Garrett's side."

His expression softened.

"Staying with Alex because you have no one else is not a good reason to throw your future away. Maybe you could use the time you normally spend with him working. I'm sure I could help you find something. . . ."

Chills ran down my spine.

"Yeah, I'll think about it," I said, getting out of my seat. "Are we done here?"

His eyes narrowed, thinly veiling the frustration he felt at my dismissal.

"I'd like to follow up about this issue soon. Until then, I'll let your teachers know you need more time with your assignments."

"Thanks," I mumbled on my way to the door.

"Kylene," he said, hesitating a bit. "You can come to me about anything. I'm here to help."

Yeah . . . help exploit me, maybe.

"Got it."

I walked out of his office, my pace quickening with every step. In all our investigating, I'd never wanted to believe that Principal Thompson was involved. That he was too nice—too cool—for that. But after that meeting with him, I wondered if that was his angle. If he lured vulnerable students in by putting the "pal" in principal, using his position to find the perfect harem of socially marginalized girls to pimp out. I shuddered at the thought.

Regardless, I needed to talk to my deadbeat boyfriend about it and get his take. Maybe we needed to try harder to connect Thompson to the sixth girl. Maybe we needed to search his closet for skeletons, too.

THIRTY-TWO

Late-night errands were my favorite kind, mainly because nobody else was out. Even on a Friday night, store traffic was minimal, so I threw on some crappy sweatpants and a hoodie and made my way there. I needed to do a better job pulling my weight around the house for Gramps' sake.

It didn't take long to gather the groceries we needed. I was halfway to the register when someone stepped out of the nearest aisle right in front of me. I stopped short, a strange feeling of dread crawling its way up my back. Then Tyson looked back to find me staring at him. I did my best to recover and school my features, but judging by his, I failed.

"What's up, Danners? You all right? You look like you've seen a ghost."

"Yeah," I said, shaking my head as I forced a laugh. "You just surprised me, that's all."

He stared at me for a beat, assessing my answer. "You haven't been by the gym for a while."

"I know. I think I might have pushed too hard last time. I've been paying for it ever since," I replied, moving my arm to illustrate how stiff it was—or I was making it look.

"Injuries are tough. Sometimes you need to push through them. Sometimes you need to lay off. You're a smart kid. Do what you think is best."

"That's the plan." An awkward silence began to build between us—one that had never been there before. I fumbled for something to say. "So, what are you doing here?"

He held up a case of beer. "I got a date."

"With a twelve pack?"

"Nah. Those are for the date."

"Oh. Guess I should let you get to it, then."

"Yeah. Probably should." He remained where he stood, still staring at me. "You sure you're all right?"

"Yep. Never better."

"Cool," he said, heading for the express checkout. "See you around."

The cashier was still ringing me up when Tyson paid for his beer and walked out without a glance in my direction.

He should have been gone by the time I reached the parking lot, but I could see his black-on-black truck in the back row, his interior light on. He was checking his phone for something, but I didn't care about that. All I cared about was the girl sitting just beyond him in the passenger seat. The one that looked too young to be in there with him. I hoped that maybe it was just the dim interior lighting or my overactive imagination playing tricks on me, but I wasn't sure about that.

Then Dawson's words leaked into my mind, forever taunting me. *"What we want to believe and what's actually true are rarely if ever the same thing, Danners. . . ."*

Unable to clear my head of the thought that Tyson might be with an underage girl, or, worse yet, pimping her out, I ran to my car and tossed the bags in the trunk. I rode past his truck, needing to get a better look. As I neared, the girl lifted her head so the full light of the car and Tyson's phone highlighted her face. I knew instantly who she was and let out a sigh of relief. Autumn Wolfhart had been the town's Winter Festival Queen when I was in grade school. She had to have been in her mid-twenties.

I raced out of the parking lot as though I could outrun the paranoia forever looming over me.

I spent the better part of the next day doing busywork around the house. My run-in with Tyson had me spooked and I only slept a few hours. The plan was to tire myself out, nap, then wake up just in time to go to AJ's with Garrett and Tabby.

But, of course, that didn't happen.

Just as I was about to nod off, my phone started ringing. I picked it up to find Meg calling. I bolted upright on the couch and answered.

"Did you find anything?" I blurted out.

"Hello to you, too," she said with a laugh. "And my answer to your question is twofold. No, I didn't find what we need, but what I did find is a whole lot of questionable lawyering for the defense. Your dad's attorney missed a lot of opportunities to object . . . redirect . . ."

"In English, Meg. What are you saying?"

"I'm saying he was incompetent at best. He clearly wasn't capable of handling your father's case."

Oh. My. God.

"You think it was intentional? His incompetent behavior, I mean?"

"I think I want your father's files transferred over to me so that I can comb through them to see what other balls this clown dropped during your dad's trial."

"Great! Let's do it! What do you need from me?"

"Nothing from you, unless you want to be the one to get your father's signature on the paperwork required to fire his attorney and agree to retain me instead."

"Consider it done."

"All right. I'll have Marcy mail them to you on Monday. Until then, hang in there. I think we're onto something here, Ky. You just have to be patient."

"That's like asking a toddler to behave, you know that, right?"

She sighed dramatically and said, "Do I ever." Then she hung up without saying goodbye—in true Meg fashion.

THIRTY-THREE

I left an hour later to pick up Tabby and Garrett. I'd already filled them in about Alex and me officially dating again, and, thankfully, they kept the questions to a minimum. Garrett did make a point to ask me if AJ knew and my heart sank. He wasn't going to take that news well at all.

We arrived at AJ's and soon found ourselves packed into his kitchen, ransacking it for provisions. With arms full of junk, we made our way downstairs.

AJ's basement was partially finished on one side and had concrete floors with storage shelves on the other. I helped Garrett get situated on the more comfortable of the two old couches, then found a spot on the smaller one next to Tabby. AJ, without a place to sit, plopped down on the rug right in front of me, and leaned back against the sofa. I acted like I didn't notice, but when I caught Garrett's eye from across the room, it held a clear warning: *You need to tell him now.*

"Here, AJ," I said, climbing off the love seat. "You can sit with Tabby. Garrett's trying to guilt me into rubbing his feet for him." I rushed over and picked up his legs so I could slide in under them. The tension in his face relaxed a bit, and I forced myself to touch his gross socks to keep up the act.

He was going to owe me big-time.

"What should we watch?" Tabby asked, hunkering down under a blanket.

"How about that new action movie that's on Netflix?" AJ suggested.

"Nooooooo," I argued. "No dude-bro films allowed."

"Oh!" Tabby exclaimed as AJ scrolled through our options. "What about *Wonder Woman*? I still haven't seen that one. . . ."

"How have you not seen that yet?" I asked, truly shocked. "It's a classic!"

"It hasn't been out long enough to be a classic," Garrett argued. I dutifully ignored him.

"I really want to see it!" Tabby squealed with delight. "It's going to be so amazing!"

"Isn't that a girly superhero movie?" AJ asked. As if choreographed, Tabby and I slowly turned to glare at him like he'd just told us our pants made our asses look big.

"It is an action movie comprised mostly of females, led by a female," I said calmly, but that calm belied the anger rising within me, "and directed by a female, yes."

"Ah, shit," Garrett mumbled. "You stepped in it big-time, bro."

"Right. So it's a girly movie?" AJ said, genuine confusion in his tone.

"Give me the remote," I said, pushing Garrett's legs aside so I could get it. I snatched it out of AJ's hand, then stormed back to my seat. "You don't deserve this." Once I was back in my spot, I clicked on the stunning image of Gal Gadot in all her *Wonder Woman* glory. "Now, prepare to be schooled in all things estrogen-dominant awesomeness," I announced. "And if anyone in this room with a penis says ONE THING about girls not knowing how to fight or the movie not being realistic—within the confines of a superhero movie—I will single-handedly make you rue the day you were born, understand?"

Garrett and AJ, having heard similar rants in the past, kept their mouths shut and nodded in agreement.

Old habits die hard.

We couldn't have been twenty minutes into the film when one of the greatest fight scenes I'd ever witnessed broke out. Badass female warriors were putting the smackdown on the Germans. I was on the edge of my seat (taking Garrett's legs with me). I glanced over at Tabby and saw big fat tears rolling down her cheeks. She stared at the screen with a sense of sadness and wonder that only she could understand. That scene had meant something to her. Something deep and moving. AJ looked over at her and his expression softened. Then his eyes fell upon me.

"Not a girly movie," I mouthed, and he nodded.

By the time we reached the infamous No Man's Land scene, I thought I was emotionally in the clear. But when Wonder Woman, in the face of insurmountable odds, chose to fight for those who could not fight for themselves, even if it meant losing—even if it meant dying—I knew I was in trouble. She stepped out onto that battlefield alone and began running at the enemy head-on like a woman possessed. In that moment, I felt my heart stop. My chest tightened. I understood her on the most fundamental level, and seeing her conviction play out in front of me was more than I could handle. I, like Tabby only minutes earlier, let tears roll down my cheeks, too overwhelmed by the awesomeness I was seeing.

We all needed heroes. Wonder Woman was mine.

After the movie finished and I came down from my girl-power high, Tabby suggested we play some ridiculous board game that she found on one of the shelves. AJ suggested Truth or Dare, pinning a mischievous set of eyes on me. Garrett pointed out that he wasn't in the best shape for dares, but AJ dismissed him with a wave of his hand and suggested he'd best tell the truth then.

It was then that I knew the night was about to take an interesting turn.

Somehow, I never noticed that Tabby had grabbed two energy drinks from the fridge before we went downstairs and drank them both during the movie. By the time it was her turn to choose truth or dare, she was practically scaling the walls.

"I blame you for this," I said to AJ as we watched her run circles around the couches, singing the theme song to *Footloose*—and it hadn't even been a dare.

"Tabby!" Garrett shouted over her terribly off-key high note. "It's your turn!"

"Okay!" she replied, out of breath but still running.

"If she has a heart attack, I'm kicking your ass, Miller," I said, leaning in conspiratorially.

"Ky!" Tabby said, stopping before me. Her cheeks were flushed and her eyes were wild and full of mischief. "Truth or dare?"

"Umm . . ."

"Dare!" she said on my behalf. "I dare you to kiss AJ!"

If she'd been anyone else, I might have killed her on the spot.

"There will be no kissing, and Tabby is officially cut off," I said calmly. "I think you need a water break and a time-out, young lady."

Garrett scooted over on the couch so she could sit down, then wrapped his arm around her shoulder to hold her in place in case she tried to bolt and regale us with another eighties-movie soundtrack performance.

"My turn," Garrett said, shooting me a look before attempting to take the tension in the room down a notch.

"I have to pee," I replied, bolting for the stairs.

"ME TOO!" Tabby screamed. She launched out of Garrett's

grasp and raced past me up the steps, taking two at a time. Apparently, energy drinks greatly improved her coordination.

I followed in her wake, then found her dancing in the hallway, unsure of where to go.

"Bathroom's over there," I pointed. She was in with the door shut in a flash.

I shook my head and climbed the stairs to the second floor and the full bath AJ and his older brother used to share. On my way back to the basement, I passed AJ's room. The door was open, so I peeked in. Seconds later, I found myself standing in the middle of it, not remembering when I made the decision to enter.

I don't know what I expected to find in it or what I was looking for, but there I was, turning a slow circle in AJ's bedroom, taking in every change that had taken place since I'd last seen it. Every photo. Every medal. *Everything.* I wanted to see it all.

Being in there alone made me bold, and I walked around his room as though I belonged. As though we hadn't broken up over two years ago for dubious reasons. They'd been legit at the time, but once the truth surfaced, the waters were decidedly muddied.

And so were my feelings.

I walked over to look at the pictures on his dresser. Front and center was a shot of Garrett, AJ, and me from freshman year homecoming. Sandwiched between the two of them, their arms slung around my shoulders, we smiled like life was ours for the taking. Like nothing could ever come between us.

I picked up the frame and traced a heart around the three of us, remembering how much fun we'd had that night. It reminded me of how much fun we were having together in the basement. Dangerous feelings rose within me, and I quickly put the picture back down. When I turned to leave, the weight of emotions I didn't yet want to unpack on my shoulders, I found AJ standing in his doorway, staring. His green eyes were filled with things I was afraid he'd say. Things he couldn't take back once he did.

"I'm sorry," I said softly. "I just . . . I guess I just wanted to see how different your room was now." He continued to stare at me, unspeaking, then took a step closer. "I'm really sorry for intruding. . . ."

I made a move to leave, but he stood in the doorway, unwilling to step aside. He'd done that once and lost me. Looked like AJ had learned his lesson.

"I don't mind," he replied. I watched his mouth as he spoke, his soft full lips as mesmerizing as ever. "I like you in my room—I always did."

"I should go," I whispered, the words unwilling to come out any louder than that. My body wrestled against my will—my heart against my mind.

"*Ky,*" he said as he gently caught my arm in his hand. Shivers ran up my spine at the feel of its warmth. The strength it barely withheld. "Don't go." His face was near mine at this point, the two of us sharing the same air. I did all I could to avoid his gaze, but it was virtually impossible when he was that close to me. My mind swirled, the past blurring with the present. Memory blending with moment. "I don't want you to go."

I dared one look up at the face of the boy I feared I still loved, and my body won the tug-of-war.

My fingers wound through his hair, pulling his face closer until our lips crashed together. His hands were all over me, desperate to make up for lost time. He hoisted me up and carried me to his bed. The two of us scrambled onto it, doing all we could not to break contact in the process. It wasn't pretty, but it worked because I soon found his body on top of mine. The weight of it against me felt like the exact thing I'd been missing since I'd left Jasperville. Like his presence filled a void I hadn't even known I'd had.

The exposed band of skin on my stomach surged with fire when he pulled his shirt off and laid back down on top of me. I raked my fingers down the taut muscles of his back—the ones that had grown stronger and larger since I'd last been with him. Seconds later, my shirt was off, and he was kissing his way down my neck. I was lost to the sensation of him touching me—of being with him. Then the sound of pants unzipping seemed to pull me from the depths of lust I was swimming in.

Maybe it was just the distinct sound of the zipper or the hungry look in AJ's eyes when I looked up at him or the fact that Garrett and Tabby were downstairs and likely wondering where we were, but something in my mind snapped to attention and told me to stop.

"AJ," I said, my voice breathy and winded. "We can't . . ."

"I have protection," he said, assuming that was my concern.

"No," I repeated with a little more strength this time. "I mean we can't do this."

He stopped immediately, climbing off me like he'd crossed a line. "I'm sorry if I did something—shit! I didn't ask first. . . ."

"No, it's not that. It's me," I said, scrambling off his bed to go find my shirt. Once I located it, hanging off his doorknob, I slipped it over my head and wrapped my arms around my waist. "You didn't do anything wrong. I win that award tonight—I'm the one with the boyfriend."

He looked like I'd slapped him.

"Since when?" he asked.

"Just the other day. I should have told you."

"Do you love him?" he asked, standing up cautiously. His undone pants were slung low on his hips, and it was all I could do not to stare at the sharp V of his ab muscles as they disappeared into his waistband. Another upgrade that had occurred in my absence.

I forced myself to turn away.

"It's not that simple," I muttered, headed for the door. Once again, he caught me before I could leave.

"Do you love him, Ky?" he asked again, the heat in his tone unmistakable. I still couldn't turn and face him. I was too afraid he'd see right through my answer. "Because the way you just kissed me, it's hard to believe that you do."

"Whether I love him or not, AJ, we're together, and that's not going to change right now, okay?" I finally forced myself to face him. "I should never have come up here—and I shouldn't have kissed you. I was wrong—"

Before AJ could press the issue any further, footsteps echoed up the staircase.

"What are you two doing?" Garrett asked, before cresting the final step. When he did, he took one look at AJ's half-naked status and my sheepish expression and shook his head. "I think it's time to go, Ky."

I nodded, knowing my voice would betray me.

The two of us made our way downstairs to where Tabby awaited us, jacket in hand. AJ didn't bother to follow.

THIRTY-FOUR

With my mind finally clear from its AJ haze, the guilt rolled in. In reality—the one that nobody but Dawson and I knew—my feelings made no sense since Dawson and I weren't *actually* dating, but they were there nonetheless, thick enough to cut with a knife. The one I'd stabbed *Alex* in the back with, as far as my friends were concerned.

I lay awake in my bed, trying to erase the feel of AJ's hands on my body and mine on his until I surrendered to the futility of it and got up.

At 1:00 A.M., I got dressed and grabbed my car keys. Absurd though it was, I jumped in my car and drove to Dawson's. I needed to tell him what I'd done so we could figure out how to deal with it.

The light in his living room was on when I pulled up to the brick ranch. By the time I reached the bottom of his walkway, the door was opened to greet me—or ask me why the hell I was there. For once, it would have been a valid question.

"Do you ever sleep?" I asked, pushing my way past him into the house.

"Do you?" he fired back. "And do you ever text before coming over?"

I turned back to look at him and found a small, satisfied smile tugging at the corner of his mouth.

"I did something tonight," I started, figuring it best to just dive right in. "Something I shouldn't have."

"Your forte, of course." He looked at me expectantly. "Well, let's hear it. How much am I about to hate my life?"

I grabbed a pillow from the couch and picked at the fringe as I leaned against the armrest.

"I may or may not have been on a trip down memory lane when this happened, so I need you to keep that in mind."

"Just spit it out, Danners."

"I kinda, maybe, sort of cheated on you tonight," I replied, wincing away from him as I did. He looked at me for a moment like the words hadn't fully registered. Then that damn smile curled the corner of his mouth ever so slightly. He was holding back his amusement, though barely.

I chucked the pillow at his head.

"I'm not sure how I should feel about this," he said in his most serious voice.

"I hate you right now," I replied, heading for the front door.

"What? You're just going to drop your infidelity on me like that, then run?"

"I'm sorry I came over here tonight," I said, grabbing the doorknob.

"All right, all right. Calm down . . . I'm just screwing with you." He caught my arm and gently pulled me away from the door, then led me to the couch. I sat down while he perched on the edge of the coffee table across from me. "You were right to tell me. We need to get ahead of this in case kids from your school find out."

"They're not going to. AJ won't tell—"

"*AJ?*" he repeated, leaning back from me like he wanted to take in everything. Like he didn't want to miss out on any body language.

"Yes. AJ. Is that a problem?"

"I don't know. Is it?"

"Didn't seem to be earlier," I muttered under my breath.

"And now?"

Apparently, the interrogation had begun. Knowing I'd opened Pandora's box with no way to shut it, I took a deep breath and gave him the abbreviated version of what had gone down. Once I finished, he leaned forward on his elbows and stared.

"What?" I shouted. "Why are you looking at me like that?"

"Do you still love him?" he asked. So not the question I was expecting.

"Some part of me seemed pretty interested in revisiting the past, that's for damn sure."

"Does anyone else know?"

"Garrett came up and found us right after. I'm pretty sure he put two and two together, given the disapproval in his expression. He didn't say anything to Tabby, but we rushed out of there pretty quickly. She knows something's up, just not the particulars."

"Neither of them will be an issue," he said. "They're too loyal for that." His brow furrowed as he continued to stare at me, his gaze unrelenting.

"So why do you still look worried?"

"Because I don't trust AJ." I opened my mouth to argue, but he shut me down with a raised palm, deflecting my argument. "If you think he won't blab, then I'll trust *you*." I tried to hide my shock and failed. He frowned when he saw it in my expression. "But I still don't think he'll stay away." He got up and started to pace the room. "Will he keep pursuing you?"

Yes.

"No . . . I don't think so. I told him I should never have kissed him. That I was in a relationship with you."

"Like that matters in the heat of the moment."

"I promise I will make this go away if you promise to never say 'in the heat of the moment' ever again," I said with a shudder. "It sounds super creepy."

"My point is that knowing you are with me won't deter him at all. He doesn't see me as a roadblock—just an obstacle he needs to get around."

I wanted to argue with him, but I couldn't. He was right, plain and simple. I knew what I'd agreed to when I'd signed on the dotted line, so to speak, and I knew that it would limit my social life in some ways—not that I'd had much of one to start with. Those girls needed Dawson's cover intact so he could crack the case, which meant they needed me to make that possible. Was it unfair that I had to put my conflicting feelings about AJ on hold so I could do that? Yes. But it was even more unfair to leave Jane and the others to their circumstances so I could navigate whatever path AJ and I were on.

"I won't let him in," I said, sighing hard. "I'm still not one hundred percent sure I even want to."

When the silence stretched out between us, he finally came to sit beside me on the couch.

"I'm sorry you're in this position. You've been through a lot already—"

"I can handle it," I said, cutting him off. Praise from Dawson was overwhelming and beyond unexpected. I needed to make it stop before I started to overthink.

"I need you to be sure you can—"

I turned to my left to look at Dawson, who silently awaited an answer. "I've got this," I said. "I'm as invested as you are."

"Good. Now, I heard back from a buddy of mine who works for the military. I had him send me the DNA samples for Tyson and Davies. They're not matches for Danielle's killer."

I let out my breath. "Thank God. . . ."

"But I couldn't clear Matthew. He served too long before the military started saving samples for body identification."

"I thought you said those couldn't be used in criminal cases."

"I called in a favor," he said with a shrug. "And now I owe him a few."

"Well, at least it was worth it. I couldn't stand the thought of Tyson being involved."

"Between his DNA and the lack of connection to all the girls, I think he can be eliminated."

"What about Callahan? Any updates?"

Dawson shook his head. "The team is still investigating all those involved in the allegations. Nothing in the financials so far. No names of students. The only allegation made aside from his wife was by an anonymous caller. She's going to be hard to track down if it's even possible."

"But he's still a suspect, right?"

He merely nodded in response.

When the quiet settled in between us, I took the hint and headed for the door. He followed me over and reached to open it, then hesitated for a moment, the two of us standing by the exit.

"Something else you need to tell me, boss?" I asked, looking up at his earnest expression that peeked through his disheveled hair.

"I'm glad you came to me tonight—that you trusted me. *Really.*"

I stared blankly at him for a second then forced a smile. "Seemed like the kind of thing my fake boyfriend should know."

He hesitated for a moment before nodding and opening the door. "Goodnight, *Kylene.*"

"See you Monday, *Alex.*"

THIRTY-FIVE

Callahan's class on Monday morning proved to be a pressure cooker of tension between Garrett and me. Sprinkle in questions from Tabby in both study hall and gym, and I was ready to explode by the time lunch came around. Once the three of us were all seated, I decided to come clean.

"I made out with AJ in his room." Tabby's eyebrows shot up and Garrett swore under his breath. "I'm not proud of this. I already feel terrible about it, so I don't need any help with that, if you were considering it. I just—I made a bad decision. It won't happen again."

The duo sat in silence for a minute until Garrett dared to break it.

"Did you tell Alex?"

"I did. I went over there that night and laid it all out for him."

"How'd he take it?" Tabby asked, the shock of the scandal still painted across her face.

"He was upset. Confused. Disappointed in me."

"Did you break up?" she pressed.

"No. We didn't."

"Ky," Garrett said, stopping to try and collect his thoughts. The loyalist in him was having a hard time with what I'd done. Cheating was a concept he would never understand, nor condone. It just wasn't in his nature. "Why'd you do it?"

Because my relationship is a lie and I might still be in love with my ex?

"Honestly? I don't know. It just sort of happened."

His lips pressed to a thin, disapproving line. "Clothes don't just magically fly off."

"I'm aware of that, Garrett," I replied, anger seeping into my tone. "I went into his room on my way back downstairs—I just wanted to see how it had changed. I found a picture of the three of us together and it's like it transported me back to that time. Before everything went to hell." His expression softened slightly. "We never had closure, you know? We had the rug ripped out from under us and that was it. Then I moved and started over. It's weird being back here—at this school—and not being with him. Does that make sense at all? It's like if I was here and you and I weren't friends. It's all I knew freshman year. The three of us together. My mind is having a hard time now that AJ isn't public enemy number one."

I don't know when, but at some point during my explanation, tears started to roll down my cheeks. Garrett leaned forward and wiped them with his sleeve. Then he took my hands in his and said the only words I needed to hear.

"Ky, I understand. It's okay."

"Yeah," Tabby said from across the table. "And I'm sorry for needling you about AJ. It's clearly not making this easier for you, so I'll stop."

I sniffled once, then choked on a laugh.

"Maybe I should cry in front of you two more often. A few tears and you guys are total pushovers."

They joined in with my laughter, and the cloud of tension hovering over us dissipated in an instant. Navigating a great friendship wasn't always easy. It's important to have people in your life willing to call you on your shit when it's warranted. But it's equally important for them to hear your side and not kick you when you're down. Garrett and Tabby had the friend thing down pat, and I was so grateful to have them. Losing either one of them because of my actions wasn't an outcome I was prepared to live with.

On my way to fifth period, my tiny-bladder syndrome kicked in and I stopped by the bathroom. When I came out, I saw something out of the corner of my eye. I turned to see Coach take a girl by the elbow and lead her down the hall toward his office. Nothing else was down that wing other than the equipment storage and the sports teams' lockers. Judging by the look of the girl he'd grabbed, she wasn't an athlete in need of some gear.

Ignoring the bell, I quietly followed them until they disappeared behind his office door. He'd slammed it closed, but it had bounced so hard against the door frame that it popped open a crack, the latch never fully catching. I tiptoed down the hall until I stood flat against the wall, trying to peek in.

"You're takin' one hell of a risk comin' to me with this," he said, his voice haughty and angry.

"I know, but I just can't do what you asked me to do," the girl replied, a tremble in her voice. She sounded scared shitless. It was all I could do not to throw the door open and pull her out of there. But I needed to hear more—hear if anything damning would be said. "I can't do that to her—"

"You don't have a choice," he growled. I saw his silhouette lean in close to hers and she winced away. It was the first time I'd seen her face and instantly recognized it. She was the girl from Marco's Pizza. The one who had stood up for me. Her name fought hard to come to the front of my mind but failed.

"I don't want to hurt her," she said, choking back a sob.

That was it. I couldn't take any more.

I pushed off the wall, having made the decision to intervene, but a hand caught my arm and turned me around. Standing in front of me was a pissed-off-looking Mr. Callahan.

"Let's go, Miss Danners," he said, leading me away.

"No! You need to go help the girl in Coach's office. Something's not right in there!" He ignored me completely and instead hauled me back down to the main hall. Once we were there, I wrenched my arm from his grasp. "What in the hell is your problem? I know you think I'm useless and never going to amount to anything, but I want to know why. Why me?"

"Because I'm sick of kids like you. *Broken. Angry.* You think the world owes you something until it proves otherwise. I find you exhausting."

"Great, then leave me alone. Problem solved."

He narrowed his eyes at me, making him look far more menacing than I thought possible.

"If only I could. . . ."

"Is there a problem here?" Principal Thompson called out as he approached us. The concern in his gaze was unmistakable.

"She was snooping around outside Coach Blackthorn's office."

"Because I saw him drag some girl in there and proceed to all but make her cry! I just wanted to make sure she was okay."

Principal Thompson hesitated for a second, an uncertain gaze falling upon me.

"Well," he said, "let's go see about that."

He stormed down the hallway toward the coach's office and didn't bother to knock before entering. I followed with Callahan tight on my heels. When Principal Thompson opened the door, I saw Coach sitting at his desk, thumbing through his prized playbook. He looked up at us as though he had no clue why we were there, then slowly stood.

"Can I help you?" he asked, voice steady and calm.

The girl was nowhere to be seen.

"There was a complaint about you accosting a female student in here."

Coach made a show of looking around his empty office. "Ain't no female students in here. I think whoever reported that was mistaken." He made a point of staring past Principal Thompson at me, a silent "fuck you" if ever I saw one.

Thompson looked torn for a minute, his desire to believe what I'd said about Coach in stark contrast with the lack of evidence before him. Then he gave Coach a quick nod and backed out of the room, closing the door behind him. He hovered there for a moment as though he were waiting to see if he suddenly heard a female voice on the other side of the door. Like he was hoping to catch Coach in a lie. But there was no voice, so he eventually walked away, gesturing for Callahan and me to follow. Once we were out of the sports wing, he turned to me.

"Are you sure you heard what you thought you heard?"

"Yes. I saw him drag her into his office and slam the door. Then I heard him say something about doing what he told her and she kept saying she couldn't do it. She didn't want to."

Thompson's brows pinched together. "I wish I could believe you. . . ."

Those words were a blow to the gut.

"Who was the girl?" Callahan asked, butting in.

I shrugged. "I don't know her name."

He scoffed. "Of course you don't."

"Mr. Callahan—" Thompson cautioned.

"She's on a witch hunt of some sort. She's taking down anyone she's not happy with."

"Donovan tried to *kill me,* in case you forgot. And I was right about him! This isn't a weird grudge match, or believe me, I'd be gunning for you—"

"That's enough," Principal Thompson said, his tone heated. "Kylene, we've already spoken about your aberrant behavior—"

"That has nothing to do with this—"

"So, if you have no evidence, I'm going to have to dismiss this issue and ask that you return to wherever it is you should be right now."

I exhaled hard. "I'm not lying."

"Unless you can find the girl and get her to come forward, my hands are tied."

"Fine," I said, hitching my bag up higher on my shoulder. "I'll see what I can do."

I walked away, leaving Callahan and Thompson behind to have a sidebar conversation. I'm sure it was littered with asshole remarks from the former and weak attempts to cover for me from the latter. Since I couldn't do anything about that, I trudged my way to class, trying to figure out how to track down the girl Coach had gotten rid of before he could get caught.

Before she became the next Throwaway Girl.

THIRTY-SIX

I didn't tell Dawson about what I saw in Coach's office. Mainly because I had nothing concrete to tell. It was all a lot of cryptic nothing unless I could give it context. And to do that, I needed details. Details I couldn't get without the girl.

Imagine my surprise when I walked into the bathroom at the beginning of last period to find her fixing her eye makeup in the mirror. It was pretty clear by the shape it was in that she'd been crying.

"You okay?" I asked.

She looked over at me and gave a small nod before she wiped her cheeks with her sleeve.

"I never properly thanked you for the other night—at Marco's," I said. "What's your name?"

She shot me an irritated glance. "I guess you don't remember?" The incredulity in her tone was thick, and it slapped me hard. "I'm Missy Edwards. I lived in your neighborhood growing up—until my mom lost her job and we were forced to move."

I felt like a total dick. I did know Missy. We'd played together as kids. She was a couple years younger than me, but nobody cared about details like that when they were seven. She'd been a sweet, happy kid, but there was no evidence of that in her dull eyes and permanent frown. There was no joy to her existence anymore, and I couldn't help but wonder if that had to do with what she and Coach were arguing about. If maybe she, too, like Jane and Danielle, was caught up in this prostitution mess.

The conversation she'd had with Coach ran over and over in my mind as Missy stared at me. She was protecting someone—keeping someone from whatever the coach had wanted to do. A chill shot down my spine as my thoughts grew darker. Thoughts of Coach slitting Danielle's throat and putting Missy in her place—the new recruiter of girls for his sex ring. His new puppet. She'd looked so frightened when he spoke—like she knew that the consequences for not doing his bidding would be dire.

Maybe she knew he'd killed Danielle, too.

"Oh yeah!" I said, trying to save face. "I've been gone for a while. . . ." She didn't say anything in response. "Missy, are you sure you're okay? I was outside Coach Blackthorn's office. I heard you two talking." At that, she turned white as a sheet. "Is he trying to hurt you?" I asked, hoping to gently pull the truth from her. "Maybe I can help—"

"You can't help me," she said, her tone so condescending it surprised me. "You need to forget what you heard and leave it alone. I mean it."

"What does he want you to do?" I pressed, my anxiety spiking. I couldn't help but think of Jane's words and how Danielle had met her terrible fate because she'd gone against the wishes of whoever was in charge. In her case, she'd wanted to leave and start a new life. In Missy's, it sounded a lot like she didn't want to involve someone else in what she was caught up in. She fit the profile to a tee, according to what those two hillbillies had said at the pizza place. I was terrified that if I did nothing—if I didn't push a little—that she might be the next to go missing.

I wasn't willing to sit back and let that happen.

"If you're caught up in something—something dangerous—I can help you. I know about things going on in this town—"

"You can't help me," she repeated, her voice cold and low—just like the girl outside Tyson's gym that night.

Without another word, she grabbed her bag off the floor and stormed out of the room.

THIRTY-SEVEN

I spent final period feeling utterly shell-shocked. Then I ran into Dawson on the way out and that luxury disappeared. I filled him in on what happened, and all I got in return was one of his pensive stares. The kind that gave nothing away except his general level of irritation. Whether or not that irritation was with me remained to be seen.

"Go home," he finally said as we made our way to the parking lot. "I'll meet you at your place in twenty."

I opened my mouth to ask for further explanation, but he was already out of earshot. The guy walked like a man possessed.

Thirty minutes later, he rolled up in front of Gramps' house and waited for me. I got in with him and drove off.

"Where are we going?" I asked.

"The shooting range."

"Should I be nervous?"

"Shooting helps me think," he replied as though that answer was all I needed.

"Guess it's a good thing you weren't allowed to bring firearms to your tests at Quantico." I tried to keep a straight face when he turned to glare at me and failed.

"Do you take anything seriously?" he asked.

"I took Donovan pretty seriously," I fired back, uncertain why he was being extra prickly.

"Not seriously enough," he muttered under his breath.

Dick.

"Hey! I've got a wild idea," I said. "How about we actually act like a couple? Have a normal conversation that doesn't involve you being a moody jerk who always has to be right or me being forced into ultrasarcasm mode to put you in your place. Can you handle that?"

"I'm not sure what that leaves us with, but we can try."

Then the smile he'd been withholding finally broke free, and I punched him in the arm. Whether I was angry or just jealous that he could deadpan better than I could, I wasn't sure. Probably both.

I shot daggers at him as he drove. Then he launched into an unnecessary gun safety lecture that left me sliding down in my seat as my eyes rolled. He finished not long before we pulled into the parking lot.

We walked into the lobby, and I hung back while he got signed in or whatever he needed to do. Then I followed him back to the empty range. He picked a spot and started unpacking all his stuff, handing me a pair of ear protectors.

"You'll need these."

"I've needed these since the day I met you." He glared up at me and I didn't bother trying to hide my amusement.

"What happened to acting like a normal, happy couple?"

I shrugged. "I never said happy. And couples fight."

"Did your parents fight a lot?" he asked, setting his handgun up on the counter.

"Is that a serious question?" He nodded. "I mean, I guess they did, but no more than I imagine anyone else's parents do. A law enforcement family isn't always an easy one to grow up in. My mom is pretty high maintenance. I think the lack of attention got to her over the years."

"Where is she now?"

"With her new boyfriend in California. She left right after my dad was sentenced."

His eyes narrowed. "She just left you behind?"

"Not exactly. We fought over where I'd go until I told her that she could either let me live with Gramps so I could be close to Dad or I'd run away the second we arrived in Cali." Dawson's expression didn't change. "Since it was only going to be a couple of months before I turned eighteen, she signed emancipation papers for me and I came to live with Gramps."

"But you hate it here," he said. I thought I heard a note of sympathy in his tone but couldn't be sure.

"I love my dad more than I hate Jasperville," I explained. His lips pressed to a thin line as though he was trying to trap a knee-jerk response about my dad from escaping. "What about you, Dawson? What's your story?"

"That's a pretty open question. Try to be more specific if you want to interrogate someone."

"Fine. How'd you end up in the FBI?"

He took a deep breath and let it out slowly.

"Jim Reider was my next-door neighbor and my father's best friend. He used to tell me stories about cases he'd helped solve and bad guys he'd helped put away. Even though I was only about ten when I heard the first one, I can remember those stories so vividly." The faraway look in his eyes drew me in, and I took a step closer to him before realizing what I'd done. He, however, didn't seem to notice. "Reider taught me how to shoot when I was fourteen. He used to take me when things got bad at home. He'd never say anything about it—just come over like everything was fine and pull me away from the chaos.

By the time I was seventeen, I swear I was at his house more than my own."

I felt my chest tighten as realization set in. Reider wasn't just Dawson's mentor. He was a father figure when his own dad had failed him. The pain he must have felt at his death shot through me and I fought hard to keep it from my expression. He looked at me, hesitating for a second before turning away to prepare his gun.

"I'm sorry, Dawson."

He turned his head slightly to look over his shoulder.

"I guess we both lost someone that night," he said, his voice low and hollow. As quickly as the moment came, it passed. Dawson turned back around, his impassive expression back in place. "Now, pay attention."

He loaded his gun, explaining every step of the process as though I didn't grow up with an FBI father and a correctional officer grandpa. I waited patiently while he droned on until he finally finished.

It seemed like an eternity.

"Are ya done?" I asked, walking up beside him. He scowled and nodded. "Good, then watch and learn, my friend." I motioned for him to step back, then slipped on my ear protection and picked up the gun.

I took the stance my father had drilled into me growing up and took aim. With a deep breath, I relaxed my shoulders and focused on the target. Gently squeezing the trigger, I shot three times, determined to show Dawson I had skills. When I finished, I realized I fell short. Like way short.

I flipped the safety on and placed the gun down.

Dawson hit a switch that made the target sail toward us and pulled it off.

"Watch and learn, she says," he said with a laugh. "Don't worry, Danners. It's not a total loss. At least you hit it."

"One in the shoulder. One in the thigh. And one in the ear." Yes. The ear. "Pretty terrible."

"That's surprising," he said.

"Wait, what?" I asked "Why does my suckitude surprise you?"

"Because," he said, looking at me with faint annoyance, "you don't strike me as the kind of girl who's terrible at anything."

I stared at him for a moment, trying to make sense of his reply.

"Except discerning fact from fiction when it pertains to my father, right?" I couldn't help myself. The words fell out of my mouth before I could even attempt to stop them, abruptly undoing whatever moment we'd just shared.

"That remains to be seen."

"Whatever. Maybe mine weren't kill shots, but they'd wound somebody pretty badly."

"They would," he said, staring me down. "But you should never get a false sense of security because you have a gun in your hand. Guns are not always the trump card people think they are. They can be turned on you at any moment. You can't depend on them. You can only depend on yourself."

"Thanks for that PSA, Dawson. I'll keep that in mind, even though I don't plan on carrying a hand cannon anytime soon."

"Damn right you're not. You leave that to me."

Before I could reply, he walked over to the counter, slipping his ear protection on. Whether it was to keep his hearing or block me out, I wasn't sure, but either way, the latter would have undoubtedly been a perk for him. He indicated that I put mine on as well, then pointed two fingers at my eyes and then gestured at himself, telling me to watch and learn this time.

I flipped him off once he turned around.

He found a comfortable, stable stance, then took aim supporting the gun from underneath with his opposite hand. *Pop,*

pop, pop. . . . Then he put the safety on and placed the firearm down on the counter. I looked over at the target and groaned. Two to the chest and one to the head. Perfect aim, not that I was surprised. Little to nothing about Dawson surprised me.

"Nice," I said dryly. He slipped his ear protection off and looked at me confused. "I said *nice*."

"It's all about relaxation and focus. You need to be strong, but not rigid."

"Easy to say when nobody's pointing a gun at you."

"Hence the need for practice. If you can't do it under controlled conditions, you sure as hell won't be able to when the shit hits the fan. You should try again."

I stepped up to the counter and Dawson slid behind me. I took my stance training the firearm on the target. Then Dawson reached his arms around me to tweak my grip and relax my shoulders. The faint smell of his cologne invaded my space and I immediately felt my chest tighten.

Too close—we were way too close.

"You need to relax," he said, after slipping the cover off my ear.

"I'm trying to, but it's hard with you suffocating me."

"Do I make you nervous, Danners?" he asked, punctuating his question with a little laugh.

"Irritated? Yes. Nervous? No."

He scoffed then pulled away, sounding far too satisfied with himself. Then he put my ear protection back on and tapped me on the shoulder to give me the all clear. I wasn't sure I could shoot anything in that state.

I wondered if that was exactly why he'd done it.

We spent an hour there, working on my skills. By the time we left, I felt confident in my ability to wield a handgun, and I was even more convinced that Dawson had to have been a pain in the ass at Quantico. He was just too perfect for his own good and it was annoying as hell.

When he signaled it was time to leave, I handed over my ear protection and walked out to wait by the car. The sun was low in the sky, casting an eerie amber glow around the empty parking lot. Just as Dawson headed my way, the falling sun highlighting his hair, my phone started to buzz.

"Hello?" I said, putting it to my ear.

"What the hell are you doing?" Jane all but growled at me.

"Excuse me?"

Dawson shot me a pointed look and I turned away from him.

"Your stunt in the bathroom with Missy Edwards."

"What about it?"

"You grilled her about Coach and then said you knew things that went on in this town."

"So? I do, but I didn't name you and I didn't give particulars."

"You had no right to do that!"

"But nothing happened, Jane! Missy thinks I'm a nosey pain in the ass, but that doesn't affect you at all. I didn't say anything specific—I just tried to get her to admit what was going on with Coach."

"It's all she could talk about," Jane said, breathing hard. By this point, Dawson had his head leaned against mine to listen in to the call. I was thankful I couldn't see the look of disappointment that was undoubtedly on his face.

"Listen, I saw her and Coach arguing. They were tucked away in the corner of his office with the door nearly closed. Their voices were hushed but I could hear the anger in his. When I sneaked a peek, Missy looked terrified. All I could think of was Danielle's dead body and Missy's being next. Coach is one of the top suspects, Jane. I thought risking looking like an asshole in front of Missy was worth it if she needed my help. . . ."

Jane was silent for a moment and I wondered if she'd hung up on me. Then I heard her let out a breath.

"Missy isn't in the same mess I'm in."

I hazarded a glance at Dawson, and he merely nodded at me, encouraging me to ask the question brewing in my mind.

"What mess is she in?" I asked, cold seeping into my veins.

"She's knocked up."

I hesitated. "Who's the father, Jane?"

Another hard exhale. "Coach Blackthorn."

I pulled away from Dawson and stared him down. What the hell was I supposed to do with that information? I needed his guidance, but he couldn't give it to me—not without Jane overhearing.

"Jane," I said calmly, trying hard to think quick on my feet. "She has to report him. At best, he's abusing his position as a teacher. At worst, he's having sex with a minor who can't legally consent. And if he *is* the one behind everything else—what happened to Danielle—then this is our best chance at putting him away for now until we can get concrete evidence."

She said nothing for a moment, clearly mulling over my words.

"I'll talk to Missy," she said softly. "She said he told her to get an abortion—that if she didn't, he'd take matters into his own hands."

My heart stopped for a second before slamming back to life in my chest. That's the girl she was trying to protect. The baby—not the others.

"Jane, regardless of whether or not Coach is involved with what you're caught up in, she has to turn him in. And if she won't, you might have to do it."

"Me? Hell no—I'm not going to the cops—"

"This isn't about your mess, remember?"

"No way. I don't trust them. I'll talk to Missy, but if she won't turn him in, I'm not doing it. You'll have to find another way to get whatever it is you're looking for."

Before I could argue any further, she hung up. My arm fell limp at my side, phone still in hand, as I turned to face Dawson.

"I screwed up," I said, my throat closing around the words. "I think I pushed her too far. . . ."

"Maybe. Maybe not. All we can do for now is wait and see if Jane can get through to her friend. If not, we'll figure out plan B."

"How can you be so calm about this?" I asked, anger bleeding into my tone.

"Because the reality of the situation is that even if what Jane said is true, it isn't damning evidence against Coach. Sleeping with a student doesn't make him a killer."

"No. Just a pedophile."

He looked at me for a moment, his piercing gaze trying to penetrate my cocoon of growing rage. I wasn't even sure who I was mad at anymore. I was just mad and frustrated, and in desperate need of an outlet for it all.

"What's up with you?" he asked, his tone cautious.

"What's up with me? Are you kidding me right now?"

"You're yelling—"

"Damn right I'm yelling! I'm pissed! I'm pissed that I messed up that call. That Coach is probably going to get away with what he's doing just like his football players did when those topless pictures of me came out. I'm pissed that I live in a town that dictates your worth based on economic status and sports ability—that fails the very people that need their protection. And I'm pissed off because you're not pissed off enough!" His stoicism wavered under that comment, but it did little to stop me. I was in full rant mode and nothing was going to shut me down, even if it should have. "It's like you've completely forgotten that these girls are victims, Dawson—that some of them are still out there night after night, making money for some skeevy perv because they're economically marginalized and backed into a corner. I think about these students by day, hookers by night—about Jane and what she's dealing with—and then I put myself in her place and wonder how she can function. Doesn't that bother you? Doesn't that get to you somewhere inside that cold exterior of yours? Because I'm pretty damn heartless, Dawson, but even I can't shrug this off."

"Are you done?" he asked, his calm tone belying the storm brewing in those hazel eyes.

I looked away from him and tried to get control of my breathing. My anger was abating, but the adrenaline coursing through me hadn't worn off just yet. And it wouldn't when Dawson opened his mouth, either.

"Unlike you, emotions are something I can't afford to let cloud my judgment, Danners. If I'm going to help those girls, then I need to focus on the facts, of which we still don't have a lot. But if you think that means that a moment goes by where I don't think about them—that I'm not up all hours of the night, poring over evidence and researching whatever I can to try and find who's behind this before another girl goes missing or Jane gets caught—you're crazy. And maybe I can't put myself in her position as easily as you can, but I can pretend that she's someone like you—someone I don't ever want to see exploited like that—and get a healthy dose of motivation from that." He was the one yelling now, and I could feel myself shrinking under the weight of it. Without my anger as a shield, his words cut right through me. What I saw as clinical indifference was nothing more than Dawson's armor against the Luke Clarks and Coach Blackthorns of the world.

I didn't realize I was crying until his harsh expression

softened a bit and he reached over to wipe my cheek with his thumb.

"I know this case is getting to you, Kylene. I wish there was a way to remove you from it. . . ."

"I don't want to be removed. And I know you care about them," I said, pulling away from him. His arm fell slowly to his side. "I don't know why I said that."

"You're angry at the injustice of it all, and you should be. This whole goddamn town should be, and it isn't. Be mad, but channel that anger. Make it work for you. Keep fighting for those that can't fight for themselves. That's what this job is really about."

I stared up at him, thinking about how my dad had said something similar about his job once—that he was a voice for those that didn't have one sometimes. I never thought I'd live to see the day where those two had something in common.

I wondered if my disbelief was written all over my face.

"We're going to bring Coach down for what he did to Missy—and the others, too, if guilty," he said, his expression harsh.

I had no doubt he'd make good on his word.

"I should probably get home now," I said, opening the car door. "Gramps isn't working tonight. I want to hang out with him a bit. I feel like I never see him."

Dawson said nothing in response. Instead, he got in and fired up the car, pulling out onto the main road into town. We rode in silence through the rolling hillside, the last remnants of the fall colors highlighted by the dying sun. It looked like the woods were on fire.

"You can't second-guess yourself," Dawson said, drawing my attention away from the beautiful yet haunting trees. "All you can do is make the best decision possible and go with it. You did that. Try not to beat yourself up over the outcome. You can't change it now."

"Thanks," I said softly.

He gave a tight nod as we pulled into town. That was the last thing he said until he dropped me off at Gramps' house and waved goodbye. As I walked up the porch steps, it hit me that, in a strange way, Dawson had given his approval of how I'd handled the call. Praise wasn't a language he seemed fluent in, but the advice he'd given me all but implied it. As far as I was concerned, if he wasn't telling me I'd screwed up, it was a compliment of epic proportions.

One I'd gladly take.

THIRTY-EIGHT

I skipped out of school early on Wednesday—I just couldn't deal.

That feeling didn't improve when I arrived at my car to find yet another note tucked under my wipers. Whoever was behind it clearly liked to strike when I was at school. Whether that was because he was employed there or just wanted to make it look like he was remained unknown.

I unfolded it to find more of the same.

You'll be next. . . .

Fanfuckingtastic.

I stuffed the letter in my pocket, equally riled up as the time before, but with less trepidation. I knew it wouldn't have physical evidence on it, nor would it point us in the direction of who wrote it. I stuffed it away like my fear and fallout from homecoming night and locked it up tight. If someone was trying to scare me off, I wouldn't let them.

At least not until I was alone in my room at night and the bad thoughts crept in. Then, I'd freak out.

When I got home, I found a legal file in the mailbox, and a surge of adrenaline shot through me until I saw who'd sent them. The papers Meg needed signed were inside and I yanked them out to look them over. Then I tucked them into the inside pocket of my jacket and drove to Logan Hill Prison with the blind hope that my father would sign them.

"Hey, Dad," I said as the guard walked away.

"What's wrong, Kylene?" he asked, seeing my exhaustion or frustration or any assortment of other emotions I was too tired to keep from my expression.

"I'm so over Jasperville, Dad. I literally can't even with that place anymore."

"What's happened? Did somebody do something to you?"

"No. Not me." I took a deep breath and told him everything that happened with Missy and Coach—leaving the potential murderer part out of the story for the time being.

I watched as my father's face turned a shade of angry that I hadn't seen in a long time—since Boobgate, to be exact. Not even once during his trial did he ever look that ready to actually commit murder.

"Tell me he's under arrest, or has that bumbling sheriff messed things up yet again?"

"I don't think she's come forward, Dad. There's nothing Sheriff Higgins can do until she does."

"Not that he will once that happens. . . ." My father's incredulity was hard to miss.

"I'm so tired of people getting away with things in this town!"

"Ky—"

"No Dad, I mean it! This needs to stop!"

He leaned forward on the counter, resting his elbows on it.

"I'm not saying it doesn't, but you don't have to be the one to make certain it does."

"I didn't say I was," I argued. "I dropped your case like you asked me to." He quirked a brow at me. "I mean, I dropped it right into Meg's lap, but—"

"Kylene! I did not agree to that!"

"Well I did. They were my transcript copies to do with as I saw fit. Meg's already said she found reason to show your attorney was an ass clown who should have never passed the bar exam. She wants you to fire him and retain her as your legal counsel—"

"No!" my father shouted before regaining control. "No. Absolutely not. I don't want her to do that."

"Why, Dad? Because you're worried about her? Because you love the accommodations here so much that twenty-five to life sounds like a solid plan?"

"Because it's my decision to make and I say no!" He slammed his fists on the counter and the guard took a step closer. My father raised his arms in surrender, and he backed away. "Kylene, I am the adult here, regardless of where I am. This is my life and my mess to clean up, not yours or Meg's. I love that the two of you love me enough to try, but you have to respect my wishes and let me handle this in my own time and my own way."

I could practically feel the legal documents in my pocket burning me. There was no way in hell he'd cave on his stance, no matter how hard I worked to change his mind. He'd drawn his line in the sand and that was that.

Or so he thought.

"Okay," I said, smoothing my jacket and the papers beneath. "I won't bring this up again."

A promise I knew I could keep.

"I love you for trying. I really do, but you have to trust me on this, okay?"

I nodded. "Sure, Dad. And I love you, too, but I have to run. I'll be back soon."

His features tightened at my words; he knew he'd hurt me. But we were both good at ignoring the elephant in the room. We'd had a lot of practice at that over the years. I got up to leave and he waited for his escort, smiling and waving at me as I looked back.

I wondered if he'd ever smile at me again once he learned I forged those documents.

THIRTY-NINE

I was a nervous wreck the next day.

Every socially and economically marginalized girl that passed me in the hall was Jane. Every buzz of my phone was her calling to tell me that Missy agreed to turn Coach in. But when I went to gym that day and found his ugly mug staring me down, I lost hope.

Even watching Tabby do the hundred-meter hurdles couldn't cheer me up.

I blew off lunch when I saw AJ heading for the cafeteria. I didn't know where I was going to go, but I knew I couldn't eat my lunch with him. I was willing to eat in my car if I had to for as long as necessary to avoid that scenario—or at least until I got caught. Or Garrett and Tabby staged an intervention.

Dawson was present for Spanish, but in body only. His mind was clearly elsewhere. It took Mrs. Stewart three attempts to get his attention by calling his name. By the third, she was standing right in front of him. He started when his eyes focused on her, then answered her question so she'd leave him alone.

When the bell rang, he stormed out of class, staring down at his phone. I tried to catch up to him, but I was caught in the mass exodus of students. By the time the crowd thinned out, he was long gone.

I exhaled hard in frustration. After a quick stop at my locker, I hurried down the hall, texting Dawson as I walked.

Then a voice stopped me just short of the stairs.

"You dropped this," AJ said, holding out a pen. A pen that wasn't mine. The impish look on his face told me that he knew damn well it wasn't mine, too.

"That's impressive given that I've never seen it before."

"That *is* impressive," he said with a wink, putting the pen into his backpack.

"Listen AJ, I've really gotta go—"

"I know you're avoiding me, Ky, and I get why. I really do. What happened the other night—"

"Shouldn't have happened," I said as firmly as I could. It almost sounded believable. The tiny twinkle in his eyes told me so.

"Exactly." When he stood there looking pleased with himself, I turned to leave. "I can walk and talk if you'd prefer."

"You know that would make you the only male in existence capable of multitasking, right? You're like a mythical creature . . . a unicorn."

"Well aren't you lucky, then?" He proceeded to keep pace with me as I made my way to the stairs at the end of the hall. "Seriously though, Ky. I want to show you I'm capable of being your friend. To prove it to you, I'm having a party after the big game tomorrow, and I want you to come. You can call it an early birthday present if you want."

I shot him a look over my shoulder before descending the steps.

"I'm not sure that's a great idea, AJ."

"Worried you'll pick up where we left off?" he asked, the challenge in his voice plain. When I sped up, he backtracked. "Listen, I'm sorry! I know you're with what's his name. I get it. I want you to come because we're friends again. Remember?

And friends go to their friends' parties." I rounded the newel post on the second floor and kept going. "Ky, throw me a bone here. I'm sorry about how things went down the other night. I'm really trying to navigate this as best I can—to be your friend—but it's hard and you're not making it any easier."

He was right. I wasn't. Mainly because being friends with AJ wasn't easy. Not even close.

I continued all the way down to the ground floor and through the double doors before AJ stopped me with a gentle hand on my shoulder.

"Ky. Please." The pain he clearly felt when he said my name made my chest hurt. It tightened around my lungs, making it hard to breathe.

"AJ, I don't know what to say," I replied, throwing up my hands in frustration. "This isn't easy for me, either, and not because of what's his name." He stood before me, unbreathing, as though whatever I was about to say might make or break him. I feared perhaps it could. "For two years I told myself that you were someone else, and now that I know everything I believed was a lie, my mind is a scrambled mess. It makes being around you complicated." I kept it short, sweet, and believable. He'd never question the truth in my words. But what he didn't know was if he'd just barely scratched the surface of my excuses, he'd have found exactly what he wanted. That every time he smiled at me, I could feel my armor cracking. That every time his arm brushed against mine, my heart sped up a beat or two. That every time our eyes met, my body begged to move closer to him—begged to be held. Begged to do what we'd done in his room again. My hormones, memories, and rational mind were in an all-out war where AJ was concerned, and I needed to get a grip on the situation fast. Dawson was my boyfriend—or at least looked that way. The last thing I needed was an apparent love triangle brewing—the Jasperville

High gossips would have loved that. My reputation, however, would not. "What happened the other night was my fault, and I take responsibility for that. But I can't afford for it to happen again."

"Ky," he replied, an unmistakable note of sadness tainting my name. "It wasn't your fault. We were both there. We both just got a little too caught up in the moment to think clearly, that's all."

I looked at the pile of books in his hands to get a break from his hopeful eyes.

"Are you sure?"

"Absolutely."

"You promise?"

"I promise."

I let out a breath. "Okay. I'll go to the party."

"Excellent!"

"But I'll have to bring what's his name . . . ," I said, a wry smile growing.

"Yeah, I kinda figured that, which basically means I'm a saint."

"Saint AJ, Forgiver of all Dick Moves . . . ," I mused aloud.

"I like that," he said. "It has a certain ring to it."

I couldn't help but laugh. "It really does."

"Does this mean you're going to go to the game, too?"

"Don't push it, AJ." I looked up to find him smiling wide.

"Last game of the season . . ." He waggled his brows for effect, but I had no intentions of caving.

"No way. No more football for me."

He feigned a pout, then perked back up. "Hey! I just got the team pictures. Want to see them?"

"Sure." He pulled an envelope out of a textbook and handed it to me. "Don't they do these digitally?"

"They do, but you know Mom," he said. "Technology is not her friend."

"Fair point."

I pulled the stack of various-sized photos from the envelope and paged through them. At the back of the pile was the team picture, AJ sitting front and center on the bottom bleacher. For once, the photographer had gotten in close enough to actually see the faces of the players. I scanned them all, cringing when my eyes fell on Donovan. AJ must have noticed, and he started apologizing immediately, reaching to take the picture away. Just as my numb hands were about to let him, something in the photo caught my eye. I turned from AJ and held it closer to make sure I was seeing what I thought I was seeing.

"Are you okay, Ky?" he asked, concern in his tone.

"AJ, can you get me a digital copy of this?" I asked, trying not to sound as panicked as I felt.

"Yeah. Sure. I'll email it right now."

"Great!" I said, turning to shove his pictures and envelope back into his hands. "I gotta go. See you tomorrow!"

Without another word, I took off in a sprint to my car, sweat beading along the small of my back. The second I got Heidi fired up, I peeled out of the parking lot and sped toward Dawson's house. I heard the notification that I'd just received an email. I dared a glance at my phone to find it was from AJ.

I was standing on Dawson's front step not long after leaving the school, pounding on his door. He threw it open to reveal his irritated expression. But when I bolted past him, fumbling with my phone, he followed without giving me another lecture on visitation etiquette.

"What's going on?" he asked as I tapped on the attached picture. It took me three attempts to zoom in on what I wanted, but once I did, I held it up so he could see.

"Danielle was killed two weeks ago, right?" I asked. His eyes just drifted to me in response. "Varsity football and cheerleading photos are taken the same time every year. Never changes. That photo was taken two weeks ago," I explained, pointing at Coach Blackthorn. "And those right there are fresh scratches on his neck."

Dawson stared for a moment before he opened a browser on my phone and started searching for something. Moments later, those narrowed hazel eyes turned to me.

"It was cold that night," he said, a sense of awe in his voice. "About forty-five degrees. He would have been wearing a jacket when he killed her—or at least long sleeves. The only skin he'd likely have had exposed would have been his face, neck, and possibly hands."

"Holy shit, Dawson. . . ."

"Danners—I think our suspect list just got a whole lot shorter."

FORTY

It took forever to calm the storm of thoughts in my mind. Thankfully, Dawson snapped me out of it when he grabbed my hand and dragged me down the hall to his office. He flipped the whiteboard over and started scribbling notes all over it like a man possessed. As I tried to decipher his chicken scratch, he stopped and turned to stare at me.

"The girl—"

"Missy Edwards—"

"We need her to come forward. Without her, bringing him in will be tricky."

"Well, Coach was there today, so no such good luck on that front."

Dawson frowned, then started to pace the room. He seemed to always pace when he was thinking—when he wasn't sure how to solve the problem at hand.

"I need to make a call," he finally said.

"To who?"

"Special Agent in Charge Wilson. I need to see if I can bend the rules a little here to get a DNA sample from Coach Blackthorn."

"What are you thinking?"

"I'm thinking of making an anonymous report to the police.

One that will surely end with the coach in an interrogation room."

"An anonymous phone call?" I asked. He nodded. "Well, you know I excel at those."

"I don't want you to make it," he quickly said. "I don't want you involved in that part."

"Because I can't handle it?"

"No. Because if there's fallout of any sort, I don't want any of it possibly coming down on you." *Oh*. "If you hear from Jane, make sure you let her know about this new evidence. Maybe it'll motivate her, and get her to leverage Missy into coming forward—especially if she thinks Coach is the killer."

"I will."

"I need to go make that call now. I'll let you know the plan once it's clear, okay?"

"All right," I said, taking the hint. I walked down the hall to the front door and paused there for a moment.

"Something wrong?" he asked, stepping next to me.

"It's just—I mean I'm no fan of Coach, but for all his dick-headedness, I would never have pegged him for a murderer. It's just hard to wrap my mind around."

His lips thinned to a grim slash across his face.

"Murderers come in all shapes and sizes. That's something you can never afford to forget in my line of work. Something you can't take for granted."

I nodded absentmindedly, his words settling on my addled mind.

"Like my dad . . ."

He hesitated. "Yes. Like your dad." For once, there was a note of sympathy in his tone when he mentioned my father, but it didn't make me feel any better. That subject was still too raw.

Instead of saying anything, I took out my phone for the second time that night, prepared to drop another bomb on him. One that would shake the very foundation of his beliefs, just like Luke's betrayal had shaken mine. I wanted Dawson to know what that felt like.

I held up a screenshot of Reider and the mobster in Atlantic City, the one my father had taken of him while investigating the fed he'd later kill. Dawson stared at it blankly, then took it from my hands.

"What is this?" he asked. His voice had resumed its haughty indignance that it had only begun to shed a week earlier.

"That's Reider with some mob boss. I found it in a box of old papers. Striker has been looking into it and a few other things I found along with it. It was taken in Atlantic City. Seems Reider had some serious gambling debt. My dad was looking into it."

I glanced up, expecting to find Dawson's stare burning holes through my face, but instead he looked pale and empty. He didn't say a word in argument.

"He told me he'd stopped years ago," he said. His voice was so filled with disappointment and despair that I instantly felt like an ass.

"You knew he had a problem. . . ."

He nodded. "I found out when I was heading to Quantico. He and his wife were having issues, and he'd said he'd gone to the casino a few times to blow off steam and it got a bit out of hand. He'd always like to go to the races—even when I was younger—but I never thought much of it. Legal gambling and addiction aren't mutually inclusive."

"Dawson," I said softly, pulling my phone from his grasp. "The AD leverages people into doing things they might not otherwise. Do you think it's possible he backed Reider into a corner because of his debt? Do you think he could have made him manufacture evidence against my dad?" He looked at me as though I'd just slapped him in the face but said nothing. Guilt roiled in my guts.

"How long have you had this?" he asked. The hurt in his voice impaled me.

"About a week."

"Why didn't you bring it to me?"

I swallowed hard. "I didn't know what it was, if anything. I wanted Striker to look into it first."

His expression hardened. "I see."

"Dawson, I know how you feel about my dad and his case—"

"It's fine, Danners. I get it," he said, walking toward the hallway. "I'm going to go make that call. I'll see you tomorrow."

He disappeared from sight.

With a sharp exhale, I opened the door. I'd planned to let Dawson in on what I knew, but I'd also planned to do it with a bit more tact. Unfortunately, any mention of my dad from Dawson seemed to set me off, even against my better judgment. It was a knee-jerk reaction I needed to get rid of, because with one tiny mention, I'd kicked the shit out of the progress he and I had made. I wondered if, in the morning, we'd be right back to where we started: an adversarial relationship built on distrust and misunderstanding.

We didn't have time for that.

We were too close to catching the killer to let that get in the way.

FORTY-ONE

I hadn't seen or heard from Dawson all day. He didn't—or wouldn't—return my calls or texts. I couldn't find him in any of his classes when I took the hall pass each period so I could stalk him. With every strikeout, I felt worse about what I'd done.

It wasn't until the final football pep rally for the year that I saw him, and I couldn't have been more relieved. Yeah, we had other things to focus on than Reider's sketchy past and me throwing it in Dawson's face, but I needed to make sure we were okay first. I needed the feeling of grounding he provided, selfish though it was. Without it, I feared I would spiral out of control.

"Hey," he said as he walked toward me.

"Hey . . ."

"Ky!" Tabby shouted from the bleachers, her high-pitched voice cutting through the awkwardness between Dawson and me. "Up here!"

Dawson said nothing but led the way up to the riser in front of where Garrett, Tabby, and AJ sat wedged in with the other students. She removed the backpacks she'd used to save our seats, and we sat down in front of them. The leftover tension from the night brewed between us as cheerleaders tumbled across the floor to the cheers of the student body.

I leaned in close to Dawson so he could hear me over the festivities.

"I'm sorry about last night—"

"I know you are," he replied, still looking down at the court.

"It was a dick move," I said, reaching to touch him, then pulling up short. "I don't know why I did it."

He turned to reply, his stare a mix of hurt and anger, but then Principal Thompson jogged to center court, microphone in hand. The band finished playing our fight song and the crowd quieted down so Principal Thompson could begin his obligatory end-of-season pep talk.

I tuned out for that.

Instead, I ignored the vibes rolling off Dawson and scoured the bleachers to find Missy, my fingers gripping the edge of my seat. I needed to know she was okay. I needed to see that she hadn't become another unfortunate statistic.

Coach stood along the far wall of the gym, looking like his usual smug, warm-up-clad self. I wanted to smack that look off his face so badly it hurt. Unfortunately for me, I wouldn't get the chance.

Movement from the door near the far bleachers caught my attention, and I looked up to see Sheriff Higgins walk in. I turned to ask Garrett if his dad was picking him up, then stopped the second my brain caught up. The sheriff wasn't there for his son.

I leaned in close to Dawson, my lips grazing his ear so we wouldn't be overheard. "Sheriff Higgins, ten o'clock." Dawson's gaze fell upon the sheriff, and he sat up straight in his seat. "Did you make that anonymous call?" He shook his head. "Holy shit . . ." He leaned forward in his seat, but I pulled him back into me. "He wouldn't do it here, would he?"

Dawson merely nodded in response.

Holy shit was right.

With a million thoughts running wild in my mind, I blocked out everything else going on in that gym, my focus squarely on the sheriff. Somehow, everyone seemed oblivious to his presence—or maybe they thought he was just there to show his support for the team. Man, were those idiots about to get a wake-up call like a two-by-four to the head.

Perched at the edge of my seat, I looked on as Sheriff Higgins walked along the wall toward Coach. By the time he reached him, my heart was in my throat, and I was clutching Dawson's knee so tight he had to pry my hand off. When the sheriff leaned in to say something to Coach, Principal Thompson called Coach out to address the crowd. He glanced at the sheriff before dismissing him with an index finger in the air, then strolled out to the middle of the court like he wasn't about to be arrested for screwing jailbait.

Hubris like that was hard to come by.

Sheriff Higgins' face went beet red as he fumed on the sidelines. Then he lifted his hand to wave over two deputies who were discreetly waiting in the wings behind the cover of the bleachers. The three of them walked in formation to center court where Coach was droning on about how we could finish the season with pride despite all the heavy hits the team took this year. He made a point of staring at me when he delivered that blow.

I smiled back at him, knowing what he was in for.

He didn't even notice the trio until one of the deputies stepped behind him and wrenched his free arm behind his back. Coach instinctively tried to pull away, so the other deputy stepped in to aid in cuffing him. The whole student body was silent, staring at what seemed an improbable if not impossible sight before them. Even Principal Thompson looked shocked. He took the microphone away from Coach so the deputies could finish securing his arms behind him. Just as he did, Sheriff Higgins spoke.

"Coach Blackthorn, you are under arrest for statutory rape, engaging in a sex act with a minor, and—"

Principal Thompson quickly shut off the mic, but I knew how the rest went. A laundry list of charges revolving around Coach's relationship with Missy were being listed off one by one.

"I need to get out of here," Dawson whispered in my ear. He moved to get up, but I grabbed his leg to keep him still.

"Wait" was all I said in response.

"I can't believe this," AJ said behind me, the first of the three of them to utter a word. "Coach? Having sex with a minor?"

"This is crazy," Garrett echoed.

Tabby couldn't seem to find her voice. Instead, she just gaped at the coach as he was led away.

The silence in the room disappeared in a flash. Replacing it was a roar of questions and myriad outbursts ranging from outrage and indignation to applause. Poor Principal Thompson was left to try and pick up the pieces, but he looked so stunned, I was worried he, like Tabby, was at a loss for words. Finally, he just dismissed us, his bewildered expression still intact as he did.

"Let's go," Dawson said, standing up.

"See you guys later," I said over my shoulder to my trio of friends, who still couldn't reconcile what they'd just seen.

Dawson practically dragged me out of the gym, not letting go of my hand until we were well on our way to the parking lot.

"I need to get down there," he said in a hushed voice. "I need to get his DNA somehow."

"Won't they do that?"

He shot me a dubious look. "Yes, and they'll probably screw it up. So I'm going to secure my own sample."

"How?"

His mischievous smirk was answer enough. "However I can within the letter of the law . . . ish."

Before I could adequately portray my disbelief at his words, he ran off to his car and tore out of the parking lot. I watched as he drove away, then headed for Heidi. Looking at me from beyond my car, standing in front of the school, was Mr. Callahan. He stared at me with a look of contempt beyond any I'd ever seen. I couldn't shake the feeling that he somehow knew I was involved in what went down at the pep rally. That my "witch hunt" had brought down one of his colleagues.

I smiled at the thought.

As I drove away, I wondered how Dawson could get what we needed: the DNA that would bring down a pedophile and possibly put a murderer in prison. It had the potential to end Jane's and so many others' nightmares. And get justice for the Throwaways.

FORTY-TWO

About an hour after school let out, Dawson texted me; he was on his way up to Columbus with what he needed. He also mentioned that Coach broke under Sheriff Higgins' interrogation. He admitted to having had a sexual relationship with Missy—and others, including Danielle Green. Ice ran down my spine at the thought.

I wondered how long it would take for him to admit to her murder, not that it mattered. With Dawson procuring his DNA, we'd have concrete proof soon enough.

I did my best to act normal around Gramps, but it was damn near impossible. When I sat on my hands to keep them still, he finally put his fork down and shot me a look that said "maybe you should just spit it out, girl."

"I'm just excited about the big after party tonight," I lied.

He looked thoughtful for a moment, then took a long bite of his famous pot roast. I thought he'd never swallow.

"Kids treatin' you better over there now after the Donovan mess?"

"Yeah. Kinda. It's an upgrade for sure."

"Where's this party gonna be?"

". . . At AJ's."

His eyes narrowed.

"Your boyfriend goin' with you?"

"He's in Columbus right now. He said he might make it back in time."

Silence.

"You sure it's wise you go without him?"

"Because a girl can't go anywhere without her boyfriend?"

"No. Because I know how you used to feel about AJ—"

"Gramps—"

"And I'm just not sure that puttin' yourself in that situation is a good idea. It ain't fair to anyone involved, including that boyfriend of yours."

I released my hands to take a bite of food. I needed to stall.

"Gramps," I said, mouth half-full. "Alex is fine with AJ. He understands that we used to date and that the circumstances surrounding our breakup were complicated. He doesn't care."

"Maybe he should. . . ."

"Gramps!" I said, truly surprised.

"Just mind yourself, Kylene. People's feelings ain't somethin' to take lightly."

Didn't I know a thing or two about that.

"I'm well aware of everyone's feelings, Gramps, including my own, which should count for something in this equation." He said nothing in response. "I should probably go get Tabby. I finally broke down and agreed to go to the game tonight."

"Last one of the season."

"Yep."

"Hope AJ leads 'em to victory," Gramps said, the lack of enthusiasm in his expression duly noted.

"I'll be home late, if that's okay."

He nodded. "Just remember what I told ya, and it's fine with me."

I took a deep breath, then walked over and kissed Gramps on the cheek. Whatever aura of disapproval that had been there melted away in an instant.

"If it's going to be after midnight, I'll be sure to call and let you know."

"You do that."

I checked my phone incessantly through the first half of the game. Tabby was actually irritated with me, like somehow AJ could see that I wasn't paying attention and we'd lose the game because of it. Garrett, however, just shot me nasty looks, like he knew I was up to something I wasn't telling him about, which, as it turned out, was true enough. But it was also likely over.

I just needed the text from Dawson to confirm it.

My bladder acted up late in the third quarter. I practically had to run to the bathroom to avoid disaster. On my way out of the ladies' room, someone grabbed my arm and dragged me around to the other side of the building. Déjà vu slammed me hard, memories of me and Jaime behind the concession stand at the drive-in flashing through my mind. But when I looked at who'd accosted me, it certainly wasn't Jaime.

A girl stood there, glaring at me.

A girl I didn't recognize at first.

"What are you doing?" she asked, voice full of anger.

"Peeing. You?"

She snorted. "You're a piece of work." She dropped my arm to step away. It was then that I realized who she was. The *other* girl from Marco's Pizza. Missy's formerly nameless friend—her trailer park sister.

Jane.

"Why yes, *Jane,* I am."

Her expression remained unfazed.

"Coach was arrested but Missy went AWOL. She's nowhere to be found, Kylene. What if he got to her?"

"Can you reach her?"

"No. Her phone goes straight to voicemail."

"Sheriff Higgins will be looking for her."

"Maybe. Maybe not. Maybe there's nothin' left to find unless they scrape her off the bottom of the river like they did Danielle."

"Jane—"

"*Shayna*," she interrupted. "My name is *Shayna*."

"Fine. Shayna, I need you to tell me everything. When you last talked to her. What she said. All of it."

She filled me in on their last interactions, but there was nothing to glean from them, just frantic messages about whether or not she'd done the right thing going to the police.

"If he's really the guy that's running the girls—that killed Danielle," Shayna said, "then he had to have done it last night. She wasn't at school today at all."

"She could just be laying low," I suggested. It was met with an incredulous glare.

"Or she could be dead. Either way, how long do you think it's going to take for Coach to get out on bail and come looking for the girl that put her up to it?"

"You think he knows?"

"It's a small town. . . ."

"That's why you're here," I said, putting two and two together.

She nodded once. "Hard to kill me in public. I wonder if he knows that you know about what he's been doing? About the missing girls . . . ," she said, her eyes filled with hope that maybe I could assuage her concerns. But I wasn't sure I could and didn't think I should. She was right to be paranoid. Paranoia could keep you alive.

"Stay at the game tonight," I said, leaning in close. "AJ is having a party afterward. Maybe you could go to that, too?"

She shook her head. "I wouldn't make it through the door, but I'll go hang out at Matthew's Ice Cream or Marco's—somewhere open late and extremely public. I'll crash at a neighbor's tonight just to be safe."

"Okay. You text me if you need anything, okay? Anything at all."

"Yeah." She looked over her shoulder, that trusty paranoia kicking back in again. "I should go. We shouldn't be seen together."

Without another word, she took off under the bleachers, disappearing into the darkness.

I let out a deep breath, then texted Dawson, telling him what I'd learned. Minutes later, he texted back a slew of four-letter words in response. He'd get Higgins on it ASAP or the sheriff would be on his shit list yet again.

The Jasperville Badgers won the game by the skin of their teeth. While everyone around us was celebrating, Garrett looked like he was ready to pass out, so Tabby and I helped him down the bleachers and out to the street.

I told them to wait for me, and I ran ahead to get the car. By the time I made it there, I'd passed half the town and almost the entire JHS student body, teachers included. Whatever would they all do now that football season was over? Oh yeah . . . basketball.

As I ran to the car, my phone began buzzing. By the time I fished it out, it had gone to voicemail. I played it, worried what that message might contain, but for once in my life, it was good news. Missy had surfaced unscathed. She was with Jane, aka Shayna, for the night.

Two Throwaway Girls who would not meet their namesake's fate.

I texted Dawson to update him, then drove to pick up my friends. Tabby got Garrett into the front seat and I drove him home to an empty house. I got him some food while Tabby helped him to his room. He threw her out when she offered to help him get changed, and I just about dropped the plate of food I was holding. She came into the kitchen, grinning like the Cheshire Cat, and merely shrugged.

"You can't blame me for trying" was all she had to say for herself.

Once Garrett was fed and safely in bed (I took the lead on that activity since Tabby's hormones had gone rogue), the two of us headed over to AJ's to the party I wasn't certain I wanted to go to—or *should* go to, for that matter. As wrong as I wanted Gramps to be about what my presence there could mean, he wasn't. But with everything else going on, I just wanted that one night to feel normal. To be the teen I was supposed to be.

Not the crime-fighting vigilante I'd become.

FORTY-THREE

Tabby and I walked into a mob of bodies.

Music was blaring so loud I could hardly think straight. How the cops hadn't come by yet to shut it down, I didn't know. But really, I did. They had bigger fish to fry, and the neighbors wouldn't be complaining anytime soon. Jasperville was too elated with the win to shut down the quarterback's party.

"I have to pee!" Tabby shouted over the bass. She headed toward the powder room as I pushed her from behind to help her cut through the crowd. With more effort than it should have taken, we made it to the bathroom on the first floor in the hallway to the kitchen.

"I'll wait out here. No room for both of us in there."

She nodded and went in not realizing that I was guarding the door more than anything. The lock on that thing hadn't worked for years. I highly doubted they'd gotten it fixed since I'd used it last.

While I waited for Tabby to do what seemed to be the longest pee ever, I scanned the crowd. The faces were all familiar. The scene reminiscent of every party I'd ever been to at AJ's house. Like the one that had changed everything between us.

A doorknob to my back jolted my mind back to the present.

"Ow!"

"Sorry!" Tabby said, sounding more Canadian than usual. Something about apologizing really amped up the girl's accent.

"You're good. Where to now?"

She shot me an impish grin that would have made Garrett proud. "Where do you think?"

She started off toward the kitchen, and I followed behind. I never would have figured her for a drinker when I met her. But, then again, I wouldn't have expected her to try to strip Garrett, so maybe my judgment really was crap.

When she found what she'd been looking for, she grabbed a can of beer for herself and then snagged one for me from some dopey-looking underclassman. She flashed him her highest wattage smile and flipped her hair. He instantly forgave her.

She handed me the can with a nod, then cracked open her beer and took a huge swig.

"Much better than the bonfire refreshments," she said, admiring it.

"Glad they're up to your high standards."

I held my unopened can and looked around. I was uncomfortable being there for more reasons than I could count. Memories clung to every wall in that home—memories of a time that part of me wished had never ended. I'd managed to ignore the bulk of them the other night, but that night it seemed like everywhere I turned, my mind betrayed me with snapshots of me and AJ. The food fight we'd had cleaning up after Thanksgiving dinner. The wrestling match we'd had in the living room that his older brother, Matt, officiated for us. The kiss we'd stolen on the back porch before Garrett found us—the first kiss we'd ever shared.

My eyes snapped shut, trying to force the images out of my mind. I could hear Tabby talking to me, asking me if I was okay, but it wasn't she who pulled me from my memory hell. It was the hand of the person I'd once thought caused it on my shoulder that did.

"Ky, are you all right?" AJ asked, his face only inches from mine.

I shook my head in a final attempt to clear it.

"Yeah. Of course. I just have a bit of a headache and this music feels like it's boring a hole through my brain. No biggie." I added an ambivalent shrug to emphasize my sarcastic reply.

"Be right back," he said before disappearing through the crowd.

Tabby turned her focus back to me—more specifically, my head—and frowned.

"I didn't know you had a headache. We didn't have to come. . . ."

"Ah, but we did, Tabs. Because pretenses—sometimes we have to keep them up." She scrunched her features in confusion, and I sighed. "AJ and I are really trying to navigate this friend thing. If I hadn't come after his big win tonight, it would have been a bit of a slap in the face, right?"

"Yeah . . . I guess. But do you want to be here? Around AJ?"

There it was: the million-dollar question.

"I think so."

Her confusion bled to mischief. "He really is a great guy."

"I thought you were dropping that schtick, Tabby—"

"And *really* good-looking."

I let out a sigh. There would be no deterring her in that moment, so instead, I decided to play along.

Just as I went to reply, the volume of the music decreased to a tolerable level. The kind you could easily hear things over, especially if someone—namely me—was still yelling like a jet was flying over.

"AJ really is hot."

Those four words practically echoed through the kitchen. Everyone in there turned their attention to me and my rosying cheeks. In my best attempt to slough off my mortifying outburst, I simply shrugged and said, "Well, he is." That's when I looked at Tabby, whose gaze was fixed on something behind me. Judging by the size of her eyes, I knew it was AJ.

Mother. Fucker.

Slowly, like I was in a space-time continuum or vacuum or wormhole thingy, I turned to find him a few feet behind me, doing his best not to beam with victory. Apparently, he, and everyone else in a twelve-foot radius, had heard what I'd said.

"Is the music better now?" he asked, the corners of his mouth fighting hard against their desire to upturn.

"Yes . . . much."

Without another word, I cracked open the can in my hand and started chugging down its contents. The bitter taste of warm beer ran down my throat, but it was a welcome sensation. It bought me time. Time to think about how I was going to escape hot AJ, who'd just overheard me declare as much.

For a moment, I wondered if my night could get any worse.

Five seconds later, I didn't have to wonder anymore.

Just as I was about to address AJ, I heard my name called from the opposite side of the kitchen. Dawson stood in the entryway, eyeing the beer in my hand. His look of disapproval was plain.

I hazarded a glance at AJ, who did little to hide the disappointment he felt at Dawson's appearance, then looked over at Dawson. To his credit, he kept the smug satisfaction I knew he felt from his face. He was clearly pleased with himself for tracking me down.

"Sorry I'm late," he said, approaching me. "I had trouble finding the place."

That made sense, given I hadn't told him anything about the party or that I was going.

"No problem. You want a beer? I think I need another beer. . . ."

I stepped out from between him and AJ. That tension sandwich was way too much for me to handle. Tabby joined me, grabbing two beers from the fridge. We immediately opened them, clinked them together, then started chugging. When we both came up for air, I could see Tabby's eyes full of uncertainty.

"It'll be fine, Tabs," I assured her, though I felt none of that assurance myself. "We're all friends, remember?"

"Do they know that, though?" she asked, casting them a wary glance. "I mean really? Because the way AJ just went from elated to devastated the second your boyfriend walked in, I'm not sure he does."

"That's his problem to sort through. Not mine."

"Not if Alex makes it his first."

Panic shot through me, and my eyes drifted over to where the two were standing, doing their best to have a civil but unbelievably awkward conversation.

"Alex isn't going to do anything to AJ. Not if he wants to live."

I said those words a little louder than I needed to. The beat of pause in Dawson's movements told me he'd heard me loud and clear.

"If you say so," she replied, opening the fridge again. "I think we might need another of these." She handed me another can of beer with a smile. "You know, most girls would die for the attention of either one of them, Kylene. Try to leave a few for the rest of us, okay?"

I choked on a laugh. "Listen, right about now, you're welcome to whichever. I'm starting to think boys are more trouble than they're worth."

"Are we now?" Dawson said softly in my ear, making the hairs on my body stand at attention. "That's not what you said the other night. . . ."

Tabby's eyes went wide, her eyebrows shooting up to her hairline in surprise. And then she started giggling. The sound was manic and unnerving and growing in volume. Clearly Dawson had surpassed her comfort level, and she all but ran away from us, red-faced and embarrassed.

"I believe I called you a cocky son of a bitch the other night."

He shrugged. "So maybe your love language is a little rough around the edges."

I wanted to be mad at him—I really did, but it was a stellar comeback and I was two beers into the night. Two shotgunned beers at that. Instead of telling him off, I laughed. *Hard*.

I tried to ignore the distinct edge it held.

I turned in his arms to face him, wiping the tears from the corners of my eyes before they could make my mascara run. His expression was so unexpected that it almost stopped my hysterics cold. A genuine, bright smile was plastered across his face, lighting up his hazel eyes so much that I noticed the flecks of green in them. Everything around us seemed to fade away for a second: the crowd, the noise—even AJ and Tabby. I felt like I was really seeing Dawson for the first time. Not the jaded detective who had wormed his way into my life, but the new recruit who hadn't had every ounce of joy drained from him yet. A twinkle of the boy who still remained in the young man.

"Well," I said, trying once again to shake unwelcome thoughts from my mind, "I'm a little rough around the edges, so I think that's only fitting."

Mischief emanated from his grin. "I wouldn't want it any

other way. Now, shall we leave Tabby and the sad puppy alone and make our way downstairs?"

"The sad puppy has a name," I sighed.

His smile remained. "I know."

With that, he led the way down the hall to the basement door.

The basement was packed with JHS students. The unfinished portion of the basement was stuffed with drunken teens surrounding a fold-up outdoor table with bright red plastic cups decorating its surface. The occasional cheering and chanting coming from that side of the room let me know that the drinking games were in full swing over there. I made a sharp right to avoid them.

Unfortunately for me, the finished half of the basement wasn't much of an improvement. There, kids were draped all over the well-worn couches and other bodies, creating a modern-day version of some Italian fresco painting—thankfully, these people weren't naked, though. At least not yet.

I looked up to Dawson and found him grinning like a jackass. He couldn't have been more elated by my discomfort.

"Maybe being friends with AJ isn't that important," I said under my breath as I continued into the room. But Dawson waylaid me, pulling me into the tiny laundry room. My eyes went wide with surprise but as soon as I saw his business face on, I calmed down.

"Why aren't you answering your phone?" he asked, sounding mildly irritated.

"It didn't vibrate!" I pulled it out to show him only to find that I'd put it on the alarms-only setting. "I must have accidentally turned it to silent," I said weakly.

"It's fine, Danners. I tried to call to tell you that the lab is booked up. They can't run the DNA test until tomorrow. I had to cash in some favors to get it in that soon."

I couldn't help but wonder what those favors were.

"So we'll know tomorrow?"

He nodded. "With any luck, this will all be over soon." I couldn't tell if he meant the case or our arrangement. Maybe both. "Listen . . . about last night—"

"I'm sorry I didn't tell you sooner," I interrupted.

He smiled at my apology.

"Can I finish?" he asked, his tone irritated but almost playful. "I was about to say that I understand why you did what you did. I'm not mad at you."

Pigs around the world took flight.

"Okay . . . good. Glad we got that all cleared up."

When he said nothing in return, just stood there staring at me curiously, I walked out of the room, my cheeks hot and my mind flustered. I took in everyone else who was occupying the basement. The second I did, I wanted to tuck tail and run. It was all the old crowd—the kids I'd called friends before everything went wrong and I'd left town. The people who'd turned on me, calling me a liar and a slut and a raging bitch when I went to the sheriff about those photos that had been taken. Dawson didn't know all the details of that part of the story, so I kept my mouth shut and bit my tongue. It was too late to turn and leave anyway.

I'd already been spotted.

"Well I'll be damned," Heather Samson shouted when she pulled away from whoever it was she was making out with long enough to see me. "Kylene Danners. . . . Are you lost or something?"

I looked around, feigning confusion. "Isn't this the primate exhibit at the zoo?"

Her haughty expression devolved into an ugly snarl. Her

cage always had been easy to rattle. She hadn't changed a bit.

"Why don't you just leave? You don't belong here."

"Why would I leave when I'm learning so much about the mating rituals of wild animals, Heather? It's fascinating. Really. But, if it makes you feel better, I will leave if you start flinging poop."

She shot to her feet with only the slightest of wobbles. Barely noticeable, really—unless you had a pulse and open eyes.

"Why are you here?" she asked, stepping over someone who had passed out on the floor.

"AJ asked me to come, so I came. Seems pretty simple really."

She rolled her eyes. "I guess your whoring tendencies didn't get any better while you were gone playing city girl."

My eyes shot to the lap she'd just been riding and back to her. "I guess yours didn't, either."

She came to stand before me, eyeing me like she was about to throw down. Heather was a tough girl. She'd had a rough life growing up, and her right cross was a testament to that childhood. The second she stepped to me, everyone in the make-out room stopped, their attention now on us.

It was the kitchen all over again—only worse.

I could practically feel Dawson behind me, the tension in his body pressing through the air into mine. He knew he'd have to let whatever was about to go down play out in a realistic manner. He'd break it up for sure, but not before we each got in a couple of hits. Looking like a responsible adult was exactly what he didn't need.

"You calling me a whore?"

"I'm saying that it's kinda hard for you to call me one while you're riding some guy on a couch."

"At least there's only one of him, not a hot tub full of guys."

Against every ounce of good judgment I had, I let a wicked smile spread wide across my face.

"The night's early, Heather. Don't sell yourself short just yet."

Her eyes were wild with rage, but she managed to contain herself a little longer. She had more restraint than I remembered. Her fuse was usually shorter than mine.

"That's a mighty high pedestal you're on for a cheating whore daughter of a murderer, who ruined this town's chances of making it to the state football championships."

"And what a pity that is—Jasperville couldn't dope its way to victory. It really is a bummer that Garrett and I almost getting killed by that psycho Donovan put such a damper on the season."

"It sure is. Would have been better if you'd died. For everyone." Her words were shards of ice that bit into my skin, making my blood run cold. Not because I was scared of her, but because I knew she wasn't just speaking for herself. Looking around the basement, it was apparent that others felt the same way. My death would have been a welcome exchange for a state football championship in a town where the sport was practically a deity. That they didn't care about cheating a little to make that happen.

Guess I was a Throwaway Girl, too.

While I tried to calm myself enough to respond, I felt a warm arm around my shoulders pull me in tight against an even warmer body. Dawson to the rescue—again.

"It wouldn't have been better for me," he said. His voice was deep and threatening, and I knew for a fact it was the one he used while interrogating suspects. He was intimidating when he spoke like that, and, judging by the way Heather had gone from triumphant to cowed in the blink of an eye, she thought so, too. "Maybe you should get back to what you were doing." He nodded toward the couch where the guy she'd just been making out with was about to lock lips with someone else. "Before you're so five minutes ago."

He turned to walk away, dropping his arm from my shoulders. While he pushed forward through the gathered crowd, he reached back to take my hand and guide me through them, interlocking his fingers with mine. I couldn't help but look down at them, wound together in such an intimate way. In my mind, I knew what he was doing was for show—to look like the good boyfriend watching out for his girl. But deep down, my beer-buzzed inner romantic, who barely ever saw the light of day, delighted in the act. There was something so protective about it that, in that moment, I almost bought the lie. But as we made it to the other side of the basement, littered with red cups and drunken bodies, he let me go, shattering the fantasy my inebriated mind had entertained. Dawson and I were nothing more than an illusion—an inconvenient necessity. He wasn't there to protect me. He was there to stop a killer and a pimp, and nothing more.

And if the DNA results came back a match linking Coach to the body, he'd be gone.

I shook my head and cracked open the beer I'd taken from Tabby upstairs while Dawson stared at me. Under his scrutiny, I leaned against the wall in the corner of the room and drank. I watched while everyone else there ignored my presence—as if I no longer existed. As if I were dead. It made me long for Garrett, who understood what it was like to fall from grace, even if his fall was by choice. It made me wonder if anyone in that room would have mourned us at all if Donovan had succeeded. With that unpleasant thought in my mind and an empty can in my hand, I made my way upstairs to find another, then track down AJ and Tabby.

I needed to be around people who truly cared about me.

I planned to drink until I forgot that everyone else there didn't.

FORTY-FOUR

Dawson and I eventually found Tabby in the living room, delighting a group of underclassmen with her completely fictional stories about growing up in Canada: how big her igloo was, her pet moose, etc. I shook my head and laughed, leaving him behind while I headed to the kitchen. I was on a mission, and even the Canuck's tales of the Great White North couldn't derail me. But damn were they funny.

Since the stash of beer was getting low, I grabbed two cans, thinking it best to plan ahead, and turned to leave the room. I almost slammed into AJ in the process. A can fell from my hands and rolled across the tile floor. Some asshole football player, whose name I couldn't remember, picked it up and sneered at me before opening it up and chugging it down.

". . . And the Lord taketh away," I sighed, trying to ignore the fact that AJ was hovering near me. I turned and smiled at him, giving the other can a little shake. "Good thing I still have this."

"I think maybe I should take that one, Ky," AJ said, reaching for the can.

"Oh no you don't," I replied, pulling away from him. "You are *so* not the beverage police. That's Garrett's job. Not yours."

"Well Garrett isn't here, so . . ." He reached for the can again and I weaved under his arm to head back down the hall. AJ caught my shoulder and snatched the can from my hand.

"You can be pissed all you want, but I think you're done for the night, Ky."

"You know what, AJ? I think I am done for the night. Done with drinking. Done with this party. Done with everything." I yanked my arm free and made my way to the front door. I'd been yelling, which had garnered the attention of most of the first floor. Tabby came darting around the corner to where I stood, her eyes full of concern. "C'mon, Tabs. I think it's time to go."

"Go?" Dawson's voice traveled down the hall from the front door, blocking my way. "Where exactly do you think you're going?" He headed toward me down the now-too-small hallway with AJ at one end, and him at the other. The brewing tension seemed to choke off the oxygen around me, making it hard to breathe.

"I'm leaving," I said.

"She can't drive," AJ argued. "She's had too much to drink."

Dawson flashed him a hard look, then returned his stare to me.

"Can I talk to you for a second, Ky?" It wasn't really a question, so I didn't bother answering. He indicated the stairs to the basement, and I begrudgingly moved toward them, descending back into the cavern of hostility.

When we reached the bottom, he took me by my arm and pulled me into a nook next to the boiler-room door near the drinking-game side of the basement.

"What are you doing?" he asked, his eyes full of disapproval.

"Escaping this hell. What are you doing?"

"Pretending to want to be here when my mind is fixated on a lab in Columbus."

"Great! Let's bail, then."

From the other side of the room, I heard laughter. The familiar sound of girls cackling at an inside joke. Somehow, I knew I was likely the butt of it.

"Looks like the new kid is getting tired of you already, Kylene." More laughter. "Don't worry, I'm sure you can find another guy from two hours away to date when this one runs from you screaming."

I looked up at Dawson, rage fueling my stare. "I'm going to shank that bitch," I said, my words little more than a growl. When I went to make a break for it, he stopped me without effort, stepping in my path and guiding me back against the wall. To someone looking on, it would have looked fluid—almost dance-like. Almost sexual. But I felt anything but sexual at that moment. Murderous seemed more fitting.

"She would hardly be worth going to prison for," he said, his steely stare glancing over to my potential victim and back.

"I'm not so sure about that," I replied, breathing hard. "Besides, I look pretty good in orange."

"Nobody looks good in orange. And you can't let her get to you."

"I normally don't. Alcohol seems to lower my tolerance for ignorant bitches."

"Clearly," he said dryly. Then he took a deep breath and leaned in closer to me. "She's needling you because she thinks she can."

"What's your point?"

"My point is, you're better than her. Better than all of them. Don't give them what they want."

"And what is that, exactly?" I asked, still trying to calm down.

"That fiery temper of yours—the one you can't keep a lid on."

I wanted to argue, but even in my buzzed state, his words

made sense. With the wall at my back and nowhere to go, I looked up at Dawson, doing all I could to hide the frustration I felt. He was right, and I knew it, but I wasn't willing to show him that.

Punching him in the mouth would have only proved his point, but it was tempting.

"Stop scowling at me," he said, sweeping my hair to the side of my face. "We're supposed to be in love, remember?"

"Sometimes you make it really hard to."

He smiled. It was clear that he delighted in my pain. I had to refrain from kneeing him in the balls so I could delight in his.

"Only sometimes?"

"Always."

"Don't pretend you hate me, Danners. We both know that's not true."

"Do we?" I asked, staring up at him. His smug smile was reply enough. "If I don't hate you, then you need to stop pretending you can't stand me. For someone who doesn't want to, you spend a lot of time in my presence."

"We're both pretending. I'm just better at it than you are."

I bit my tongue and looked away from him to find Heather glaring at me from across the room. She said something to the kids around her before they all started laughing again. My blood boiled instantly.

Dawson followed my gaze over and frowned.

"Being just like them is starting to look like a really great plan right now, Dawson," I muttered under my breath. He caught my chin and gently turned my face toward him, breaking my death stare with Heather.

Then his hand fell away.

"Kids like her . . . they want you to fail because it makes them feel better. They know these are the best years of their lives. They peak at eighteen."

"Speaking from experience?" I asked, heat in my tone.

Darkness washed over his expression as he leaned in closer to me, his cheek brushing against mine.

"You are not the only person alive to think high school is a special kind of hell." His breath was light on my ear, and as much as I hated myself for it, my heart started to race. "If you want to beat them—really stick it to them—do the last thing they'd expect you to do right now. Show them that nothing they do can touch you." He pulled away just enough to pin deadly serious eyes on me, his face still so, so close to mine. "Make them eat shit and thank you for it." Before I had time to think it over, my hands drifted up to the small of his back, my fingers gripping his waist. "Even if it's a lie," he continued, "even if it's all pretend, don't ever let them see that they're getting to you."

My breath hitched in my throat as his forehead rested against mine.

"The last thing they'd expect . . . ," I mused as a flicker of mischief pulsed through me. I pulled his body so tight against mine that not a part of us wasn't touching. His head pulled away from me for a second, his eyes wide. "I bet they didn't expect this. . . ."

In a flash, my lips were on his, my tongue deep in his mouth. I ran my hands up his shirt, digging my nails into his back. After a moment's hesitation, he pressed back against me so hard that I could barely breathe. For a solid ten seconds, we kissed in the basement of AJ Miller's house.

And nothing about it felt pretend.

FORTY-FIVE

Given my less-than-sober state by the time we left, Dawson drove me home, lecturing me on the perils of teenage drinking, like the responsible law enforcement officer he was. He took Tabby home first, then started off toward my house on the other side of town, which left my car at AJ's overnight. Apparently, I'd have to figure out how to get that later.

And come up with a nonscandalous reason for it still being there.

I hated seeing Tabby walk up her front steps, tripping on them in classic Tabby style before fumbling her way inside. The second she had exited the car, the tension seemed to double. Dawson and I drove halfway home in silence, neither one of us knowing what to say. When I faked being asleep, he finally spoke.

"So, Danners . . . about that kiss," he drawled.

My eyes shot open. "New subject."

Seeing my instant anxiety, he started in on me.

"Don't get me wrong, It wasn't half bad—"

"Not really interested in your feedback—"

"But I'll admit, I didn't see it coming."

"Beer makes me do things. It's evil and should be destroyed."

"It makes you do things you don't have the balls to do when sober."

"You'd like to think so, wouldn't you?"

"Admit it, you've wanted to kiss me for a while now—"

"Please stop—"

"You've been dreaming of me at night—"

"Help me, Jesus—"

"Maybe next time will be better if—"

"Next time?"

"Yeah," he said as though I was the one who'd taken leave of my senses, not him. "The next time we break your PDA rules."

"Do you have your gun?"

"It could happen, you know. The case isn't closed yet. We might have to keep this ruse up for a while still. . . ."

"Please shoot me. I'm begging you."

He finally cracked a smile, unable to suppress his delight in the knowledge that he'd gotten the better of me.

"Calm down, Danners. I'm just messing with you." I slumped down in my seat with a mighty exhale. "But seriously, that can't happen again."

"Not gonna be a problem, hotshot."

"It's not just an age thing . . . there are too many reasons to count—"

"Shhhhh . . . it's quiet time. No more talking. You're much cuter when you're not talking."

"Cuter, huh?" *Ugggggh*. . . . Me and my stupid drunk mouth. "You think I'm cute?"

"I think you're still talking. . . ."

"Don't run away from your feelings, Danners."

"I'm not running, I'm trying to pass out and forget this night ever happened. The only thing I feel right now is nauseous."

"No puking in the car."

"Then you'd better drive faster."

"Are you serious right now? Are you really going to puke?"

"Will it get me home faster if you think I am?" The car slowed at least ten miles per hour. "I'll take that as a no."

He grew quiet for a moment, which made me nervous. A quiet Dawson was a thinking Dawson, and little good could possibly come of that.

"Tell me something: Do the kids at your school really hate you that much?"

I let out a mirthless laugh. "Yep."

He hesitated for a moment. "All because of Donovan?"

"Because of Donovan and my father and the topless picture scandal. And because they're a bunch of narrow-minded hicks that dream of being prom queen and having eighteen babies before they're twenty-five. I don't fit in here. . . ." I turned my gaze out the window. "I don't know if I fit in anywhere."

Silence fell upon us again, but this time, it was less welcome. I don't know why I'd told Dawson that. He wasn't exactly a bastion of sympathy. But maybe I hadn't realized—or been willing to acknowledge before that moment—that it bothered me as much as it did. Without Tabby and Garrett—possibly AJ—I had no clue how I would survive.

"Good," he said. His voice was firm but softer than normal. I turned to face him, ready to tell him what an asshole thing that was to say, but he cut me off at the pass. "Do you want to fit in with people like that? Derail your track in life to appease them?" My tongue went limp in my mouth. "Because if you did, you wouldn't be the kind of girl capable of clearing her father's name."

It felt like my heart stopped for an instant.

"But you still think he's guilty."

He nodded. "I do, but I'm slowly becoming convinced that you might just find a way to prove me wrong."

"If you really believe that, why aren't you trying to stop me?"

He pulled up at a stop sign about a quarter mile from

Gramps' house and turned to face me. "Because a small part of me wants to see you succeed."

"So I can prove you wrong about who my father is?"

"No," he said. "So you can prove me right about who I'm starting to think you are."

While my swimming mind tried to wrap itself around the subtext of Dawson's words, he pulled away from the stop and headed toward Gramps' house. The trip seemed to pass in a blink. He rolled into the driveway, killing the lights while the car idled.

"Thanks for the ride," I mumbled under my breath as I reached to open the door. My arm felt heavy, like it was resisting my commands. Like something in me wanted to force me to stay—to reply to Dawson's earlier words.

"Like letting you drive after drinking was ever an option," he said, a hint of teasing in his tone.

"Yeah. I guess it wasn't."

I finally managed to push the passenger door ajar and swing my leg out. Right before I stood up, Dawson caught my arm.

"Do yourself a favor and eat something before you go to bed. A lot of something, actually. You'll thank me for it in the morning."

"I'm sure I will."

His expression tightened as he looked at me across the dimly lit interior of his car, but he let me go a moment later, and I all but bolted away on unsteady legs. And they weren't weak from drinking. Dawson's words had shaken me. No matter how I tried to spin them, I couldn't find a hidden, snarky connotation. Nothing sarcastic underlying them.

I could hear the faint purr of the motor as I made my way up onto the porch and to the front door. It remained until I had the door unlocked and open. The car shifted into reverse and started to pull away, lights still off. I turned to watch Agent

Dawson back out of Gramps' driveway, his expression visible only with the help of the full moon above. Something about it was different. Concern creased its way into the set of his brow—the corners of his eyes. Maybe he was worried that he had said too much in the car. Maybe he felt guilty for what had happened between us at the party. Or maybe something else was brewing inside the hotshot detective that even he didn't understand, and his inability to comprehend it was what bothered him the most.

FORTY-SIX

I woke up with an uncontrollable desire to hit things. Sadly, it wasn't an uncommon event, but the party had my head spinning in too many directions to focus. I needed to get my shit together before the DNA results came. If the sex ring shut down, Dawson and I could drop our charade and he could go back home. Because that's what I wanted. Him gone. Long, long gone.

At least that's what I kept telling myself.

Confusion, along with the barrage of other emotions I didn't feel like unpacking at that moment, nagged at me until I was out of bed and getting dressed for the gym. I walked outside to find my car waiting for me. I tried not to think about the person who'd likely brought it home.

My phone buzzed in my pocket, and my adrenaline spiked out of reflex. I fished it out to find Meg's name on the screen.

"Hey, Meg. What's up?"

"Just wanted to let you know I got the signed papers, and I sent them off."

"Cool. Do me a favor—let me know when the files arrive. Before you call my dad."

Silence.

"Why would I need to do that?" she asked, her tone dubious.

"He's not happy about any of this, Meg. I don't think we

should discuss anything with him until you have something concrete, that's all."

I prayed she couldn't hear my heart beating wildly through the phone.

"You sure that's why?"

"Yeah."

Another pause.

"I'll be in touch, kid."

I hung up and released the breath I was holding. Meg was no fool; she knew something was up but was smart enough not to press the issue. Plausible deniability for the win.

The door to Tyson's gym squeaked loudly as I pushed it open, drawing attention from those already warming up. I got nods from a few, including Mark, who was kneeing one of the heavy bags. I waved, then ran in, kicking my shoes off. My head was already beginning to protest me being there, a headache brewing, but whether or not it was about to explode was beside the point. I still needed to hit something.

"Glad you could drag your ass out of bed in time to only be five minutes late," Kru Tyson shouted over the music. "You look like hell. Rough night?" I nodded, hating how my head pounded with the movement.

"So rough," I replied, walking over to grab a jump rope. "Apparently, when you drink too much, you get this thing called a hangover . . . who knew?"

He laughed at my response. Then he turned the music up louder.

"This'll help."

I spent the next thirty minutes wishing I hadn't been born. Two emergency trips to the bathroom to empty the contents of my stomach later, though, things were looking up. At least until I heard Tyson greet someone while I whaled on the heavy bag.

"Hey man, can I help you with something?"

"I'm looking for somebody," Dawson replied. There was a beat of pause in their conversation before Dawson spoke again. "And there she is. . . ."

I could practically hear Dawson's smile in his response.

I looked over my shoulder to find him standing in the small entry area, staring me down.

"You know him?" Kru Tyson asked, shooting me a curious look.

I sighed heavily. It wasn't an act. "Yep. That one's mine."

Tyson's eyes drifted back to the young fed, dressed in workout clothes, and gave him a thorough once-over. Tyson's mouth pressed to a thin line; he didn't seem to be overly impressed.

"Shoes off if you're coming in," he said before walking away, shooting me a "do you want me to make him leave?" look. I shook my head as Dawson approached.

You still have to pretend he's your boyfriend, I repeated to myself over and over under my breath.

"Hey, I've been trying to reach you," he said, coming to stand next to me. Too close to me. I took a step back, and he eyed me curiously. So did Tyson.

"Sorry. I'm smelly. Why are you trying to get a hold of me this early on a Saturday?" The irritated quirk of his eyebrow was answer enough. I took back the space between us that I'd just retreated and lowered my voice. "Did the DNA come back?"

"Danners!" Kru Tyson shouted. "You're either training or you're leaving, Your choice."

"Sorry!" I replied, turning to face the bag. With a jerk of my head, I told Dawson to get behind it. "You hold; I kick. Got it?"

"I can manage that," he replied, gripping the bag. I uncorked a switch kick on it that got his attention, and he held it tighter. "The test results aren't in yet. They should be soon though. I just wanted to let you know that as soon as we get the match, I'll be out of your hair." He hesitated for a second, staring at me over the bag. "No need for any repeat performances of last night."

I kicked the bag again.

"Well that's a relief," I said, not sounding nearly as relieved as I should have.

"Agreed." Silence fell between us for a minute until he thankfully broke it. Kicking and kneeing weren't doing nearly enough to release the tension I felt in that moment. "But then I think about what you told me the other night—about Reider. I can't let that go. I can't know that and walk away."

I stopped kicking.

"What are you saying?" I asked him, thinking back to our heated conversation and his unwillingness to see the truth I'd slapped down right in front of him.

"I'm saying, I need to see it through. Good or bad, I need to know what really happened that night."

"Even if it means you were wrong?" I asked, my voice soft and full of surprise.

"If your dad was framed, I can't, in good conscience, let him stay where he is. I want the real person responsible for Reider's death in prison, whoever that may be."

While the two of us stared at each other, Tyson yelled, "Switch!" My body moved out of sheer muscle memory, wandering to where Dawson stood behind the bag. He didn't budge. I looked up at the determination in his face as he stared back at me, jaw flexing.

"So, what do you say? Are you in or not?"

"Danners!" Tyson shouted again. "I mean it!"

"Sorry!" I replied, shoving Dawson around to the other side of the heavy bag.

"That's not an answer," Dawson said, taking his stance. "Are you in?"

A mischievous grin overtook his serious expression, and I couldn't help but mirror it.

"Hell yeah," I replied. "I'm *so* in."

The two of us walked out together half an hour later, sweating like crazy and laughing at how I'd dropped one of the heavy-weights with a leg sweep while we were sparring. Apparently, Dawson found the sound he'd made rather entertaining and couldn't let it go. Or maybe he just had a lot of pent-up stress that needed to come out, too, and that event set it off. Either way, there was something amazing about a laughing Dawson. Something my mind couldn't quite interpret.

He walked me to my car, standing on the passenger side as I threw my gear in the backseat.

"Kylene," he started before the sound of my phone ringing interrupted him. I rummaged through my bag until I found it. I didn't recognize the number on the screen.

"Hello?"

"It's me.".

"Jane . . . I mean, Shayna!" I said, popping out to stare across the hood of my car at Dawson.

"Something's wrong," she said, her voice full of panic. She started rambling on so fast that I could barely understand her. Seeing my distress, Dawson was at my side in a flash.

"Slow down! You need to slow down and say all that again."

She took a few breaths to compose herself, then started over.

"It's not Coach," she said plainly, regaining some of her typically irritated tone. "It can't be Coach."

"You can't know that yet. The DNA hasn't—"

"I *can* know that because I just got a text saying I have to meet someone at Marco's tonight." My eyes went wide. "And it looks like a normal meet, but I have never gotten a message like this—not with this short notice—something's wrong."

Oh. Shit.

"Okay," I said, turning to Dawson. "We need to talk—in person. We have to come up with a plan."

"What if it's the guy who really killed Danielle?" she said, her panic taking over again.

"Do you trust me?" I asked her.

"What?"

"Do you trust me?"

She took a second to reply. "Yes."

"Great, then I need you to meet me at 68 Willow Lane in an hour. Okay?"

"Yeah . . . yeah, I can do that. But Ky?"

"Yeah?"

". . . . I'm scared."

I took a deep breath. "I know. I am, too. But we're going to get this guy. . . . I'll see you in an hour."

I hung up, hands shaking, and turned back to Dawson, who was staring at his cell phone.

"What?" I asked. "What is it?"

"The DNA results," he said, disbelief in his voice. "They're not a match. Coach didn't kill Danielle. . . ."

"I know," I said softly. "The killer just texted Jane, I mean *Shayna*." He looked at me strangely and I realized I hadn't filled him in on that detail. "Long story. Anyway, she said her pimp set up a date for her tonight, but she doesn't buy it. She said everything about the normal protocol is off. She thinks someone's luring her there to take her out like he did Danielle."

"That's not going to happen," he said, storming over to his

car. "Go clean up and come straight over. We need to go back over all our evidence. We've missed something somehow. Maybe if we take Coach out of the running, we can better see who the killer really is."

He peeled out down the street, and I wasn't far behind.

FORTY-SEVEN

Shayna showed up at Dawson's looking wary as could be. She asked to use the bathroom and took off down the hall. Dawson and I used that time to have a hushed conversation about our informant.

"I'm not sure she's ready for this," I whispered.

"We don't have any other options. I talked to the sheriff. The risks have been addressed."

I didn't hear the bathroom door open—Dawson and I were too embroiled in our quiet argument to notice. It wasn't until we heard her gasp that we realized where Shayna had gone. We raced down the hall to where she stood in the whiteboard room, her mouth agape. Dawson took that opportunity to explain to her who he really was. She blinked a few times before her face regained some measure of animation, then she turned her attention to the intricate wall of suspects and evidence and we lost her all over again.

"We've narrowed down the suspects using the information we could find on the names you gave us," I said gently. "You're the reason we were able to do that."

"Lot of good it did," she muttered under her breath, reaching to touch Danielle's name. She followed the line that Dawson must have just drawn—the one connecting her to Coach.

Dawson started explaining the plan for the night, how he'd

arranged for the sheriff's department to stake out the parking lot with plainclothes officers to secure the perimeter of the building. He and I would follow Shayna there and enter the building a few minutes after she did, looking like a couple of teenagers on a date. He devised a signal for her to give if someone made contact with her via text, and myriad other precautionary measures that he'd come up with to make sure we wouldn't be blindsided by anything. In truth, we had the upper hand in the whole thing. Whoever was after Shayna didn't know that we knew.

At least, that was our hope.

By the time he finished, I was pretty sure she hadn't heard a damn thing he'd said. She was still staring at the whiteboard, presumably trying to make sense of all she saw.

"This ring here indicates the most likely suspects," I explained, pointing to the one containing names like Callahan, Coach, and Principal Thompson. "They're categorized by how many known connections they have with the girls. Coach and Callahan are six for six. Thompson has five. The rest have fewer."

She scrunched her face, then looked closer at the connections made and reasoning given. Then she pointed to Angela's name and tapped the board twice.

"This one," she started, pausing for a second. "Why isn't she tied to Principal Thompson?"

"Because she graduated before he took over the school," I said, thinking back over the timeline I'd created. "Thompson's first day was the beginning of the school year—we confirmed that through records at the School Administration Building. I also cross-referenced it with Principal Haynes' final day before he retired. He finished out the summer, then passed over the reins."

"Right, but Angela had summer school—"

"Which was done by the time Thompson started to transition into his new role," I said, not seeing where she was going.

She shot a dirty look over her shoulder. "It *was*, but that's not the point. I knew Angela from the trailer park. She used to get us booze and cigarettes. The neighborhood kids all used to hang out behind her place and party. Anyway, I remember one night sittin' there with her, she was in the best mood. The woman that had been teaching her English class for most of the summer had gotten mono or something and they'd had to find a replacement. I would never have remembered this if it weren't for how she went on and on about how hot he was for a teacher and how mad she was that he'd be the principal at the school right after she graduated."

My body went numb.

"Thompson has a degree in English," I said, my voice low and soft and full of disbelief. "I saw it in his office the other day."

Shayna nodded. "Angela was most definitely tied to Thompson. He taught her through the rest of the summer."

"And she died a few months later," Dawson added. "Do you know how long she was a part of the prostitution ring?"

Shayna shook her head. "Not exactly, but it wasn't very long. I know that much. Do you think it's him?" she asked, her eyes darting back and forth between Dawson and me.

"Not necessarily," Dawson replied.

"He's the right build. The right height. He has ties to all the girls—"

"And he'd have access to all their personal files," I added. "Their social histories. Information on where they lived, who their parents were. He'd also know if they were having problems at school, who their friends were, if any. He had everything he needed to profile those girls." My eyes drifted over to Shayna. "Have you had much interaction with him?"

Her face went pale.

"Yes. After my mom had her back surgery—when she got addicted to pills—and everything fell apart, I met with him pretty regularly. He wanted to check up on me, see how things were going. . . ."

"How much did you tell him?" Dawson asked.

She exhaled hard. *"Everything."*

I looked to Dawson as he weighed her words, his brow furrowed and eyes narrowed.

"How long after that did you start . . . *working*?"

"About the time we stopped meeting," she said, her voice low and distant. "I was a junior."

My stomach churned.

"Do you know if any of the other girls had the same relationship with him?" Dawson asked. She shook her head, and he frowned. "It doesn't matter. We don't have time to figure that out now. We're going to follow through with the plan tonight. Hopefully when it's over, we'll know exactly who's behind it all."

Before I knew it, it was time to leave. Shayna went and got in her car, which made Heidi look like a dream come true, and Dawson and I got into his sedan. We would trail her at a distance to Marco's and wait in the parking lot for a few minutes before going in just in case someone had any suspicions about her being followed.

As I watched her walk into the pizzeria, I wondered if I was capable of pulling off this high-stakes plan or if my paranoia and lack of sleep combined with the rising anxiety I struggled to keep at bay would get the best of me. I could feel my mind spiraling with doubts—my heart racing with adrenaline. Even through the anxious haze, I knew I couldn't afford to screw up that night. If I did, the consequences would be dire.

"So now we wait?" I asked Dawson, whose eyes were pinned on where Shayna sat inside.

"Now we wait."

Silence.

"She's going to be okay, right?" I asked, hating how small my voice sounded. I needed to pull myself together.

"She is. We have every part of the parking lot covered by deputies. Higgins himself is inside eating. We'll be there, too. There's no way this guy is getting to her without us knowing."

"Okay . . ."

"It's going to work out, Danners. Just breathe and try to remember that once this is over, Shayna and the others can start to get their lives back—things can go back to normal." *Normal.* I had no clue what that meant anymore. When I didn't respond, he hazarded a glance my way. "Isn't that what you want? To get your old life back?"

What a loaded question that was.

I contemplated it for a moment as I watched Shayna hunched over her soda. Could anything go back to normal after all that had happened? After dead bodies and murder attempts and topless pictures? After an imprisoned father and a turncoat mother and a town that abandoned me?

No. No it couldn't.

But even deeper than all that was an implication I couldn't ignore. One of the boy I used to love and may love still. AJ was a piece of that normalcy Dawson was hinting at, and the fact that he did gave me pause. Maybe AJ could help balance my life—help fill a gaping void that had existed since I left Jasperville—but something about Dawson suggesting that hurt. Like he was happy to pawn me off on someone else. Like he wanted to bail after all we'd been through together. He'd suggested it so casually, like it didn't faze him in the least.

That stung more than it should have.

"Yeah," I said, voice soft. "It'll be great."

He said nothing for a minute, then opened his car door.

"It's showtime, Danners."

He waited for me at the back of the car. When I stepped up beside him, he could clearly see my nerves fraying, so he reached over and took my hand in his to lead me into the restaurant. In that moment, his hand was a lifeline, a grounding force that I needed. His confidence was contagious, and I could feel it easing my fears with every passing second.

We got settled into a booth on the far side of the pizzeria and waited to be served. Dawson was positioned with his back to the door so he could better keep an eye on Shayna. I let my eyes drift around the place, casually scanning the faces of everyone there. It didn't take long for that activity to spike my blood pressure.

It seemed like every potential suspect was there.

Gotta love small towns on a Saturday night.

Callahan was in a corner booth surrounded by a few other JHS staff. He caught me looking at him and his expression soured. I quickly looked away.

Principal Thompson wasn't with them, which was a relief in some ways and not in others. If he really was the guilty party, I needed him to show himself so we could get this over with.

Just as I finished assessing who was there, Mr. Matthew walked out of the hallway that housed the bathrooms and made his way to a table. He picked up his leftovers box and headed past us to the door. He noticed me along the way and smiled.

"You comin' by the shop for an ice cream after this?" he asked.

"Maybe. If I leave enough room," I said, trying to steady my voice.

He laughed and shook his head. "There's always room for ice cream, Kylene. At any rate, I'll leave you kids to your date. Tell your gramps I said hello again for me."

I let out an exhale as he disappeared through the entrance.

Dawson ordered something small when the waitress came, but I didn't pay any attention. I just kept running over the possibilities in my mind as I looked at everyone in the restaurant. Was it Callahan? Or was he working with someone else? Was a woman involved, too? Or was it Principal Thompson after all? Or Coach, even if he wasn't the killer? Or maybe it wasn't any of them at all. Maybe Tyson really was involved, even if he didn't kill Danielle. Maybe that was a one-off somehow. Maybe he really had killed the others.

Or maybe we'd overlooked someone altogether. Someone like Marco, who had a criminal record and access to everyone in town. Surely one or more of the girls could have worked there, too? Maybe under the table? I looked over to find Marco's hulking frame turned toward where Shayna sat, his eyes clearly pinned on her.

My mind started to race even more.

I was wound so tight that I nearly screamed when Dawson reached across the table and rested his hand on mine.

"I just got a text from Shayna. She said that her date is over fifteen minutes late and that never happens."

"Okay," I said, taking a cleansing breath. "So now what?"

"I'm going to go pay for our food, and we're going to head outside. She'll be out right behind us. Wait here."

The cold sweat of realization ran down my spine. Nobody was coming for Shayna. We'd either been made or Shayna had been wrong.

"Time to go," Dawson said, leading the way to the door.

Once we were by his car, I found my voice again.

"Do you think someone tipped him off? One of the deputies?"

"It's possible," Dawson replied. "Which is going to be a problem for them tonight when I threaten to tear their lives apart until I find out who, if any of them, it was."

Shayna strolled outside, looking calm and collected. She gave us a little wave like we were old friends and she'd just noticed us, then came over to Dawson's car.

"Now what?" she asked, her eyes filled with fear.

"We go back to my place and regroup," Dawson said.

"You should go with Shayna," I suggested. "She shouldn't be alone right now. I'll take her car and follow you."

"No!" Dawson said brusquely before lowering his voice. "You take my car. I'll drive Shayna's. I don't want you alone in her car. If someone follows, they could mistake you for her."

"But if she's in her car—"

"She'll have me," he said, his expression stern. "And I can handle it." I worked through the potential downfalls to his plan and found very few. He was right, so I did as he asked. He threw me the keys as he headed to Shayna's car with her at his side. "And Danners?"

"Yeah?"

"I don't want to see so much as a scratch on it when we get to my house, got it?"

I opened my mouth to launch into a rant about my perfect driving record but stopped when he looked back at me and smiled.

It was all I could do not to key it right then with him watching.

"I won't promise that," I replied, mimicking his expression.

"Stay behind me, and keep close, got it?"

"Got it. I'll be right on your bumper."

I climbed in as Dawson backed Shayna's car out. He rolled toward the exit, waiting for me to follow. I went to stick the key in the ignition, then realized there wasn't one—just a push button to start it.

"What the hell is this?" I asked, pushing the button to no avail. I frantically searched for an explanation on how to fire up his fancy new car.

A knock on the window startled me, and I turned, expecting to find a pissed-off Dawson staring at me, prepared to mansplain how his old-man car worked. Instead, I found Principal Thompson gazing through the window at me, a familiar smile on his face.

My body went rigid.

He motioned for me to roll down the window, but I couldn't get that to work, either, so I just shrugged at him instead.

"Do you need help with your car?" he asked through the closed window.

"It's not mine. Just trying to sort out how to start it."

I looked down at the button again and saw that it gave all the instructions needed.

"Why don't you step out and let me show you," he said, trying the door handle. But I'd already locked that—force of habit.

"No, thanks," I said, pushing the button while slamming my foot on the break. When the car finally roared to life, I flashed him a nervous smile and threw the car in gear. I damn near ran over his toes as I backed out. Dawson was still waiting for me at the end of the parking lot. As soon as he saw his car pull up behind him, he turned onto the street. Before I did the same, I looked in the rearview to find Principal Thompson staring me down, his brow furrowed.

I fumbled with my phone as I drove, wanting to call Dawson, but I was way too hopped up on adrenaline after that encounter, and I dropped it.

"Shit!" I yelled, trying to reach across to the floor to retrieve it. When I nearly swerved off the road, I decided to pass on that and live instead.

I tried to slow my breathing and calm my mind. I was okay. Shayna was okay. It was all going to be all right.

With Dawson ahead of me, we took a shorter route to his house. One that led us around the perimeter of town to save time. We were the only cars on the road, which helped calm my anxiety, but I wouldn't feel better until we were all back at his place.

He was probably a quarter mile or so ahead of me, headed for the train tracks. Not long after he crossed, the lights began to flash and the guards came down. I was tempted to speed up and go under them but thought better of it. I didn't want a lecture from Dawson about me endangering myself and his pristine car. Instead, I slowed my approach, in no hurry to get to the roadblock in my way.

I took that moment to grab my phone off the floor and call Dawson.

"Hey," I said the second he picked up. "Thompson was there tonight. He came up to your car when I was trying to start it. He tried to get me to step out under the guise of wanting to help."

"How was he acting?" Dawson asked, his voice tight.

"Normal, which made it that much creepier."

The blast of the train's horn cut through the night air, nearly deafening me. I could see Dawson's taillights on the far side of the barricade, waiting for the train to pass so I could catch up. It was a comforting sight.

"If Thompson is behind this, we're going to get him," he said. I couldn't tell who he was trying to reassure.

The train finally roared past, blocking my view of Dawson and Shayna. Just as I settled back in my seat, waiting for it to pass, a flash of light from my left temporarily blinded me. I turned to see headlights barreling toward me from a remote railway access road. I reached for the gear shift to throw it in reverse, but my hand fumbled with it, the setup in Dawson's car different than Heidi's. Before I switched gears, those headlights were upon me. With a terrible crash, Dawson's car was T-boned and pushed toward the edge of the road. I screamed as it rolled over the adjacent embankment, the crunch of metal and glass breaking, drowning me out. The car rolled until it hit the bottom, slamming to a stop. While I sat there for a moment, stunned but alive, the strangest thought flashed through my mind. As my vision swam and darkness encroached, I wondered what Dawson would say when he found me.

He was going to be so pissed about his car.

FORTY-EIGHT

"Time to go," Dawson said, pulling me into his arms. The ringing in my ears made his voice hard to recognize, but his hands were not unkind as he hauled me away.

"What happened?" I asked, my head woozy, my speech slurred.

"You were in an accident," he said. I let my aching head loll against his chest. Sleep called for me—raged for me to join it. The night wrapped around me like a blanket, tucking me into the arms of my partner, and I relaxed in his hold, taking a deep breath to help clear the pounding in my head. When I did, something niggled in the back of my mind, just out of reach. Something familiar.

Something wrong.

"Where's Shayna?" I mumbled against his chest.

I felt it rumble beneath me, a deep vibration of a laugh coursing through him into me. *That's not funny*. . . . my mind thought, feeling swimmy and disconnected from my body. *Why does he think that's funny* . . . ?

"I'll get her soon," he replied, the rough sound of gravel reverberating as he laughed again.

My brain caught hold of the sensation in the back of my head and yanked it forward, parading it in front of my mind's eye. That wasn't Dawson's voice. That wasn't Dawson's laugh.

Instinctively, I began to struggle against his hold, but it tightened around me like a vise.

"The hard way it is, then," he said, dropping me to the ground with a thud. My head knocked against the concrete, making my vision dance again as I struggled to get my bearings. A kaleidoscope of tires swirled before me and I reached out to grab one and haul myself up, but an arm wrapped around my throat, choking off my air supply. Like a novice, I pawed at his forearm, panicking as the darkness moved closer, narrowing my vision. "You just don't know when to butt out, do ya? Well, this time, it's gonna cost you."

"Dawson," I croaked, my voice more of a desperate wheeze than the cry for help I'd hoped it would be.

With that final word, the darkness swallowed me once again.

When I tried to open my eyes, I found more darkness waiting for me in the form of a blindfold. It was too tight against my throbbing head, but when I tried to remove it, I realized my hands were bound behind my back. I sat propped up against a cold, hard surface. The musty smell in the air around me told me I was underground.

But at least I wasn't dead—not that kind of underground.

My first inclination was to scream for help, but the plea fell dead on my tongue. Whoever had gone to all that trouble to capture me was hardly going to stash me away where my calls for aid would be heard. No, I'd be tucked away somewhere far from anyone who could rescue me.

While panic rose within me, I tried to recall all the details of the ride home. Keeping my mind busy was the only way I knew to hold it together. It was also the only way I had a chance at figuring a way out of the mess I was in.

Thankfully, I hadn't lost any pieces of that evening in the

crash. I worked my way through the facts as I knew them one by one. What we'd done before going to Marco's. Who'd been there that night. That we couldn't have gotten far before Dawson found his wrecked car.

My mind clawed frantically to hold onto that thread of hope, but continually came up short. I didn't know if Dawson and Shayna were safe. I didn't know who my captor was. I didn't know where I was or how I got there. All I did know was that whoever it was had been two steps ahead of us for longer than I liked to think about, and that didn't bode well for me.

And Dawson . . .

He was probably going out of his mind trying to find me.

"Dammit!" I whispered, wriggling against my bonds. My feet were free, but that did me no good. I couldn't exactly untie my hands with them. But I could search the room with them. . . .

Swishing them like I was doing half a snow angel, I worked my way around, hoping I'd eventually run into something. I continued the awkward movement, scooching along on my butt as I did. It seemed to go on forever, but I eventually ran into something solid. The distinct sound of foot on wood echoed through the space. The sound was short-lived, letting me know the room wasn't that large. *A home basement?* I wondered, as though that detail was super helpful. I kicked at the wood and it inched away from the contact, dragging along the concrete floor. Table leg. But more helpful than that realization was the distinct sound of metal objects clanging atop it at the reverberation. Those were going to be my ticket out of captivity, assuming at least one of them was sharp.

I managed to get to my feet only to crash over again, my equilibrium clearly off from the accident. As I lay on the ground, breathing hard to quell the nausea, I heard Kru Tyson in my mind: *You get knocked down, but you don't stay down. You fight. You fight until the fight is over. . . .*

"The fight's not over yet," I muttered to myself, rolling onto my side. Again, I forced myself to my feet in an awkward and unsteady motion, but this time I remained upright. Without my sight to help focus on the horizon, it took an insane amount of effort just to take a small step forward—then another, and another—until my hips were pressed up against the square edge of the table. Using it to help keep my balance, I slowly turned so that my hands could roam the table for something sharp.

The second my fingers grazed something, my heart stopped cold.

One by one, I took inventory of what lay on top of that table. Yes, there were definitely tools there that would be able to free my hands from the ropes binding them, but my mind was too focused on what else they could be used for to care. Gardening shears, tin snips, and a variety of other outdoor and construction paraphernalia were neatly aligned across the table. Had they been more haphazard, maybe I wouldn't have jumped to the worst conclusion possible. But they weren't, so I did. Whoever had put them there had taken steps to line them up in a precise and organized fashion, like a surgeon would his implements. I wasn't in a basement at all.

I was in a torture chamber.

FORTY-NINE

My blood pressure skyrocketed.

"Oh my God . . ."

I repeated those three words over and over again while I fumbled around the table behind me for something I could use to free my hands. I settled on what I thought were pruning shears—the kind that were perfect for snipping off fingers. With that morbid possibility settling upon me, I held them in my right hand and hooked the sharp edge against the ropes. My sawing motion was jerky and awkward and made the muscles of my forearms burn within seconds, but I could feel progress being made, so I kept at it despite the pain. Having those shears used on me in other ways promised to be far worse.

When I felt one of the twisted fibers let go, I muffled a cry of joy. Biting my lip, I ground the blade against the remaining rope as hard as I could, though my arm screamed at me to stop. *Almost free* . . . I thought as cord after cord snapped. I could practically smell the crisp fall air and feel the bite of its wind on my face.

Then reality punched me in the gut.

A distant sound interrupted my fantasy—the sound of crunching leaves and gravel under the weight of a vehicle. My captor was coming.

I hacked at the remaining rope, slicing my skin in the process, the sharp sting of the cuts doing nothing to slow me. The slam of a car door made my heart jump and I bit my lip to contain the yelp of fear that nearly escaped. "Come on . . . come on . . ." I begged the rope to let me go. Finally, with a desperate slash, it released me from its hold and fell to the ground. A second later, I had my blindfold off, scanning my surroundings for a way out.

The ceiling was low—much lower than a normal basement—with a stumpy wooden staircase leading to the floor above. Footsteps echoed outside, and the jingle of keys punctuated their stop as my abductor paused to unlock the prison he held me in. Panic gripped me, but I shoved it down into a pool of black somewhere in my gut, praying it would stay there long enough for me to get myself out. I could melt down later, but the present required all my attention.

Heavy-soled feet fell upon the wood floor above me, forcing me into action. I knew it wouldn't be long before he was downstairs and ready to implement the menagerie of tools he had laid out for his pleasure. I had no interest in that.

I scrambled around the room, which was barren except for shelves lining the circumference of most of it and the table in the middle. There were no doors—no windows—to be seen. The only exit I knew of was the one at the top of the stairs that would deliver me right into the hands of my captor.

I had no interest in doing that, either.

Grabbing some pointy object from the table, I quietly worked my way around the room, trying to find a place to hide. I was small enough to tuck myself away into tiny places. Maybe if he'd thought I'd already escaped, he'd leave to go find me. If not, I would have the element of surprise on my side, which was about the best I could do under the circumstances. Quickly and quietly, I scurried through the room trying to find something on the shelves to use for cover. I pulled boxes down, doing my best not to make any noise in the process, but it was hard. One that proved far heavier than I expected came crashing to the ground. The dirt floor did a lot to absorb the sound, but I knew it hadn't been enough. The immediate pause of footsteps mulling about above spoke to that fact.

Fear like I'd never felt before slammed into me.

I was going to die.

I looked up to the heavens, prepared to beg for my soul, when the soft glow of light fell upon my closed eyes. They shot open to find sunlight pouring in through a small, filthy window. One small enough for ventilation but little else. One I was about to try and cram my ass through.

I climbed up the shelving, prepared to smash out the glass, but upon inspection I could see the casing had rotted away. With one rough tug, the entire pane came loose. I tossed it on top of the shelf and scrambled through the opening. I managed to get my upper half through without issue, but once my legs were unable to push off the shelving, my body hung from the not-so-egress-window. I was stuck.

"No no no no . . . ," I muttered under my breath, wiggling wildly. I clawed at the loose dirt and moss surrounding the building, doing everything I could to pull myself out. It was then that I heard the muffled opening of a door. I knew in my heart it was the door to the basement. I was about to be caught.

No longer afraid of making noise, I grunted hard, releasing my breath like I so often had in Muay Thai to conjure as much strength and power as I could. To land a fight-ending blow. Like a war cry, it left my mouth, and my lower half shot through the window. I was on my feet in a dead sprint seconds later, the angry shouting of a man the soundtrack to my escape.

I was at a clear disadvantage—I had no idea where I was or where I was going, but I knew enough to just keep running. The one advantage I had was a head start, and I needed to milk that for all it was worth and pray that my abductor's cardio was lacking. A lot.

The sun was far higher in the sky than I'd expected. It was afternoon from what I could tell, and I was heading west toward the falling sun. The hills around me were dense with firs and birch and pine, and they bit into my skin as I ran. I hadn't even realized that my coat had gone missing somewhere between the car accident and my escape. It left me horribly exposed and vulnerable to the elements. Another hurdle I hadn't needed but was given nonetheless.

I pumped my arms and legs faster, jumping over downed trees and brambles and branches, praying that I wouldn't stumble upon the bodies of the missing girls along the way. Morbid, but true all the same. Denial was elusive in that moment. I knew all too well what fate would have in store if I was caught. I wondered if Dawson was alive and if he'd ever find me, or if I would be yet another disappearing girl turned forgotten headline. I really would become the next Throwaway Girl of Jasperville County.

No . . . I thought as a rogue branch snagged my ankle and dropped me to the leaf-covered forest floor in a heap. *No* . . .

Over the rushing blood in my ears and my jagged breaths, I could hear something in the distance. A soft rumble. A quiet thrum of an engine. Somewhere out there was a vehicle, one far bigger than the one my attacker drove. A semitruck? Maybe a construction vehicle. Definitely something large and diesel consuming.

My ticket home.

I shot to my feet and continued my blistering pace toward nothing and everything, clinging to the hope that I wasn't imagining things—that I really was near a road or quarry or mine. Something with people. People who didn't want to torture and kill me.

The ground beneath my feet started to angle downhill, but the density of trees was unrelenting. I couldn't see where I was headed, but I could still hear the occasional rumble of an engine in the distance. And they were getting louder.

As I ran, sunlight started to pierce the canopy, streaming welcome rays to light the way to safety. Going as fast as I dared, I descended the steep embankment, heading to a break in the trees—a clearly man-made break. With a strangled cry, I broke through the tree line, almost hurtling my body right out into the road. The paved two-lane didn't look familiar to me, but it looked glorious nonetheless. I opted to head north, hoping to see a sign or crossroad that I recognized. Something to give me some sense of where I was. Because really, I could have been anywhere. I had no clue how long I'd been unconscious or if I'd been drugged. For all I knew, I was in another state.

I knew staying out in the open was a risk, but I felt it was one worth taking. I had no idea if my kidnapper was following me on foot or in a vehicle. I had to make a decision, so I went with the one that allowed me to get my bearings. I ran along the shoulder of the road, headed toward some signs posted far off in the distance. Cold wind bit at my skin as I ran, trying to pull me from my adrenaline high that allowed me not to feel much of anything. I did what I could to ignore it, thinking about getting to a phone and shelter instead.

I was close.

So, so close.

In the distance, I saw a car come into view, headed my way. I sighed with relief. The cavalry had arrived. I was going to be okay. I was going to be saved.

In dramatic cinematic fashion, I stood in the middle of the road and flagged down the vehicle, tears running down my face. If I didn't get hit, everything was going to be okay. It would all be over.

The nondescript silver sedan pulled to a stop well shy of where I stood, and the driver's-side door opened. Relief flooded through me as I started toward the car, already rambling an explanation of who I was and what had happened and where I needed to be taken. But I stopped short the second I saw the driver. Something in the back of my mind screamed "*Danger,* Will Robinson. *Danger* . . ."

I knew that warning voice.

It was never wrong.

"Kylene," Mr. Callahan said as he approached. "Good Lord . . . are you okay? The whole town is looking for you."

I stared at him blankly, taking slow, cautious steps in retreat. My mind scrambled to put together the pieces of the puzzle as I did. He'd had access to all the girls that had gone missing over the years. He had a past that could be leveraged. He was at Marco's the night I was taken. He was smart and vindictive and not a big fan of mine—or girls just like me.

In so many ways, I fit the profile of the others.

"Get in the car, Kylene. . . ."

Fat fucking chance.

"I know it was you," I said, my voice cold and hollow and warning.

"I tried to warn you," he replied. "I told you this would happen. My friend and I have been trying to help those girls out of their bad situations for a long time."

Numbness and cold filtered through my system at his words.

"I'm sure you and Coach tried to help lots of girls that we don't even know about, but no more. You're done, Callahan! They found Danielle's body. . . ."

He eyed me strangely.

"You're not making any sense, Kylene. You must have hit your head." He reached his hand toward me and I recoiled, taking another step backward. "Just get in the car . . . please."

Callahan could gaslight me all he wanted, but there was no way in hell I was going anywhere with him. If I did, I was as good as dead.

Instead, I sprinted up the embankment just enough to get around him and his vehicle, heading back through the woods, my head reeling.

My physics teacher had kidnapped me.

Mr. Callahan killed those girls.

FIFTY

I could hear him yelling after me as I ran, but I tuned it out. I wished I'd gotten a better look at wherever it was he'd kept me bound in the basement. That would have been helpful information for the sheriff. When you get far enough into the backwoods of southern Ohio, it's easy to keep secrets and hide things, like unpermitted cabins or homes—or bodies. So easy to bury them deep among the trees that would never tell. I chastised myself for not thinking like my father would have. I couldn't afford to let Callahan get away with what he'd done.

I ran just inside the tree line, Callahan still in pursuit. He wasn't gaining on me, but he wasn't fading, either. I tried to think while my head throbbed and the blood pounding in my ears created the rhythm of my survival. I'd either outrun Callahan and live or be forever lost.

There was a bend in the road up ahead, and as I neared it a shiny black car came around. I threw myself in the middle of the road and darted straight for it. I dared a glance back to Callahan. He had paused on the side of the road. As soon as the car came to a stop, he took off running.

I darted to the passenger door, threw it open, and climbed in.

"My name is Kylene Danners and I've been kidnapped," I said before landing in the seat. I looked over to find a familiar face staring back at me with disbelief.

"By God, Kylene. What are you talkin' about?" Mr. Matthew asked, looking pale. "*Kidnapped?*"

"Yes. I need you to take me to the sheriff's department right away. Do you have a phone on you?"

He scoffed in the same way Gramps did when technology was involved.

"It's in the trunk with my things. I can go get it or I can just take you where you want to go."

"Where are we?" I asked, scanning the hills around us.

He looked at me strangely. "You don't know where you are?"

"No. I said I was kidnapped."

His eyes narrowed for a second then turned toward the road as he put the car into park.

"Sheriff's gonna have all kinds of questions for you when you get there," he said, staring south. "You sure you're up for that?"

"I don't have a choice."

He nodded. "I'm gonna go get that phone so you can call the sheriff and let him know you're all right."

He popped the trunk, then got out. Seconds passed before he returned with phone in hand.

"It's a shame," he said, reaching the phone toward me. "Girl like you . . . got next to nobody lookin' out for her. That's how bad things like this happen. . . ."

That voice in the back of my mind perked up, telling me to hear his words—to grab the phone and run. I reached for it slowly, controlling my shaking hand and breathing as I did.

"Bad things like what?" I asked, slipping the phone from his grasp.

His sideward glance met mine and I saw the devil in it.

"If you don't already know, you're about to find out."

Just as I threw open the car door to launch myself out, his outstretched arm wrapped around my neck, pulling me back against him. A cloth soaked in some chemical pinched over my mouth and I could feel my mind grow fuzzy. Unconsciousness came slowly but welcomed me like an old friend—one who secretly hated me and wanted me dead. Because that was what I was going to be when Matthew was finished with me.

Dead like the rest of them.

FIFTY-ONE

I awoke in a drugged haze.

My eyes fluttered—lids and lashes heavy as concrete—while my head swam. I had no idea what he'd given me, but it was damn effective. When I tried to move, I couldn't. Fear crept up my immobile spine.

"The dead has arisen," a voice called from somewhere in the room. "Nice of you to join me. I don't like workin' on the unconscious ones. Takes all the fun out of it."

Doing my best to ignore his words, I forced my eyes open enough to assess my situation. I was lying on my side against the wall of the basement with the window I'd escaped through. The stairs were on the far side of the room, taunting me. I had no chance of making it to them in my nearly paralyzed state. I could only assume that was why my hands and feet were untethered. No need to bind someone who can't move.

I tried to think clearly—to form some kind of plan, but my mind was still hostage to whatever chemical he'd given me. Something was clawing at the back of my brain, but the drugs seemed to shush it into submission. I watched Matthew saunter around the room, a new table positioned next to the one with all his torture implements, and I choked back a sob. This was it—there really would be no escaping.

"I have to tell ya, Kylene. Your gramps would have been

mighty proud of how you managed to get out of here. Real proud, indeed. Course, that don't matter much since he won't ever know what happened to you. Sure, there'll be suspicion of foul play, but good ole Sheriff Higgins will lay that to rest. That's the nice thing about having a dirty cop around. My hands can stay clean as a whistle."

When his back was to me, doing something in preparation for my murder, I took a deep breath and tried to move my hands. A twitch of my index finger—a firing of the tiniest synapse—gave me hope. I tried again with my other hand. All five of those fingers wiggled, too.

"You gave me a real scare there for a second with your escape, young lady. I'll give you that. But I know these woods like the back of my hand. I saw which way you'd run and I knew where you'd end up. Only took me three passes down that road to find ya." My right foot flexed. My left knee bent. "And now we're here." He looked over his shoulder at me, his smile wicked and full of bloodlust. "It's just about time."

I stifled my flinch, not wanting him to know his cocktail was wearing off. Not wanting to play the only card I held. Instead, I lay as still as I could while I attempted to speak, mumbling something incoherent, letting drool run from my mouth as I did.

"Easy there, girl. That chloroform can really take it out of ya, especially followed up with a healthy dose of ketamine. Might have given you a bit too much. You petite things barely got enough meat on your bones to live." He turned back to his tools, methodically placing them around his table of doom. "I got real good at estimating things like that in Nam. Medics never had any fancy equipment or anything. No scales to weigh patients. We could figure how much juice to give a soldier. But you ain't a soldier, are ya, Kylene? You're just a girl. A girl too much like her daddy for her own damn good." He turned his body toward me, steely eyes glaring. "And you're gonna pay a price for that, just like he did."

He stepped toward me, hands empty, and I stifled every instinct in my body telling me to fight—to run. Freedom was still too far away, and I knew it. I needed to get closer. I needed more time.

Matthew bent down, scooped me up under my legs and shoulders, and carried me over to the empty wooden table. The one likely to soon be painted in my blood if I couldn't figure a way out. He placed me down, arranging my hair around me, but I couldn't focus on that. All I could feel was the bite of sharp metal into my lower back. Right where I'd tucked garden snips before I'd escaped. The pain helped me think—helped me clear my head and focus on how I could use them.

Matthew thought he'd given me too much sedative—thought I was just a waif of a thing—but what he hadn't bargained for was my percent lean body mass. Was I small? Yes. Was I strong? Definitely. And I'd once read that things like roofies and other date rape drugs didn't always work well on athletes and extremely healthy people. Their systems burned through them too quickly for the desired effect to take hold as deeply. I prayed whoever had written that article was right. That it wasn't some junk piece on *HuffPost*.

Because I was about to bet my life on its accuracy.

One shot, I thought to myself. I had one shot at him. If I succeeded, I escaped. If I didn't, I died. It was really that black and white—that cut-and-dried.

With his back turned to me again, muttering to himself about which instrument to use on me first, I made my arm silently creep up the table to my back. It took some effort, but I managed to dislodge the shears from my pants so they were loose behind me. Doing what I could to lift my hips out of the way, I pushed the tool down behind my leg to where I could more easily grab it. Then I let my arm lie lifeless beside me, though a touch closer to my body than it was before.

When Matthew turned his attention back to me again, he had a gnarly saw in his hand. I panicked at the sight.

"You know I had to amputate a lot of limbs back in Nam. It was real gruesome. Sometimes we had enough meds lyin' around to sedate the poor bastard. Sometimes we didn't." He looked at the rusted saw whose teeth were bent at all angles and ferocious looking, and smiled. It was a look of longing. A look of nostalgia. Whatever he'd done overseas, he'd clearly grown to enjoy it, and it made me question if all the soldiers he'd worked on had actually needed their limbs amputated. Or maybe Matthew just needed to scratch his psychotic itch.

Right then, I knew it was now or never.

My lips quivered, a jerky uncoordinated movement that drew his attention, just as I'd intended. He took a step closer, his pelvis in line with my waist—above where my hand was slowly creeping toward the shears. Once again, I tried to force words out, letting a tear slide down my face as the garbled, choking sound passed my lips.

He leaned in closer still.

"Shhhh . . . ," he said, trying to quiet me. To calm me. My adrenaline surged. "We've still got time before you can talk. And I want to do as much as I can before I have to strap you down. I like them awake and immobilized. Tying 'em down always did seem like cheating to me. . . ."

Another tear escaped, and he bent over the top of me, his hand reaching to intercept the tiny droplet. I gripped the handle of the shears and unfastened the safety. I felt the handle widen and knew the blade was exposed.

"It's better this way," he said softly, whispering in my ear.

One shot . . .

He pulled away to smile down at me, his teeth yellowed

with coffee and age—his scars puckering—and anger rushed through me. This wasn't just for me. It was for every girl he'd ever touched. Ever exploited. Ever killed.

One shot to end his reign of terror.

Without hesitation, my arm sliced through the air with every ounce of strength I had. It slashed across his face, catching the hooked edge of the blade on his cheek and dragging it across his nose into the opposite eye. He shrieked in pain, falling back. As he laid on the table of tools, I saw the butt of a gun peeking out from the hem of his shirt. I reached for it with my other arm, wrenching it from his waistband before I fell off the far side of the table. I collapsed to the ground, but I held the gun tight. From my position on the floor, hands shaking, I released the safety and pointed it at him.

"Don't you fucking move!"

He looked over his shoulder at me as I scooted back to use the wall as support. My legs felt weak and heavy but fight or flight had kicked in, helping me get to my feet. His face looked ghastly, all bloody and dripping. And his eye . . .

"I'm going to flay you, ya little bitch!" He took a step toward me and I discharged the gun, the bullet whizzing past to embed in the rock wall behind him.

"Do you think I'm screwing around, you sick bastard?" I sidestepped toward the stairwell, my back still pressed against the wall. He mirrored my movement around the far edge of the table I'd been laid upon only moments earlier. "I'm getting out of here and getting help. Hope you can run fast, you old bastard. Because once they unleash the dogs in the woods, it won't take long to track you down."

"They won't take me alive . . . ," he said. An icy finger slid its way up my spine. Death by cop. He was willing to die just to avoid his punishment—or avoid retribution from whomever he answered to. With his knowledge of Sheriff Higgins' situation, it had to be the AD.

"I don't care how they take you," I replied, inching closer and closer to the bottom of the rickety stairs. "In cuffs or a body bag, it makes no difference to me. Try me and see. I grew up around here and my daddy's a cop. Wanna find out how good my aim is?" I steadied the gun with both hands as I climbed the first step, which was wonky and too high. My shaking leg could barely haul me up.

As if to taunt me, he took a large step forward. I dropped the barrel of the gun at his foot and fired. Again, his cries echoed through the basement as the bullet pierced it.

"You'd better hope you get out of here, little girl. . . ."

I took aim and shot him again, wounding his other foot.

"That's where I'm headed now. And my guess is I can get there faster on two wobbly legs than you can on those."

I took another two steps as he hobbled toward the stairs.

"If I'm dead then you'll never know the truth about those girls," he said, giving me pause. "Or your daddy . . ." My feet fell still. His creepy, pain-filled laughter floated up to me, begging me to come back down and face him. And I knew I should try to run. Every fiber of my being was screaming at me to, but the small part inside of me that sought justice for the girls and freedom for my father said he wasn't bluffing. He was baiting me, but if there was any chance that he knew something about either, I needed to hear it. To risk it. If not, the truth would die with him.

"Talk," I said, stepping down a riser. I wanted to come down enough to see his face. To try and see if he was full of it or not. I could always read people—or at least I thought I could. My confidence in that ability had been shaken over the past couple weeks, but I was certain it wouldn't fail me in that moment.

But damn did all that blood make it hard.

"Your daddy was framed."

"No shit."

"You know who did it, do ya?"

"Like you do. . . ."

"I know the AD." My body froze. My suspicion confirmed. "The man behind the curtain—the great and powerful Oz."

My hands started to shake, and I reset my grip to try and quell it. But it was a losing battle. I was too shocked to control my system.

"You work for him?" I asked. He nodded. "How did that happen?"

"He came to me," he said, inching toward me. "The first girl I ever killed—I was sloppy that time, and he knew about it. Figured out I'd done it. He sent me a letter giving me a choice: either I did as he asked—ran his whoring operation for him—or he turned me in."

My addled mind grasped for pieces of the puzzle too far out of reach.

"Who did you kill?" I asked, scared of the answer.

His maniacal smile did little to assuage my anxieties.

"I think you know. . . . Your daddy never solved that one."

Sarah Woodley. . . .

He smiled when he saw realization dawn in my eyes.

"Who else?" I demanded, regaining a fraction of my composure. Thinking of the girls steeled my spine. "I know there were others."

"Well now, that's true."

"What did you do with them?" I asked. "Where are the bodies?"

His gory stare was distant and wistful as he looked past me as though the wall were a window and the answer to my question lay just beyond.

"These hills are riddled with bones," he said, voice distant. "I like having them nearby. . . ."

I shuddered at his words. "Then why did you sink Danielle in the river?"

His beady eyes focused on me, the anger and hatred in them so bold and raw that it forced me back against the wall.

"She was special to me—not like the others. But she crossed me. Said she wanted to leave me. Letting her go just wasn't in the cards," he replied. His tone was as venomous as his expression. "The great thing 'bout women, though, is that they're dispensable. I learned that while over in Nam. Learned how easy it is to kill there, too. . . ."

"So you just killed your recruiters when they wanted out and replaced them?"

He nodded. "They're all replaceable, especially in these parts. Ain't no shortage of girls in rough circumstances that need cash, willin' to sell their friends out to get extra."

My mind flashed back to his job offer the night of the double date from hell, and bile rose in my throat. Danielle hadn't lied about working for Mr. Matthew. She'd just lied about what she'd done.

What he would have had me do, too.

"Well you fucked up this time because I'm not one of those girls. I'm high profile. I'll be missed. And the feds are already on to you."

"I don't imagine that'll be a problem," he said with a confidence that shook mine to the core. "Didn't help Sarah Woodley now, did it?" Ice ran down my spine. "She thought she could toy with me too—found out the hard way that you shouldn't dangle a promise you ain't willin' to follow through on in front of a man."

All the pieces finally fell into place. Sarah was his first kill—the result of toxic masculinity gone awry. The skeleton the

AD had used to leverage Matthew into running the seedy sex operation. Matthew had buggered that murder up, and he knew it. He'd learned from that and gone to great lengths to make sure it never happened again. Until me.

"Regardless," he continued, inching closer, "the AD will make sure this is all cleaned up once I'm done."

"Killing you might be part of that cleanup, you know?"

"Maybe . . . but I know killing you most certainly is."

I stared at him for a moment before realization tackled me hard. "The AD told you to go after me, not Shayna. . . . *Why?*"

His eerie smile widened. "Didn't ask why. I'm a military man, Kylene. I do as I'm ordered. But you're on his radar now, girl." He laughed to himself, throwing his head back until he started coughing up the blood that rolled down his face and into his mouth. "He's gonna make you wish you were never born."

"As soon as the cops find you, you're going to wish you'd never been."

His eyes narrowed as he shifted his weight forward. "Like I said, they won't be taking me alive. . . ."

I couldn't let him die if he knew who the AD was, but I couldn't afford to let him leave, either. I just needed a phone so I could call Dawson. Everything would be fine once he arrived.

I eased myself up the stairs backward so I could call the cavalry. But as I shifted my weight onto the next riser, it gave way. My leg sank in up to my knee and my arms went wide to catch whatever they could to brace myself. Seeing his chance, Matthew darted toward me. I fought as hard as I could to get up, but the second my leg was free, he was on me, throwing his body at mine.

I tried to train the gun on him, but it was too late. He was already reaching for it. It discharged twice in our struggle, hitting the ceiling, raining dust and wood chips down around us.

"You shoulda left when you had the chance," he snarled, bloody spittle spattering my face.

I grunted as I tried to get rid of the gun before he turned it on me. With a twist and a jerk, I pulled it free of his grip. It fell down into the basement with a thud. When he turned to see where it had gone, I sliced his bloody face with an elbow—my favorite up-close maneuver. His head fell back and to the side. I tucked my knees up to my chest and shot them out with every ounce of strength I had left right into his gut, knocking him ass over teakettle down the stairs.

I rolled over and dragged my way up the steps with the singular focus of getting out of there. I barely heard the crackle of gravel outside the cabin as I burst through the basement door and into the main living space. Gunshots rang out behind me and I ducked while I crawled toward the front door. I flung it open and fell outside, where a fleet of sheriff's department vehicles were parked everywhere, men in uniform jumping out of their cruisers and reaching for their sidearms.

My arms flew up in a flash.

"Gun!" one of the deputies shouted as bullets rang out from inside.

"Don't shoot him!" I screamed as I scrambled forward. A man in a green shirt and tan pants grabbed me and hauled me to my feet before shoving me out of the way.

I turned just in time to see the gory sight of Matthew smiling at me, his weapon trained on my head. Then a barrage of guns began popping all around me, the sound nearly drowning out my cries. Silence fell as Matthew hit the ground only feet away from the cabin, his arms and legs askew. His chest had been peppered with bullets, those wounds taking both his life and the identity of the AD with them.

"Kylene," a familiar voice called as strong arms hefted me up to my feet. Then Sheriff Higgins' face was in mine, a look of terror contorting his features. "Good Lord, Kylene. I was scared we'd never find you."

"I'm okay," I said, trying my best to assure us both that was true. "I'm okay. . . ."

He looked up at the other officers and started barking orders, but his hands never left my shoulders. Whether it was for my benefit or his own, I wasn't sure, but I felt better with them there, so I didn't fuss. Then a deep, booming voice called out over the din and I wrenched my head to find the man it had come from. It wasn't hard to spot Striker in a crowd.

"Striker!" I cried, running over to him. He scooped me up in his arms and hugged me so tight I thought he was the second man that day to try and kill me. "What are you doing here?"

He looked down at me like I'd lost my damn mind.

"The second I heard you were kidnapped, I was in my car. I was hardly going to leave these hillbillies with badges to track you down alone. I have resources they don't. And I have far more motivation. . . ." He let his words trail off and let his eyes roam over me, assessing what kind of shape I was in. How damaged I was.

"Where's Dawson?" I said under my breath.

"I don't know but it doesn't really matter because I'm pretty sure I'm going to rip him apart with my bare hands when he gets here."

"This wasn't his fault," I said.

"The hell it wasn't! He had no business involving you in this!"

I hesitated, wondering how much Striker knew of Dawson's case.

"He didn't have a choice. One of the girls reached out to

me—would only talk to me." Striker's dark brown eyes narrowed. Then rage slowly filled them and he searched for Dawson.

"I know all about it. He told me everything when he called to tell me what had happened. . . ."

"There was no other way, Striker."

His lips pressed into a thin line. "Your father said that to me once. Now he's in prison."

"I get it, I get it, I'm my father's daughter. I already know that. Why does everyone insist upon beating that fact to death?" I asked, anger moving in to squash the other emotions building within me.

"Because we don't want you beaten to death because of it," he snapped in that angry father tone that always startled me when my dad used it. Seems he wasn't the only one who possessed it. Then he exhaled hard and hugged me again. "I'm sorry, Kylene. I'm just—I'm taking things out on you that I shouldn't. Listen, I want you to come and sit down while I deal with this mess." He ushered me to a fallen tree near one of the vehicles. "The ambulance should be here in a bit. I want them to check you out." I absentmindedly nodded in agreement, knowing arguing would be in vain. "Good. Stay here. I'll be right back."

As he disappeared into the crowd of deputies, the sound of more tires on leaves and gravel drew my attention. I looked up to see an unfamiliar car skidding to a stop near the train of parked vehicles. Not far behind it was a very familiar truck.

Dawson was half out of a sedan before it came to a full stop. Garrett's truck ground to a halt right behind him before AJ, Tabby, and Garrett jumped out.

"What in the hell are you kids doin' here?" Sheriff Higgins yelled, blocking them from the scene. But Dawson had already gotten past him, headed right for me. I could hear Garrett say something about a call put out on the police scanner at the house, but I had a hard time focusing on anything else while I watched Dawson storm toward me, his angular features taut with what appeared to be anger. He stopped just short of me and pinned his arms tight to his sides. All I could see was heat in his stare and tension in his face.

"You're supposed to be happy to see me," I said softly, trying hard not to squirm under the weight of his gaze. The one I couldn't read.

"I am."

"But you look angry. . . ."

"I am."

"You look like you want to kill someone. . . ."

His hands flexed wildly at his side as his eyes drifted from me to the dead body at the entrance to the cabin. When they returned to me, realization began to creep in.

"Because I do."

For a moment, we stood silent, looking at each other. So much hung between us unsaid, but I didn't think we needed to speak those things aloud. Maybe ever. What acknowledging them would do to us was more than I could handle. Dawson, though on occasions a thorn in my side, had become someone I could depend on. I didn't want to mess that up by telling him how I'd nearly gotten myself killed.

"We should probably hug or something . . . if we're still trying to keep your cover intact."

Without a hint more of invitation, Dawson stepped forward and snatched me up in his arms, squeezing me against his chest. It felt warm and wonderful, and I had to try and push away from him before I fell apart in the safety it surrounded me with.

But his hold was unyielding.

"Kylene," he said softly enough that no one else could hear him.

"Yes . . ."

He pushed me away just enough to look me over, assessing something I couldn't understand. Something more than my well-being.

"Ky!" Garrett shouted, startling me away from Dawson's hold. I tugged at the hem of my shirt like a kid who'd gotten caught doing something she wasn't supposed to. Moments later he was practically diving at me—which had to have hurt him—so he too could wrap his arms around me like he'd never let go. Knowing Garrett, that was a solid possibility.

He said nothing, just held me tight, rocking back and forth slowly in a calming motion. My cheek was pressed to his chest, my face turned toward Dawson, whose tight expression had returned as he stared. Something in him looked like it was about to boil over. Then AJ and Tabby joined in the hug and blocked him from view.

"Garrett," the sheriff shouted over at us. "You kids need to get out of here. This is a damn crime scene."

"We're leaving, Dad," he said with a sigh, his arms still locked around me. The three of them slowly peeled away, AJ and Tabby still silent—not qualities either of them inherently possessed. My disappearance had shaken them badly if they were both at a loss for words.

Each of them gave me a sympathetic look as they walked back toward Garrett's truck, AJ looking over his shoulder for the better part of the trip. Then I heard Sheriff Higgins say something to Dawson, and I pulled my attention back to the standoff brewing.

"I'm not going anywhere," Dawson said, his voice low and cold and certain.

"What did you say, boy?" the sheriff asked, casting the young fed a sidelong glance.

"I said, I'm not going anywhere. I go where she goes. That's nonnegotiable."

Sheriff Higgins started toward us with a bit more speed than I was comfortable with. I stood slightly in front of Dawson, hoping to bar the way enough that he didn't get his ass handed to him by the local cop, but I wasn't holding my breath. Higgins looked pissed.

"Until I hear from your boss that we are no longer to support your undercover work," the sheriff said under his breath, "you'll do what I tell you to do, and that's final."

"*No,*" Dawson said, not budging an inch.

"Do you want me to arrest you for interfering with an investigation and disobeying an officer?" Sheriff Higgins said loudly enough for the other cops to hear. Striker, realizing Dawson was there, started toward us. I shook my head at him and he stopped, but I could tell that Dawson was in for a world of hurt when Striker finally got him alone.

"Do what you need to do," Dawson replied, still unmoving.

"Maybe you should just go, I'll meet you—"

"*No,*" he repeated, now staring down at me. "I'm not leaving you again."

Those few words said so much.

"You never left me," I said softly, hating that the sheriff was there to overhear. "Just go. Striker is here. There's no danger anymore. I'm fine, really. . . ."

Dawson looked at me, then Striker, then me again. He seemed unsatisfied with my reply, but he nodded once and made his way over to his borrowed car. He looked back at me over his shoulder as he did, and though the light was fading through the trees, I thought I saw a glint of pain in his eyes. Then he climbed in and drove off.

"Kylene," Striker said, walking over. "I need to take your initial statement. Then we'll go to the precinct and you can walk us through everything. We need all the details . . . even if they're hard to share."

"I know how this works, Striker."

"Of course you do," he said gently. "I wish you didn't."

"I'll be all right," I said, looking over to the sheet-covered body lying near the cabin. "I could be a hell of a lot worse."

FIFTY-TWO

The sheriff's department was a total clusterfuck. A melee of deputies scurried around while Sheriff Higgins barked orders at them. Just as I expected, Garrett, AJ, Tabby, and Dawson sat waiting for me, all of them jumping up the second I walked in with Striker at my side. They made a move for me, but Striker held them off with an outstretched hand. Actually, he held off Garrett, Tabby, and AJ. Dawson, however, was having none of it.

He was at my side in a flash.

"You're making this difficult," Striker growled under his breath. "And you're already on thin ice as it is."

"If I'm supposed to keep my cover, then I'm going in with her. It kills two birds with one stone. I get briefed on everything that happened while I play the dutiful boyfriend."

"You know I'm still here, right?" I asked as the two talked over the top of me.

"You good with this plan?" Striker asked. Apparently, he'd put together early on that Dawson and I had little love lost between us. But what he didn't know—what he couldn't have known—was that Dawson and I had fallen into some sort of bizarre partnership. A dysfunctional one, albeit, but a partnership nonetheless.

"It's fine."

"Then you two take a seat in there while I get the sheriff." He opened the door to the interrogation room and gestured toward the metal chairs awaiting us. With a hard exhale, I stepped into the tiny room with mint-green-painted cinder block and took a seat.

"How did you find me?" I asked, my voice thin and shaky.

"Callahan. He gave us your last known location and the plate number of the car you got into. Without his help—"

"You wouldn't have gotten to me in time."

He nodded. Silence fell upon us for a moment.

"The 'DG' in his daybook stands for *Daily Gazette*. He's been working with a reporter there—he suspected foul play in some of the other girls' disappearances. He wanted to do something." Suddenly Callahan's words when he found me had context. If only I'd gotten in his car. "Apparently he sent you warnings—notes meant to scare you off." I looked to Dawson and his hazel eyes flashed with anger, then cooled. I merely nodded in response. "This isn't going to be fun, Kylene, but you need to answer Sheriff's questions honestly and directly." His boyfriend tone was gone, sounding all federal agent in that moment. It distanced him somehow—I didn't like it. "They just need to know what happened."

"I know," I said, sounding distant and slightly annoyed even though I wasn't. He was too intense—too serious all of a sudden—and I longed for Garrett to come in and say something wildly inappropriate to make me laugh. Something about being a drama queen and the lengths I went to for attention. I would laugh and say he was just jealous because I stole his thunder.

I smiled to myself as I stared at the one-way mirror on the other side of the room while Dawson looked at me, undoubtedly trying to sort out what I found so amusing. It made me smile harder. Then the door swung open and the sheriff walked in with Striker.

My expression fell—*hard*.

"Okay, Kylene . . . let's start from the beginning."

By the time I said, "And that's when I crawled out of the cabin right into you guys," it had been well over two hours. It was late, and I was exhausted.

"I think that's all we need, right, Sheriff?" Striker asked, though it was clear the question was rhetorical. We were done, plain and simple, so sayeth Striker.

I was relieved to be excused from what I could only describe as the worst oral exam in the history of oral exams. The questions were grueling and detailed, and demanded far more attention than I had left. Dawson sat by my side throughout the whole thing. I remember him grabbing my hand under the table when I recounted the part of my botched escape and what Matthew had planned to do to me. What he alluded to having done to many before me. Dawson stopped breathing when I talked about the struggle for Matthew's gun. I knew because what had been a pounding pulse in his hand slowed dramatically. It was distracting, which turned out to be serendipitous, given that I didn't want to relive that particular moment. Dawson had told me that guns gave you a false sense of security, and he was right.

Not that I planned to share that tidbit with him.

When Striker shut down the interrogation, I rose to leave, then realized Dawson was still holding my hand. That's when I remembered that Sheriff Higgins told us that nobody would be watching the interrogation. That he had made sure of it. Striker and Higgins both knew who Dawson really was. There had been no reason to pretend.

"I need to go," I said, pulling my hand from his. He did nothing to stop me but followed me out of the room to the main lobby. Instead of just Garrett, AJ, and Tabby waiting for me there, I found them with a very weary and terrified-looking Gramps.

"Junebug!" he cried before hurrying over to hug me senseless. "Oh my sweet girl . . . I thought—" He stopped himself short, not wanting to admit the dark thoughts that had plagued him in my absence. But his expression betrayed him. It was the same he wore the night Sarah Woodley's remains were found

"I know, Gramps," I replied, voice breaking slightly. "I'm here. . . . I'm still here."

"What happened? All they'll tell me is that you were kidnapped and Grant Matthew is dead. I don't understand how those two things go together. Who did this? Is he here, because if he is, I'm gonna—"

"It was Mr. Matthew, Gramps." My words stopped him cold. "He's been exploiting and killing girls for years. He somehow figured out that I was helping one of them. . . ."

"He's dead now, sir," Dawson added, hoping to assuage the poor old man before he had a heart attack.

"Grant did this?" he said, voice full of disbelief. "How—how could he? I've known him for decades—fought beside him in Nam. How could he hurt you? He knows you're all I got."

I closed my eyes, fighting back the tears that I knew would make the whole scene worse. My need for some shred of control in that moment was fierce.

"He fooled everyone, Gramps. Whoever you thought he was, he wasn't. That's all I can say."

"Christ on the cross, I just don't understand it. I'da taken a bullet for him back then."

"Please don't try to make sense of this, Gramps. You'll make yourself nuts in the process."

He looked down at me and forced a smile. "Ain't no sense

in tryin' to sort out crazy, is there?" I shook my head. "All I can say is if he weren't already dead, I'da killed him myself."

"I think there would have been a long line for that privilege, sir," Dawson added.

Gramps gave him a pointed nod. "Damn right. Now, let's get you home, Kylene. You need some rest."

As he ushered me out, I realized he was still wearing his correctional officer uniform.

"Gramps, did you come here from work?"

"I was goin' in when the sheriff called the house."

I took a deep breath, knowing that what I was about to say wouldn't be taken well. But I was going to say it all the same. The thought of Gramps—or anyone—fussing over me and worrying in plain sight made my skin crawl. I just wanted to be alone, if for no other reason than to prove to myself I could be—that Matthew hadn't taken the last bit of mental stability that had recently been eroded. My strength and independence had long defined me.

Without them, I wasn't sure I knew who I was.

"Please don't stay home on my account, Gramps. I'll be fine. I promise. You've missed so much work because of me already. I don't want you to lose your job . . . you can't afford to."

"If the warden wants to fire me over this, he's welcome to," he replied, steel in his tone.

"Gramps—"

"No, Kylene!" he shouted. "This is the second time since you've been back here that you've damn near been killed. Don't you dare try to tell me what to do!"

My heart crashed into my shoes. "Gramps, I'm sorry but you can't shelter me. And losing your job doesn't make things any better—or me any safer."

His expression hardened.

"No, maybe it won't, but it'll keep you from doin' somethin' else that puts you in danger, like chasin' a chance that you can find the people responsible for your daddy's incarceration."

I steeled myself against my pounding heart and the hurt I knew my words might cause.

"No," I said, taking a step back from him. My temper was rising, shoring up the holes in my crumbling emotional wall. "It won't."

"*Kylene*," Dawson said, his voice teeming with warning.

"No," I said, wheeling on him. "This is my life. I'm technically an adult now, and I get to make my own choices. If I get hurt trying to free my father because I can't possibly live a life with him in prison, then so be it."

Anger. Anger was exactly what I needed to mask my vulnerability and guilt in that moment. Anger would see me through this, but at what cost? It was a relationship killer, and I knew it. Even as I said those hurtful things, I was aware of what I was doing—but that didn't make it stop. I was fresh out of coping mechanisms and devolving quickly.

Before that night, Gramps thought I hung the moon. But after I was finished with him, I wasn't so sure anymore. The look of pure shock and sorrow on his face put the fear of God in the shred of soul I had left. If Gramps abandoned me, I'd be all but orphaned.

An adult-sized consequence for adult-sized choices.

Gramps eventually pulled himself together, masking his emotions with an expression I didn't recognize on him.

"I love ya, Junebug. More than anything. And I hate that you're hurtin' right now and pushing me away. I know that's why you're actin' out. But you're right. This is your life. And if you want to throw it away, I sure can't stop ya. But you can't expect me to sit back and watch you do it."

With that, he hugged me again and kissed me on top of my head before he walked out of the sheriff's office to return to the prison, leaving me behind with a roomful of staring eyes and a mountain of shame. The crowning glory to my evening.

"I think it's time I take you home," Dawson said, moving toward me. He was wise enough not to overplay his hand and touch me. Smart, that one. So, so smart.

"Yeah," I muttered under my breath, balling my hands into fists to keep them from shaking. "Let's go."

"Are you going to stay with her?" AJ asked, reminding me that he'd been there to witness how much of an asshole I'd just been to the man who loved me unconditionally. Garrett and Tabby, too.

"Yeah, I'll stay—"

"The hell you will," I said, whirling around to face Dawson. "I don't need to be babysat. I'm alive. I'm fine. Matthew is dead. I don't think we have to worry about his corpse coming for me. And if we do, we've got a zombie apocalypse on our hands. I think that's a problem your presence won't solve."

"Ky—"

"I mean it! Can we just go? Please?" I stormed toward the door as I dug my fingernails into my palms. I stopped short when I heard Garrett say something to Dawson. Something about defense mechanisms and deflection.

"No, Garrett. Not you," I said, my voice almost a growl. "Not. You."

He put his hands up like I was pointing a gun at him.

"We're all just worried about you," Tabby said softly, using a calm and soothing voice. Unfortunately for her, I was well past the point of that parlor trick working.

"I'll be outside," I said, shoving the door open. "When you all are done deciding what's best for me, we can go."

The bite of cold air was welcome, and I breathed it in, letting the burn in my lungs numb me. I was spiraling out of control, and the worst part of it all was that I knew. I knew what

I was saying was awful and mean and done with the express purpose of hurting those around me, but I couldn't stop myself. Whatever stress I'd felt that day—combined with the emotions I'd been repressing—were coming out loud and ugly and full of venom. I needed to get a hold of myself. I needed to take back some measure of control.

I needed to not feel like a victim—victim didn't sit well with me.

Dawson came out not long after I did, walking past me to his rental car. I remained where I stood, breathing so deeply that it felt like I had ice in my belly. A minute later, he pulled up next to me.

The window rolled down. "Get in," he said. No "please." No placating tone. Just an order.

"You're not staying at my house."

"Wouldn't dream of it, Danners. Now get in the car."

I did as he said, and we rode to Gramps' house in silence, me staring out the passenger window, praying that daylight would soon come, and Dawson doing whatever it was that Dawson did when he was eerily quiet. How quickly we'd fallen back into our old roles. How quickly we'd erected the wall between us. But that was my fault, not his.

He pulled into the driveway and got out without a word. I started up the sidewalk after him, prepared to argue, but before I could, he turned to me and said he was just going to do a sweep of the house first. Standard protocol, he explained. Nothing special.

"Okay," I said, a knot in my stomach tightening.

"We're clear," he announced as he came down the hallway. He hovered in front of me, jaw working furiously as he ground his teeth. I stared up at him, still wondering what went on in that mind of his sometimes. "If you need anything, you know how to reach me."

"I'll be okay, Dawson," I replied. "I *am* okay."

He opened his mouth, then snapped it shut, giving me a tight nod before heading for the door. He exited without looking back.

The knot pulled tighter.

To distract myself, I got ready for bed, leaving practically every light on in the house as I did. Then came the time to shut them off and I hesitated for a moment. *He's dead*, I told myself, flicking the first of the switches down. One by one I made my way to my room, the shadows chasing me through the door until only one light was left. I lay down in my cot and stared at the tiny lamp next to me. I was desperate to leave it on, but if I did, then Matthew won. He killed a part of me vital to my survival, and I couldn't let that happen.

With a deep breath, I steeled my nerves and reached for the switch. The click echoed through the dark room as I settled back into my bed, burrowing deep into the blankets. No matter how enveloped in them I was, I was still freezing. I tossed and turned forever, wondering when I would be rid of the cold that seemed to permeate every cell in my body.

I fell asleep wondering if I'd ever feel warm again.

FIFTY-THREE

I shot awake in bed, drenched in sweat.

Mr. Matthew's words ran rampant in my mind. *These hills are riddled with bones*. . . . I could hardly breathe.

On shaking legs, I climbed out of my cot and hurried out of my room. It was too small. Too similar to the cage I'd just escaped. And the silence around there was undoing me second by second. I couldn't stay there; that much was obvious.

Where to go, however, was not.

I snatched a hoodie off the kitchen table and my car keys from the hook by the entrance. I was out the door, still slipping a boot on, then running to the driveway, only to find it empty. My car was probably still at Dawson's where I'd left it. I pulled out my phone that Sheriff Higgins had returned to me at the station and stared at it. It was two in the morning, and I had nowhere to go.

I felt like I was going to explode.

Without a thought, I took off in a sprint, unsure where I was headed but needing to burn off some of the nervous energy threatening to break me—if it hadn't already. I was on the main road in town before I realized which direction I was going. Instinct had kicked in, my mind and body seeking safety. There was only one place I could find it. One person who understood.

Rain started to fall just as I arrived at Dawson's tiny ranch home, panting hard and sweating. I stopped up in front of it and did my best to compose myself before I walked up the front sidewalk, hands wrapped tightly around my waist. I told myself it was the cold and the rain outside—that's why I was doing that—but even I couldn't lie that baldly to myself. The cold I felt had nothing to do with the weather.

I raised my hand to knock on the door, but it swung open before I could, revealing a shirtless Dawson with weapon drawn. I flinched at the sight of the gun and he quickly put it away.

"I heard footsteps," he said, his eyes assessing me. I clutched my waist tighter. "Danners?" When I didn't answer right away, he took a step closer, rain gliding down his skin as his hand fell gently on my arms where they held me together. "Did you just run here?" I didn't bother to respond. "*Kylene* . . . talk to me. Please."

"I'm not okay," I finally said, my voice cracking on the final word. My head started shaking side to side, small movements at first that only grew with the swell of emotions I'd tamped down—the ones I no longer could. They were about to crash down on us both. "I'm not okay . . . I'm not okay . . ." My body racked with sobs as I stood there on Dawson's front steps and completely fell apart. Though my head was down, I could feel him staring. Then his arms were around me, firm and sure, dragging me into his body.

"You will be," he whispered. "I promise that one day, you will be. Now, come inside."

Never fully letting go, he ushered me into his house and closed the door. He peeled off my wet sweatshirt, then got us both towels. He wrapped one around my shoulders, then went to the kitchen to get me a glass of water.

I did my best to control my outburst, but it took effort—a lot more than I had the energy for. Hovering awkwardly in the foyer, shaking with cold, I tried to keep telling myself that it was over. That nobody could hurt me now. But, for whatever reason, my mind had a hard time accepting that reality.

"I'm sorry—" I squeaked out before sniffling. "I didn't want to come here but I didn't know where else to go."

He stopped in his tracks. "You don't need to apologize to me, understand? You have nothing to apologize for. I didn't want you to be by yourself tonight anyway. Being woken up is the least of my worries."

I forced a smile through the tears. "I probably should have called first. I forgot that running up on you in the middle of the night might get me shot." I laughed a little, but it lacked any hint of amusement. Judging by the harsh expression on Dawson's face, he'd noticed.

"Do you want to talk about it? About what happened?"

I shook my head. "I'd rather pretend it didn't."

"But pretending never works, Kylene. It only makes life worse when you can't anymore."

I drew the towel across my face to wipe it off, my tears having slowed to a near stop.

"I think you underestimate me, Dawson."

His gaze sharpened as he took a step closer. "I used to." He reached toward me, offering the glass of water. "I don't anymore."

Not knowing how to reply, I gladly guzzled down the water instead. The weight of his words pressed down on my too-tired mind, and it felt like they would alter it in a way that I just wasn't ready for. I almost wanted him to insult me or tell me I was crazy or anything that felt normal. I needed some normalcy in that moment.

When I was finished, I handed him the glass. Then a morbidly amusing thought crossed my mind, and, in Tabby fashion, it came flying out of my mouth before I could stop it.

"I guess we both knew it was only a matter of time before I started acting like a normal teenage girl. I'm probably your worst nightmare right now, huh?"

His whole body tensed at my self-deprecating remark. Then he spun quickly away from me, his arm with the glass in hand swinging hard in the opposite direction. A crash sounded through the room before the tinkle of shattered glass on tile echoed behind it. Dawson's back was to me, but I could see him breathing hard, the muscles of his back tensing as he raked his hands through his wet hair. He apologized, then stormed away from me and the broken glass, into the tiny living room. He paced around and around the coffee table until a path was worn into the carpet and my chest was so tight I could barely breathe.

After what seemed like an eternity, he stopped.

"My worst nightmare, Danners, is that I'd failed you—failed my *partner.* That I wouldn't find you in time. That something would have been done to you that couldn't be undone. That I'd find your body . . . that you'd be dead." He slowly turned to face me. I didn't dare move. "I've never been more terrified in my life."

"I didn't mean to—"

"That sounds a lot like the start of an apology," he said, walking toward me. He stopped only inches away, his body still coiled with anger—anger at himself.

"I wasn't trying to. I just wanted to say that I didn't come here to make you feel bad. I really thought I could handle it, Dawson. I really did, but then I kept hearing Matthew's words in my sleep and I woke up in the dark and I felt like the world was compressing and I had to get out. And I know that's because I'm in way over my head. I mean, who am I kidding? I'm not my dad . . . I'm not *you.*"

He cupped my face in his hands, holding it gently.

"You listen to me, Danners, and you listen well. I've seen seasoned agents fall apart after things less traumatic than what you've been through, so as far as I'm concerned, you're just as strong as anyone I know in the bureau. Got it? I'm amazed by what you did on your own, by how you got out of there. I don't know that I would have." I tried to pull away from him, the intensity of his gaze becoming too much for me, but he held me in place, unwilling to let me go. "There is no shame in breaking down about this. None. If you want to sit on my couch and cry for the next five hours, I'll sit with you. You're not acting like some dramatic teenager. You're acting like a cop who just went through some serious shit."

Silence drew out between us, making me uncomfortable. There were only two ways I knew how to fix that: humor and anger. And after what he'd just said to me, I had no room for the latter.

"Crying makes my head hurt—which I don't need help with at the moment—so I think I'll pass on the five-hour bawlfest, if that's okay with you."

His expression lightened a bit, a small curl tugging at the corner of his mouth.

"Great. In truth, crying girls aren't really my specialty."

"Can we maybe just watch some TV until I crash on your couch?" I looked away from him, desperate to escape the vulnerability I felt. "I don't want to think right now."

He didn't reply, but instead headed down the hall to where the bedrooms were. A minute later, Dawson appeared with a shirt on, a dry one for me, and an armful of pillows and blankets.

"Here," he said, handing them to me. "Make yourself at home."

So I did. I shimmied out of my wet top while he turned his back, then I put a pillow against the arm of the couch and laid my head on it, curling the rest of me up in a tight ball on my side so I could watch the TV. When I gave him the all clear, Dawson draped a blanket over me, and I burrowed myself into it, making sure every inch of me was covered. It smelled like him—I tried to ignore how safe that made me feel.

Without a word, he plopped himself down on the far end of the couch and turned on the TV, flipping through the channels until he found some eighties movie with Tom Hanks. Something about him turning into a kid again. I was jealous of the idea. What I wouldn't have given to go back in time to when life was simpler and far less frightening.

"I know you don't want to talk about it, Danners, but . . ." He hesitated for a second. "I just need to know one thing so my mind can stop playing over the possibilities." I craned my neck to look over at him, silently agreeing to answer his question. The look in his eyes was painful, like he was being tormented by what might have happened to me in that cellar. By what likely had. "Did you leave anything out of your statement?"

"Like what?"

Silence. "Did he . . . did he *touch* you? *Hurt* you?"

I closed my eyes and took a deep breath. "No. Not like that."

The couch creaked under his weight as he relaxed back into it.

"Thank God."

"I'd have found a way to kill him if he'd tried."

I opened my eyes to find Dawson staring at me again. "Good."

I hesitated for a moment, thinking of one detail Dawson needed to know. One I hadn't had a chance to tell him away from an unwelcome audience.

"Matthew knew the AD's identity." He turned slowly to look at me with wide eyes. "That lead died with him."

He nodded once.

"We'll find another way" was his only reply before he turned back to the TV, letting me know that there'd be no more talk of Matthew that night—maybe ever. I snuggled back into the blanket farther and closed my eyes, letting the sound of the movie drown out the thoughts in my mind. Eventually, sleep took me.

And my dreams were far sweeter.

I awoke to the sound of clanging and scraping.

I opened my eyes, totally disoriented by what I saw until I remembered recent events—where I was. Groggy and sore, I pushed myself up to sitting and took a moment to get my bearings straight. As I surveyed the living room, memories of a broken glass and Dawson's pacing came to mind. Then I saw a pillow and blanket lying on the old recliner across from me—the perfect place to watch over me from while I slept.

"You're up," Dawson said, coming around the corner from the kitchen. "You hungry? Breakfast will be ready in a minute." I nodded, still staring at the chair. "About that," he said, looking uncomfortable. "I didn't want to leave you alone out here—in case you woke up afraid."

By the look on his face, I couldn't help but wonder if it was as much for his peace of mind as it was mine.

"Thanks," I said, my voice rough and scratchy.

I got up and made my way to the bathroom to get cleaned up as best I could. My eyes were bloodshot, with mascara pooled beneath them like a rabid raccoon. I tried washing the black rings off with water, then brushed my teeth with my finger to get the foul taste out of my mouth. My hair looked like it had been in a fight and lost, so I threw it up in a messy bun and opened the bathroom door.

"Yes, sir. She's okay. She came here late last night. She was pretty upset," Dawson said. I peeked down the hall to see him pace by, my phone in his hand. "I think she does, too. I'll talk to her about it. Maybe I can convince her to meet with her again." Silence. "You're welcome, sir."

Dawson stopped at the end of the hall and hung up. I stepped out of the bathroom and he tossed me my phone.

"Your gramps texted you last night to see how you were doing. I replied from my phone to let him know you were okay and that you were here. He just called and I didn't want to bother you. I know things were left pretty tense between you two last night. . . ."

"I was awful to him, Dawson. He didn't deserve any of that."

"He'll forgive you. Don't worry. Family is good for that." With no further explanation, he turned and started for the kitchen. "Coffee?" he asked. I followed him into the room where he stood holding a mug.

"Do I seem like someone who should be caffeinated to you?" I asked. He cracked a smile. "Water is fine, but feel free to put it in a mug so I can look all mature and cool like you while I drink it."

"As if that's even possible," he muttered under his breath. "Glad to see your sarcasm has returned."

"Me, too." I took a sip of the water he'd given me, then noticed the amazing aroma wafting toward me from the stove. "Smells good in here, Dawson. What are we eating?"

"Waffles."

"Ooooh . . . fancy. Do you make those for every girl that shows up at your place crying?" His movement paused for just a second before going back to what he was doing, his back facing me. "Sorry . . . I didn't mean it like that. I was trying to be funny."

"I'm laughing on the inside."

Just as I was about to try and dig myself out of the hole, he turned around with a plateful of waffles and strawberries with whipped cream on top. That alone was pretty impressive, but what stopped my heart for a single beat was the candle burning on top of it all.

"Happy birthday, Danners."

He hesitated for a moment, then brought the plate of birthday awesomeness over and placed it on the table before me. I stared at it like it was the most amazing thing I'd ever seen. And, in some ways, it was. It was more than just a birthday breakfast. It was a gift. A peace offering. A do-over. In all that had happened, Dawson had remembered my birthday when even I'd managed to forget it. That spoke volumes about who he was as a person.

And how much he cared.

I looked up at him with tears burning the backs of my eyes and smiled.

"I really prefer raspberries. . . ."

For a second, he looked like he wanted to murder me, but when I winked at him through a teary eye, his smile returned.

"You're a piece of work."

"Shut up and help me eat these, would you? There's enough here to feed Striker."

He shook his head and grabbed a fork, sitting down across from me. The two of us dug into the waffles that were so much more than just breakfast and ate until the plate was clean. We were a team now—a partnership, as he'd called it—and I knew from that moment on, we'd work together to bring down the AD and anyone else that got in our way. Maybe we were doing it for different reasons, but that didn't matter to me anymore. Dawson wanted to bring down whoever had targeted his mentor, and I wanted to free my dad. Either way, we had a common goal.

Justice for both men.

And punishment for the AD.

FIFTY-FOUR

EPILOGUE

News vans were parked everywhere outside town hall. Reporters jockeyed to get near the makeshift podium at the top of the steps, which was decked out with a microphone and a tiny American flag that nearly blew away in the harsh fall winds. The unseasonably cold weather didn't keep half of Jasperville away from the press conference about to be given. News of Matthew's death had traveled like wildfire. It buried Coach's impending trial in the headlines.

Apparently, for once, the townspeople wanted the real story.

Sheriff Higgins and Mayor Applewood stood behind the podium, talking quietly between themselves. Behind them was a wall of deputies—basically the entire force. And next to them stood Dawson in all his official FBI jacket-and-ball-cap glory.

Garrett, AJ, Tabby, and I stood amid the crowd, the three of them discussing what they thought the cops had found. Not one of them had spotted Dawson in the back row. I didn't bother to point him out. His cover would fall the moment he stepped up to that microphone, and I was happy to put off their collective interrogation a few minutes longer. I was too exhausted to explain.

Mayor Applewood glanced at his watch then stepped up to the mic, raising his hands to shush the murmuring crowd.

Silence fell like a blanket upon us, tucking us in for what promised to be a wild ride for everyone there. Everyone but me.

"I'd like to thank you all for coming out today. Sheriff Higgins of the Jasperville County Sheriff's Department and Agent Dawson of the FBI will be addressing the events that took place here over the past two days, then they will be available for questions." The mayor looked back to Garrett's father. "Sheriff Higgins . . ."

"Thank you, Mayor Applewood."

As the sheriff began to talk, my mind shut down. I heard him speaking; on occasion a word would slip past my defenses and register in my brain. Words like *Amber Alert, kidnapping, police shoot-out,* and *deceased suspect—prostitution, johns,* and *ongoing investigation.*

I felt Garrett's arm wrap around my shoulder, Tabby's head rest against mine, and AJ's body press against my back when the sheriff detailed what was found in the basement of Matthew's cabin. Then I felt them all go stiff as Higgins introduced Agent Dawson and the guy they knew as Alex Cedrics stepped up to the mic.

"Thank you, Sheriff Higgins," Dawson said, glancing back at him. Then he turned his attention to the crowd of cameras just steps below him. "As the sheriff has stated, this event was not an isolated incident. The FBI has been investigating a prostitution ring in Jasperville County for the past few months. That investigation led us to the murder of eighteen-year-old Jasperville High School student Danielle Green, whose remains were recovered two weeks ago from the Marchand River.

"The suspect in the abduction of Kylene Danners, Grant Matthew, has been linked through forensic evidence to Danielle's death. He was also the primary suspect in the disappearance of at least four other young females from Jasperville County. Our extensive investigation has now linked

Matthew to at least twelve missing girls over the past ten years, including Sarah Woodley, who appears to have been his first victim. Matthew admitted to that crime before he was shot and killed by the sheriff's department. We may never know exactly how many lives he took over those ten years, but the FBI, with the help of local law enforcement and volunteers, will be searching the woods around the Matthew property for human remains."

He continued on, connecting the dots between the sex ring and the dead girls for the press. Just when it looked as though he was finished and ready to take questions, he paused for a moment. Then his eyes fell on me.

"Before I finish up and open the floor for questions, I want to take a minute to acknowledge two people who aided in solving these crimes. First is a young woman who was involved in this sex trade and reached out for help. I will not name her for various reasons, but without her knowledge and willingness to come forward, the FBI would not have been able to connect the missing girls to the sex ring, nor would we have known about Danielle Green's death or where her body could be recovered. Second is the person who that young woman reached out to. Kylene Danners has been an asset in solving this case, and, as a result of her efforts, put her life in great peril to do so. This hometown girl is nothing short of a hero. Both Jasperville County and the FBI owe her a debt of gratitude." He hesitated for a moment, his eyes pinned on mine. "Lastly, we know that at least some of the girls presumed to have run away over that ten-year period were used and thrown away by Grant Matthew. What makes this even more shameful is that nobody in this town even noticed. Danielle Green, Kit Casey, Rachel Fray, Angela Mercy, and Samantha Dunkley—those girls were someone's daughters, sisters, cousins, and friends. Remember their names, Jasperville. Remember them so that this town—and its children—never fall prey to someone like Grant Matthew ever again." Silence. "Now I'd like to invite Sheriff Higgins to come join me at the podium so we can answer your questions."

Not surprisingly, the press shouted over one another, each trying to get the best sound bite for their employer. But my friends and I all stood silently alongside the townspeople that had come out that day, the weight of Dawson's words pressing down on all of us. The shame among the crowd was plain. Jasperville had been complicit in those girls' disappearances in one way or another. Their blood was on all our hands.

Garrett took a deep breath and leaned in closer to me.

"Do you want to go now?"

I nodded.

"I'll drive her home," AJ offered. Garrett looked down at me. I nodded again.

AJ led the way, pushing through the tightly packed crowd. I followed behind him with Tabby, then Garrett on my heels. We hadn't gotten far when the silence lifted, and whispers began. My hackles went up in an instant, my armor clicking into place. But, when I actually listened to them, I heard what those whispers said: *She's a fighter . . . survivor . . . hero.*

I felt AJ take my hand in his, and I looked up to find him staring back at me, a sense of awe in his eyes. He continued on until we were finally clear of the mob. As the four of us walked away from the spectacle outside town hall, I glanced back over my shoulder to where Dawson stood by the podium, answering questions like a seasoned vet. His mentor would have been proud.

AJ led me to his truck and hovered next to the passenger door, my hand still firmly held in his. He looked like he wanted to say so much but he didn't know where to start. The strongest sense of déjà vu shot through me—hurt and love and guilt.

I found myself needing to apologize for so much that the word "sorry" felt weak and inadequate. I wondered if it was a scene we were destined to relive forever.

Instead of speaking, the tears I'd been holding back broke through my guard. They rolled down my cheeks until AJ pulled me into his chest, his shirt absorbing the watery signs of distress.

"What am I going to do with you?" he whispered against the top of my head.

I let his question go unanswered.

I didn't have one for him anyway.

While AJ sheltered me from the crisp fall wind, I looked back to town hall where Dawson and the sheriff were still busy with the press. Dawson's gaze was beyond the reporters and crowd, aimed at where I stood. I gave a little wave, and he—mid press conference—gave me a quick nod in return. I smiled to myself, knowing that Dawson and I were far from through with each other. We were too close to learning the truth about the night his mentor died and my dad became a murderer to walk away.

That left me caught between two lives: the one any normal high school senior should live and the one I had. I wasn't sure there would be any going back from what I'd experienced, no way to be the college-obsessed student I was supposed to be. And the longer I watched Dawson at the microphone, I wasn't sure I wanted to. My life had all the purpose I needed.

My partner and I were going to bring down the AD.

ACKNOWLEDGMENTS

I always find writing these things stressful because I am certain to leave someone (or *someones*) out. It takes a lot of input from various individuals to really put a book together—far more than I ever would have thought possible when I started writing. So, with that said, I'm going to try not to screw this up too badly.

To Amy Stapp, Jessica Watterson, Ali Fisher, Shannon Morton, Marty Mayberry, Caden Armstrong, Kristen Bronner, and the entire Tor Teen team, thank you for helping craft this book from beginning to end. I couldn't have done it without you.

To the lovely mods at TBR and Beyond and the amazing readers in that group, thank you for being so supportive of this series and me, and for making my TBR list even more unruly than before. You guys kick ass.

To my Baan Muay Thai family, thank you for helping to bring Ky's character to life.

To my family, who constantly endures my random outbursts and incessant notebook carrying (because inspiration LITERALLY strikes at any moment), thanks for tolerating the voices in my head when they spill over.